Over You

LUCY DIAMOND lives in Bath with her husband and their
three children. When she isn't slaving away on a new book
(ahem) you can find her on Twitter @LDiamondAuthor or
Facebook at www.facebook.com/LucyDiamondAuthor.

What Lucy's fans say . . .

'Wonderful characters and the stories are
always great, with twists and turns'
Gemma

'Lucy's books are as snuggly as a blanket, as warm
as a cup of tea and as welcoming as family'
Cheryl

'Full of friendship, family and how when life throws
something at you, you have to fight back!'
Emily

'A skilful writer with the ability to
place herself in anyone's shoes'
Sue

'Lucy's books make me smile, cry and give me
happiness, a little bit of escapism from everyday life.
Page-turners I just can't put down!'
Mandy

Lucy Diamond

OVER YOU

PAN BOOKS

First published 2008 by Pan Books

This edition published 2016 by Pan Books
an imprint of Pan Macmillan
The Smithson, 6 Briset Street, London EC1M 5NR
EU representative: Macmillan Publishers Ireland Ltd, 1st Floor,
The Liffey Trust Centre, 117-126 Sheriff Street, Upper
Dublin 1, D01 YC43
Associated companies throughout the world
www.panmacmillan.com

ISBN 978-1-5098-1111-3

9 8

A CIP catalogue record for this book is available from the British Library.

Typeset by Set Systems Ltd, Saffron Walden, Essex
Printed and bound by CPI Group (UK) Ltd, Croydon, CR0 4YY

Visit **www.panmacmillan.com** to read more about all our books
and to buy them. You will also find features, author interviews and
news of any author events, and you can sign up for e-newsletters
so that you're always first to hear about our new releases.

To Hayley and Kate,

with lots of love and weekends away

Acknowledgements

I'd like to thank the following people, who helped me with this book.

Jo White, Jo Thulborn, Hayley Bangs and Kate Tilley all read early drafts and gave me brilliant feedback and encouragement. Liz Withers helped enormously too – thank you all so much.

Super-agent Simon Trewin gave sound editorial advice and great pep-talks – cheers, Simon!

Imogen Taylor and Trisha Jackson at Pan – thank you for the title, and for persuading me (in the nicest possible way) that the X-rated office scene of the first draft needed to go – you were so right, as always!

Cheers to everyone else at Pan – Ellen, Emma, Fiona, Steph, Anna, Michelle and all the other lovely people there who make publishing seem so glamorous and such fun.

The Novel Racers and Bloggers with Book Deals are my cyber-colleagues – thanks to all of you for your

Acknowledgements

constant support, advice and enthusiasm, especially Kate Harrison and Milly Johnson.

Thanks too to everyone who bought the first novel and wrote to say they enjoyed it – I can't tell you how much I appreciated those emails.

Hugs to my mum and dad, who are on good terms with every bookseller in the East Midlands by now, and thanks to Phil, Ellie, Fiona, Ian and Saba.

Big kisses to Hannah, Tom and Holly Powell for bringing such sparkle and laughter to my life.

And finally, lots of love and thanks to Martin, as ever. You're the best.

Chapter One

It was too tight. Far too tight. The perfect, to-die-for top that Josie had fallen in love with on first sight was — there was no doubt about it — boob-jammingly, belly-clingingly, flesh-pinchingly tight. Yet it had definitely said Medium on the label. Josie grimaced at her reflection in the changing-room mirror. Why did they always have to *lie* on the labels anyway? Was it just to make you feel bad?

Typical! It had seemed the ideal top for a girly night out, too, back when she had first spied it on its hanger. It had ticked all of Josie's boxes, being black (flattering), with a plunging V-neck (minxy), made of floaty, chiffony material (feminine), with tiny shiny beads stitched into the bodice (a bit glam — although a bugger in the washing machine, she guessed).

She sucked in her tummy and looked at herself side-on. Oh God, even worse. Roll upon roll of flab. The seams were straining. All she needed now was for Trinny and Susannah to burst in with a camcorder, laughing hysterically as they mauled her around, grabbing spare bits of flesh.

Josie realized she was turning purple and let out her breath hurriedly. She did *not* want Nell and Lisa to see her in this tomorrow. They would think she had let herself go, big-time. She hadn't seen them for ages – at least a year – and had been hoping to look good in a seemingly effortless hasn't-Josie-done-*well*-for-herself? kind of a way. If she wore this, though, Nell would probably launch into a round of 'Who Ate All the Pies?'.

The three of them had been flatmates, soulmates and best mates back in their twenties, living it up in London together in a succession of grotty rented flats. It seemed like a lifetime since they'd parted to go their separate ways – herself into marriage and kids, Nell into travelling and failed romances, Lisa into career glory and the salary premiership.

Finding the photo of the three of them tucked away in one of her books had been the prompt for Josie. It was a picture that – what was his name? Dale? Dave? One of Nell's many exes anyway – had taken one New Year's Eve when they'd all been dressed in their finest, ready to hit the West End for booze and snogging. They had looked so happy with their arms around each other and, damn it, so fresh-faced and young, that a lump had swelled in Josie's throat. She could conjure up even now the singeing smell of Nell's curling tongs as she'd styled everyone's hair that night, could remember the exact way the floorboards of that dismal Kilburn flat had shuddered to her own *Dance Anthems* CDs, and she could practically taste the siren-red lipstick on her own lips, as if it had been yesterday. It must have been eight or nine years ago, though. A reunion was way overdue.

And so, thanks to Josie, within a week or two the whole thing had been arranged. Weekend for three at Lisa's posh new pad (Josie could hardly *wait* to see it).

But what the hell was she going to wear?

Well, not this, for starters. Josie wrenched the top over her head with relief. Her skin was flushed and clammy-looking, and her ponytail was wisping out all over the place. The changing-room lighting was so bright it showed up the dull flatness of her hair, and every line and bag under her eyes. She could smell her own sweat.

God. Josie Winter. What *happened* to you, anyway?

Josie swung away from her reflection and pulled on her baggy cream jumper and coat. The boys always called it her Miss Hoolie coat, much to Josie's dismay, even though she was quite sure she looked absolutely nothing like Miss Hoolie from *Balamory* when she wore it. It was just a sensible, everyday coat. Just a plain, ordinary coat.

She zipped it up, feeling glum. It was a mum coat,

wasn't it? With its stupid hood (for rainy days) and quilted lining (for cold days) and big pockets (for gloves and small toys and fir cones and interesting stones . . .).

Oh God. What had *happened* to her?

She put the black top back on its hanger, tried to smooth it a little, then opened the curtain and handed it to the over-made-up assistant.

'Any good?' the girl simpered.

'No,' Josie replied. 'A bit on the big side actually.' Sod it, she'd got her coat done up, hadn't she? Underneath that she could have the body of a goddess, for all the assistant knew.

Did Nell still have such a slinky figure? she wondered, leaving the shop without bothering to try on anything else. Lisa had always been the chunkiest one of the three – not fat exactly, although she was always moaning that she was. She was just . . . well, 'nicely covered', as Josie's mum put it. 'Thighs like a footballer,' Lisa had frequently sighed, 'and bum like the back end of the number seventy-three bus – that's me.'

But Nell had always been knock-out slim with good legs and a nice little bottom. Plus she had those gorgeous long blond curls too – with the help of a bottle, mind, but dazzling in a Pre-Raphaelite, shampoo-advert kind of a way.

Maybe Nell had put on a few pounds these days, thought Josie hopefully, now that she was shacked up with – what was his name? Gareth? It did sound romantic, the two of them in that remote cottage somewhere in north Wales. Perhaps Nell had taken to hogging loads of comfort food in front of their log fire, now she was loved-up and content. She probably didn't have the most rocking social life these days any more either – calories no longer burned off by the thousand every weekend by dancing in sweatbox clubs all night. And maybe she'd stopped bothering to touch up her roots too . . .

Well, Josie would find out tomorrow, anyway. Tomorrow! She found herself grinning as she went into Marks and Spencer and began loading up a basket with provisions for the boys. If the truth be told, she was secretly *dying* to know how Pete was going to manage without her. Their four-year-old twins, Toby and Sam, weren't exactly naughty or difficult children, but they were rather – how should she put it? They were *lively* boys. Energetic. She tossed three ready-to-cook spaghetti bologneses into her basket and smirked. They let you know they were around, those boys of hers. And tomorrow, for the first time ever, the pleasure of looking after them single-handed for the weekend would be all Pete's. Whereas she, on the other hand . . .

She'd be living it up in the big city, just like she'd done all those years before. It would be like stepping back in time.

Josie was on her way back to the car when something caught her eye. There in front of her was a heavily pregnant woman, bump so rounded you could see the faint outline of her pushed-out belly button where her top stretched over it. The woman was showing a friend a romper suit she'd just bought, holding it carefully over one arm, her face animated.

Josie felt herself staring, footsteps slowing. It was a cerise romper suit, with a pale pink cherry design embroidered on one pocket. 'I just couldn't resist it,' the woman was saying, folding it up again and patting it affectionately before she slid it back into the bag. 'Girls' clothes are so sweet, aren't they?'

Josie felt a pull in her own belly and rolled a hand over it. Her pulse quickened. And then, almost before she knew it, she'd wheeled around, straight through the doors of Baby Gap behind her. She just couldn't help herself, marching straight through to the racks of teeny pink and white clothes. Fleecy dungarees, frilly skirts, little buttoned cardigans ... The woman was right. Girls' clothes – especially baby girls' clothes – were utterly, heart-meltingly gorgeous.

Josie stroked a pair of dungarees, size 0–3 months. They were so tiny and fleecy and *pink*. Candy-floss pink, perfect for a newborn. She unhooked them from the rail and put them reverently over one arm. Her mouth was dry suddenly, and she licked her lips. Next, she picked up a packet of vests that had a fairy print all over them. So, so cute! Oh, she just *had* to have them. And how about the pink knitted cardigan, even if it *was* hand-wash, the kiss of death for baby clothes? Just gorgeous, though, with the teeny mother-of-pearl buttons. I couldn't resist, she told herself in her head. Look, and there was the most darling little plum-coloured hat! It was adorable!

Josie rubbed her thumb across a pair of soft white tights, imagining small chubby legs tucked inside, kicking and twitching in that random, unintended newborn way. She added them to the selection over her arm and then, after a last brief look at a display of pink cot blankets – no, she'd probably got enough of those for now – she turned towards the till.

The girl behind the counter rang up her purchases without comment, even though Josie was more than ready for the usual questions. *When's it due?* she wanted the girl to ask. *Thought of any names yet?*

A few months to go yet, Josie would reply, patting her belly with a contented smile. *And we're going to call her Rose.*

Rose! the girl would say. *Such a gorgeous name!*

I know, Josie would nod. *It's our favourite too.*

Nothing of the sort, though, unfortunately. The girl was only young, nineteen or twenty at a guess, chewing something, her eyes bored. No doubt she was thinking of where she'd be clubbing later that evening, what she'd be wearing, how she'd do her hair. Exactly the kind of things that had occupied Josie's waking mind for so many years – Hmmm, pointy high shoes or boots? – until the boys had been born and looking after them had consumed everything else.

The girl tissue-wrapped the clothes and placed them in a bag. 'That's forty-two pounds please,' she said, shifting her wedge of chewing gum to the other side of her mouth.

Josie handed over her card, eyes fixed on the dark blue bag. There we are, Rose. Won't you look lovely in that lot? My little sweetheart!

Then she saw the time. Christ! She'd be late for playgroup kicking-out time if she didn't get going.

She ran to the car, stuffed the bag in the boot and started the engine.

'Look, Mum, I done a ambulance for you. There's its light, there, and this is the driver. And he's going really really fast cos there's somebody *dying* in the back and there's loads and loads of blood and they've got to get to hospital before he *dies* and . . .'

'Lovely, darling,' Josie said automatically to Toby, trying to wiggle his coat sleeves on to his arms without him noticing. 'Hello, Sam. Had a nice morning?'

Sam flung himself bodily against her legs, small arms wrapping tightly around her. She bent down and kissed his head, breathing in his delicious salty boysy smell of Play-Doh and warm trainers. Sam always seemed so relieved whenever she reappeared to take him home that it was impossible for Josie to smother a niggle of doubt about him being at playgroup. Maybe Pete's mum had been right all along, maybe it was a mother's duty to stay at home with her children until they were old enough to vote, instead of having the nerve to put them in playgroup a few mornings a week . . .

'Those precious years,' she'd sigh, eyes up to the ceiling, whenever Josie said anything about it. 'You'll miss them when they've gone. You mark my words!'

Barbara was very fond of making such pronouncements. Josie had had to mark Barbara's words on all manner of things over the years. She was the expert, it seemed, on teething, potty training and tantrums, as well as state childcare. With a pursing of her lips and her fat arms folded meatily over her chest, she liked nothing better than to tell Josie where she was going wrong.

'They *enjoy* playgroup, though, Barbara,' Josie had tried to argue several times through gritted teeth. 'And I like them being there. It's good for their independence – and mine.'

The plan had originally been for Josie to return to work on these mornings. She'd been a designer, pre-kids, a good one too, rising to a senior position in a large children's charity. She'd held out for the boys' starting playgroup as the moment to claw back some time for herself, to kick-start her brain and build up a portfolio of work once more before job-hunting. But it hadn't quite worked out like that somehow. Three mornings a week was not long enough to get the housework and shopping done, let alone anything creative. And almost every time she'd fired up the Mac and started playing around with ideas, she'd been conscious of the minutes slipping past. One hour left before the boys needed picking up. Twenty minutes. Five ... And that had been that.

No matter. There was plenty of time to start work again once they were at school, come September. Josie wasn't in any hurry.

'Did you paint an ambulance as well?' she said to Sam, ruffling his hair.

He shook his head. 'I done a frog. For you,' he said. 'But it's still wet.'

'You did a frog! Well done,' Josie said, trying to sound surprised. Of course he'd done a frog. All Sam ever wanted to paint was frogs. 'We'll pick it up next week. Let's get your coat on now and we'll go home.'

Once the boys had been strapped into the car, Josie pulled out on to the main road, half listening to Toby's chatter about killing pirates and half worrying she'd forgotten something for the weekend. *So for lunch tomorrow, they can have those rolls and tuna*, she found herself musing, *and for tea, the spag bol, and . . .* She forced herself to stop. This was ridiculous! There was a corner shop at the end of their road! If Pete needed anything, he could easily make his way there and sort it out. She was being patronizing, really. Pete was perfectly able to cope. He was a grown man, for goodness' sake! And even if he hadn't been very keen on the idea of Josie going off with the girls, he was just going to have to live with it.

'And I'd whack him over the head with my sword, right, and . . .'

She glanced at Toby in the mirror as he gestured some bloodthirsty bit of violence or other. She'd never imagined herself to be the mother of boys. Never thought she'd have to learn the intricacies of model pirate ships, or try to explain how rockets worked. She'd never dreamed that she'd be the one having to referee punch-ups over whose turn it was to go on the swing, or that she'd end up walking any number of different ways home so that she and her sons could solemnly inspect the yellow JCBs that were carving up nearby roads.

Josie had always pictured herself hand in hand with beaming daughters; had imagined plaiting their hair with shiny bobbles, taking them to ballet lessons, throwing fairy parties and decorating cupcakes with pink icing and jelly tots.

It wasn't that she wasn't crazy about the boys. Quite the opposite. She'd fallen in love with them the second she'd laid eyes on them, even though they resembled wrinkled, blood-covered rat babies, so tiny and mewling, coming as they had six weeks early. It had been like the strangest, most surreal kind of dream – she'd been bleary from all the drugs they'd given her pre-Caesar, the very air seemed a hallucination, shimmering and rippling as first one little rat baby then another was mysteriously pulled from within her belly.

'A boy!' Pete had cried, holding Toby, first out of the bag.

'And another boy!' the surgeon had cheered, handing Sam over to Josie. She could still hear the way he'd snuffled in her arms like a small vernix-covered puppy, could still remember exactly how he'd felt against her bare arms, skin to skin, warm, wet and jittery, with those dark blue eyes opening just a crack to inspect her.

And oh, it had been love at first sight. Even though she now accepted they must have been hideous to an onlooker, so shrivelled and greasy from the waxy white vernix, hardly a scrap of hair between them, arms and legs as tiny as sticks. They were beautiful to her. Her boys. She had *sons!* As she held them both to her chest, their miniature hearts pulsing on top of hers once again, she felt as if she might very well combust with sheer joy.

'Mum! Why aren't you stopping?'

Toby's voice jerked her out of her thoughts, and Josie slammed on the brakes. She'd almost driven straight past their house, so wrapped up was she in baby memories.

Once home, she went upstairs with her precious bag of goodies and stowed it at the back of her wardrobe. There was already a mobile of pastel-pink bunnies there, plus a pile of fuchsia blankets, still in their cellophane wrapping, and a sweet little white teddy with pale pink ears. *All for you, Rose. When you're ready, sweetheart.*

She came back down to see that the boys were out in the garden. Sam's face was set in deep concentration as he swung up the climbing net, a frown rucking his eyebrows. Toby, sure-footed as a cat, was already at the top, shooting imaginary enemies in the forsythia.

Josie started making lunch, peeling sausages from their packet and sliding them under the grill, and putting on a pan of water for the potatoes. She froze as there came a familiar chittering sound, and the glossy-winged magpie flew down to next door's cherry tree. *One for sorrow.* Again!

It was always on its own, that sodding magpie, living out a lonely bachelorhood in the pale pink froth of blossom, flaunting its bad luck each time in clear mono-chrome. Why couldn't it find a partner and settle down, so that Josie could have 'two for joy' for a change? Or, better still, invite a couple of mates over so that she'd have 'three for a girl'?

Her period had started eight days ago. Eight days. That meant an egg was silently ripening inside the red darkness of Josie's ovary right now, on the verge of detaching itself and rolling headlong down a tube into her waiting womb. And there it would lie, still and quiet, half a possibility, half a person. Half a daughter, with any luck. Half of *Rose*.

She breathed in hard, and put her arms around herself. *Come on, Rose. What's keeping you?*

She and Pete had been trying for a daughter for so long now. Too long. And Pete had absolutely no idea she'd been stocking up with baby things in preparation. He'd probably think she was mad.

Maybe she was.

Josie peeled a couple of potatoes and slung them into the pan of water. So if we have sex on Sunday night, she reminded herself, and every day until Wednesday, then maybe, just maybe...

She would cook something with shellfish on Sunday, she decided, so that she could boost Pete's sperm with a bit of zinc – did a prawn curry count? Maybe she could order in a takeaway – nothing too chilli-tastic, just something to get them in the mood...

Josie checked how much wine they had in the rack. Three bottles of white, four reds, some bubbly. Well, she couldn't see Pete polishing that lot off on his own tomorrow night, however knackering a day he'd had, so there would definitely be some left for Sunday...

She grimaced. It wasn't like she *needed* alcoholic help when it came to seducing her own husband but ... you know, anything to oil the wheels was a bonus. She could even dig out some of the sexy underwear that he always bought her for birthdays (uncomfortable, chafing, cold) – even if, truth be told, big Primark knickers were the finest thing since chunky Kit-Kats in her opinion.

Josie watched the magpie flap away and felt a twist of sadness that she and Pete had once been unable to take their hands off each other, yet nowadays, he would paw at her hopefully once the lights were off and, nine times out of ten, she'd sigh and say, 'Oh, sorry, love, I'm just sooo shattered tonight,' or whatever. Headache. Not in the mood. *Must* get an early night because of blah-blah-blah tomorrow.

She always hated herself during the moment of silence as he took his hands off her and rolled over, rebuffed, but then felt nothing but blissful relief as she shut her eyes and said good-night into the darkness.

Sunday night, however, would be different. He'd love it!

There was a scream outside and suddenly only Sam was on the climbing frame, white-faced, his mouth one enormous, shocked 'MUM!'

The sausages were burning. The smoke alarm shrieked.

Snap out of it, Josie, she told herself savagely, racing outside to her oldest boy. His face was a sickly *eau-de-nil* as he lay sobbing and shaken on the grass. Catch a grip! Look where daydreaming gets you!

The unpredictability of the traffic, late-running meetings and post-work drinks all made the equation of Pete's ETA home dificult to calculate on any given evening. Sometimes, very occasionally, he'd be back in time to give the boys a bath after their tea, which meant an orgy of splashing, whooping and speedboat noises. Other times, also relatively occasionally, he wouldn't be in until they were asleep under their dinosaur quilts, an arm or leg flung over the side of the bunk bed, hair fluffed against the pillow. Most nights, they would hear his car pull up, the engine die and the *clunk* of the central locking outside as Josie was reading the boys their bedtime stories. It was pretty much Josie's favourite time of the day. Her sons, in their pyjamas, smelling of soap, hair damp and sticking up, both leaning into her as she read them *The Smallest Dragon* or *Pirate Peg-Leg*, or whatever had been chosen. Gone was all the bravado of the daytime. As twilight fell, they seemed to regress to babyhood, clambering on to her knee, sucking their thumbs, wanting cuddles.

On this night, she had just opened her mouth to read the first line of *Where's That Monster?* when there was the usual *clunk* from outside the window. Both boys whipped their heads around immediately, monsters forgotten.

'Dad!' cheered Toby, leaping off her knee.

'Daddy!' echoed Sam a second later, racing after his brother.

The front door opened and Josie leaned back against the sofa, listening to them contentedly. Her three boys. Team Winter all present and correct!

'Dad, I fell off the climbing frame!' Toby was boasting. 'Right from the top, like a dive-bomber. Can you see my plaster? Look! There was loads of blood. Loads!'

'Dad, I can hop on my own – look!' Sam's voice was next, with accompanying thumps. 'See, Dad? Can you see I'm hopping? Toby can't do it yet, just me. He still has to hold on to the wall. Look, Dad. See that?'

'Excellent, excellent.' Pete sounded distracted. It often took him longer than the commute home to leave the office behind. Josie felt an anxious ache inside at the thought of Sam's proud, hopeful face, and crossed her fingers that it hadn't melted to disappointment, mouth turned down, triumph unheeded.

'Good day?' Josie asked, getting up as he came into the living room. He looked tired, she noticed – grey-faced, eyes slightly pouched – but just as handsome as he'd been when she'd met him eight years ago.

'Not bad,' he said, pulling his tie off and tossing it on to the sofa.

He still hadn't looked her in the eye. Still hadn't pulled her in for a kiss. *Something's wrong*, she thought uneasily.

'Everything all right, Pete?' she asked. 'Shall I get you a drink?'

The boys were swarming all over him and at first she thought he hadn't heard her. It was only when he'd swung Toby up around one shoulder and was dangling Sam upside-down that he glanced across to where she was hovering. 'Love one,' he said. 'Glass of red would hit the spot.'

'OK,' she said, walking into the kitchen. This was all about her going away tomorrow, she thought, with a flash of annoyance. A pre-emptive sulk to make her feel bad about leaving him with the boys for one single night, even though he'd disappeared on business trips for days on end, and had stayed in London loads of times when his meetings had run over unexpectedly. 'Nell and Lisa?' he'd echoed when she'd announced her intentions. 'But ... Well ... You should have asked me first. I might have been busy that weekend!'

'Well, you're not,' she'd replied. 'I checked on the calendar. Oh, go on, Pete, it's only for one night...'

He'd huffed and puffed a bit, tried to joke about Nell and Lisa being a bad influence on her (as if!), but for once Josie had dug her heels in. She really, really wanted this weekend. And the more he went on at her, the more determined she was to have it. It wasn't too much to ask, was it, that he looked after the kids on his own for once?

She gritted her teeth as she took down a glass for him, then, as an afterthought, one for herself too. They'd been over this already. They both knew she was going. He didn't have to make such a fuss about it all over again now, did he?

And here's me, trotting into the kitchen like an obedient little wifey to pour him a drink! Josie thought, yanking out a wine bottle from the rack. Well, as from tomorrow morning, Josie Winter, obedient wifey, is temporarily history. And Josie Bell, party animal, can bloody well make a comeback – and about time too!

Chapter Two

'Bye then, boys. Be good,' she said. It was Saturday morning and Josie was crouched in the hall, holding her sons tightly as if she were trying to imprint their shapes on to her body.

'Are you going to bring us back a present?' Toby wanted to know.

Josie laughed and kissed his freckled nose. 'Maybe. If you're really really good for Dad...'

'Yeah!' he cheered, confident already. 'Thanks, Mum! Come on, Sam, let's get the pirate stuff out.'

Toby ran out of the room, but Sam stayed close to Josie as she hugged Pete goodbye. 'Have fun,' she said. 'I'll ring you later, OK?'

'OK,' he replied. 'And have fun yourself.'

'I'm going to, don't worry,' she said. Then she picked up her bag. 'I hope I've got everything,' she muttered, fighting the urge to undo it and check.

Pete rolled his eyes. 'What are you like? You just need

PMT – pants, money, toothbrush. That's all anyone ever needs.'

Josie hoisted her bag up on to her shoulder and stuck her tongue out at him. 'For starters, no self-respecting woman calls them "pants" – and for seconds—' She smiled, feeling light-headed all of a sudden. 'For seconds, I'm going to be late. Bye, Pete. Love you. And don't forget – tomorrow's you-know-what day.'

He frowned. 'What?'

Josie flushed. He *had* forgotten. Well, she wasn't about to remind him right now, what with the boys' ears being so finely tuned to anything remotely personal. 'Nothing. I'll see you tomorrow. God, that sounds weird, doesn't it? I can't remember when I last said that! I—'

'Josie – train,' Pete reminded her. He opened the front door for her. 'Go get.'

'OK, I'm going, I'm going.'

'Bye, Mum!' Sam shouted, leaning against the door-frame.

'Bye, love,' she said, a lump rising in her throat at the sight of his pale little face. Come on, she told herself, walking down the drive. It's not like you're *leaving* them. It's not like you're never coming back. This is one night away – one well-earned night away – and you'll be home tomorrow. And then before you know it you'll be sucked back into real life, and this will just be a single blip of excitement that once happened. End of.

Josie felt her stride picking up as she went down the road. There she was, clip-clopping along in her high-heeled brown boots and nicest pink coat, looking for all the world as if she was quite unattached. Quite free.

A grin slid over her face. Free. It wasn't a word she'd used to describe herself for a long time. But today she was free from the kitchen sink, and the washing machine, and the—

Oh, bollocks. She knew there was something she'd forgotten. She fished in her pocket for her mobile and dialled home.

Pete answered on the sixth ring, breathlessly beating the answerphone. 'We're all right! We're surviving!' he told her before she'd even said hello. 'Nobody's injured or crying yet!'

Josie laughed. 'Sorry,' she said, 'it's just I remembered I left my coat in the washing machine, and I put it on the synthetics programme, so when it stops, you need to take out the coat and give the rest a spin. Oh, and—'

'Hang on, let me write this down,' Pete said. 'Synthetics, coat, spin ... OK, got it.'

'And don't let the boys play with the furry collar from it, will you?' Josie added. 'They pretend it's a fur snake and . . . Well, anyway, I took it off before I washed it – it's a detachable one, it just buttons on and off – and I've put it on one of the shelves on the dresser. So . . .'

'OK, got it,' Pete repeated. It was hard to tell whether he was bemused or on the verge of irritated. 'Anything else?'

Josie licked her lips, then whipped her tongue back in her mouth before she removed all her new lippy. 'Um . . . No. Sorry. That's it,' she said.

A shout went up from Pete's end of the phone, and Josie strained her ears to tell whose voice it had been. Sam or Toby? Was one of them hurt?

'Better go,' Pete said. 'Bye, Jose.'

'Wait – who's——?' Josie started, but the line went dead. She held the phone to her ear for a moment, half wondering if she should call again in a minute to find out if either of the boys was injured, and if she needed to rush back home to wait for the ambulance, and . . .

No. Don't, she told herself, stuffing the phone back in her pocket. She strode forward assertively. The boys shouted all day long. In fact, the more she thought about it, the shout she'd heard just then had sounded like a fighting-pirate kind of shout, rather than a broken-bone kind of shout. She hoped.

OK.

Back to the weekend. Yes!

London, here she came!

Josie could hardly sit still as the train approached King's Cross. It was all so familiar and yet so strange. She'd actually lived near King's Cross for a while (although, of course, she'd told everyone it was Islington) and had loved being in the thick of everything. Yeah, sure, there were smackheads and prostitutes on every corner, there were burger wrappers blowing in the wind, plastering themselves around your ankles anywhere you walked, and there were the hustlers too, always on the look-out for dumb tourists with cameras hanging off them and pinchable wallets in pockets. That came with the territory. But there were some good pubs, too; it was close to everything, she could walk to work, and it had made her blood leap with happiness to feel part of the city bustle and pace.

Now, obviously, she couldn't imagine anything worse than having to live here. Too dangerous, too hectic, too scary. Which was why she and Pete had upped and left for the suburbs as soon after the boys had been born as they could manage it.

The 'burbs. She had a love–hate relationship with where she lived, the bland Toytown streets and houses with their neat Identikit gardens and people-carriers on the drives. Their house was only ten years old, and Pete had jumped at it during one of their house-hunting missions, especially as his new job was just a few miles away. In hindsight, Josie hadn't been in a fit state to pass judgement, having only recently given birth. At that point she'd been sucked in by the big, clean kitchen, the stretch of lawn, the safe, secure feel of the place. She'd been too tired to traipse around any more houses with the babes mewling in the double buggy. 'OK,' she'd said, without any real conviction. 'Let's buy it.'

Sometimes she wondered if it had been the right choice. However hard she and Pete had tried to imprint their own style on the house, with their soft furnishings and painted walls, it still looked like a box to her, with its square rooms and boring brick frontage. She wouldn't choose it if they were house-hunting now. No way.

But hey. It was only brick walls and a roof. It didn't matter that much, at the end of the day. And Pete still loved living there, so . . .

The train wheezed into the station, and she felt her heart step up a beat. She was really here, in London, on her own. Her phone bleeped and she grabbed it quickly. A text from Nell.

Can't w8 2 c u babe. Am here, Ks X. Where r u?

Josie grinned. No time to reply. She was here too, and Nell could see that for herself in a few minutes. She stood up as the train rattled to a stop and waited impatiently for the automatic doors to hiss open. Come on, come on!

Sssssssssssssssssss!

She was released from the smelly carriage, and jumped down on to the platform. 'Hello,' she said to the city under her breath. 'I'm back.'

They'd arranged to meet outside WH Smith in the station, where half the population of London seemed to be hanging out too. A wild-haired woman with a tatty blue sleeping bag around her shoulders was asking for money, one hand outstretched. A gaggle of Japanese girls were poring over an *A–Z*, all talking at once. A manic-eyed lad leaned against a pillar staring at his own hands as if they were newly sprouted from his wrists.

Josie scanned the crowd for Nell's blond curls. And then . . .

'Hey! Over here! Josie!'

She spun around at the sound of her name and there was Nell hurrying towards her, Nell with the same wide grin and sparkly blue eyes, her hair in a new jagged urchin crop, but still as slim as ever – God, she looked fit! – in a dark denim skirt and biker boots, assorted beads slung around her neck and fuchsia feather earrings. She also had on a pink coat. A much nicer one than Josie's – shorter and brighter and louder. Josie's coat looked the pale insipid relative next to it.

All these thoughts whirled around Josie's head as she rushed into her friend's arms. Nell might not feel the same to hug – no bobbing curls going ticklingly up the nose any more – but she still wore the same perfume, and Josie breathed it in as if she were hungry. It was a smell of friendship and good times.

Then they were standing apart and looking at each other, grinning like fools. 'God, you look great,' Josie blurted out, trying to keep the envy from her voice. 'I love your hair – it's so funky! I almost didn't recognize you!'

'Cheers – it was a bit of an impulse chop,' Nell replied. 'I don't recognize myself any more either.' She grabbed Josie's hands and squeezed them. 'Oh Josie, I am so excited about this weekend,' she cried. 'I can't believe we're back together in King's Cross like this. You're a star to have sorted everything out. We've left it too long, haven't we?'

'Too, too long,' Josie agreed, unable to stop smiling. 'And here we are, in our pink coats – yours is much nicer, of course – and—'

'Don't be daft,' Nell said affectionately, giving her a nudge. 'It's not a competition. Yours looks much posher than mine. I bet yours didn't come from the Oxfam shop either. Now – where's that Lisa-Lou? Eyes peeled for the old city slicker . . .'

Josie laughed. Suddenly the coat didn't matter. So what? Actually, it gave her a feeling of solidarity. Sisters, comrades, put on your pink coats and they shall know us . . . She and Nell had always swapped clothes, back in the flat-sharing days. Although tonight . . . Josie sneaked another quick glance at her friend's slender limbs. No. There was absolutely no way on earth she'd be able to fit into anything of Nell's any more. Not unless Lisa had a liposuction machine at her place that Josie could borrow, anyway.

'There she is!' Nell said just then, and Josie stared into the distance, following her friend's pointing finger. 'God, look at her! The glamour-puss!'

Josie's eyes widened in surprise as she clocked the confident, sassy woman who was approaching them, waving and smiling. Lisa's long dark hair now had gorgeous plum-coloured highlights blended in, and fell in shining waves around her shoulders. Her skin looked sun-kissed, with just a hint of eye make-up and dark lipstick. And she was the picture of classy chic in her camel-coloured suede jacket, fitted at the waist, her plain white T-shirt, dark jeans and wedge-heeled sandals.

'Bloody hell,' Josie said, trying not to gawp. Lisa looked sensational. There was no other way to describe it. She seemed so groomed and polished, Josie half expected to see an army of personal stylists slinking back to their headquarters behind her, high-fiving each other and saying, 'Good job!' at their work.

'Hiya,' Lisa said, her mouth breaking into a grin. 'Nell – your hair! Where's it gone?'

Nell laughed and hugged her. 'The same place as your arse, by the look of things,' she replied.

Lisa grinned and gave a little wiggle. 'And long may it stay there,' she said, before turning to Josie. She seemed to hesitate for a split second, then pulled Josie in for a hug. 'Hi, darlin',' she said. 'Long time no see.'

Josie's mouth was suddenly full of Lisa's musky perfume and her thick, soft hair – had she had extensions put in? There was so much of it! – and she was momentarily lost for words. It *was* a long time no see, way too long. They'd bumped into each other a year or so ago at a friend's wedding, but despite Josie's best attempts, she'd barely had five minutes alone with Lisa, who seemed to be working the room like a woman on a mission. And before that ... Josie couldn't think straight. Lisa had certainly come to see her when the boys had been born, but Josie couldn't remember her visiting since then.

'Lise – you look amazing,' she said bluntly, once she was able to speak. 'You've lost so much weight! You just look . . . incredible!'

'Thanks,' Lisa said. 'Two stone gone, can you believe? And I still want to lose a bit more.' She patted her flat, verging on concave, stomach. 'Must get rid of this pot belly.'

'What pot belly? There's nothing there!' Nell scoffed. 'God, you cow. You look far too gorgeous for me to hang out with you. Can't you put a bag over your head while we're together or something?'

Lisa laughed again. 'The only bags I'm planning to see today are shopping bags, filled with mucho purchases,' she said. 'Shall we get out of here?'

'Definitely,' Josie said. She followed Lisa's confident stride across the station, slightly stunned. Talk about a transformation. She'd never seen Lisa so sparkly and self-possessed before, never. People were staring at her, and you could tell they were half wondering if she was a celebrity, with that head-high, I-know-I'm-fabulous march. Back when they'd been living in each other's pockets, Lisa had never been the one to lead the way, had never strode ahead like that. Now look at her!

It was disconcerting, Josie thought, heaving her bag higher on her shoulder as she trotted after her friends. The dynamic had shifted. Once upon a time it might have been her, Josie, strutting ahead, taking control. But she didn't feel like that Josie any more. She'd morphed into a follower, just as Lisa seemed to have morphed into the leader.

For a second, Josie had the urge to dodge into WH Smith and hide behind the newspaper stand. Had this been such a good idea? Did she really have anything in common with Nell and Lisa any more?

Nell looked over her shoulder and saw her hovering. 'Come on, Jose,' she said, waiting for her to catch up. 'It's not like you to hang about when there's shopping to do.'

Josie smiled and nodded. These were her friends, after all. These were pretty much her oldest and closest friends, who'd seen her pluck her own nostril hair, heard her snore and held her hair back for her when she'd vomited up ten strawberry daiquiris over that minging Kilburn toilet. 'Don't worry,' she said. 'I'm coming.' And even if she *was* taken aback by Lisa's transformation, they were all grown women, right? So she'd leave all that she's-prettier-than-me stuff back in the school playground where it belonged, wouldn't she? Right.

The plan for the day had already been discussed. Forget the West End or Oxford Street for grown-up shopping. If they were going to have a proper reunion, they needed a Saturday afternoon at Camden Market. Back in the old days, the three of them had made regular weekend pilgrimages there for cut-price clubby outfits, bargain boots and all sorts of tat to adorn the grotty flats. It had also been a favourite place for a mid-afternoon pint, which had often stretched well into a drunken evening.

Where else could they possibly head this afternoon than Camden Town? It would be an essential nostalgia trip, an excellent starting point for the weekend. 'And if we get there and realize that everything in the market is hippy crap that we wouldn't be seen dead in these days, we can always go somewhere else,' Lisa said as they left the station and headed around the corner towards a bus stop.

Nell grinned. 'There's nothing wrong with a bit of hippy crap,' she said. 'Don't knock it, Lise. Hippy crap has served me well through the years.'

Josie definitely fancied Camden over any grown-up shops Lisa might have been thinking of too. She'd had enough of swanky boutiques for skinny people yesterday, thank you very much. 'Anyway, we can always go for a ... drink, if we have to,' she said. She'd been on the verge of saying 'a cup of tea', but had bitten back the words just in time. Although she never usually touched the booze until the boys were in bed (not unless it was a really, *really* trying tea-time, anyway), she was quite sure Nell and Lisa had no such rules.

'Well, I suppose so, if we're *forced* to go to the pub, at gunpoint or something . . .' Lisa said.

'Or if someone threatens to poke us in the eye with joss sticks,' Nell giggled.

'Here,' Lisa said, pulling up by a bus stop. 'This is our one.'

'So,' Nell said conversationally as they waited with a couple of acne-scarred Goths and a smooching couple, 'how did you do it, Lise? How did you lose all that weight?'

'Well, believe it or not, it wasn't through the sleep diet or the puke diet,' Lisa replied, her eyes crinkling at the edges as she grinned.

'Oh God! The puke diet! I'd forgotten that,' Josie laughed. 'Eat whatever you feel like, knowing you'll get so lashed later you'll puke it all up anyway.' She winced at the memory. 'We were so gross, weren't we?'

'The sleep diet was a good one, though,' Nell reminded her. 'Stay in bed all day so that you don't consume any calories . . .'

'Even if does mean you lose your job, remember, Nell?' Lisa pointed out, raising a perfectly shaped eyebrow.

'Oh yeah,' Nell nodded. 'I knew there was a downside. No calorific gain, but lots of financial pain.' She shrugged. 'Still, it was a crap job anyway, so . . .'

'But forget our tragic diets,' Josie interrupted, turning

to Lisa. 'How *did* you do it? I feel blobby just looking at you.'

'Spinning,' Lisa replied, pulling a face. 'And stress. Too much work. Lots of shagging. Being too lazy to buy food . . .'

'What's spinning?' Josie asked.

'Shagging who?' Nell chimed in.

'Spinning is basically torture in Lycra,' Lisa replied with a grim expression on her face. 'Spinning is like gym hell.'

'God,' Josie replied, none the wiser. She couldn't help eyeing up Lisa's slim flanks as she leaned forward to flag down the bus. 'Well, whatever kind of torture it is, it works. In fact, I'm going to book myself in for some as soon as I get back home. I need to be tortured at once!'

'And the shagging?' Nell prompted. 'And please don't reply, "*Heaven* in Lycra" or I'll have to push you into the traffic.'

Lisa grinned and whipped out her travelcard. 'I think that's a conversation for the pub, don't you?' she replied.

Chapter Three

The smell of Camden hit Josie as soon as they got off the bus on the High Street. Incense, kebabs, patchouli oil ... It was all exactly the same. The pounding bass-y reggae; the shops full of buckled biker boots and outrageous platform heels; the clusters of skanky teenagers smoking roll-ups, clad in their uniform of ripped black bullet belts and piercings; the cannabis flags fluttering like bunting from shop windows ...

It made her feel old. It made her feel like a middle-aged mother. Which, of course, she was. But she wished she didn't *look* quite so much like one.

'Right,' Lisa said, looking around as if they'd just landed on a different planet. 'God, Camden High Street. So here we are again. I think I need a drink already.'

'I think I need some food,' Josie said, eyeing a bistro across the road.

'I think I need to hear who Lisa's been shagging,' Nell

said, steering them to the pedestrian crossing. 'Twelve o'clock's not too early for a drink and lunch, is it?'

'Not in my belly it isn't,' Josie replied. She suddenly felt anxious as she saw Lisa consult the watch on her slim, slim wrist. Oh no, Lisa wasn't going to sit there and just *watch* them eating while she picked at a single grain of rice or something, was she? Josie couldn't bear it when people did that. Talk about killing off everybody else's fun. Today she just wanted to enjoy herself, not be reminded about calories and spare handfuls of flesh.

'Looks like wine o'clock to me,' Lisa said, 'and I'm absolutely ravenous. I forgot all about breakfast this morning, I was so excited about seeing you two.'

The crossing started bleeping for them to go, and Josie pressed her lips tight shut together. She'd been excited about the weekend too, but that hadn't stopped her wolfing down two rounds of toast and the boys' leftover bacon. How did anyone *forget* to eat, anyway? Was it actually possible? She always suspected models and celebrities were lying when she read statements like that in magazines. Surely nobody was *that* forgetful? Ever since she'd had the boys, Josie's whole life had been charted by mealtimes. 'Mum, is it nearly lunchtime?' 'Mum, what's for tea?' 'Mum, I'm starving! I'm THIS hungry!'

They crossed the road and went into the café. It was vaguely familiar, and Josie struggled to think why. 'I'm sure I've been here before,' she said, staring around. It was gloomy inside, but cosy-gloomy, with lamps on the wall, leather armchairs and an open fire in the front. Further back were scruffy, chipped tables and chairs. 'I've got major *déjà vu*. Ringing any bells for you two?'

'No,' Lisa said. 'Not even a tinkle. Hello?' she called over to a waiter.

Nell started to laugh and elbowed Josie. 'You *have* been in here – and so have I,' she said. 'Don't you remember? We came in here for lunch – well, actually, it was probably a late breakfast for us in those days – and we met those awful blokes. Yours was a poet. Mine was an artist, I think.' She shook her head. 'Must have been ten years ago or so. Jesus!'

Josie racked her brains. A vague shadowy memory flickered in her mind, of an earnest, brown-haired guy trying to sneak his arm around her back on a slippery leather sofa. 'I remember,' she said. 'Didn't they keep trying to get us to look at their etchings?'

'Something like that,' Nell said. 'I think we just let them buy us drinks, then made a swift exit.'

Josie stared at the sofa in one corner, as if half expecting to see a ghostly image of herself still there, giggling and flirting with some poor sod. 'What mercenary bitches we were,' she said, feeling guilty and amused at the same time.

Nell grinned. 'Thank goodness we're so mature and sensible these days!' she said, wide-eyed.

'Table for three, please,' Lisa said crisply to the waiter, as if she were in a grand hotel instead of a dive-y little café.

'Anywhere you like,' he said, pressing a pile of greasy menus into her hand.

Once they were settled with a beer each, Nell planted both elbows on the table and leaned forward. 'So, Miss Lisa,' she started, 'back to your love life . . .'

'Oh God, do we have to?' Lisa moaned.

'You might as well tell us now, before you get too drunk and lose all your inhibitions,' Nell pointed out. 'At least this way you can give us the edited highlights while you've still got your wits about you.'

Josie laughed. 'And we'll winkle the really juicy bits out of you later on,' she said, tilting her bottle of Peroni and taking a long, cool gulp. Delicious. She raised an eyebrow. 'So, let's guess. He's your personal trainer on some kind of two-for-one deal.'

'Cheeky cow!' Lisa said, spluttering on her beer. 'My personal trainer is as gay as fairy lights. No, it's . . . Well, there's nothing serious. I'm just dating, you know.'

'Anyone particularly falling-in-lovable?' Nell pressed.

Lisa shook her head. 'There hasn't been for ages,' she said, suddenly looking down at the table. 'Years. No, these are all just casual flings. A bit of fun, you know the score. Excellent sex, now bye, who's next?'

'Sounds good to me,' Josie said, even though that was a complete lie. The thought of still having loveless shags with dates who didn't set her heart racing filled Josie with dread and pity – how could Lisa *bear* it, not having met the right man and settled down with a family by now? How could she stand sleeping alone all those nights, with nobody putting their arms around her? But she certainly wasn't going to say as much.

'Do you ever hear from – what was his name? – Guy?' Nell asked.

Lisa shook her head. 'Nope. *Nada.*' She tipped her head back, avoiding Nell's questioning gaze, and had a long slug of beer.

Josie had a swig of hers too, wondering what was going on in Lisa's head. She could tell there was no chance of getting any more answers about Guy or anyone else right now. Lisa's private life had always stayed far more private than Josie's and Nell's, even during their most drunken confess-all girly nights in. Josie had known via Nell that Lisa had had her heart broken really badly a few years ago by this bloke Guy, but Josie had never even met him, and hadn't heard the full story. Besides, at the time it had happened she was still in the throes of early motherhood – the boys were probably no more than a year old, and her mind was full to its brim with their lives. Long heart-to-heart sessions about anything else had not been possible. Nell, too, had been away somewhere hot and Third Worldish, so hadn't been able to fulfil her best-friend comforting duties either. Josie felt bad that Lisa had had to go through her heartbreak without her two closest allies beside her.

'Anyway, what about you?' Lisa asked, turning to Nell. 'How's it all going with your boyo in the valleys? Any plans for sprogging or vows or anything serious yet?'

Nell shook her head, her mouth in a funny little twist. 'Nope, *nada*,' she parroted. 'It's all over, me and Gareth. As of last week, I am an eligible bachelorette once again.'

Josie put down her beer harder than she meant to and it banged on the table, sending a surge of bubbles fizzing up its green neck. 'What happened? Why didn't you say something earlier?' she asked.

Nell shrugged, a cagey expression slipping over her face. 'Just because,' she replied. 'I don't really feel like talking about it. So . . .'

'OK,' Lisa said, her dark eyes on Nell.

Josie leaned over the table and squeezed Nell's hand. 'Are you all right?' she asked. 'Change the subject if you want, but . . .'

Nell's mouth turned up in a smile shape but a light seemed to have gone out of her eyes. 'I'm cool,' she said.

41

'And don't even think about asking me if I want to do a Ten Reasons Why He Was a Wanker Anyway list, all right?' She grabbed a menu and opened it up in front of her face. 'Right, let's choose some food.'

Josie and Lisa exchanged glances as they took menus themselves and flipped them open. OK, so Nell's love life – or recently extinct one – was clearly out of bounds. And judging by the way Lisa had shut down so completely when quizzed about relationships, so was hers. So that just leaves me, thought Josie, rolling her eyes. And who wants to hear about my marriage? It would seem like boasting if she started talking about Pete now. *Yes, we're coming up to our seven-year anniversary – I know! I can hardly believe it either. Yes, we're still madly in love. Well, you know – comfortable together, rather than tearing each other's clothes off all the time, but that's what happens, I guess, when you're settled down. The honeymoon doesn't last for ever! Anyway, we're trying for a little girl now, a sister for the boys. Oh, it'll be lovely. Rose, we're going to call her. We've got it all worked out!*

Josie grimaced behind the safe shield of her menu. No. Definitely not the time to start reeling all that off. Not unless she wanted to be slapped around the head with a Peroni bottle, anyway.

'How about another beer while we decide?' she suggested, to break the awkward silence. Somehow or other she'd finished hers already.

'Definitely,' Nell and Lisa chorused. Then they both smiled, a little self-consciously, and Josie felt relieved. So certain subjects had been flagged up as off-limits for now ... but it was still early. Hopefully, by the end of the day, Nell and Lisa would have warmed up enough to ease back into best-mate-intimacy mode, and everything would be back to how it used to be.

The waiter brought over three more bottles and set them on the table.

'Cheers,' Josie said, lifting hers. 'To friendship.'

Nell clinked her bottle against Josie's. 'To friendship.'

'To friendship,' Lisa chimed in, raising her own bottle. 'And food. What shall we eat?'

Josie stared into the rust-flecked mirror and groaned at the sight of her flushed cheeks and bloodshot eyes. Christ. She felt half-pissed already and it was still only one-thirty. It wouldn't have been so bad if either Nell or Lisa were even a tiny bit tipsy, but they seemed completely unaffected by the beer. Unlike Lightweight Josie in the wobbly corner. At this rate she was going to be passing out before three o'clock. Surely they wouldn't want to continue boozing the whole afternoon and then all evening? She'd never be able to keep up.

Josie splashed cold water on her face, trying to cool her hot cheeks. What she really fancied right now was a nap. A lie-down on one of those comfortable-looking sofas at the front of the restaurant, with her head propped on one of the fluffy cushions. Mmmm. Just for half an hour or so . . .

She shook her head at her reflection. No way. She already felt like the frumpy one of the trinity. She certainly wasn't going to compound that by proposing an afternoon snooze like an old granny. Maybe she could suggest they had a cup of coffee instead. She certainly needed *something* to jerk her out of this beery blurriness.

In a sudden clutch of paranoia, she wondered if the other two were discussing her right now. Were they laughing about how red-faced and pissed she was looking? Had they noticed that her make-up seemed to have melted away to nothing already, that she'd spilled salsa down her top from a particularly drippy nacho? Oh God – what if they were regretting coming to meet her, boring old Josie? Was she cramping their style?

The bathroom door creaked, and in lurched Nell. 'I am enjoying this sooo much,' she declared. She came over and put her arms around Josie's neck. 'Who would have thought it, eh, Jose? Me and you back in Camden together. We just need our poet and painter and it'll be as if those ten years never happened.'

Josie felt faint with relief. 'You're not . . . bored, or

anything, are you?' she asked. Three beers ago she wouldn't have said the words, but they just fell out of her now.

'Bored?' Nell echoed. 'Of course I'm not bored! What are you on about?' She elbowed Josie. 'Are you trying to tell me something? Have I been rambling on too much about India?'

Josie shook her head, smiling. 'No,' she said. 'Just . . .' She shrugged, feeling daft. 'Ignore me,' she said. 'I can't take my beer any more.'

Nell went into one of the loos. 'I think I've had enough for the time being too,' she called through the door. 'Afternoon drinking wipes me right out these days.'

'Me too,' Josie said, thankful at the admission.

Nell came out and washed her hands. 'It's a bit of a time-warp this, isn't it?' she asked, applying some fresh lipstick. 'Like, it's all the same, yet not. And we're all different too, yet kind of the same.' She blotted her lips and threw the tissue in the bin. 'Think I should definitely stop drinking. I'm talking rubbish, aren't I?'

Josie shook her head. 'No, I know what you mean,' she said. She leaned against the cool tiled wall, trying to string the right words together. 'Being here in Camden, I keep expecting to bump into Nick, or your ex David, or someone else we used to know. Almost as if I've forgotten that I don't live here any more. And then I see you and Lisa, and you've both changed so much, to look at, and...'

'Haven't we just,' Nell said. She peered into the mirror and pulled a face. 'Honestly – do you *really* like my hair? Or were you just being kind when you said so earlier?'

Josie turned to her in surprise. 'Of course I like it,' she said. 'I mean, I loved your old curls but I think it looks really cool cropped like that. Honest.'

Nell fiddled around with the strands at the front. 'I did it after me and Gareth split,' she confessed. 'Because he always adored my curly hair, so it was kind of two fingers up at him.' She snorted, her expression hardening. 'Which is totally ridiculous because he hasn't even seen me since, so it was all for nothing. But...' She shrugged. 'I feel different for it. Like I'm a new person, not the same person that he...' She broke off and looked away. 'Anyway, thanks for being nice about it,' she said after a moment, and went past Josie to the door. 'Shall we get the bill and go shopping?'

'Yes,' Josie said, following her. She couldn't help wondering what Nell had been about to say. *Like I'm a new person, not that same person that he...*

The same person that he *what*? Josie mused. What had he done to her? Or was it that she couldn't bring herself to say 'dumped'? Nell had never been dumped by anyone, it was always she who called things off. The terminal finisher, Nell was.

That had to be it, Josie decided, sliding back into her seat and getting her purse out. Gareth had instigated the split, and Nell was in denial over it. Or something.

Camden Market was loud, hectic and bustling after the dingy calm of the bistro. The three of them made their way over the bridge that spanned the canal, past the middle-aged punks who were charging people to take their photographs. 'Sad bastards,' Lisa commented loudly, and Josie couldn't help agreeing.

'Not tempted to get a snap of yourself and that one with the green mohican, Lise?' Nell giggled. 'I always thought you suited green.'

'Not snot-green like that I don't,' Lisa said firmly, steering them through the crowds. 'And besides, he's forty if he's a day. I like my men to be a bit more professional than that.'

'You never know,' Josie teased, 'he might scrub up nicely in a suit . . .'

Lisa rolled her eyes. 'God! I'm not desperate, you two. Leave it out!'

'Nobody said you were desperate!' Nell retorted. 'We were only having a laugh.'

'Yes, but . . . Oh never mind,' Lisa said. Her mouth

twitched as if she wanted to say something else, but she fell silent.

'What's everyone after today then?' Josie asked, changing the subject. 'Shopping-wise, I mean,' she added quickly, in case Lisa thought she was still talking about men.

'Summer dresses,' Nell said, running her hand through a rack of colourful strappy numbers on a nearby stall. 'These are nice, aren't they?'

Josie paused to rummage through a pile of tops on a table. 'I like this,' she said, holding up a smocky kind of top, with a drawstring scoop neck and floaty sleeves.

Lisa wrinkled her nose. 'Bit mumsy,' she said dismissively, turning to a tray of sunglasses.

Josie felt her cheeks flame. Mumsy — was that Lisa putting her in her place? She tried to pretend she hadn't heard. 'I don't really wear pretty things like this any more,' she said. 'It's practical all the way these days. Jeans, jeans and more jeans. And boring old tops that can be washed two hundred times without falling apart.'

Lisa was trying on some sunglasses in front of a mirror and pouting at herself. 'God, I couldn't bear that,' she said. 'Don't you get sick of it?'

Josie shrugged. 'I suppose,' she said. To be honest, though, she hardly thought about what she wore. She had enough to do every morning, getting the boys fed and dressed, without stopping to agonize over which outfit to put together for that day. Which was why, more often than not, she grabbed whatever was on top of the clean-washing pile.

She put the scoop-necked top back on the pile and turned away from it. Anyway, it wasn't as if she *needed* to dress up like a mannequin every day, was it? She was hardly out there on the pull any more, trying to dazzle the guys with her shag-me outfits. She'd done all that and got through to the other side, husband in tow, hadn't she?

She saw a rail of skirts in bright jewel colours and felt a wistfulness steal over her. Back when she'd been a designer, she'd worn clothes like that. Loud, look-at-me clothes. You could get away with wearing quirky, funky stuff and statement jewellery if you were a designer. In fact, she could even remember lying in bed in the mornings, not being able to throw off the duvet until she'd planned exactly which ensemble she was going to wear. It had all mattered so much then. Her clothes had defined her. She had cared.

They made their way slowly through the market, past the jewellery stalls, the painted crockery, the mosaic-framed mirrors, the decorated light-bulbs and kooky hat stalls. Nell bought some flip-flops with large pink flowers over the toe straps. Lisa bought a bottle-green vase for her sister's birthday present. Josie bought two painted wooden dinosaurs for the boys and a retro silver clock to go in the kitchen. The boys had broken the last one with a badly aimed Frisbee that came in through the back door.

The sun had emerged from the clouds and was glinting off the canal. Josie was carrying her coat as well as her overnight bag, and suddenly felt hot and tired. 'Anyone want coffee?' she asked hopefully as they passed a stall.

'Definitely,' Nell said. She was laden with her coat and bag too, and was fanning herself with one of her new flip-flops. 'Good idea.'

'Could you get me a latte?' Lisa asked, pressing a two-pound coin into Josie's hand. She was holding her BlackBerry. 'I'm just going to send a quick email to the States. Something's come up.'

'Sure,' Josie said, rather taken aback that Lisa was still together enough to even think about work, three beers into a sunny Saturday afternoon.

She and Nell joined the queue for coffee, as Lisa perched gingerly on a metal chair nearby and started typing. 'So, what are your plans now?' Josie asked Nell as they waited. 'I mean, will you go back to Wales, or stay in London for a while? Have you left your job?'

Nell put a hand to her head as if she were going to tuck a curl behind her ear, then dropped it again. The habit clearly hadn't quite left her. 'Yeah,' she said, 'but it was only a temporary thing. I'm not sure what I'm going to do now. My first instinct was to get a plane ticket somewhere – anywhere – just to escape for a few months and...' Her eyes slid away from Josie. 'You know, lick my wounds. Distract myself from my broken heart with an adventure.' She spoke the words lightly, but there was a brittle edge to her tone. Then she smiled properly. 'But being back in London feels fab after a year in the middle of nowhere. I quite fancy a summer here, the more I think about it.'

'Oh good,' Josie said warmly. She loved the thought of Nell being closer at hand. 'Well, if you want somewhere to stay, come to ours any time. You don't even need to ring, just turn up. There'll always be a bed for you.' She rushed on before Nell could say no. 'I mean, I know we don't live in London, just boring suburbia, but it's commutable if you're working and...' She stopped herself as they reached the front of the queue. 'You know what I'm saying. Any time.'

'Cheers,' Nell said, smiling at her. 'I might just do that.'

The boys had floated up into Josie's head periodically throughout the afternoon, but as abstracts largely, in the back of her mind, rather than for any particular reason. It was only on the bus rumbling towards Lisa's house that she realized the time – almost four o'clock – and had a pang of missing them. Almost their entire day had gone by now, without her. That had hardly ever happened before.

Lisa and Nell were chatting about something in the seats in front, and Josie couldn't resist pulling out her mobile, just to see how her boys were doing without her. She pressed the home number – the one number she hardly ever dialled because she was so rarely away – and listened to the burr of the ring-tone. *Ring-ring, ring-ring . . .*

She could imagine their white phone on the corner table in the living room, its aerial crooked and stuck together with gaffer tape where one of the boys had bent it, falling on it in a fight. *Ring-ring, ring-ring . . .*

What would she be interrupting? she wondered with a little smile. Maybe Pete had got the pirate stuff out and they'd been immersed in a long, bloodthirsty game all afternoon. Maybe they were watching *Star Wars* together, deaf to the shrill of the phone, as Luke Skywalker grappled with Darth Vader. Or perhaps they were out in the garden being knights and dragons, and Pete was having to pelt through the house to get to the phone, a ridiculously small helmet still jammed on his head . . .

Her own voice spoke to her.

'You have reached Josie, Pete, Toby and Sam. We

can't take your call right now, so leave us a message and we'll get back to you as soon as we can. Thanks. Bye!'

She turned away from the woman next to her and spoke, hunching over her phone. 'Hiya, it's me,' she said, smiling again as she imagined them listening to her words sometime later. 'Hope you're all having a lovely day together. Been thinking about you loads. I'll try you again before bedtime, OK? Love you. Bye.'

She clicked the line dead and dropped the phone into her bag. She couldn't help wondering where they were. It was odd, not knowing, not being in the loop. Had Pete taken them out to the park all day, perhaps? Or to the cinema? They'd be having a brilliant time together anyway, she was sure. She should have done this before – given them their own space, the three of them, to do boys' stuff without her.

They got off the bus at the end of St Paul's Road, a long curving street lined with genteel three-storey Victorian houses.

'This way,' Lisa said, leading them along. 'Not far, promise.'

'Thank God for that,' Nell said. 'My arms are about to drop off with all this stuff.'

'See that silver Merc up there?' Lisa asked, pointing ahead. 'Well...'

'Is it *yours*?' Josie gulped. She knew Lisa was flying high at work, but she hadn't known she was flying *that* high.

Lisa shook her head. 'In my dreams,' she said. 'It's Roger's. He's my neighbour. No, I was about to say, my house is just there, near the Merc.' She laughed. 'My car's that really badly parked Honda.'

Right, thought Josie as they walked past it a few moments later. That brand spanking new baby-blue Honda must be the one then. O-k-a-a-ay. Lisa clearly *was* raking it in these days. She really had turned into alpha-minx of the pack while Josie hadn't been looking.

Nell let out a long whistle as Lisa stopped in front of a house with a black-painted door. 'Is this *all* yours?' she asked. 'The whole house?'

Lisa nodded. 'Yep,' she said proudly. 'The whole shebang. Come in and have a look.'

'Wow,' Josie blurted out as she followed Nell and Lisa up the front steps and into the hall. 'Wow, Lisa. This is so...' She swallowed, not able to think of a suitable superlative. The hall was long and wide, laid with the original Victorian floor tiles – small black and white squares in a checked pattern. The walls were painted a warm cream, and there was a huge gilt-edged mirror on one side and an antique console table with elegant curving legs on the other. 'So gorgeous,' she said, with a sigh of envy.

'Just dump your stuff and I'll put the kettle on,' Lisa said. 'There's a cloakroom under the stairs for your coats,' she added, walking along the hall in front of them.

'Bloody hell, Lise,' Nell said. 'I feel like I'm messing up your house just standing in it!'

'Don't be daft,' Lisa's voice floated back to them. 'Come down to the kitchen and tell me what you want to drink.'

Josie unlatched the cloakroom door and hung her coat on a peg. There was a selection of Lisa's coats and shoes in there, with several hooks still empty. Josie found herself thinking of her own coat rack, with the boys' green winter Parkas on it, plus their navy-blue raincoats and a variety of hooded tops for warm days, all fighting for space with her and Pete's things. That's the pay-off, she was ashamed to find herself thinking. Lisa's got a nice house, but she doesn't share it with family. Not like me.

She shoved the thought out of her head as quickly as it had popped up. That was a horrible thing to think. 'I am so jealous of this house,' she confessed to Nell in a whisper.

'Tell me about it,' Nell said. She hung her coat on a

peg, kicked off her boots and shut the door. 'How do you think it happened?' she asked as she and Josie walked to the kitchen. 'I mean, we all started off the same, didn't we? Fresh out of college, with our rubbish boyfriends, bad haircuts and crappy temping jobs. And now look at us.'

'Exactly,' Josie said. 'Wow, Lise. If I had this kitchen, I would just live in it, I think.'

The kitchen was long and wide, and stretched down to French windows at the far end, through which Josie could see a decent-sized garden. The walls were white-washed and had a rough, country look to them, as if they were really the walls of a farmhouse in Provence. The large windows were hung with cheerful striped roller blinds, with slate tiles on the sills. The units looked like solid oak, and were topped with black granite work surfaces. Everything shone like a Flash advert – the espresso machine, the chrome juicer, the silver Alessi kettle . . .

'No, I mean, you as well, Jose,' Nell was saying. 'You're a success story too, with your man and two kids and nice home. And Lisa's shot off the scale in career terms, with—'

'Hardly,' Lisa said, filling the kettle with water.

'Darlin', compared to me, you are in the outer strato-sphere,' Nell told her bluntly. 'And here I am, having started in the same place as you two and look at me! I'm homeless, jobless, boyfriendless...' Nell pulled a face. 'What am I doing wrong?'

'Nothing!' Josie said indignantly. 'Hello? Reality check! You've been all over the world, seen tons of amazing things, had loads of adventures ... Nell! Not many people have had even half the exciting times you've had. And you've got no strings! You're free! Nobody's holding you back from doing whatever you want to do!'

Josie stopped abruptly, aware of the note of yearning in her voice.

'I know that,' Nell said, perching on the edge of the table. 'And it's good, being free, but it's just ... Well, I think I'm doing all right, but as soon as I compare myself to you two ...'

'Don't even go there,' Lisa said. 'Yeah, so I've got a nice house and car, and can buy whatever I want to right now, but I've slogged in the City for years. I've worked late nights, weekends, I've dealt with shit from all the blokes there every single day. I've put everything on hold – family, friends, men, babies, all the rest of it – to climb the greasy pole. And take it from me, there have been plenty of times over the last few years when I've had a postcard from you, barefoot in Bali or Bolivia or Brazil or wherever, and I've thought exactly the same thing: What am I doing? Why aren't I seeing the world like

Nell, or having babies like Josie, or . . .' She put the kettle down suddenly, and took a breath. 'Maybe I should open some wine,' she said. 'This is all getting a bit serious.'

'Maybe you should,' Josie agreed. She was trying to catch Nell's eye but Nell was staring out into the garden.

'I just don't know what to do now,' Nell confessed, her blue eyes far away. 'At least you two have some kind of game plan. You can see where it's all going next in your lives. Me, I haven't got a clue. Not a fucking clue.'

'But that's not so bad, is it?' Lisa said, opening a cupboard door and squatting in front of rack upon rack of wine bottles. She pulled one out and considered it, then pushed it back in and selected another. 'Red all right for everyone? This should be a good vintage. And would you really have it any other way, Nell? You'd hate my life. You'd resign from my job within seconds.' She raised an eyebrow. 'And it's all very well having a nice house but you have to keep up the mortgage payments. Which, let me tell you, are a ball and chain in themselves.'

'I suppose,' Nell said, nodding.

There was a silence while Lisa uncorked the bottle and poured three generous glasses full.

Nell took the glass Lisa handed her and held it up. 'Cheers anyway. To all of our futures. Whatever's around the corner – let's hope it's something exciting.'

'Definitely,' said Josie, raising hers. *Let's hope it's Rose,* she thought immediately, a hand stealing around to her belly. That would be the best kind of excitement.

Nell started talking rather more enthusiastically about the places she still wanted to visit — Sumatra and Zanzibar and Guatemala and a great long list of others — and Josie's thoughts drifted homeward. Excitement wasn't exactly something that her family did in spades, she realized, sipping her wine. She and Pete had been a lot more reckless before they'd had kids but now they existed in a safety chamber. They holidayed in the south of France now, or Cornwall, rather than anywhere tropical that required jabs or malaria tablets. Week in, week out, it was work for Pete, and playgroup, swimming lessons, gym club and trips to the park for her and the boys. Sunday dinner at the in-laws'. Maybe a child's party to go to. It was all very . . . pedestrian, really. No excitement whatsoever.

Josie took a larger slug of her wine and leaned back in her chair, listening as Nell talked about the wide African skies she'd camped under, the vibrant coral reefs she'd scuba-dived, the noise and smells and bustle of her favourite market in India . . .

She was envious, she realized. She'd come here this weekend feeling as if she had the perfect life all wrapped up, but suddenly she was starting to doubt her conviction. There she'd been at lunchtime, worrying that her friends might think her smug, that they might covet her life, her husband and children. Now she wondered if they actually pitied her for taking the motherhood path while they'd flung themselves into adventures and professional triumphs instead.

She had nothing to contribute to this conversation, she thought helplessly, no adventures of her own to report. She couldn't join in knowledgably when Lisa spoke about boardroom dramas. She couldn't add anecdotes to Nell's travelling stories. Her life had become so safe, so predictable, so *boring* in comparison! She'd been somebody's wife, somebody's mum for too long, lost her sparkly Josieness, lost her bottle . . .

She sipped her wine again. Still, it wasn't too late to change things, was it? She didn't have to spend the rest of her life like this. Now that the boys were older, maybe she and Pete could afford to be more impulsive, take a few risks? Maybe they could all go on an adventure together!

She grinned to herself. Yes. She'd suggest it. They should definitely break out of the safety chamber and go somewhere exciting before Rose was born. That way, next time she and her friends met up, she'd have tales of her own to tell again, wouldn't she?

Chapter Four

'Smile!'

Josie beamed into the camera and blinked in the flash that followed. She, Lisa and Nell were the only people left in the Italian restaurant now and their waiter had taken a break from pointedly sweeping up around their table to snap a photo of them with Nell's camera.

'Thanks. That's one for the family album,' Nell said, winking at him. 'Could we have the bill, please?'

'I'll get this,' Lisa said, skimming through a wedge of credit cards in a smart Mulberry wallet. 'My treat.'

'As if,' Nell said, planting a twenty-pound note in the centre of the table. 'We should be treating you, for being our hostess with the mostest tonight.'

Lisa batted away Nell's money. 'You two paid train fares to come to London,' she countered. 'So this can be my contribution.'

Besides, I'm loaded and this paltry bill is nothing to me, a nasty little voice added in Josie's head. 'Well, we'll pay for the cab back,' she said quickly, trying to shut out her uncharitable thoughts. 'Won't we, Nell?'

'Cab back? We haven't started yet,' Lisa said in surprise. 'I thought we were going clubbing after this!'

Josie gulped. The thought of going to a hot sweaty club now, where you had to shout over the pounding music to make yourself heard and where everyone was fifteen years younger than her (and better groomed, and in sexier clothes), and where it cost a fiver for a single drink ... Oh God! She really *really* didn't want to go clubbing! But there was no way she could say that in front of the other two. No way! If Nell had the stamina to go on somewhere too, then Josie would just have to bite the bullet and join them.

She turned to Nell, trying to keep the desperation from her eyes.

'Do you really want to?' Nell asked Lisa. 'Only ... I was kind of wondering about getting some chocolate and having a cup of tea in our PJs back at yours, Lise. Like the good old days ...'

'Josie? How about you?' Lisa asked.

Josie felt a wave of relief. 'Chocolate and PJs have my vote too,' she said apologetically, standing up to get her coat. 'Sorry, Lise – is that really boring of us?'

'No! Course not!' Lisa said. The waiter came over and

she handed him her credit card. 'Put it all on there,' she instructed.

'Well, we'll definitely pay for the cab then,' Josie said. 'And all the chocolate.'

Nell shrugged on her jacket. 'And that alone will be a small fortune, if I've got anything to do with it,' she laughed.

Once Lisa had paid, they strolled out of the restaurant, arm in arm. As well as aching feet and a feeling of having drunk far too much for one day, there was another reason Josie wanted to go back to Lisa's – to check for messages. She'd called home a couple more times that evening, only to keep getting her own answerphone. Pete's mobile had been switched off too, every time she'd tried it. Where were they?

Josie kept telling herself that everything was sure to be fine, they'd just got caught up having a great time somewhere or other and hadn't managed to call her, but it felt horrible, not being able to say good-night to the boys.

She slipped her arm out of Nell's and checked her mobile again for messages as they walked – ahh, and there was a text from Pete. At last! She must have missed the phone's bleep when it came through. She read it quickly.

Sorry – missed yr calls. All fine. See u tomorrow.

All fine. Thank goodness. Oh, thank goodness! It was only then that she realized how much she'd been worrying about them, how tense she'd felt. She tried dialling his number but it switched straight to voicemail. Maybe he was having an early night. It was gone eleven now, after all.

She put the phone back in her bag, and took Nell's arm again. 'I am having such a good time,' she blurted out, as she was flooded with joyful drunkenness. 'I am so happy that I'm here with you two. My two best friends.' For a second, she thought she might cry. 'Life is great, isn't it? Life is just great.'

Back at Lisa's, Josie stepped out of her boots and sank into the sofa, massaging the balls of her feet thankfully. Lisa lit some stout white church candles on the mantelpiece and put on a CD. 'We should really be drinking Baileys now if we're going to indulge in the complete nostalgia trip,' she said, 'but I don't know if I can face it. What does anyone else fancy? Tea? More wine?'

Josie bit off the end of a Twix and crunched it. 'I could go another bottle of wine,' she said. Hell, why not? Now that she was curled up on Lisa's squashy sofa with chocolate melting in her mouth, and her bed only a stair-climb away, she could feel a second wind coming on. It wasn't as if she had to drag herself out of bed to make the boys breakfast at six-thirty the next morning, after all. For once she could lie in bed until midday if she felt like it.

'Go, Josie!' Nell cheered. 'Me too. Sorry, Lise, we should have picked up another bottle while we were out.'

'No worries,' Lisa said easily. 'How about something bubbly? I've got some champers in the fridge. I meant to open it earlier but we ended up drinking all that red instead.'

'Champagne would be just *lush*,' Josie said, resting her head on the back of the sofa. 'Oh, Lise, do I have to go home tomorrow? Can't I just come and live with you instead? I'll do all your cooking and cleaning . . .'

Lisa laughed. 'I'll get some glasses,' she said, and left the room.

Nell was staring into the candle flames from where she was curled up at the other end of the sofa. 'Everything all right?' Josie asked, nudging her with a foot.

Nell nodded. 'Just thinking,' she said, without looking at Josie.

'About Gareth?' Josie prompted before she could stop herself.

'Kind of,' Nell replied. She leaned against a cushion and closed her eyes. 'It's been a bit of a mad few weeks. I—'

She stopped abruptly as Lisa came back into the room with a fat green bottle misted with cold, and three champagne flutes clinking between her fingers. 'Right – who wants to pop the cork?' Lisa asked.

Josie flicked her eyes across to Nell, a little irritated that Lisa had come in at that second. She was sure Nell had been about to tell her more about Gareth and what had happened between them. Now the moment had gone. 'You do it, Lise,' she said. 'I always get nervous it's going to spurt everywhere.'

'Said the actress to the bishop,' Nell drawled, sitting up and opening her eyes. 'Oh God, what am I going to do without sex?' she moaned suddenly. 'That's the worst thing about breaking up with someone, those single nights with nobody to put their arms around you.'

'Nell, it's only been a week,' Josie reminded her. 'You might even be able to patch things up, you never know.'

'Nah,' Nell said, shaking her head. 'No, I won't. It's over, that one.'

'Sex is the easy part anyway, if you ask me,' Lisa said, pulling the champagne cork out with a flourish. A thin wisp of vapour spiralled into the air, then vanished as she began pouring. 'Getting the buggers to stay around the next morning, that's the tricky bit.'

'Sex isn't everything,' Josie put in. 'If you must know, I'm really looking forward to sleeping on my own tonight, without Pete trying to pull my knickers off as soon as the lights go out.'

'Oh, don't, you're making me feel worse,' Nell groaned, taking the glass that Lisa was holding out. 'Smug cow.'

'I'm not being smug!' Josie replied. 'OK, so I've got it when I want it, but most of the time I don't want it.' She took the second glass of champagne from Lisa, and stared at the vertical lines of tiny bubbles rushing up to the surface, one after another. 'And then I feel bad for not wanting it, like I'm letting him down, when I'm just so knackered all I want to do is shut my eyes.' She leaned forward conspiratorially. 'Once I even pretended I thought I'd caught nits off the boys to keep him away from me.'

'Evil!' Nell laughed, spluttering as she took a sip.

A small frown appeared between Lisa's eyebrows. 'I don't get that,' she confessed. 'You're married to him – but you never want to sleep with him?' She gave a small hiccup. 'Don't you worry that he'll just go off with someone else?'

Josie shook her head. 'Absolutely not,' she said firmly.

'He's not like that. No way.' She took a mouthful of bubbles, enjoying the sensation of them fizzing on her tongue. 'Anyway, I'm not saying I *never* want to sleep with him,' she went on. 'Sometimes I do really fancy him. It's just . . .' The sentence hung in the air, unfinished. *It's just that I only fancy him at certain times of the month, that's all. Like, when he can make me pregnant.* 'Are we going to have a toast with this bubbly or what?' she demanded, not wanting to discuss it any more.

'Course,' Nell said, raising her glass. 'Cheers, ladies. Here's to me forgetting all about Gareth and meeting somebody fabulous soon.'

'Cheers,' Lisa added. 'Amen to that. And here's to me meeting—' Her BlackBerry started beeping urgently, and she rolled her eyes. 'Sorry, guys, I'd better just get that.'

'It's almost midnight!' Josie said in surprise. 'Who's going to be emailing you now?'

Lisa checked the screen. 'Just another work thing from the States,' she said, her fingers flashing over the keyboard. 'I'll be two minutes.'

'Are you not allowed to have a life?' Nell asked, exchanging raised-eyebrow glances with Josie. 'Can't you just tell them to sod off?' She laughed. 'You were right, I'd be sacked from your job within the hour, Lise,' she said. 'Me and my bad attitude. I couldn't be doing with all that prisoner-of-my-own-technology stuff.'

Lisa pressed a button to send off her message and picked up her glass again. 'Dahling, I'm so *essential* to their business, they can't manage without me, even at weekends,' she replied. 'And don't worry, I'm billing them for every minute. In fact, they just bought us another bottle of that vintage champers, so don't knock it.' She said the words jokily, but there was a kind of defensiveness in there as well, Josie thought, mentally backing away from the subject.

'What were we talking about?' Lisa went on breezily. 'Oh yes, our sex lives.' Her eyes rested on Josie. 'Well, it sounds as if I'm the only one who's getting my rocks off these days.'

Her words felt like an attack, and Josie blinked. 'But you're not in love,' she countered before she could rein herself in. 'And haven't been for years, according to you. So I know what I'd rather have.' Her reply came out sharper than she'd intended it to.

'What, a loveless marriage, and two brats? No career, no life? Stuck out in Dullsville, with your wardrobe full of jeans and boring tops?' Lisa's words were sharper still, cutting right to the quick.

'They're not brats!' Josie cried, her voice rising in indignation. 'And it's not a loveless marriage!' she added hastily.

'That's not what I heard,' Lisa muttered.

Nell held up her hands. 'God, calm down, you two! It's not a competition!' she said.

'What do you mean, that's not what you heard?' Josie demanded, ignoring Nell. She could feel the blood surging around her at Lisa's criticisms. 'Who's been saying that, then?'

Lisa looked tired suddenly. Her make-up was smudged, her top was crumpled and her hair had lost its sheen. 'Oh, nobody,' she said, waving a hand as if in surrender. 'Sorry, I shouldn't have said that. Below the belt.'

'Yes,' agreed Josie, stung, 'it was.' Way below the belt – below the bikini line, actually – and totally out of order. 'And they're not brats!' she felt like saying again. She knew Lisa didn't particularly like kids – she hadn't been interested in Josie's two from the start – but to call them *that*, when she didn't even know them ... It was a swipe too far. She shook her head angrily.

The CD ended and there was an uneasy silence in the room. 'This is still about Nick, isn't it?' Josie burst out, unable to stop herself. 'You still carry a grudge! Just because he fancied me, not you. Just because *I* went out with him, not you. Admit it, Lisa. You've always held it against me.'

'No!' Lisa protested, but her cheeks were flushed. 'This has nothing to do with Nick. That was years ago.'

'Exactly,' Josie said. 'Which is why I can't believe you're still resentful about it now, after all this time.'

'I am *not* resentful!' Lisa shouted.

That silence again. Josie didn't know where to look. The truth was, she had always felt bad about what had happened with Nick, even though it was going back ten years at least. Nick had been Lisa's friend originally, she'd met him through the legal firm where she'd worked. He had been one of the junior lawyers there, and he and Lisa had had a few post-work drinks where they'd gossiped about their colleagues and compared notes, but nothing more had happened.

Josie could tell that Lisa *wanted* more, though. It was nothing specific she'd said about him, but Josie had noticed a particular look in her eyes, a little smile playing around her mouth whenever she mentioned Nick's name. And then, almost overnight it had seemed, Lisa – who'd always been a bit of a scruff back then – had started wearing perfume to work, had taken to spending ages applying her make-up first thing instead of slouching in front of GMTV with a coffee, had revamped her wardrobe and hair … Josie had known it had been for Nick's benefit. It was screamingly obvious that Lisa had a full-blown whopper of a crush on him.

A month or so later, it was Lisa's birthday and she'd organized a pub get-together for Saturday night. She'd invited Nick and a couple of others from her work along, and Josie and Nell were both nosily looking forward to meeting them, especially Nick. What Josie hadn't counted on, though, was the overwhelming *whoomph* of lust she'd experienced when she'd seen him come in through the door. It was like a match dropped in petrol, the suddenness of it, the heat and intensity.

Nick was something special. He sparkled with charisma. He walked into a room, and people noticed him. He was sexy without seeming to know it, carried himself with an effortless kind of grace. He had strolled straight up to Josie at the bar and given her such an easy, friendly grin that she'd literally had to hold tight to the wooden ledge to stop herself keeling over.

Less than two hours later, she was back at his flat, being shagged senseless, tingling from head to toe with lust.

Lisa had never said anything – anything at all – about Josie and Nick leaving her birthday do so blatantly early. And when Josie had returned to the girls' flat the following morning, bright-eyed and loved up, it only took one glance at Lisa's face to give her the guilty feeling of having trespassed on her friend's property.

Lisa had barely commented on Josie and Nick's relationship, even when it had progressed to a serious thing lasting over a year. But the gleam had faded from her eyes, Josie noticed. The post-work drinks ended abruptly, to Nick's surprise. (He, being a bloke, hadn't got a clue about Lisa's feelings, of course.) The make-up was toned down, the skirts went back into her wardrobe and her boring trouser suits reappeared. Lisa threw herself into her blossoming career as if it were the only thing that mattered. And Nick had always been the unspoken, taboo subject that stood between them, even after all these years.

Lisa got up to change the CD. 'I am not resentful,' she repeated in a quieter voice. It was almost as if she was trying to convince herself, let alone the other two.

'It all happened such a long time ago,' Nell said. 'To be honest, I'd totally forgotten about Nick.'

Josie glanced over at Lisa, who was flicking intently through her CDs. *We hadn't forgotten, though, had we, Lise?* she felt like saying.

'Mmmm,' Lisa said non-committally. 'It's all water under the bridge now, I suppose.'

'Yes,' Josie said, her cheeks cooling from the sudden rush of anger. 'Sorry, Lisa. I shouldn't have dragged it up. It was just what you said about my boys, I felt really—'

Lisa finally looked her in the eye. 'I shouldn't have

called them brats. I'm sorry, too. It wasn't a personal thing, I tend to call all kids brats.' She gave a small smile. 'I'm sure your boys are perfect little angels.'

Josie forced a smile too, grateful for the peace offering. 'Well, I wouldn't go that far,' she said. 'But thanks. And about Nick ... this is all too late, and we should have had this conversation at the time, but for what it's worth, I'm sorry if I was insensitive, going off with him and—'

'Oh, don't,' Lisa said hurriedly. 'Honestly, there's no need to say anything about it. What happened happened. And you two were great together, while it lasted. It wasn't like I had any exclusive rights over him.'

Nell picked up the champagne bottle and went around filling their glasses. 'Right, that's that, then,' she said. 'Nick – finally dealt with and laid to rest. Not literally, obviously, but...' She giggled. 'Let's talk about something else now anyway. Something less emotive. Anybody been watching *'Stenders* lately?'

Josie rolled over in bed, dimly aware of morning noises filtering into her mind. It was strange, not hearing the usual sounds of her boys shouting and fighting, the birds singing in the rowan tree outside her bedroom window, Radio 5 burbling from Pete's bedside clock...

Lisa's house sounded different. Josie could hear the faint buzz of traffic from the road outside instead. A bus rumbling as it slowed at the lights. Muffled voices from people walking along the pavement.

She was in one of Lisa's guest rooms – there were two – at the front of the house, with wisteria branches framing the window in a woody tangle. If you were going to wake up with a hangover, this was about as soothing a place as you could hope to be in, Josie thought, with its cream walls and large antique bed, its thick oatmeal curtains and honey-coloured waxed floorboards.

She opened her eyes a crack to see sunlight streaming through the gap in the curtains where she'd drunkenly only half closed them the night before. The light was dazzling, and she shut her eyes again immediately as a dull, heavy pain thudded inside her skull.

Ouch, that had been a bad idea. How much had she drunk yesterday, anyway? Her own body weight in beer, wine and champagne, if the pounding of her head was anything to go by. Ugh. *Ugh.*

Her face felt hot. Her eyelashes were clumpy where she hadn't bothered to take off her mascara the night before. Her hair reeked of Nell's roll-ups, and her skin had a sour, sweaty tang to it. And to think she had to get all the way home on a train later. She was so going to throw up on it, she knew already.

Josie lay still for a few moments while the hangover raged around inside her. She could hear some kids shouting in the street outside and had a pang for her own two. How would they have got on, waking up without her this morning?

She smiled, despite her headache. They were probably loving it. They'd be sprawled out on the sofa, no doubt, still in their Spiderman pyjamas, watching *Return of the Jedi* and doing their Chewbacca impressions. She couldn't wait to see them again.

Ahh. There was Lisa's voice floating up from downstairs, so she and Nell must already be awake. Josie rubbed her eyes sleepily, then sniffed the air, suddenly feeling more alert. Mmmm. That was definitely the unmistakable scent of bacon drifting up from the kitchen . . .

Bacon! All of a sudden, Josie was starving. A mug of tea and a bacon sarnie, dripping with butter and ketchup . . . Just what she needed. *Exactly* what she needed to see off this hangover. Good old Lisa had thought of everything.

Josie sat up, swinging her legs out of bed. The sudden movement made her head spin, and she clutched a hand to her temple, knocking her make-up bag over on the side table as she did so. 'Oh shit,' she muttered, as her lipsticks bounced on the floorboards and rolled away under the bed. Her foundation, her eye pencils, her silver pocket mirror . . . they were cascading out of the bag like a cosmetic fountain.

Josie grimaced. She had never been the most co-ordinated person to start with, but a hangover always made her ten times clumsier. Bollocks.

She took a slurp of water from the glass on the bedside table – thank goodness she hadn't knocked *that* everywhere too – and got down on her hands and knees to pick up all her bits and pieces. Ouch. It hurt, bending her head so low. Josie groaned aloud. Why had she drunk so much? And oh God, she'd just remembered that row with Lisa about Nick. Why had she dredged his name up after so long? Why hadn't she just left it buried?

Josie shut her eyes as the memory slammed into sharper focus. Oh no, and she'd said all those awful things about Lisa being on her own, and resenting her, and . . . Oh, help. She was a total liability after a few drinks. A nightmare friend, as well, to come out with such stuff. What were the chances of Lisa suffering a memory block and having no recollection whatsoever of the conversation?

Josie rolled her eyes. Zero, at a guess.

Still, the rest of the evening hadn't been so rancorous at least. They'd all hugged each other good-night when they'd finally run out of steam, so things had ended up

OK. And didn't all the magazines say that it was the sign of a good friendship, when you could be honest with them, sort things out and move on, still friends?

Josie picked up her lipsticks and stuffed them back in her bag. She, Lisa and Nell would always be friends now, she reckoned. They just had too much history for that to change. It was reassuring, when other things in life were forever shifting, that you could have your best friends as constants, through thick and thin, good times and bad . . .

In went the eyelash curlers and the tweezers and the eyeshadow pots and the nail varnish. Not that she'd used any of that last night: Nell had made Josie up with a load of freebies Lisa had donated to them. There was the foundation and the perfume – phew, mercifully un-broken. Was that everything? Where had her little mirror landed?

Bending her neck stiffly, Josie peered under the bed. Christ, even the space under Lisa's spare-room bed was tidy and ordered. Josie lived in horror of anyone seeing the cardboard boxes crammed with stuff, and fluffballs like tumbleweed under the bed she shared with Pete.

Not so in Lisa's case, though. Of course. There were several rose-patterned storage boxes stacked up neatly right at the back, and a smart black suitcase. Was that her mirror next to it? She stretched an arm under the bed, groping around for where she'd seen the tell-tale flash of silver. Her fingers closed around something – oh, it was the edge of another storage box – and then she managed to knock *that* over. God, what was wrong with her? She was a right oaf this morning!

She peered under the bed again and sighed. Now there were heaps of Lisa's stuff all over the floor. Bloody hell. She was never going to get her bacon sarnie at this rate. She swept her arm around it, dragging everything out into the light. There was the mirror – oh, and another eye pencil she'd missed. And there . . .

She blinked uncertainly. There, in a small round frame, was a photo. Of Pete.

She stared in surprise, her brain racing to make sense of the discovery. Why on earth was there a picture of her husband under Lisa's bed? How had it ended up there? It wasn't even a photo she recognized. In fact, she was quite sure she'd never seen it before.

There he was, Pete, gazing up at her from her hand, as if he could tell the answer to the riddle, smiling into the camera, his eyes crinkling at the corners. The photo had been taken a few years ago, she guessed, because he was wearing a top that he'd loved to death one summer – when was it? She couldn't think suddenly. His hair looked different in the photo, too. Slightly shorter than it was now.

Josie frowned, confused. She didn't recognize the

photo. She was sure *she* hadn't taken it. It had been cut small to fit in the tiny frame, so she couldn't see the background, couldn't give it a context. He looked happy, wherever he was. He looked really happy. Josie could tell by the brightness of his face that the sun was shining, and he had a wide smile, head slightly tilted, shoulders relaxed, as if he were on holiday.

But who was he smiling at? And why was it making her feel so unsettled to look at it?

Josie took another slurp of water and got to her feet. Still holding the photograph, she went downstairs to the kitchen, head spinning with questions. She felt as if she was in a strange dream, where everything was muddled.

She opened the kitchen door, and Nell and Lisa both turned towards her, smiles on their faces.

The bacon was sizzling. The kettle was whistling. Lisa was at the hob, holding a spatula as she turned, and seemed to be saying something, but Josie couldn't hear it. Couldn't take it in.

Josie stood there in her pyjamas and bare feet, hair sticking up on end. She held up the photo in front of her. 'I found this under the bed,' she said, the words sticking to the sides of her dry mouth. 'Why was this under your bed, Lisa?'

Chapter Five

Lisa blinked. For a split second, her face changed, a ghost of an expression crossing it fleetingly, and then it was gone. Closed book. She shook her head. 'I have absolutely no idea,' she said briskly, her features wrinkling in a frown. 'How weird. Coffee?'

'It *is* weird,' Josie said warily, her eyes fixed upon Lisa. The smell of bacon turned her stomach now, and the photo felt heavy in her hand. That look in Lisa's eyes, that flicker of reaction – Josie had caught it before it was wiped clean. Something was going on. 'I mean, I've never even seen this picture before. When was it taken?'

'How should I know?' Lisa asked, pouring coffee into a mug, her back to Josie. 'He's your husband, not mine. I can't keep track of him!'

'Yes, but I found it in *your* house,' Josie said uncertainly. She was trying to catch Lisa's eye but Lisa was busying herself stirring in milk and rinsing the teaspoon.

'Where did you find it?' Nell asked, coming over to Josie. 'Can I see?'

'It's just a photo of Pete,' Josie said, handing it to her. 'It was under the bed. I wasn't poking around,' she added hastily. 'I knocked my make-up bag off the side and everything spilled, and I was just gathering all my bits and bobs that had rolled under the bed, when—'

'There you are, then,' Lisa put in, flipping the bacon deftly.

'What?' Josie asked.

'It must have been in your make-up bag,' Lisa replied. She put down the spatula and handed Josie the mug of coffee. 'Don't you see? The photo must have been in your bag all along, and fell out with your other things. Pete obviously put it in there before you left, to surprise you. How sweet!'

'How sweet,' Josie echoed uncertainly, warming her hands on the mug. Could that really have been what had happened? She wanted to believe Lisa was telling her the truth. But wouldn't she have noticed the photo last night when she was getting ready to go out?

'Aw, how romantic is that?' Nell said, passing the photo back. 'He didn't want you to miss him. Bless!'

Josie sipped her coffee, trying to make sense of it all. If the photo had been right at the bottom of her make-up bag, there *was* a chance she wouldn't have seen it last night. After all, she'd brought tons of slap with her, most of which she hadn't even used. So the photo could easily have been underneath it all, unnoticed, she supposed . . .

And, if she was honest, she did like the idea of Pete choosing a snapshot of himself, trimming it to fit in the small frame and hiding it in her bag. It was the sort of thing he might have done back when they were first seeing each other, in those heady romantic days. The thought that he could have done it again, after seven years of marriage . . . Well, it was lovely, wasn't it? What a thoughtful gesture.

Lisa was right. It *was* sweet. Romantic.

'Bacon sandwich?' Lisa asked pleasantly, and the conversation was closed.

Josie stared out of the window as the city sped past. It was eleven-thirty now, and the sun glittered on the Thames, bouncing off all the glass riverfront buildings with a thousand different sparkles. It tricked you like that, London, showed you its best side just as you were leaving it behind.

Now the train was hurtling through a maze of terraces, thundering through Battersea and Wandsworth Common and on towards Crystal Palace. Rows and rows of streets and houses and lives, all packed in together. She saw a barbecue in one garden, children playing on swings in another. A barking black Labrador bounced after a ball on somebody's lawn, washing lines were full and fluttering, back doors and windows open to let in the sun. Lawns were being mown, flowerbeds tended. Inside, in the coolness of shaded rooms, young couples would be entwined in bed still, curtains drawn against the day. And in busy kitchens, Sunday lunch was being chopped and boiled and roasted, while children wound about their parents, droning, 'Is it nearly ready? I'm starving! I'm THIS hungry!'

Josie took out her mobile, planning to call Pete and let him know when her train was due in. She'd originally thought she'd have lunch with her friends and head home this afternoon, but Lisa had made her apologies after breakfast, claiming to have hours' worth of reading to plough through before a meeting tomorrow, and Nell had already arranged to go to her mum's for Sunday dinner. So she was returning earlier than she'd guessed, but that was cool. She was looking forward to it.

Josie was just about to dial when she stopped herself and put the phone down. Actually, it would be more fun to surprise them by rocking up when they weren't expecting her, wouldn't it? She could almost hear the excited shrieks from the boys as they mobbed her. It made her smile just to think about it. She couldn't wait to hold them again, to put her arms around their wriggling bodies and feel their twin heartbeats thumping against her own. And, of course, there was Rose to gear up for now! Tonight was the night, after all. Perfect timing – a romantic reunion with Pete was the very thing to top off the weekend, especially if there was some insemination as a Brucie bonus!

Her phone bleeped as a text message came in. It was from Nell.

Had such a fab w/e with u – loved it. N x

Josie grinned and texted her back.

Me too. Come and stay soon, she wrote. Love you.

Oh, it had been great to see Nell again. The two of them had shared a cab to King's Cross, then had a long affectionate hug on the concourse. It was only as they'd been about to part that Josie remembered the photo of Pete. 'Nell, you don't think...' she started. She paused, searching for the best way to phrase the question. 'You know that thing with the photo this morning? Was it me, or was Lisa being a bit ... odd?'

Nell hesitated. 'I'm not sure,' she replied. 'I could hardly think straight, my hangover was such a shocker, so the whole thing rather passed me by. But it did feel as if there was a bit of a strange atmosphere. Tense.' She shrugged, then nudged Josie. 'What, do you think she's got a bit of a crush on your Pete or something? D'you reckon there was a stash of love poems under her bed as well?'

Josie wrinkled her nose. 'No, I . . .' She felt stupid for having asked the question now. 'It was probably nothing. I'd only just woken up, maybe I was reading too much into it. She seemed a bit . . . defensive, that's all. Like I'd rattled her.' She tried to remember the expression that had flitted across Lisa's face, but it was hard to dredge it up in her mind now. Then a thought struck her. 'Oh God! I wasn't thinking. Maybe she was being cool with me after all the Nick stuff last night!'

Nell nodded sagely. 'Could have been. It did go a bit heavy, didn't it?' She rolled her eyes in a comical way. 'I bet Nick's ears were well and truly on fire, with all that arguing over him.'

'It wasn't arguing over *him*, it was just a drunken lapse,' Josie retaliated. 'It wasn't like either of us still carry a torch for him.'

'Well, I dunno,' Nell put in. 'Lisa seemed very touchy on the subject.'

'Mmm,' Josie said. The more Josie thought about it, the more her hunch seemed plausible. 'All the more reason why that must have been it — the tension this morning, I mean. She woke up, remembered the set-to with me and was feeling a bit humpy about it. Then I burst in, brandishing Pete's photo in her face all accusingly, and . . .' She giggled, relieved that she'd worked it out. 'No wonder she wasn't exactly chummy.'

Nell raised an eyebrow. 'By Jove, I think she's got it. Listen, I'd better fly, anyway. Back to my mum's for the Spanish Inquisition on why I haven't settled down with my two-point-two children and mortgage and sensible job yet . . . God, how am I going to cope?'

Josie laughed. 'You don't have to,' she reminded her. 'Spare room at ours whenever you need it.'

Nell gave her a last hug. 'Mrs Winter, you are too kind,' she said. 'I'll probably be on your doorstep before the week's out.'

An hour or so later, Josie pushed open the front door and dropped her bags. 'Hello! I'm back!' she called. 'Anybody home?'

There was silence. Not the breathless, we're-hiding kind of silence she knew from the boys, but a proper, dense, nobody-in absence of sound. 'Oh,' Josie said aloud. She glanced back out of the front door, and realized that Pete's car wasn't on the driveway. She'd been so excited about surprising them with her appearance she hadn't even noticed.

She closed the door, unable to keep her shoulders from slumping. It was something of an anti-climax, coming back to find nobody home. Her arms swung empty where she'd hoped they'd be full of her boys and man. Where were they?

Maybe they'd all gone out to pick up a Sunday paper and some milk. Or maybe, as it was sunny, Pete had taken them to the adventure playground, and any minute now they'd come belting back in for lunch. So in the meantime she should make the most of it, have a quiet coffee, sit in the garden on her own and enjoy the peace and quiet.

The answerphone was bleeping, she realized. Maybe Pete had left her a message telling her to come and meet them somewhere?

Beep! 'Hi, it's me, Lisa. I've been trying your mobile but couldn't get through. Give me a ring when you get this, OK? Bye.' *Beep!*

Josie pressed Delete. She was always doing that, leaving her mobile off. She'd call later – she'd probably just left a pair of dirty knickers under the bed or something equally classy. Now ... coffee. A strong one was definitely in order. Her hangover was still thundering about in her head, stubbornly resisting the Nurofen she'd thrown at it back in London.

She walked into the kitchen – and groaned out loud.

What a tip! The breakfast things were still all over the place, the washing machine had finished its run and needed emptying, and ... Josie's eyes locked on to it and she let out a moan of dismay. She could see a wet, beige mass through its door and knew straight away what it was. Her bloody Miss Hoolie coat, which she'd put in to wash yesterday morning!

She tutted in annoyance as she went to wrench the door open. Ugh! So the whole load of wet washing had been sat here all day yesterday, and overnight! It smelled damp and mouldy already, and would need rinsing all over again. Bloody hell! Couldn't Pete have hung it out? Was he really that incapable of doing a bit of housework off his own bat? When she'd specifically phoned to remind him as well!

Sighing, she turned the dial to Rinse and switched it on. The machine hummed into life and water poured into its drum. Honestly! What a welcome home. No hugs, no 'Missed you's, just yesterday's washing to redo. Great. Thanks for that, Pete. Missed you too, sweetie.

Josie filled the kettle and put it on to boil. Then she went to get her favourite mug out of the cupboard, the one the boys had decorated in red and khaki splodges at a pottery-painting shop last year. But it wasn't there. She swivelled back towards the sink ... to see it dumped on a toast plate, waiting to be washed.

Her eyes narrowed and she stormed over. The mug still had a lipstick print on one side, and a swirl of cold tea at the bottom. For goodness' sake – it hadn't been washed since she'd used it yesterday morning! What was Pete playing at? The breakfast things piled up at the sink were from *yesterday* – they'd obviously been left there all night!

Josie filled the washing-up bowl with hot water and squirted in some Fairy. Out of habit, she began sorting the glasses to go in first, then the plates . . .

Hold on. Something was wrong. The breakfast things were all here from yesterday, yes – but nothing else. No lunch plates with uneaten sandwich crusts, or empty yogurt pots. And no dinner plates either, smeared with sauce, or bedtime milk cups.

She ran to the fridge door and pulled it open. Three cartons of spaghetti bolognese stood exactly where she'd unpacked them, on the middle shelf. Josie stared at their cheerful packaging, taken aback. So . . . if Pete and the boys hadn't eaten here since breakfast yesterday, where had they been? And where were they now?

Her mind in a whirl, she raced upstairs to the boys' bedroom. Their beds hadn't been slept in, and the bedtime teds were missing. Some of the drawers were pulled out at angles, as if clothes had been taken from them hastily.

What was going on? Where *was* everybody?

Horrible thoughts collided in Josie's head, and she grabbed at the chest of drawers, feeling giddy. Oh Christ! The boys had been rushed into hospital after some horrible injury, and Pete hadn't had time to leave her a note. He'd slept on the floor next to their hospital beds and—

No, stop. He'd sent her that text, hadn't he? *All fine.*

Maybe Pete had run away with them. He'd taken them off to live somewhere else with him, because ... Well, why? Why would he do that?

Oh, no – what if they had been abducted at gunpoint? What if someone had broken into the house yesterday, just after she'd left, and ...

'Hello? Josie? Are you back?'

Josie thought she might pass out in relief at Pete's voice calling up the stairs. 'Yes – where have you *been*?' she cried, stumbling out of the room. 'I was starting to worry, I was ...'

'Mum!'

'Mummy!'

And there they were, shock-headed and grinning, her sons, her darlings. She raced down the stairs as they scrambled up, meeting them in the middle in a tangle of hugs.

'Oh, I've missed you!' she cried, sitting on a step and

kissing them in turn, her arms tight around them. Their hot breath on her neck, their pulses against her skin, their soft hair on her cheek ... it was heaven. And to think that for a moment she'd been imagining ...

'So where *were* you?' she asked, looking up at last.

'We went to Nanny's,' Toby told her, bouncing on her leg. 'And she gave us sweeties!'

'To Nanny's?' Josie echoed in surprise. 'Did you really?'

'And we helped her make biscuits,' Sam said, pressing himself into her side. 'I made a specially nice one for you, Mum. Only I ate a little bit in the car because I was hungry. One teeny nibble.'

'No, it wasn't! It was two nibbles. It was seven nibbles,' Toby said.

'Well, thanks anyway, sweetheart,' Josie replied automatically, but she was hardly listening. Since when had Pete been planning to take them to Barbara's anyway? Why hadn't he said anything?

She got to her feet, unwinding herself from the boys after a last squeeze, and stepped down towards Pete. 'Hiya,' she said, hugging him. 'I thought you were going to do stuff here this weekend?'

He held her for a moment. 'The car packed up,' he said. She could feel his throat vibrate as he spoke into her hair. 'And rather than have the boys hanging around with me in the garage while I waited for it to be fixed, I thought they'd have more fun at my mum's, so I took them there, and . . .'

'Oh, right,' Josie said. 'What's wrong with the car?'

Pete launched into a long description of something technical that went straight over Josie's head, as he steered her into the kitchen. 'Anyway, enough about that boring stuff,' he said. 'Sorry it's a mess in here, by the way, I wasn't expecting you back yet.' He flashed her a smile. 'But how was your weekend? Did you do anything outrageous?'

Josie smiled faintly. 'Not quite,' she said. 'It was great. It was just a bit weird, coming back to . . .' She waved a hand over the dirty dishes, and the spinning washing machine. 'Well, this lot. I was getting panicked, thinking you'd all run off together or something.'

He was still smiling at her, but she didn't feel re-assured. In fact, if she was honest, there was a small part of her that felt let down. She'd been really looking forward to Pete experiencing boy-care single-handedly for a day, just so that he'd realize it wasn't quite as easy as he thought. She'd been half hoping to come back to him groaning and saying, *How do you do it, every day of the week? Looking after them for just twenty-four hours has brought me to my knees! You are a saint! A goddess among mothers!*, etc. Obviously not.

The boys galloped into the kitchen at that moment and insisted on unpacking their overnight bags to show her the biscuits they'd made and the drawings they'd done and . . .

Something was bothering Josie. Something was nagging away at the back of her mind, but she couldn't quite reach it. And then, before she could even properly try, she was having to admire the drawings and biscuits and everything else, and lunch was demanded as they were starving, THIS hungry, and then the thought was gone, spun away from her in the whirlwind of everything else.

It wasn't until that evening, when the boys were in bed cosy and kissed, both still clutching their new dinosaurs as they drifted into sleep, that Josie's thoughts turned, with a shiver of excitement, to Rose. She'd already done the maths. If Rose were to be conceived sometime over the next few days, she'd be born in February next year. Lovely. Not too close to Christmas, not too near the boys' birthday (April) either, not too late in the school year to be the youngest in the class . . .

And oh, she and Rose would be able to snuggle up and see the winter out together, warm at home for a while, before spring burst into bloom. Josie could imagine herself pushing along one of those Silver Cross Mary Poppins prams with a darling dimpled face peeping out at her from the pink blankets. And there she'd be, showing Rose the daffodils and spring lambs, lying her on a blanket in the back garden when it was warmer, watching her bend and kick those gorgeous chubby thighs under the apple tree . . .

But she was running ahead of herself as usual. Mustn't get her hopes up. She had to get pregnant first, and that was taking long enough . . .

Josie undressed quickly, swapping her plain cotton knickers and bra for a pretty pink matching set, all lace and ribbons to undo – Pete could never resist those – before dressing again, with a little smile on her face. She squirted some perfume into her cleavage, and tried to muss up her hair into a sexy, tousled look.

She hummed to herself as she went downstairs. The weekend now felt like the best kind of catalyst for their new improved lives. She'd broached the subject of taking a trip abroad, all together, while the boys had been having tea, and they'd been wildly excited, even if Pete had seemed more reluctant.

'Well . . . I'm not sure if, financially . . .'

'We can borrow some money,' Josie had interjected. 'Let's just go and have some fun, and pay it back later! Australia would be amazing, wouldn't it? What do you reckon, boys, fancy seeing some kangaroos bouncing about?'

'Yeah! Cool!' the boys had shouted. 'And polar bears!'

'They don't live in Australia,' Josie had laughed. 'Polar bears live in the Arctic.'

Pete was tight-mouthed. 'Australia? That would cost a fortune! There's no way we could afford that, Josie, absolutely no way!'

'Well, somewhere nearer then. Thailand sounds exciting. Or South Africa.'

'Disneyland!' Toby put in at once.

'Or India...' Josie suggested, imagining the four of them riding a bejewelled elephant.

'You know what my stomach's like,' Pete had moaned. 'I'll have the trots the whole time if we go to Asia. And what about all the gun crime in South Africa? It's far too dangerous. What's got into you, Josie?'

What had got into her? A reality check, that's what. A wake-up call, loud and clear. Attention, Josie Winter! Your life is passing you by. Do something with it!

Anyway, one thing at a time, eh? She had Rose to think about tonight. Maybe she could bring up the subject of foreign expeditions again when they were snuggled up in bed later, post-coital and lovey-dovey...

Now. What to eat, to get them in the mood? The boys had had scrambled eggs for tea earlier, but Pete had claimed not to be hungry after the huge lunch at Barbara's.

'Great,' Josie had said brightly, 'you and I can eat together later. It's a date!'

She didn't fancy the spag bol she'd bought them for yesterday – not romantic enough – so she grabbed the sheaf of takeaway menus. There was wine in the fridge, they could share some nice Indian or Chinese food, then get down to business. Rose – prepare to leave that limbo of unborn souls! You are on the verge of being created, my little darling!

She went into the living room, where Pete was sitting staring into space, and spread the menus in front of him like a fan.

'Pick a card, any card,' she said. 'You choose.' As long as it's prawns, she thought. She knew, from devouring every article ever printed about getting pregnant, that zinc was good for men's sperm count. She'd already bought in the supplements, and had cooked up enough eggs and shellfish in the last few months to send his zinc levels sky-rocketing, but a last top-up tonight wouldn't hurt. In fact, would it be too deceitful if she secretly ordered everything to have prawns in? She could pretend the restaurant had cocked up the order so that when his beef in black bean sauce turned out to be prawn chow mein, she'd—

He was sighing and shifting around in his armchair. 'Josie ... um ... I'm not that hungry. Sorry.'

She stared at him in surprise. 'What's wrong? It's not like you to turn down a takeaway. There's some wine in the fridge, I thought we could...'

He still hadn't looked at her properly. Now he was fiddling with his wedding ring. 'Josie,' he started, then put his head in his hands.

'What?' she asked. I'll order him something anyway, she thought distractedly. He was bound to be hungry when the food arrived. Chinese would be nice. And she knew from her pregnancy-magazine addiction that if a woman wanted to conceive a girl, she should eat calcium-rich food, green vegetables and fish. Let's see, maybe she could start with...

'Josie,' he said again, then cleared his throat. 'Josie, I can hardly bear to do this to you, but...'

It wasn't exactly the best way to start a sentence to your wife, Josie thought, turning sharply towards him. Not the most cheering words to hear at any given point. Zinc and spring rolls disappeared from her mind at once, and a creeping horror spread through her at his pale face, the way his eyes were so dark and haunted-looking. And what was going on with the wedding-ring thing?

'But what?' she prompted hoarsely.

'There's somebody else,' he said. 'I've met somebody.'

Josie's mouth moved but her brain seemed to have jammed with some kind of mechanical fault. 'Well...'

she heard herself saying, 'well, everybody meets new people all the time! I mean, I met the new woman from number twenty-three the other day, Joanne, she's called, and . . .'

She wasn't being deliberately obtuse, she just couldn't equate Pete's words with the truth. He hadn't really said that, surely? Slip of the tongue, it had to be. He hadn't meant to say *that*. The somebody-else thing.

He *couldn't* have said that.

'Josie!' He sat up, a flash of irritation crossing his face, then seemed to think better of it, and bit his lip. 'I'm trying to tell you — I'm trying to say that I've met someone else. I've *fallen in love* with someone else. And I'm . . .' He looked at the floor for a second, then full in her eyes. 'I'm leaving you.'

Chapter Six

It had been a gorgeous wedding. Absolutely gorgeous. Gold September sun beaming through the windows as she teetered up the aisle of the seventeenth-century stone chapel. Her killer-heel shoes, the pinching corset, the tightness of her hairstyle were temporarily forgotten as she saw him there in his tails, a single white rose on the lapel. Those brown eyes on hers – slightly anxious at first, then, as she got nearer to him, a wink and a grin.

On the video you could hear a low, sighing chorus of *oohs* and *ahhs* as she walked up – not to mention her nan exclaiming loudly, 'Well! What a beauty!' in a particularly surprised sort of way – but Josie wasn't aware of any of that at the time. She didn't hear a note of 'Here Comes the Bride'. She didn't smell the perfumed lily-of-the-valley tied in little posies by each row of seats. Pete was all she could see, dear, kind, lovely Pete, with his one white rose and his brown eyes.

'Do you, Josie Catherine Bell, take this man, Peter David Winter, to be your lawful wedded husband?'

'I do.' Damn bloody right I do! she'd thought, shocked that there could be any doubt. Who in her right mind *wouldn't* take Peter David Winter to be her lawful wedded husband, with his low chuckle, his saucy cocked eyebrow and his penchant for sex in public places?

'You may now kiss the bride.'

Josie had never particularly liked that line. What about the bride? Didn't she get a say in it? Today, feminist annoyance was put to one side.

You may now kiss the groom, she told herself as Pete's mouth came towards hers. My husband!

On the video, her eyes were shut. She was smiling as she kissed him. He had a hand on her back, as if he was steadying himself. Or was he steadying *her*? Pete had never been nervous in his life. Confidence ran through him like blood.

One kiss, and they were married. It was perfect. *Perfect.*

Josie often thought about their wedding day. Dusting the framed photos always made her smile. Driving past the old rectory where it had all happened, remembering the marquee on the grass, friends in colourful dresses and hats gathered in clusters on the lawn like late-summer flowers ... she could conjure up the memories in a flash, and they always left a melting warmth inside her.

Often, when Pete was away at a business conference or a stag weekend, she sat down with a glass of wine, put the video on and watched herself marry him all over again. It gave her the most delicious shiver, seeing them so young and happy on her own TV screen. So in love.

And now...

Now...

'It's Lisa, isn't it?' she said. It all clicked into place in a second. Josie felt as if she'd been punched in the stomach as the images crashed into her mind. The photo under Lisa's bed, the flash of guilt in Lisa's eyes, the message on the answerphone. It was meant for Pete, surely, to warn him that...

'Lisa?' Pete repeated. He was staring at her, with a look of fear. 'What did she ...? I mean, why do you ...?'

She gulped. So it was true. It was really true. It was written all over his face.

'I'm not stupid!' she snapped. 'I worked it out all by myself. And you just confirmed it, looking at me like that.' Tears sprang to her eyes, and her fingers trembled uncontrollably. She had spent twenty-four hours with her friend – her so-called friend – Lisa, and all the while this had been on the cards. It was breathtaking! 'So ... what are you saying?' she managed to get out. 'That you're leaving me for her? That you're leaving me for *Lisa*?'

He shook his head, a strange uncertainty in his eyes. 'Josie, it's not Lisa,' he said slowly, as if he was speaking to a child. 'That was just a stupid mistake. It's—'

Josie nearly fell off her chair. 'What?' she cried, her voice rising in shock. She couldn't keep up with this. 'What? So you *had* an affair with Lisa – but now you're leaving me for someone *else*?'

She could hardly take it in. Finding out about Lisa was a sucker punch on its own. That had all but knocked her to the floor. But now – this? There was *more*?

Words were coming out of Pete's mouth. Spilling out, as if he couldn't control them. Awful words. Terrible words that she'd never expected to hear him saying. Not 'Till death do us part' after all.

Stale.

No sex drive.

Outgrown one another.

Boring.

Then came even worse.

'She makes me feel alive.' Wham! A knife in the back.

'She makes me laugh.' Thud! A kick in the guts.

'She makes me feel like a teenager . . .'

'When you were a teenager, you were as miserable as sin,' Josie reminded him waspishly. There were only so many clichés she could take. She buried her head in her hands. *Go on, say it*, she wanted to scream. *She makes me come twenty times a night. She makes me horny as hell. She makes me hard just by cocking her little finger* . . .

'You know what I mean,' he said helplessly.

'No, I don't fucking know what you mean,' she shouted, remembering too late the boys asleep upstairs. 'You're thirty-five, Pete. You're not *supposed* to feel like a teenager any more. Remember?'

She was weeping, though she couldn't remember starting to cry. She dashed the tears away, almost surprised to feel the wetness sliding down her cheeks. Don't cry, don't cry, she told herself fiercely. Don't let him see you cry.

'You're meant to feel like a grown man,' she went on, staring at him, this person she'd loved for so long. He suddenly looked like a stranger with his blue T-shirt and guilty eyes. 'You're meant to feel like a *married* man. A dad! And now you're telling me that you went off with Lisa, and this other slag . . .'

'She's not a slag,' he said wretchedly. 'She's . . . I love her.'

Josie thought of the Baby Gap bag still sitting in the bottom of her wardrobe, full of its cheery pinkness and promise. That was the worst blow of all, straight to her belly, her softest, most vulnerable part. 'But what about Rose?' she said, her voice breaking on the name. 'What about—?'

'There *is* no Rose!' he shouted. 'She doesn't exist –

and I'm sick of you going on about it! Can't you see, that's what's driving me away, you being so . . .'

He didn't finish his sentence, he held off from the adjective at the last moment, leaving the unspoken accusation hanging between them.

Josie felt as if she'd been slapped. She felt winded, out of breath. There was a long, horrible silence.

'But . . . you *can't* love her,' she said, in the end. 'This other woman. You're supposed to love *me*.'

She looked up at him, but he said nothing. He turned away.

'I . . .' she began. 'You . . . You can't just leave like that,' she said. She felt as if she were floundering through an awful dream. 'You can't just *go*. What about the boys? What about me? What about our marriage, our home, *everything?*'

The words were coming out wrong, half choked, half spat. She was crying harder, almost unable to speak.

'I'm sorry,' he said. 'Josie, I'm really sorry.'

'Well, that's all right, then, isn't it?' she sobbed. 'That makes everything just fine, if you're sorry!' She put her arms around herself, holding each elbow tightly as if it was the only thing that would stop her falling to pieces. 'How many others have there been?' she asked, not daring to look at his expression. 'Two? Three? Ten?'

'Josie . . .' he said pleadingly, but she was on a roll.

'Go on! Tell me. Twenty? And who's the latest one, anyway? Hey – I've guessed it, it must be Nell. Are you doing the rounds of all my friends? Is it Emma? Harriet? Joanne from number twenty-three?'

He was shaking his head. 'Don't be silly, of course it's not them,' he said.

'What do you mean, don't be silly? It didn't stop you with Lisa, did it?' she roared. Suddenly, she hated him. She absolutely hated him. He had betrayed her, humiliated her. She could hardly bear to look at his lying face.

'I told you, Lisa was nothing. Honestly. It was just a stupid mistake and I've always regretted it.' He gazed at her beseechingly, and for a second – just for a single second – she actually felt sorry for him. He genuinely seemed to mean it. Then he ruined everything all over again. 'She's called Sabine,' he said haltingly.

'Sabine? *Sabine?* What sort of name is that?' Josie shrieked, sympathy out of the window. 'Is she French?' she demanded. 'Is she?' *Please don't let her be French*, she thought despairingly. That sexy accent, chic wardrobe, adventurous sex romps, all that va-va-bloody-voom … Josie knew Sabine would win hands down if she were French. How could she, Josie, with her British pear shape, ever compete with *la belle Sabine* and her *je-ne-sais-quoi*, her '*Oh, encore, monsieur!*'?

'No,' he said. 'She's not French.'

'Well, where did you meet her? How old is she? What does she look like?' she asked. The sobs were giving way to a sneer. She wanted to know everything about her, everything – yet at the same time there was a part of her that wanted to know nothing, just needed to cover her ears and run away.

'I met her at a conference,' he said, his voice a sigh. A sigh of what? Sorrow? Nostalgia? Lust? 'She's thirty. And she looks . . .' He shook his head. 'Actually, I don't think that's important.'

'Why? Too scared to say that she's sexier than me? Better-looking than me?' Her voice rose to a scream. 'Better in bed than me?'

'Josie . . .' he said, putting a hand on her arm.

She threw it off, rounding on him. 'Did you ever think about *our sons*, while you were shagging her? Our boys? What about them? What am I going to tell them?' Her voice wobbled and broke as she thought about their earnest pink faces, the lack of comprehension. What words can you use to four-year-old boys who think their dad is the all-time superhero of the universe to tell them that, in actual fact, he's nothing but an out-and-out . . .

'Tosser,' she said, fresh tears springing to her eyes. 'You *shit*. You've wrecked everything, you and your stupid dick. Had to go and conquer something else, didn't you, had to go and—?' She stopped again, hands over her face, weeping uncontrollably.

'Maybe it's best if I just go,' Pete said. 'We can talk about it when you've calmed down.'

The coward! 'What, so that's it?' she asked incredulously. 'It's all over – easy as that?'

He stood up awkwardly, not sure what to do with his hands. They stretched out in her direction as if to comfort her, but then he snatched them back, as if that was beyond his remit now. 'I'm sorry,' he said again. 'But . . .'

'You're not bloody sorry,' Josie spat. 'If you were sorry, you wouldn't be saying all these things, walking out on me, while upstairs our sons – *our sons* – are asleep.' Her voice was shaking; the thought of the boys made her feel furious. How could he do it to them?

'I'm sorry,' he repeated, like a cracked record. Josie imagined him using the same calm tones when he fired people, or told them he was making them redundant. Sorry – but not that sorry. *Sorry, but I'll have forgotten your name after fifteen minutes. Sorry, but I've been shagging your mate, and now I'm leaving you for another woman.* 'I never wanted to hurt you, or the boys.'

'Too late for that,' Josie snivelled. Tears streamed

down her face, snot too, but she didn't care. 'Too bloody late for that, mate. You just did! You just have!'

'I'll call you,' he said. 'I know it's a shock. We can talk about everything when you've had time to think.' He took a cautious step towards the door, as if worried she was going to rugby-tackle him if he tried to escape. 'I'll just grab a few things then go.'

Josie sank down in the chair as he went upstairs. Go after him, beg him not to leave, a voice urged in her head. Maybe if she calmed down, stopped swearing at him and calling him names for two minutes, she could talk him into staying. Promise him whatever he wanted – more sex, more fun, less moaning, less 'I'm too tired' – anything. *Anything.* Just send Sabine packing – and stay. *Please.*

Yet it was as if she couldn't move. While she knew that she should be up there with him, pointing out all the great things about their marriage, all the reasons why he should stay rather than slink off to foxy Sabine, she just couldn't do it, didn't have the energy. Not when she knew she'd just be humiliated all over again with his rejection.

Minutes later, Josie heard his Audi rumble to a start, saw his headlights beam through the curtains at her, watched them swing away across the wall and then disappear. She shook uncontrollably. This is not happening, she told herself. This is not my life. My life is safe and certain. I'm the smug cow, the happily married one, remember? Bad things like this don't happen to me. They don't. They just *can't*!

Her heart was thudding painfully. Her throat was dry. It was all a mistake. He'd made a mistake. She forced herself to stop crying, then picked up the phone and, calm as you like, ordered Thai for two. Yellow chicken curry for Pete, his favourite. Pad thai for herself. A couple of crab cakes with chilli dipping sauce too, please. Oh yes, and don't forget the prawn crackers. How long would that be? Forty minutes? Lovely. Thank you!

She opened a bottle of wine and poured a large glass. The wine was greenish-yellow, expensive. No doubt from one of Pete's internet wine clubs. The wine glass had been a wedding present from – who was it again? Her Auntie Jackie?

She drained it in one go. Who cared? What did it matter now?

She poured herself another, quickly. He'd be back soon, she told herself. He'd come back and take her in his arms and say . . .

What would he say?

I can't believe I nearly walked out and lost you, Josie Bell, the best thing that ever happened to me.

It was madness to think I could leave you. Sheer madness!

Sabine means nothing to me. You are my life, Josie. You and the kids.

I'm so sorry. I'm so, so sorry. Can you ever forgive me?

And Josie? She would cry with happiness. She would sob through that blue T-shirt of his, and say, *It's OK, baby. You're back now. Curry's on the way. Would you like a glass of wine?*

And they would sit down and watch telly and he would check the sports news on Teletext every time there was an ad break, and she would start on the ironing pile. And they would go to bed, their king-size sleigh bed, which had been a joint wedding present from about fifteen of their friends, and they would hold each other all night, and he would say, *I'm so sorry, Josie. Do you think we can forget this ever happened?*

And she would close her eyes and breathe in his scent and say, *Yes, my love. As long as you promise never, ever to do that again.*

And he would say . . .

Josie jumped out of her reverie at the gentle knocking at the door. She knew it! He'd come back!

'That's fifteen-fifty, please. Enjoy your meal.'

*

It only ever took Josie a couple of glasses of wine to get giggly. Pete used to find that endearing, she knew. *Sweet little wifey has such a low tolerance, bless her, aren't women amusing?*

She'd already downed two large glasses by the time the Thai delivery boy dropped off her fragrant, steaming food. 'Keep the change,' she told him earnestly, pressing a twenty into his hand. 'Treat yourself. Do something nice. Seize the day.'

He was backing away with the money, not interested, not making eye contact, despite Josie's best efforts. 'Thank you. Enjoy your meal,' he repeated.

Josie sorted herself out a plateful of food and another glass of wine, then put the lids back on the takeaway containers for Pete. She was sure he'd be back soon. He absolutely would be.

A tear rolled down her cheek, and splashed into the wine as the doubts swam up in her next breath. No, he wouldn't. She knew already that he wouldn't. He'd left her. Nobody walked out on their wife and children on a whim, did they?

Face it, Josie. He's left you. He's gone. Had enough of boring wifey. Off to the new sex kitten now.

She picked up the foil containers and moved towards the bin with them. Stupid cow, ordering so much food. Living in a dream world, like that conversation with Pete hadn't just happened. Wise up! This lot would all get thrown away. What a waste!

She flipped up the lid with her foot and held the food over the bin, but at the last moment couldn't quite bring herself to let go. She turned around and put them back on the worktop. Just in case. He still might come home. He really might. He had to come back sometime, didn't he? It wasn't like she was never going to see him again.

I am pretending that everything is going to be all right, she said to herself miserably, because everything has gone so wrong.

The smell of curry was making her feel sick. How had she ever imagined that she'd be able to eat? Was she mad?

She grabbed her wine and left the food to cool stickily on its plate as she marched into the living room. Suddenly she wanted to question Lisa. She wanted to know. The conversation with Pete already seemed like a blur. He'd moved so fast on to Sabine – slaggy Sabine! – and wanting to get out of the house that he hadn't said much about Lisa, only that it had been a mistake. But when had the mistake been, and how long had it gone on for? Had it started before they were married? After? Recently?

She wrenched the phone from its base, and punched

in Lisa's number. Bile rose in her throat as she thought back to Lisa standing in her kitchen just that morning, telling her that *Pete* must have put the photo in Josie's bag, and that was how it had ended up under her bed. Ha! She'd probably had a good old laugh about that piece of quick thinking since Josie had left. Smart move, Lise. Wormed your way out of that one nicely with your quickfire legal brain, didn't you?

And all the while the photo had been Lisa's. She'd propped it by her bedside, no doubt, when the affair was on, gazing into it every morning and night when Pete was in his own bed with Josie.

God. The thought made her feel sick.

'Hello?' Lisa said.

Josie squeezed her eyes shut for a second. She could just imagine Lisa in her slouchy Sunday cashmere, curled up in an armchair in that luxurious front room of hers, mohair cushion under her bum, pile of work on her lap ... 'It's Josie,' she said, in a strangled-sounding voice.

'Hi, Josie,' Lisa chirped. 'Everything all right?'

'I got your message,' Josie replied, in as casual a way as she could manage. 'You said to call?'

'Oh! Oh yes,' Lisa said. The brightness slipped from her voice momentarily. 'Um ... It was nothing really, just to see if you'd had a good trip back and to say thanks for coming.'

Josie pressed her lips together. For a few seconds she couldn't speak. Then the rage powered up inside her and she opened her mouth and said, 'Don't lie. I know who your message was really for.'

There was a pause. 'What ... what do you mean?' Lisa asked carefully. Ever the legal bloody eagle.

Josie shook her head at the question. What do you mean, indeed. Nice try at deflection, Lise. Not happening this time, though. 'I think you know *exactly* what I mean,' she spat. 'I knew you were lying about the photo this morning. I knew it! And now I know the truth. Pete's told me all about it. Everything.'

'Oh God,' Lisa said, a tremor in her voice. 'Oh, Josie, I'm so—'

'Leave it out,' Josie snapped. 'I don't want to hear it. You backstabbing cow. You were supposed to be my *friend!*'

She slammed the phone down with a crash. Her throat was suddenly tight, as if she was going to choke.

The phone started ringing, but she ignored it. Lisa, no doubt, to grovel and kiss her arse. No chance. She was so sacked as a friend! How could she have been so cold-blooded?

The answerphone kicked in. 'You have reached Pete, Josie, Toby and Sam...' her own voice said, and Josie switched it off before it could go any further. No messages, thanks, Lisa. Save it for someone who cares. The deceitful bitch! She'd stood there in her kitchen telling those bare-faced lies about that wretched photo! The lying, sneaky, conniving slut! She and Pete deserved each other. She was well shot of both of them!

Josie sat down on the sofa, the adrenalin subsiding as quickly as it had rushed through her. Oh God. Was this actually happening? Had she really just made that call?

She shivered as her eyes fell upon a framed photo on the mantelpiece. There they were, Josie, Pete and the boys, in the perfect Happy Families pose, arms around each other on a Cornish beach, sun low in the sky behind them. They were tanned and freckled, in shorts and T-shirts, smiling and holding one another. We Are Family!

Not any more. Not now. So much for her plans of them all going off on adventures together! The nuclear family had just gone into meltdown. How on earth would she tell the boys? It would break Sam's heart. And Toby, how would he feel about his number-one alpha-male role model abandoning him?

Josie started to cry again. And Rose, she thought. Darling Rose. Now I'm never going to see you. Never going to hold you. Never going to dress you in candy-floss pink . . .

She stumbled upstairs, tears dripping off her chin. She

opened the wardrobe and there it was, her bag full of hope. She could hardly bear to look at it.

Josie pulled out the pink dungarees and held them to her face until her tears soaked through the material. Then she bent double with the pain, and howled.

Two hours later, she lay on the bed, still fully dressed, listening to the silence. It was ten-thirty, and she knew that the rest of the street would be brushing their teeth and getting under the bedcovers like good little residents, all ready for their eight hours' kip. By rights, Josie should have been lying here in her sexy undies, waiting for Pete to finish in the bathroom and come in and find her, watching for that smile on his face as he realized that for once she was up for it. Wa-hey! Impregnation coming up!

Instead, the house was quiet. Horribly, unusually quiet. It was all wrong. Everything was wrong.

Where was Pete now? Were he and Sabine celebrating somewhere? It all fell into place now, like the reveal of a magician's trick. *That* was why he'd dumped the boys on his witch of a mother – so that he could spend the night with Sabine! Josie had known something didn't quite add up. It was seeing the boys with their overnight bags like that, as if Pete had intended them to go to his mum's all along, rather than a spontaneous resolution to the car-in-garage situation. And of course there was nothing wrong with the car in the first place. Another lie. God, he was good at it. They just dropped from his mouth, those lies, like breath. He'd had Josie fooled all this time.

It was shocking, his nerve. The sneaky, snidy, lying git! Oh, and she could just imagine the conversation he and Sabine would be having right now:

Darling, I feel so free now that I've finally told her!

You won't regret it, Pete, I promise. Let me show you just how much I appreciate this...

Oh, baby, that's good. That's so good. That's...

Josie got up unsteadily, not wanting to think about it any further. 'Screw you, Sabine,' she said. 'You slag. What about sisterhood, eh? Never heard of that?'

Oh God! Please let me wake up from this! Please, please let this all be a horrible dream!

She wandered into the boys' room and sat on the floor in the darkness, comforted by the sound of their breathing. She leaned her head against the rocket-papered wall. Surely Pete wouldn't really be able to leave *them*? She knew that she couldn't. There was no way she could walk out on her children, her own flesh and blood, to go off with another partner. How did anybody do that?

Toby stirred in the top bunk. 'Ready, steady, go,' he muttered drowsily, and Josie felt her body flood with love for him. Of *course* Pete would come back. Of *course* he would realize his mistake. Sex on tap with a lover just didn't compare to seeing your child sleeping peacefully night after night, arms flung out on the pillow, lips slightly apart, long lashes resting on those perfect peach-like cheeks. Nobody would realistically turn their back on that, would they?

They would have to be mad. Desperate.

Or, of course, really, really in love . . .

Josie stumbled downstairs, not sure what to do with herself. There was no way she could sleep, not with Pete's words still echoing around her head, not with the image of Lisa's guilt-charged eyes on her. But . . . what, then? What did one do when the unimaginable happened?

Josie sat down at the kitchen table in the darkness. Their family table, where they ate their meals, where she'd sat for hours with the boys, making Play-Doh men and cutting out biscuits and painting frogs and all the rest of it. She pressed her cheek against its cool wooden surface and cried into its oaky knots and whirls. Would Pete take this table away if he and Sabine got a place together? He'd inherited it, after all, from some grand-parent or other. It was his to take, wasn't it?

Josie cradled her head. She couldn't bear the thought of slaggy Sabine eating breakfast off this table. Mind you, she probably didn't eat, full stop. She was probably whip-thin, all cheekbones and legs. She probably only used tables for having sex on.

Don't. Don't think about it.

What else would Pete take? The plasma-screen TV, his pride and joy? Surely he couldn't survive long without that. The remote control was practically an extension of his right hand. He'd sit there, holding it lovingly throughout an entire programme, guarding it, practically. Oh, the TV would go with him, no question. She was surprised he hadn't bundled it into the car when he'd left that evening. Video, DVD, stereo system . . . oh yeah. He'd have the lot. He'd leave Josie her *Friends* video boxed set to gather dust on the shelf, take everything else. *Mine, mine, mine. Worked for it, earned the money, bought it, mine.*

Josie was grateful for the chair beneath her, keeping her upright as she calculated his inventory. The chair — would he take three of the six? Half the cutlery? One of the armchairs? One of the matching walnut wardrobes? God, she hated the thought of it being filled with Sabine's stuff. All gorgeous designer outfits, no doubt. She'd have a separate shoe rack, Josie guessed, for the sheer volume of sexy strappy shoes she owned, and . . .

Oh God! Why was this happening to her?

She wasn't sure how long she sat there. Long enough to drink another large glass of wine, eat the rest of the chocolate biscuits and work her way through half a box of tissues anyway. Outside, the night seemed black-poster-paint dark, and she shivered as the stars wobbled smudgily through her tears. She dreaded it when Pete was away at night. Even though they had Christ knows how many security alarms and deadlocks everywhere, she hated lying there in bed alone, listening to a solitary car thrum by, or the wind gusting at the letterbox.

Well. Better get used to it, girl. Welcome to the future.

She stood up, swaying and holding on to the tabletop for support. God, she was horribly pissed. All the chocolate was making her teeth ache. She grabbed the phone and dialled his number. Time to tell her stupid, deceitful husband just what she thought of him.

Ring ... Ring ...

Answer it, you wanker.

Ring ... Ring ...

'This is the voicemail for Peter Winter. Please leave a message after the tone.'

Josie licked her lips. Suddenly she felt very tired.

Beeeeep.

'It's Josie,' she said. 'Just phoning to tell you that ...'

She stopped. She didn't even know what to say.

She swayed; tried again. 'To tell you that I really, really, REALLY hate you.' She gazed out into the dark garden until her eyes lost focus. 'I can't believe you're doing this. I can't believe you—'

Beeeeep. 'Thank you for your message.'

Bloody hell. Even his mobile was against her. It was all a conspiracy.

Josie replaced the receiver. She put her solitary wine glass in the sink. The fridge was humming loudly, the clock ticking the minutes by. Time for bed. She was wrung out. She just didn't want to be awake any more.

She hesitated by the front door before going upstairs. Usually Pete slid the bolts across before they went up to bed, a comforting *thunk, thunk,* locking them in from the night. That was his job, same as buying the wine, putting out the bins, washing the cars. Her fingers refused to push the bolts along tonight. What if he came back in a few hours, contrite and grovelling, and she'd locked him out?

She leaned against the door, struggling with the problem. Pete, just come back, she begged silently, feeling a headache begin to thump into life. *Please.*

What would he be doing now? Had he gone to Sabine's? A mate's house? Was he driving round and round the M25, wondering what he could do to make things up to her?

She sighed after what seemed like an age, and peeled herself away from the door. She locked the mortice instead. That way he could still get into the house but she and the boys would be safe. She felt light-headed with relief that she'd done it, solved the problem by herself.

Before she went upstairs, she left Pete a note. For when he came back.

Gone to bed, she wrote. *Curry in fridge if you want it. I taped* Match of the Day *for you. Josie x*

Chapter Seven

'Where's Dad?'

Josie opened her eyes to see Toby two inches from her face. For a second it felt just like any other morning. Then everything came back to her with a horrible lurch.

Pete had gone. THUD.

Pete had left her. THUD.

Pete had fallen in love with somebody else. *Sabine.* THUD.

Josie put out a groggy arm to rub her son's back. Whatever happened, she had to keep his world a safe place for as long as possible. 'Um ... he went to work early,' she said. 'Want to hop in for a cuddle?'

His eyes brightened, as she'd known they would. 'Yeah!'

Josie held up the cover so that he could scramble in beside her, and put her arms around his wiry little body. He smelled of sleep and shampoo and innocence; the exact things that a four-year-old should smell of. She held him as his breathing slowed and he nestled into her. She felt as if her heart were breaking. How could she tell him? It would tip his whole life upside-down.

The world according to Toby was: Mum, Dad, Sam, running, jumping, climbing, bad jokes, farting in the bath, sausages and baked beans, strawberry Petits Filous, his battered blue teddy bear, Power Rangers, his fireman bike, chocolate buttons, Lego. Small things but important. They made up his universe, they defined him. Take away one of the pieces and it all fell apart. How was she going to do it to him?

Josie stroked his hair. The events of the night before seemed like a dream – or rather a nightmare. The worst losing-control nightmare possible – more terrifying than the exam-she-hadn't-revised-for nightmare, or the no-clothes-in-public nightmare. It was worse, even, than the can't-find-the-boys nightmare that made her wake in a pale sweat, heart thudding, eyes wide in fear, each time.

Josie. Pete. Even their names sounded wrong on their own. She'd been part of Josie-and-Pete, Pete-and-Josie for so many years. Who shall we invite for dinner? Oh, Emma-and-Will, Laura-and-Matthew. Josie-and-Pete.

Now she was just Josie. Or rather, Josie-and-the-boys. If Pete didn't come back, she'd have to be everything to them, mum *and* dad. After Pete's revelations, she couldn't count on him for anything. She'd never trust another person again.

You think you know me? Boom! Wrong!

You think I meant all those promises we made, all those vows? Boom! Wrong!

Joke's on you, Josie, you loser. You fool.

She felt cold and clammy under the bedclothes, and rested her chin against Toby's head for comfort. Monday morning, and all over the country mothers like her were making breakfast, sorting out school lunches and PE kits, finding shoes, going through the routine of just another ordinary day . . .

Not in this house. The rules had changed, the outlines of life shifted. She'd never woken up and had to think about single parenthood or maintenance payments before. Had never opened her eyes and felt sick with worry that she was going to ruin her children's lives, break their hearts.

She could almost visualize a ghostly image of herself pulling on her dressing gown, carrying Toby downstairs, his arms tightly around the back of her neck, into the kitchen. The ghostly Josie flicked on the radio, changing it as usual from Radio 5 back to Radio 1, put on the kettle, made Weetabix for Toby, hugged Sam, who was trailing through the door bleary-eyed, and sat him on his chair . . .

She could almost hear her down there, that other self of hers, humming along with the radio, chattering to the boys about everything and nothing. Did you sleep well? What did you dream about? It's sunny, isn't it? What would you like to do today?

She shut her eyes, feeling hopeless. Why had she never appreciated the normality of it all before? Why had she ever been so keen to leave it all behind for a weekend in London?

The hours stretched emptily ahead of her. It wasn't a playgroup day today. Somehow or other she had to fill the time with stuff, things to do to keep the boys busy, but she couldn't think of a single idea. She just wanted to pull the duvet over her head and stay there all day.

Josie felt a sick ache spread through her as she thought about Pete. Was he waking up with Sabine, their sheets rucked up over their naked bodies after a night of liberated passion?

Was he whistling as he showered, another hard-on springing into life?

Maybe he was making Sabine a coffee – she probably drank it black, and skipped breakfast, Josie thought glumly. And then later he'd be dressing for work, driving a different, new way to the office, singing along to a CD with a smile on his face . . .

He should be with *her* right now, Josie, spooned the

length of her, arm slung across her body, breathing into the back of her neck. That was where he *should* be. Even if one of the boys crept into their bed, he liked to slide a hand up her belly, still pretending to be asleep, until his fingers just brushed the underside of her breast. He knew it drove her crazy – knew she wouldn't do anything saucy with Toby or Sam nearby – but he still tried it on, every single time.

Nobody would ever touch her like that again, Josie thought miserably. She'd be a dried-up old spinster, a lonely husk of an ex-wife. Those same breasts, that same belly, they'd wither and pouch and sag, with nobody ever seeing them again.

She remembered with a wrench all the times she'd pushed his hands off her. 'Not tonight, darling.'

'Not this morning, babe.'

'Oh Pete, I'm trying to sleep' . . .

She'd give anything to have him back. Even sex on tap, whenever he wanted it. Anything.

He would come back, though, wouldn't he? Surely he would come back!

Josie stroked Toby's hair, glad he couldn't see the grief on her face. Whatever happened, the boys had to come first. She'd make it up to them by becoming their whole world, if that's what it took.

But it wasn't just the parenting she'd have to do alone,

was it? It was the works. The mortgage and bills – Pete had always taken care of those. And the house … would he want to sell up? It was a joint mortgage, but there was no way she could pay it on her own. She hadn't worked for the last four years. And Pete would need somewhere to live, wouldn't he? What if he wanted to sell the house and buy himself a new flat with his share of the proceeds? He'd be perfectly entitled to.

Ripples of dread spread queasily through her. She'd have to put the boys in full-time nursery and get a job, so she could afford the payments on some squalid little bedsit for her and them, miles out of the catchment areas for all the good primary schools. They'd have to rent somewhere, and she'd be back to the days of complaining to anonymous landlords about unreliable boilers and damp patches; lying in bed listening to the *clack-clack* of other people's feet walking above her head, the muffled shouts of other people's arguments, other people's sex. She'd thought those days had long gone, but now she was staring them full in the face again, only this time with two huge boy-shaped responsibilities, too. Oh Christ. Had it really come to this? What was she going to do? What was she going to *do*?

'Too hot,' Toby muttered, squirming beside her.

'Sorry,' she whispered, releasing her grip on him, smoothing back his hair. 'Sorry, baby.'

She was so, so sorry. A tear trickled from the corner of her eye down into the pillowcase and she scrubbed it away as Sam came into the room, his hair tufting sideways, pyjama top twisted, sleep still in his eyes. His ears were slightly more sticking-out than his brother's, and he was half an inch shorter, but otherwise his mirror image. Peas from a pod.

'Where's Dad?' he asked. Straight in with the big question. Ka-boom! No mercy!

Josie took a deep breath. Anything she said would be loaded with deceit. But she couldn't break the news to them yet – Pete might be home before bedtime, wringing his hands and apologizing. It might still be OK.

For now, she would bluff. She would get through this day as best as she could. 'Work,' she said briskly, avoiding his gaze. She shuffled up to a sitting position, pulling Toby on to her knee and making room for Sam to scramble in beside her.

The room swung around horribly, as if she were on the waltzers at a fairground. Oh God, she'd drunk so much the night before. Again.

She licked her lips, suddenly starving. 'Now – who wants a cooked breakfast this morning?'

The whoops of joy that followed were almost enough to bring a smile to her face. But not quite.

*

Ten minutes later she was dishing up bacon, eggs and toast. Exactly the kind of breakfast that would have had Pete muttering about childhood obesity and cholesterol levels as he devoured his morning muesli and blueberries, no doubt. But he wasn't here, was he? So sod it. And sod him.

A slice of sunlight fell on to the kitchen wall, and Josie felt herself staring at it. Cheesecake, the paint shade was called, she remembered. When they'd moved in, the house had been brilliant white throughout – shiny white, dazzling and harsh, the sort of thing you'd get in a student gaff. Repainting had been the first step to making it their place, differentiating it from every other brilliant-white house on the street. She and Pete had decorated together, newspapers on the floor, heaving the stepladder round from wall to wall, jars of murky turps on the windowsill overnight. Yellow seemed right for a kitchen somehow, they'd agreed. Cheerful and warm. Yellow for the kitchen, Summer Blue for the bedroom, rocket wallpaper for the boys, Soft Caramel for the living room and Sweet Violet for the spare room. Not that any of that mattered any more.

The letterbox rattled, and Josie went out to the hall. She wasn't sure what she was expecting – a forgive-me letter? Some kind of token? – but her heart raced as she approached the pile of post.

There were a couple of brown window envelopes she guessed were bills, and a computer-labelled MR AND MRS WINTER white envelope with a local postmark. She stuffed them in her dressing-gown pocket and trudged back to the kitchen.

'Stop pushing.'

'*You* stop pushing!'

'You pushed me first.'

'No, *you!*'

Josie raked her fingers through her hair wearily. 'Don't fight today,' she said. 'Please.'

There must have been something in her tone, something unusually desperate-sounding, for the boys stopped their argument mid-sentence and went back to their food. Miracle of the year, Josie thought, dragging her finger under the white envelope's seal. Then she felt bad for crushing their high spirits. The last thing she wanted was for them to pick up on her grief. Weren't the TV psychologists always saying that miserable parents produced damaged children? What if this was the start of her ruining their lives, screwing them up completely? They would be repressed, depressed, on Prozac before they were out of short trousers . . .

She pulled the letter from the envelope and registered the council logo at the top of the sheet then read:

Dear Mr and Mrs Winter,

I am writing to inform you that Toby Winter and Samuel Winter have been allocated places at Redwood Primary School from September this year. The term dates are as follows:

She read it through again. Redwood! They'd got into Redwood! Only the best primary school in the area, the one that all the middle-class parents fought over! If your child got into Redwood, it meant the best teachers, the best facilities, an ASBO-free childhood practically guaranteed!

A few days ago, Josie would have been overjoyed, bounding around the room, cheering and phoning up the other mums she knew to see if they'd been so lucky. Now she just felt ... sick.

Where might they be living in September now? Some crappy little plasterboard-walled box with no central heating and an infestation of cockroaches probably, miles from Redwood sodding Primary School. She'd have to get them into a different school, but only a crap one would have places left now. All the decent ones were oversubscribed every year.

She gulped back the rest of her coffee, barely noticing the way it scalded her throat on the way down. *Shit*. In a matter of hours, their whole future had been wrecked, as well as hers.

'Mum,' Toby asked, mouth full of bacon, 'when are we going to Australia?'

She couldn't speak suddenly, couldn't get a single word out.

'Mum,' Sam asked, swivelling around on his chair to peer at her, 'why are you crying?'

Somehow or other she managed to eat a slice of toast without throwing it all up again. Somehow or other she tidied the kitchen, threw away the cold, congealed Thai food, washed the breakfast things, mopped the floor and put on a load of clothes to wash. She hoovered the living room and stairs, and made the boys' beds. She persuaded them to get dressed, then put on a *Fireman Sam* video for them to watch while she finally peeled off her seduction undies (might as well throw them in the bin now), had a long hot shower and scrubbed her body until it was bright red and tingling.

She had squeaky-clean hair and sweet-smelling skin and minty-brushed teeth, she had fresh underwear and clothes on, but she still felt awful. And it was only ten-thirty in the morning. Pete would be at work now, probably humming smirkily and sending rude texts to Sabine.

Don't think about it. Don't think about it.

Meanwhile, what else was she going to do today? She had to keep busy, had to keep moving. The minute she sat down, she knew that the reality would crush her to pulp. It would blitz her, destroy her. She'd never be able to get up again. So what else could she do?

She stared out of the window. Last week, she'd vaguely planned to take the boys out today, to a new farm that had opened nearby with a big play area and lots of animals. If she could muster up enough energy to drive them over there, it might be just the thing. Fresh air, loads of distractions, and a bit of space for her to sit and watch them enjoying themselves.

She stared at herself in the mirror. She looked broken and old. She looked miserable and kicked-in. She looked exactly like the sort of wife that got left.

Don't you ever worry he'll go off with someone else?

Lisa's voice was a taunt in her head. The snidey bitch.

She swung away abruptly before she could see herself cry again. She had to keep going for the boys' sake. She couldn't just shut down completely, much as she wanted to. 'Boys!' she called. 'Get your shoes! We're going out.'

Was it possible to use up your entire reserve of tears? Josie wondered, clumsily backing the car into a space. Surely she couldn't keep up this rate of fluid loss for ever. She felt dehydrated already, not even twenty-four hours after Pete had walked out. Christ alone knew how she'd managed the drive to Fulton's Family Farm, whose slogan boasted *Guaranteed fun for ALL the family!* She'd barely had the brainpower to reverse the car out of their drive, let alone stay focused through the entire journey.

She pulled on the handbrake and wiped her eyes with a soggy bit of tissue. 'Here we are!' she cried brightly. Here they were for a morning of guaranteed fun, for ALL the family. Fat chance.

Josie shivered as she opened the car door and swung her feet down on to the grassy field that served as the farm's car park. It had been a mild May morning when they left the house, weather that promised new blossom opening, tulips unfolding in the sunshine, maybe even jackets off and lunch outside. Now a battalion of threatening clouds scudded dully across the sky, and a low wind flattened the grass, bouncing a faded crisp packet along the ground. Great. And there she was in Capri trousers, sandals and a T-shirt. She rubbed her arms, feeling the goosebumps that were already prickling along them.

'Mum, the wheels are really wonky,' was Toby's critical assessment of her parking once he'd clambered down from his car seat. 'Look!' He kicked one of the tyres that was skewed out at an ungainly angle, and Josie flinched.

'Who gives a toss?' she replied tightly, gripping her cold arms and wishing she'd brought a cardigan. While she was at it, she wished too that her eldest son didn't have to be such a Nazi about her driving. Today of all days she just wanted the world to be nice to her, for people to treat her gently, like a fragile ornament. Any more criticisms and she'd shatter into hundreds of pieces, impossible to glue back into any sort of useful shape.

'Come on,' she said, wincing at the startled look on Toby's face as she zipped up his jacket. It's started already, she thought glumly, following their racing figures towards the farm entrance. They're going to notice something's up any minute.

Fulton's Family Farm was a rural pocket of child heaven. There were miniature goats to pet, a stamping carthorse, three fat saddleback pigs (one with a litter of piglets), harrumphing ruminative cows munching hay and completely ignoring all the children, ducks, chickens, sheep, guinea pigs, rabbits and even a mangy-looking, rather smelly donkey that gave rides (and flea-bites, no doubt). There was also an enormous field full of climbing frames, swings, sandpits, trampolines and slides.

Josie bought herself a coffee and sat down thankfully at a picnic bench as the boys careered off towards a scary-looking twisty slide.

OK. We're here. The boys are happy. So far, so good. No need to do anything but sit here and drink coffee and let the time go by.

For some reason she was counting hours, as if that proved anything. It had been fifteen hours since Pete had walked out. Fifteen hours and she was carrying it off, putting on the performance of her life. You're doing OK, she told herself, sipping coffee. You are doing absolutely fine. Fifteen hours in, and you're keeping going.

But her fingers were trembling traitorously on the Styrofoam cup. For how long, though? a voice wailed in her head. How long would she be able to keep it up before the façade cracked and she revealed all the messiness and fear underneath to the world? Sixteen hours? Twenty hours? A whole day?

She was exhausted. She could feel the caffeine skidding through her bloodstream, attempting to give her a buzz, but it just made her feel even more sluggish. She wished she still smoked so she could chain her way through a packet of twenty, just for the comfort, just for something to do. She'd spent the whole night lying in bed running through her last conversation with Pete and rewriting it so that she got to say things like:

This is ridiculous. I refuse to let this happen. Call Sabine right now and tell her that it's over. I mean it!

Or, when she was feeling less feisty:

Let's talk about where we went wrong, and try to fix things. We can make it work again, Pete. We owe it to each other. And to the boys.

Or sometimes, when the desolation and alcohol hit her in a particularly potent combination:

You scumbag liar! You are SO going to pay for what you've done to me!

She wished now that she'd slapped him. Hard, right across the face. *Whack!* Take *that!* How satisfying it would have been to have heard the crack of his nose, the ringing slap against his cheek! How gratifying it would have been to see the look of cold shock on his features! She had never hit him before – had never hit anybody in her whole life – but her palm smarted at the thought. If only she had sliced open his pink fleshy cheek with her wedding ring – the irony would have been supremely comforting.

She took another sip of coffee, vaguely registering the woman who was striding up towards her, face set, lips pinched in a tight line. A crying child was attached to one of her hands, snot running into her mouth, features crumpled.

'Are those your boys over there?' the woman said grimly as she swam up into Josie's line of vision.

Josie blinked, then tried to focus on where the woman was pointing a chapped red finger. Toby was hanging upside-down from the climbing frame, arms dangling, face slack. Sam was astride one of the top bars, shouting something or other.

'Yes,' Josie replied. 'Why?'

'*Why?*' the woman repeated. 'They've just pushed my Shannon off that climbing frame, that's why! Don't you think you should be keeping an eye on them?'

Josie opened and shut her mouth a few times. Shannon scuffed a trainer along the ground, red lights flashing on the side panel of her shoe as her foot moved. The girl was smaller than the boys, long hair tangled by the wind, and her eyes were red from crying, but Josie could muster up no feeling towards her. She was numb inside.

Shannon wiped her nose on a bare goosepimpled arm, and Josie stared mindlessly at the shining snail trails she left behind.

'Sorry,' Josie muttered, more to Shannon than Shannon's mother.

The girl turned her eyes down to the ground, pressed herself into her mum's side, sniffed again.

'I'm really, really sorry,' Josie said, and then the wretched tears were back, spilling out of her. She dashed them away, but her eyes felt so sore, so gritty and tired and tender, that more tears just leaked down in their place.

There was an awkward pause. 'Um ... Is everything

OK?' the woman asked, her tone reduced from bollocking mode to merely gruff and embarrassed-sounding.

'No,' Josie replied. It was a relief to be honest at last, to let the truth tumble out of her. 'No, everything is awful. Everything's gone wrong. My husband—'

She stopped. What the hell was she doing? What was she saying?

Sam's waving arm caught her eye and she pushed a smile on to her face automatically, felt her own arm lifting itself from the table to wave back. A pink, cold limb moving back and forth like a windscreen wiper. How odd to feel so completely detached from one's own body, she found herself thinking. How peculiar that my arm knows what to do when the rest of me doesn't.

'Look at me, Mum!' she heard his thin voice call, carried by the wind.

'Well done, love!' she bellowed back. She blew her nose, and glanced up cautiously to Shannon and her mum. 'Sorry,' she said again, and wiped her eyes. 'I'm fine, honestly.' Her voice was wobbling, and she drew breath and said it again, a little louder. 'I am absolutely fine.'

Cornwall had been one of Josie's best ever holidays. Forget the five-star luxury the other mums she knew yearned for. Forget the far-flung adventures she'd so recently been craving. Pure happiness for Josie had been that fortnight last July when the four of them had rented a little cottage in St Ives. It had been the first summer that the boys had been old enough to truly appreciate digging moats in the wet sand, squealing in excitement as the sea curled in ever nearer at the end of the day and dissolved their castle walls. It was the first time the boys and their armbands had been in the sea, too – and they'd loved it. Pete had bought a junior surfboard and spent ages teaching them to float on it, pushed along by the waves. Josie had watched them from the warmth of the beach, a fat sand-sprinkled novel in her hands, and had been filled to the brim with love and joy. This is as good as it gets, she had told herself. My husband, tanned and gorgeous in his trunks, making our boys shriek with laughter in the sea. Yes. As good as it gets.

The sun had shone down every day. They'd eaten out most evenings all together, before shoulder-riding the boys back up the hill to the cottage. And then she and Pete had drunk wine in the tiny, fragrant back garden as the sky reddened, their skin tingling from the day's sunshine, crickets chirruping from the undergrowth.

They'd held hands over the wonky-legged white metal table, whose top was patterned like a doily, and had talked, really talked. They'd set the world to rights.

They'd made plans. And they'd decided that they'd try for another baby.

Josie had fingered the petals of the cream shrub roses near her seat. 'Do you like the name Rose, if it's a girl?' she'd asked.

'Yes,' Pete had replied.

And Josie had breathed in the perfume of the roses, and smiled across at her husband. 'Let's have us a Rose,' she'd said.

The phone was ringing as they pulled into the drive later that afternoon. Josie was quite sure of it, could hear it over the dying mumble of the engine. She jerked on the handbrake, pushed the car door open and sprinted into the house. The hall was still as she rushed in, and something about the stillness forced her to stop dead. The air rearranged itself around her shape while the slow sliding tick of the grandmother clock cut into the quiet. She felt cheated, tricked. She could have sworn she'd heard the phone; had been positive Pete was trying to get through.

'Mum!' she heard the boys chorus from the car. 'MU-U-U-UM!'

Josie cocked an ear and glanced up at the stairway. Had that been a creaking floorboard she'd heard up there? 'Pete?' she called breathlessly, head tilted towards the ceiling. 'Is that you?'

She struggled to remember if the door had been double-locked when she'd opened it. She'd been in such a hurry to get to the phone, she couldn't think clearly. Or had she left the mortice unlocked herself? Probably. She'd been in such a daze that morning, it was surprising she hadn't left the bacon pan on the stove, smoking away over the cheerful blue flame.

Josie put her arms around herself and shivered. Pete's car wasn't in the driveway so of course he wasn't here. He'd still be at work, remember, stupid? It was Monday afternoon. Life was going on everywhere else in the world, children traipsing home from school, office workers surreptitiously looking at their watches and sighing, babies being born, husbands cheating on wives . . .

Wake up, Josie! Just because she was out of sync with the world didn't mean that everyone else was too.

'Mu-um! Mu-um!'

'In a minute,' she called tonelessly without moving. 'Just coming.'

The house seemed dead, a mere receptacle of dust motes and static objects, with no life or movement, just the creeping of time. Just the slow withering and dying of plants, the desiccation to brown husks of flowers in their vases, just the leftover food slowly growing mould in the fridge to show that hours and days were passing by.

'MUM! Let us *out!*'

Josie turned and went to unstrap her children, both straining wildly against their seatbelts, red-faced and indignant at being left. The house needed them more than ever, running through its rooms, stirring up the stale air, knocking and dislodging things in their rushing wake.

She locked the car, double-checking all the windows were shut. She hadn't even switched the headlights on, but she checked that they were off anyway. Handbrake on? Check. Was the boot locked? Emptied of all valuables? Yes. Keep it together, keep it together, she told herself. If the car was safe, that was one less thing to worry about. It was the kind of comfort she needed right now.

While the boys embarked on a noisy game downstairs, Josie went up to her bedroom, just to make sure that everything was the same as she'd left it. She was pretty sure Pete wouldn't do anything as cowardly as sneak into the house when it was empty to collect his things without contacting her first, but who could say what he'd do now? She'd never dreamed that he could even give the eye to somebody else, let alone sleep with them, become so bewitched by them that he left her, his wife of seven years, and their children. Nothing would ever surprise her again, she thought, tramping heavily up the stairs. Nothing.

She pushed open their bedroom door. It only took a cursory glance to take in his half-read thriller still by the bedside table, the alarm clock turned towards his side of the bed, for her to realize he hadn't been. She sank down into the softness of their quilt, relieved that she hadn't missed him.

Then relief became doubt. So if he hadn't come by today, when *would* he? What did it mean, him not coming to collect more of his things? Maybe he'd had second thoughts, and was planning to come home that evening. Or maybe he and Sabine were joking about him having to borrow pairs of her knickers, her dressing gown, her toiletries. Was it more of a thrill, casting off his possessions temporarily? Casting off his whole *life*?

Josie sank backwards on to the bed. Calm down, she told herself. He was at work, that was all. Pete wouldn't take time off for something so trivial as his marriage breaking down. She should have known that.

She rolled on to her front so she could smell him on the covers. Pete. There was just a trace of his aftershave lingering on his pillow, and she wrapped her arms around it tightly. Come home, she urged him. Come back.

Josie swallowed hard – and there it was. The metallic

taste in her mouth that only meant one thing. She was ovulating. She imagined her milky white egg faithfully rolling along its path where it would lie and wait for fertilization . . .

Right. Like that was going to happen now.

'Three more to go and we've got a five-a-side team,' Pete had joked the day the boys had been born. He'd been crouching low to look at her, a proud protective arm – a dad's arm! – laid across her in the operating theatre.

'Three more, eh?' she'd laughed. 'I think these two will be enough to get on with for now.'

The comment had come back to her time and time again over the next six months as she'd entered the twilight zombie world of twin babies: endless night feeds, puke-cleaning, bum-wiping and heaving double-buggy manoeuvres. Three more? Not likely, a voice muttered in her head. Never again would she put herself through all of this. Not for anybody. Never ever *ever* . . .

People forget, though, don't they? Mothers forget. Little things – car keys, sun hats, spare nappies. And big things – pain, sleepless nights, crying at breakfast every morning because she was so hideously exhausted. It had been hard, bloody hard. She had felt as if her whole identity had been sucked out of her as she battled through the days and weeks. She didn't wear make-up for a whole year. She didn't get a lie-in for even longer. She no longer yearned for new shoes or bags. She yearned only for sleep.

Yet it passed. And last summer, she'd felt that her batteries had finally been recharged. She was ready to do it all over again.

So they'd tried, Pete and Josie. How they'd tried to make Rose. Flat on her back, legs in the air, Josie would lie there each month, willing on the sperm to swim into the right area, to do the right thing. Sex became mechanical, something to be ticked off.

'We have to do it tonight. I know you're tired, but I'm sure this is the night, I've counted in my diary and . . .'

'Wait, Pete! Let me put a pillow under my bum! Apparently it helps the sperm get there faster.'

'Have you taken your zinc supplement? You know it's good for your fertility, don't you?'

She'd lie there afterwards, hoisting her bottom in the air, uncomfortable and sticky, not daring to move. Half an hour, it said in her book. Lie on your back, legs raised, for half an hour. If nothing else, she was getting her stomach muscles back, she joked. Pete's smile never quite reached his eyes.

Then the finger-crossing would start. And the date consultations. Her last period had started on 22 February, so if she was pregnant now, the baby would be due on ... She'd follow the line of dates in her pregnancy book. 28 November. Lovely! Just in time for Christmas!

The alcohol would stop. Just in case.

The positive thoughts would start. Just in case.

She'd dream about her daughter. Rose Winter. Beautiful, strong, feisty Rose! A baby in the family again. She'd have to dig out the high chair and baby clothes from the loft, buy a brand-new single pram. No more dark blue or red or khaki – for Rose it would be pink and lilac all the way. She'd need muslins and nursing pads, a new sterilizer, a nice girly mobile to hang above the cot ... She would create the perfect world for her daughter to come into.

If only Rose would just hurry up and *come!*

That was the problem. Josie's imaginary daughter was feisty enough not to come when she was called. She ignored *all* the calls, in fact, for month after month after month, until sex had become a chore and Josie's period was a peak of sheer misery every four weeks.

Then the sex stopped altogether. Pete told her he felt depressed, that he couldn't give her what she wanted. Maybe if they stopped trying so hard, had fun again, it would happen. Hence a carrier bag full of Agent Provocateur lingerie and what-have-you. Anything to get things going!

But now she'd have to face facts. The baby stuff gathering dust in the loft might as well go to the next playgroup jumble sale, or the charity shops. She wasn't going to need it now, was she?

The phone jerked Josie out of her thoughts. A hiccup caught in her throat, and she passed a hand nervously through her hair. Right, OK. If it was Pete, what was she going to say?

She grabbed the receiver without thinking anything else. Better answer quick before he bottled it and hung up.

'Hello?'

'It's Barbara,' announced a voice. 'Is Pete there?'

Josie felt her whole body tense. Did her mother-in-law really have to be so damn rude on the phone? she wondered. No 'Hello, Josie.' No 'How are you, Josie?' Not even a 'How are my darling grandsons, Josie?'

'Hello, Barbara,' Josie said, unable to stop the sarcasm sliding into her voice. Sod it. She could be as rude as she liked in return today. 'I'm very well, thank you for asking. No, Pete *isn't* home. Actually, I'm surprised you're trying to get hold of him here. I thought he'd have told you himself.'

Silence. There, gotcha, Josie thought. Didn't see that one coming, did you?

'Told me what?' Barbara asked.

'That he's left me!' Josie replied. Her voice didn't sound like her any more. It was a voice she'd put on for interviews in the past: tinny, artificially bright. Chirpy, even. 'I can't believe he hasn't told you, Barbara. He's left me and the boys for his new fancy woman. So why don't you call him on his mobile and ask him to tell you all about it? I'm sure he's dying to tell you what a spineless shit he really is. Goodbye!' The word was practically a trill as she slammed the phone down, the breath panting out of her in hot painful spurts as if she'd just been running.

Please don't call back, she thought. Then, almost immediately afterwards, she thought, Please call back. I need to talk to somebody about Pete, even if it is just horrible Barbara.

The phone lay silent beneath her clammy fingers. Barbara had probably had a seizure at the revelation, coupled with Josie's rudeness. Or if not, she'd be punching the Quickdial button for Pete's mobile, rolling her eyes at her husband. *I said she was no good, that Josie. Didn't I always say? And now he's left her. She obviously drove him to it. You should have heard how snippy she was to me on the phone! Roy! Roy, are you listening? Go and sort the spare room out. The lad will need somewhere to stay, won't he?*

Chapter Eight

Josie would never forget the day she'd met Pete. It was a momentous occasion, in the same league as their wedding and the boys' birth. She liked imagining their lives, hers and Pete's, as two dots on a satellite screen, travelling in their own circles for so long without being on one another's radar, then finally hurtling towards one another and ... boom! ... colliding in a golden mist of attraction.

It had been approaching a year since she'd split up with Nick, and Josie was in a rut. Since Nick had dumped her (for his career, he'd said ... for the platinum blonde, the grapevine had it), Josie had had a few dates, a few flings, a few one-nighters, but she hadn't met anybody who even came close to Nick. It made her shudder now to remember those men – complete strangers, most of them – that she'd allowed into her bed, into her body, and then turfed out again the next morning. She'd told herself at the time that she was taking control, satisfying her own needs, but with hindsight she'd just wanted to be held and desired again, even if only for a few hours. She'd been lucky to escape lightly, with just a few lovebites and some stubble rash to show for it.

Weekends had been worst, back then. It was summer, and Josie felt by rights she should have been cavorting saucily in a poppy-splashed meadow with somebody handsome, or taking day-trips to the sea with other couples, or sitting in pub gardens until her nose turned pink and freckly, or all those other things that twosomes did together.

Instead, she felt uncomfortably alone. Nell was in the joined-at-the-hip honeymoon period with a new man, Andy, and had barely been in the flat for weeks. Lisa was away for conferences and business trips all the time. Josie literally didn't know what to do.

Then, one Sunday, she'd woken up feeling different. The lethargy that had weighed her down recently had disappeared. *Something is going to happen today*, she'd said to herself over breakfast. *I just know it.*

She washed her hair and blow-dried it, slathered sweet-smelling moisturizer into her skin and put on a ditsy little summer dress and sandals. She was starting to feel tingly with anticipation. *Something is going to happen.*

She took a bus to Islington. It was as good a place as any. The sun was warm on her bare shoulders as she wandered towards the Green, picking her way around breakfasting couples at pavement tables. She could smell coffee and croissants, and the sharp stink of cigarette smoke. A lightness had settled upon her, as if she'd broken free from her misery over Nick at last. Her eyes fell on a sign for a new gallery just off the main road, and on the spur of the moment she decided to take a look.

Just like that. She stepped into the cool dim foyer and changed everything. In that split second she steered her life in a whole new direction, with Pete, marriage and motherhood all lined up in front of her, like glittering treasures waiting to be discovered. Just like that.

The gallery was small, only a couple of rooms really, but it felt calm and quiet, a bubble of tranquillity away from the buses and chattering Islingtonites outside. It was light in there, all big windows and bleached wood, and the walls were filled with paintings by local artists.

She was staring at an abstract design – lots of shades of red in overlapping squares, thick brush-strokes of paint visible in ridges – when she heard footsteps behind her.

She smelled him before she even saw him – a light, woody cologne. He smelled fresh, like summer. Without even clapping eyes on him, Josie found herself thinking about cavorting in the poppy-dotted meadow. With *him*.

It was mad. It went against all the rules. But it was chemistry.

She held her breath. *Something is going to happen. Any second ... now.*

'Nice,' she heard him say. She turned to acknowledge the remark and saw him then, with his brown eyes and long lashes, his short dark hair, perfect skin, even white teeth. He wasn't looking at the painting. He was looking at her.

'Very nice,' Josie replied, gazing straight back at him. She couldn't help herself. He had a face that demanded to be flirted with.

His eyes crinkled at the edges when he smiled. She found herself checking out his hands in case he wore a ring. He didn't.

'Like art, do you?' he asked.

'I do now,' she replied. Her heart hammered under her floaty dress, she felt as if her nerve endings were all responding to him, with thousands of individual tingles. Thank goodness I shaved my legs, she found herself thinking, then pushed her gaze away from him, feeling prim and proper all of a sudden. Stop it, Josie! You don't even know the man!

'Me too,' he said. And then he grinned. Leaned in, like a conspirator. 'I've got a lovely pair of Pollocks I could show you, if you're interested.'

Josie burst out laughing. So cheeky! So rude! She loved him for it. 'And I've got a very nice Constable, if *you're* interested,' she managed to splutter.

He took her hand. Just like that, in the gallery, as if they'd known each other for years. 'I'm Pete,' he said. 'Can I buy you a coffee?'

'I'm Josie,' she replied, suddenly demure. Her hand felt tiny in his warm brown fingers. 'Yes please.'

She should have known from the start, really. He'd been so slick, so sure of himself. How many other women had he charmed like that? How many other women had been flattered by that smile, that super-confidence? 'I've got a lovely pair of Pollocks . . .' I mean, really!

But back then she'd been swept along by him, utterly bowled over. Hadn't she been thinking to herself all day that something would happen? And something had. She had come alive again at his appearance, as if he'd enchanted her, or freed her from a spell. He was so funny, so quick, so good-looking.

Bloody fantastic in bed, too. She'd hardly finished her coffee before they'd been at it like sluts, back at his hot, messy flat.

That seemed a long time ago now. A different Josie had lain naked on his rumpled sheets smirking at him afterwards as he went to fetch glasses of water and fags.

A different, fearless, bolder-than-brass Josie. That was who he'd fallen in love with, the Josie whose knickers were dangling from the cheeseplant where they'd been tossed in the midst of all the passion.

She could hardly equate that saucepot – 'a very nice Constable', indeed! – with how she was now. And Pete meanwhile had moved on to his next conquest, leaving Josie and the boys washed up in his wake like battered pieces of driftwood.

Josie sighed as she ushered her sons into playgroup. It was Tuesday morning, the second day that she'd woken up without Pete. She'd had to dish out another string of lies in answer to the big 'Where's Dad?' question. He still hadn't called her. Not a word. The hours he'd been away felt like a chasm between them now.

'Hello, Toby, hello, Sam, we're painting mugs for Father's Day today!' chirped Maddie, one of the playgroup staff. 'Get your aprons on and sit down, that's it. What's your daddy's favourite colour, then?'

Josie winced. Of course. Father's Day in a few weeks or so. What an irony.

'Red,' Toby said decisively, splodging a brush into the paint with gusto.

'Green,' Sam said in the next instant, grabbing a brush from the tin.

'Bye, boys,' Josie said, kissing their heads and stepping

back as the paint started flying about. 'Have fun, see you later.'

'Hey, guess what, Maddie?' she heard Sam say as she turned to go. 'We're going to Australia! To see polar bears!'

She winced at his words but she couldn't bear to correct him. She walked past the Lego table and the Play-Doh table and the little cloakroom, saying hello as brightly as she could manage to Zach's mum and Daniel's mum. She stopped as she saw her friend Emma bundling her daughter Clara through the doorway.

'Josie, hi!' Emma said, smiling at her as she whipped off Clara's sun hat and hung it on a peg. 'Are we on for a coffee this morning?'

Josie hesitated for a second. Emma lived a couple of streets away and the two of them often stopped at the deli just opposite playgroup on their way home. Over many, many coffees and slices of cake, she, Emma, and a couple of other local friends, Laura and Harriet, had discussed the minutiae of their lives. They'd been taking it in turns over the years, it seemed, to get their lofts converted, their kitchens done, their halls recarpeted. One of them always had a new car, new baby or new holiday lined up. Four nuclear families: well-to-do and doing well. Until now. Now Josie had gone and broken all the rules, hadn't she? Her own nuclear family had ... well, gone nuclear.

But she needed to talk. She'd been existing in a goldfish bowl of shock since Pete had left. She hadn't told anybody yet – apart from Barbara, of course, but that old bag didn't count for anything.

'Yes,' she said, after a few moments. 'Coffee sounds good.'

'I'll be two minutes,' Emma said. 'Come on, Clara. Oh, look! Painting mugs for Father's Day! Do you want to make one for Daddy?'

Josie tried not to listen to Clara's bright chatter. It hurt too much. Clara still had a daddy at home, after all. And, come Father's Day, Clara and her big sister Millie would be helping Emma upstairs with the breakfast tray, Clara's pigtails bouncing as she jumped around saying, 'Happy Father's Day, Daddy! Look what I made for you!'

'Are you all right, Jose?'

Josie snapped out of her thoughts to see Emma right next to her, a puzzled expression on her face.

She tried to smile, but could feel the tears gathering again at the kindness of Emma's voice. 'Not really,' she said. 'No, I'm not all right.'

Emma took her arm as they left the playgroup building. 'What's up? You sound like you've got a cold,' she said sympathetically.

Josie sniffed. If only she had a cold. If only that was all she had to care about! 'No,' she said. 'It's ... It's something worse than a cold. Pete...' Oh God, say it, just say it. The words were hard to get out when she wasn't using them to attack her mother-in-law. Said to a friend, they stuck in her throat. 'Pete's walked out. He's left. He's ... He's got another woman.'

There was a stunned silence, and Emma stopped walking, right in the middle of the pavement. 'He's *what?*' she asked, incredulous. 'You mean ... You mean he's having an affair? *Pete?*'

Emma was right to sound shocked. Nobody in their group of friends had ever done anything quite so soap-opera-esque.

Josie swallowed. 'Em, I don't know what to do,' she whispered. 'I'm really scared.'

Emma looked as if she didn't know what to do either. 'How did it happen?' she asked, aghast, steering Josie to the crossing. 'I mean, are you sure it's not just a mid-life-crisis thing?'

Josie shook her head as they waited for the lights to change. 'I don't know, Em. I hope so. I'm floundering about trying to make sense of it all.' She wiped her eyes with the back of her hand. 'All I know is that he said he'd fallen in love with someone else – *Sabine*, she's called – and that he felt we'd...' She bit her lip. 'That we'd outgrown each other. That things had gone stale between us.'

'Outgrown each other?' Emma echoed indignantly. She lowered her voice as they neared the deli. 'Stale? Honestly! Me and Will are as dull as hell yet we jolly along together...' She stopped. Not helping. Try again. 'I mean, you can't expect it all to be fireworks and weekends in Paris when you're our age.' She sighed and pushed open the door of the deli. Their favourite table, the one by the window, was empty, and she guided Josie over to it. 'Wait there. I'm going to get you some food. Have you eaten anything lately? Did you have any breakfast?'

Josie shook her head. 'I forgot,' she said, picking at a loose flake of skin on her thumb.

'You *forgot*? No wonder you're so pale. Wait there, I'll be really quick.'

Josie stared at her fingers while Emma went up to the counter. It seemed so long ago that she'd been amazed at Lisa forgetting to eat, back on their London weekend. Aeons ago. It was hard to believe it was merely a matter of days. Back then, she'd thought it incredible that someone should actually forget to put food in their mouth and swallow it at regular intervals. Now, she understood perfectly. Food was nothing. Everything was nothing.

Emma bustled back again with a tray of lattes and an almond croissant each. 'Here,' she said. 'Eat.' She eyed Josie anxiously over the rim of her cup as she sipped her coffee. 'Josie, I'm so sorry,' she said. 'I still can't believe it. You must be completely blown apart.'

Josie peeled off a piece of croissant to nibble. 'I am,' she replied. 'I'm in bits, Em. Bits.'

'What can I do to help? I mean, do you want me to come and look after you for a few days? Or do you and the boys want to stay with us?' She thought quickly. 'I could put Millie and Clara in together, if the three of you don't mind squeezing into Clara's room? Or...'

'No,' Josie said hurriedly, before Emma spun off into a duvet count. 'No, I think we need to stay put. I haven't told the boys anything yet.'

'Of course not, no,' Emma said. There was a silence. 'Have you spoken to him since he ... you know, since he went?'

'No,' Josie replied. 'I'm half expecting him to walk through the door any moment, tell me it was all a mistake and...' Her voice trailed away. Pathetic, wasn't it? 'Or phone,' she added miserably. 'I've tried his mobile but it's off. I left a drunken message the other night when I was...' She forced a laugh. 'When I was feeling a bit sorry for myself.'

'Babe, you've got every right to feel sorry for yourself,' Emma said. She leaned over the table and took Josie's hand in her own. 'What's he thinking of? The wanker!'

She blushed to her hairline. 'Sorry – shouldn't say that. But honestly, it's mad. What's he playing at?'

Josie shrugged. She felt so tired, she could barely follow the conversation any more.

'Well, you two need to sit down properly and talk,' Emma went on, a firmness coming into her voice. 'If you think you can handle it, I reckon you should try calling him again. Talk it through. You can't leave things as they are: you'll go mad, wondering where he is, what he's thinking.'

'Yes,' Josie said, feeling her treacherous eyes well and dampen all over again. The tears plopped on to her croissant, glistening on the pastry.

'It's a seven-year itch, mid-life crisis, that's what this is,' Emma said in a hearty, practical sort of a way, as if she were trying to convince herself as well as Josie. 'Although why he couldn't just get a new car ... Anyway. He's probably just flipped out, freaking about turning forty in a few years. It's what men *do*, isn't it?' She bit into her croissant with sudden force. 'Call him. He probably feels a right plonker, saying all that stuff. He's probably thinking of ways to make it up to you. Well, you tell him from me – Tiffany should do it.'

Josie laughed feebly. She knew Emma was trying to make her feel better, but jewellery was about a million miles from where she was right now. Who cared about jewellery anyway? Who cared about *stuff*? It was all landfill at the end of the day.

Emma was warming to her theme. 'Tiffany, an early summer holiday, and some new shoes. Sod it, a whole summer wardrobe. He owes you big-time for this.'

Josie blew her nose. 'He does,' she said. 'But do you know what? I'd take him back like a shot, without any of that lot. I just want him back.' A tear rolled down her cheek and splashed into her cup. 'Oh, Em,' she said, her chin trembling. 'I just want him *back!*'

It was hard work, being dumped. Exhausting. Josie felt as if she'd been through the wringer over and again. Living it was bad enough, but having to talk about it, having to *tell* people about it ... it made it all horribly real and immediate, every time. When she got back from the café there was a message from her mum on the answerphone, and Josie cringed. How was she going to tell her parents about this? They'd been married for *ever*, coming up to forty years. Jesus. They would be devastated.

She picked up the phone and pressed the call button, then put it straight back on its base. No. She couldn't bring herself to tell her mum just yet. The whole thing might blow over, like Emma had said. Pete might still come back, not with a rock from Tiffany, nothing that extreme, but he still might reappear. He *would* reappear, he had to. So what was the point of putting her mum through such misery, if it all came good tomorrow?

She made another coffee instead and washed her hair. There was dandruff flaking all along her parting, she'd noticed that morning. Dandruff! Where had that come from? She hadn't had dandruff since she'd been an acne-splattered teenager. Her scalp itched and felt tight as she blow-dried her hair, and white speckles of skin fell softly like snow on to the wooden floorboards in the bedroom. God! She'd have to get that sorted before Pete came home. He hated things like that. Hairy armpits, pimples, dandruff – he thought they were all gross. She'd never get him back if she let herself go.

She gazed into the mirror anxiously. Her face seemed to be falling apart too. Her skin was dry and red around her mouth and above her eyes, however much moisturizer she pressed into it. What next? Would her hair start falling out as well? Would her internal organs start packing up one by one?

Two coffees later, with clean hair and half a tube of the boys' E45 sunk into her face, she finally plucked up the courage to pick up the phone. Like Emma said, she and Pete needed to talk. And if he was too chicken-shit to face up to the responsibility, then it was down to her to arrange a crisis meeting. She'd win him back. She'd *woo* him back. Hell, she knew the buttons to press with her own husband. Sabine would be no match for *her*.

'I'm sorry, Mr Winter's out of the office for a few days,' his secretary, Sara, said, picking up the call. 'May I take a message?'

'Oh!' Josie blurted out in surprise. Taken a few days off? 'Well, where *is* he?'

There was a moment's hesitation. 'Josie, is that you?' Sara asked in confusion.

Josie coughed, embarrassed, her cheeks flooding with colour. 'No,' she replied, trying to disguise her voice with a huskiness that wasn't usually there. Her eye fell on a *Star Wars* video box that was on the sofa next to her. 'No, this is ... Leia. Leia ... Lucas. I'll call back next week.'

She banged the phone down and stared unseeingly out of the window. Where was he? What was he doing? Why wasn't he at work?

She punched the sofa, suddenly furious with him. He'd gone away with Sabine for a shagging holiday, she just knew it. Right now, right this minute, while she was sitting here, Pete and Sabine would be strolling down the Ramblas in Barcelona together, or snogging in a Venetian gondala, or sunbathing on a Greek island ...

'You can afford to take *her* somewhere exciting then,' she said aloud. No wonder he had blanched at her idea of an exotic trip away. His credit card was already maxed out, she guessed, paying for this little jaunt with Sabine.

With a deep breath she tried his mobile, but the call went straight through to voicemail. She hung up without leaving a message – she'd only end up ranting like a maniac – and sent a text instead.

Where are you? Ring me. Boys suspicious. We miss you.

She sat quite still in the middle of the sofa holding the phone in case he texted her straight back, but nothing happened. She leaned back heavily and her eye fell upon the painting that hung above the mantelpiece. Pete's wedding present to her – the very picture she'd been staring at when they'd first met. It had been a symbol of love back then. Now she could hardly bear to look at it.

He phoned on the Friday. Finally. She was going out of her mind with worry by then. She couldn't believe he'd actually let the best part of a week go by without contacting her at all. Not even one little call to say good-night to the boys, or a text to say that he was still alive. Nothing.

God knew how she'd got through the week single-handedly. She'd busied herself every day, doing the usual sociable things with the boys and her friends on automatic pilot, but all anyone wanted to talk to her about had been Pete walking out. She was getting sick of the sympathetic expressions her friends pulled, their hearty reassurances, their offers of help. She was sick, too, of her own voice saying that she was sure it would all work out. She wasn't sure about anything any more.

The boys were asking a lot of questions now. She was certain they'd guessed something was wrong. Sam kept flicking anxious little glances her way, his eyes troubled, and Toby was doing a lot of kicking. Sam had even wet the bed on Thursday night, something he hadn't done for months. Oh, they knew something was up, all right. But what was she supposed to tell them? She didn't even know what was happening herself.

As each day ticked through the minutes and hours, she felt as if she was dying inside, like a neglected plant. Every morning she told herself that this would be the day that he'd ring, or come round. And then, as the hours slipped away without the phone ringing or the doorbell's chime, she slowly lost her conviction all over again. He wasn't coming back after all. He wasn't going to phone.

On Friday, she woke up feeling sick with misery. The weekend loomed ahead of her and she was dreading it. Weekends had always been their precious family days, where they all went swimming together, or to the park, or took the bikes out. But now the weekend seemed like the loneliest time of all. Her friends would be busy doing their own family things, she knew. There was no gym club, no playgroup, no coffee mornings.

And then the phone trilled on Friday afternoon, and at last it was Pete. The relief she felt when she heard his voice quickly gave way to trepidation. Was he ringing to say he was coming back? Or not?

'How are you?' he asked. 'Sorry I haven't called,' he went on, without waiting for her answer. 'I've been away. How are the boys?'

'All right,' she replied, her mouth dry. She'd thought up so many things she wanted to say to him since he'd gone — some imploring, some bitter, some practical — but in an instant they disappeared from her mind, leaving her disarmingly blank. 'They miss you,' she said. Understatement of the year, she thought miserably. From Wednesday onwards, they'd asked when he was coming back home every half an hour on average. The weight of having to reply, 'I'm not sure,' again and again, like a jammed CD, had been like the most excruciating kind of torture.

He sighed down the line. 'I miss them,' he said. 'I was wondering if I could see them tomorrow? Take them out somewhere?'

Josie felt panicked by the question. The hand that wasn't holding the phone stole around her middle as if for comfort. 'Do you mean...' She licked her lips. 'Do you mean, without me?'

He hesitated. 'Yes,' he said. 'Without you.'

Her mouth was so dry she could hardly speak. 'Is *she* going to be there?'

'No,' he replied, and she thought she might keel over with relief. She didn't want Sabine to get her filthy paws on the boys. They were Josie's. Sabine had already stolen Pete. She wasn't going to let—

'Not tomorrow, anyway,' Pete went on, and Josie stiffened. 'Plenty of time for that. There's no rush, is there?'

Josie clenched her fists. 'No,' she managed to say. 'No rush.' She swallowed hard, as if there were a painful, solid blockage in her throat. 'We need to talk, though. You and me, I mean. Because I don't think we should just give up on ... us. Could we maybe ... try again?'

There was an agonizing pause. 'Josie ...' he began, and then stopped. 'Let's just give each other some space now, yeah?'

She bit her lip. 'What did I do wrong?' she asked, brokenly. 'I thought we were happy together.' And then she was crying again. 'I thought we were happy,' she sobbed.

'We were.' His voice was softer suddenly. 'But don't you see? It had changed. We'd grown apart, hadn't we?'

'No,' she said, tears rolling down her face. 'I *don't* see. I thought everything was fine.'

He hesitated. 'But that's the problem, isn't it? Because I wasn't fine. I felt . . . trapped.'

She put a hand up to her face, unable to speak. Thank God the boys were out in the garden and not able to see any of this. *Mummy Loses the Plot* (Part One). Part Two: *Mummy's Nervous Breakdown*, coming soon!

'Look, I'll talk to the boys tomorrow, OK?' Pete said, not waiting for a reply. 'That's the most important thing.'

'Yes,' she said dully. So important that he'd waited all week to get in touch with her. They could have been in hospital beds for all he'd known. 'What . . . what will you tell them?'

Again, that hesitation. Not long – a few seconds, tops – but long enough for Josie's mind to be rushing with panicky thoughts.

Sorry, boys, but I don't love Mummy any more.

Hey, kids, I'm getting married again!

Guess what? Me and Auntie Sabine are going to have a new baby soon – would you like a brother or a sister?

'Just that I won't be coming back to live with you – with them. That we're separating, I guess. God, I don't know. It's really difficult.'

Josie was holding herself so tightly she could hardly breathe. It sounded so final. It sounded so ... painful. 'Do you have to tell them that?' she burst out, with a sob in her voice. 'It sounds like it's over, like we're never going to get back together again.'

'But Josie, that's what I'm trying to say,' he replied. 'We're not.'

Josie couldn't take her eyes off the clock. Two o'clock, Pete had said he'd be here, and the boys had been in a state of great excitement since breakfast. It was two-thirty now, and the excitement was waning fast. Toby was kicking the sofa and throwing all the cushions off, his eyebrows hooded over his eyes. Sam was banging about upstairs, noisier than was strictly necessary.

'You said he'd be here by now,' Toby muttered, glaring at her as if it was her fault.

Josie reached out for him but he dodged away, not wanting to be comforted. 'Well, I'm sure he'll be here soon,' she said lamely. 'Shall we read a story while we wait?'

Toby shook his head, mutinous. 'No,' he said. 'I don't want a story. I don't want you. I want my dad!'

Josie was starting to feel angrier and angrier with Pete. She'd been in a state all morning herself. She wanted to display an Ideal Home scenario to him when he arrived, and Ideal Wife to boot, to remind him what he was missing. The house was spotless — well, apart from the discarded cushions — and she had spent a stupidly long time dithering over what to wear. Nothing black — the dandruff was still pattering down from her scalp every time she moved her head. And half a ton of foundation was a given, seeing as her skin was still spotty and dry. Was the tight white T-shirt he'd always fancied her in too obvious? Should she wear a skirt, flash a bit of leg?

He'd blown it now, though. She was feeling as petulant as the boys, no longer cared what she looked like. Come *on*, Pete! What was he doing? Surely he hadn't forgotten? Surely even *he* knew that you couldn't be late for your own kids?

She put her hand on the phone, then snatched it off again. She wasn't going to remind him to pick them up. Let him be really, really late. Then they'd hate him for it. Then they'd love *her* even more. And ...

'I want Da-a-ad,' Toby whined again, punching the arm of the sofa. His bottom lip was curled out sullenly. His eyes were downcast.

Josie grabbed the phone at once. She couldn't play games like that. She wasn't going to get into the who-do-you-love-best? thing, it was out of order. She would phone Pete right now, and demand that he come round this minute!

Ding-dong!

'Daddy!' Toby cheered, his face alight once more as the doorbell pealed. It was like the sun coming out, seeing his expression change.

Sam thumped down the stairs, almost tripping in his haste. 'Is it Dad?' he asked, pushing past Josie without waiting for an answer.

Josie tucked her hair behind her ears self-consciously as she walked towards the door. She felt nervous, as if she were about to go on a first date. How ironic was that?

'Have you got your shoes on? Well done. Here are your sun hats, OK?' She was trying to keep her voice normal and light — *Hey, this is no big deal, kids!* — but there was a horrible wobbly sound to her words. Don't cry, whatever you do, she ordered herself. Do not cry.

Her hand felt shaky on the doorhandle as she lowered the latch. A part of her wanted to fling open the door and drag him bodily into the house with her. *You will stay with me, you will! You're not allowed to go again, do you understand?*

And then there he was, Pete, on the wrong side of the doorstep, like a total stranger. She was about to speak when the boys charged past her, one either side, headlong into Pete's arms. He crouched down and caught them, burying his face in their hair, and Josie had to turn away, unable to look.

It was going to break their little hearts. It was going to destroy them!

'I'll bring them back by five, yeah?' he said, finally raising his eyes to hers.

He looked different. Not the man she'd married. He smelled different too. New aftershave. New T-shirt.

Josie folded her arms around herself, suddenly feeling cold, and nodded. 'Have a nice time, Tobes, have fun, Sam,' she said, bending down to kiss them. 'Be good for your dad, won't you?'

But they were already turning away from her, and Pete was hoisting a boy up on to each shoulder, and they were all laughing together. All except her.

At the last moment Sam turned his head to wave goodbye, his brown eyes anxious as he saw her tense expression.

With her last ounce of strength, Josie managed to plaster on a big smile and blow him a kiss. Then she shut the door, and there was silence.

'Why doesn't Daddy want to live with us any more?'

Josie stared at Sam, trying to get the right words together. Her mouth moved, but nothing came out. The very question she'd been dreading. 'Well, it's not that...' she began, but Toby was too quick for her.

'Cos he doesn't love us no more, silly!' he told his brother, scooping up an armful of foam with a practised sweep.

The boys were in the bath now, having returned (late) from their afternoon with Pete with grass clippings in their hair and cut knees after football in the park. Josie, meanwhile, had spent the three hours they'd been gone in a kind of trance, bereft, as if they'd been snatched away from her for ever.

'That's not true,' she said quickly. 'Toby? Are you listening? Your dad does love you, very much. Of course he does.'

Sam looked at her, his face tilted to one side. 'Doesn't he love *you* any more then, Mum?'

God! Out of the mouths of babes and all that. She took a deep breath. 'Me and Dad will always love you two,' she said. 'Always. But now he...' This was so difficult. They never taught you this bit at childbirth classes. 'Now he wants to live with somebody else.' She crossed her fingers behind her back. 'For a while,' she added in the hope of softening the truth.

'Bean?' Toby asked. He was swishing his arms through the bubbles with a fierce kind of concentration. 'Oh yeah, Dad told us all about Bean.'

Did he now?

'Her name's Sabine,' Josie said, through gritted teeth.

'I don't like that name,' Sam said, loyal to the end. He was looking at her carefully, as if desperate to say the right thing and please her.

'I don't either,' Toby said. 'It's stupid.' He did a karate chop into the water, and Josie dodged away as it sprayed everywhere. 'Meany beany Sabin-ee!'

'Toby, don't call her names,' Josie said, tempting though it was to join in. 'She might be very nice.'

'*I* won't like her,' Toby said confidently.

Sam was reaching for her, his fingers wet and bubbly on her arm. 'Don't worry, Mum,' he said. 'We still love you best.'

Josie put her arms around him, and his little damp hand crept around her back. 'Thanks, sweetheart,' she said, trying not to choke on the words. How did children manage to do that anyway? Wrench at your heart just with a simple pronouncement? 'Thanks, pumpkin. I love you two best, as well.'

The next day was Sunday, and there was actually something on the calendar that they could do, even if it was only lunch at her mum's. It was the first time Josie could remember for months where she was actually pleased at the prospect, rather than it seeming like a chore, dragging the kids out to Guildford. She'd managed two mother–daughter phone calls during the week without telling her mum anything of what had been happening. Why put her through it? She'd tell her when she had to, and not before.

Never had the sight of her mum's lace curtains twitching as she pulled into the drive brought such relief to Josie. Even better, Stu, her younger brother, was due to be there with his new girlfriend too, so the focus would be temporarily off her own life. There was no way Josie's mum would pass on the chance for fully grilling any prospective daughter-in-law.

It was a close, sultry day, and the air inside the house seemed to be boiling with the heat of the oven and the stifling smell of roast chicken. No matter that it was almost June, Mrs Bell prided herself on serving up a full roast week in, week out.

'Can I help, Mum?' Josie asked as the boys charged straight out into the garden where their grandad had set up the sprinkler.

Mrs Bell fanned her flushed cheeks. She was standing in front of the cooker, lifting saucepan lids and releasing great jets of steam as she assessed the progress of each item. 'Almost done,' she said. 'You could lay the table for me, love.'

The doorbell rang and Mrs Bell replaced the final lid

and smoothed down her apron. 'That'll be Stuart and Melanie,' she said, patting her iron-grey curls into place. 'Coming!' she carolled as she bustled out to the door.

Melanie was petite and slender with smoky grey eyes and olive skin. Her long dark hair was bundled back into a ponytail, with a couple of daisy hairclips wrestled into it for good measure. She had on a white crop top that showed a flat, tanned belly, and a pale floaty skirt. 'Hi Josie, I'm Melanie,' she said, walking into the dining room where Josie was laying out the knives and forks.

Stu came in and kissed Josie on the cheek. He looked like the cat who got the cream, Josie thought to herself in amusement. And he smelled different, too – had the after-shave been a present from Melanie? she wondered. Oh, to be back in those heady days of new love, she thought with a pang. Love tokens and presents and edging into one another's lives, all shiny and new and sexy . . .

She took a deep breath. 'Hi, Stu. Nice to meet you, Melanie. Pete's playing golf today, some business thing.'

She'd given her mum the same line. There was no way she was going to talk about what had really happened over roast sodding chicken.

Mrs Bell arrived in the room then with a steaming dish of vegetables. 'Go and wash your hands, you three,' she ordered, as if they were children again. 'Almost on the table.'

Melanie pressed her lips together as if she wanted to giggle but obediently went to the kitchen with Stu to scrub up at the sink. 'Boys!' Josie called into the garden. 'Lunch!'

The roast chicken was succulent and tender, the roast potatoes just the right side of crunchy, the broccoli, carrots and peas all steamed to perfection. They had gravy in a gravy boat, plates on place mats, matching cutlery and a full set of wine glasses. If it wasn't for the boys kicking each other under the table and flicking their peas at one another, Josie could almost have believed she was seventeen again, and living at home.

Josie ate and ate. She could see her mum raising her eyebrows as Josie piled on the chicken and gravy, helped herself to another slithering white dollop of bread sauce, another spoonful of potatoes. She could almost read her mum's mind: *Eating for two, hmmm? Something to tell us, hmmm?*

Hardly. Eating for a broken heart, more like. Eating for comfort, eating to carb out the permanent hangover she seemed to have had since Pete had broken the news to her. So much for heartbreak making you thin. At this rate, Josie was going to be busting out of everything in her wardrobe before the day was up.

'So, Melanie,' Josie's dad said genially, pouring himself another glass of red wine, 'what does your father do?'

'He's dead,' Melanie replied, lifting a forkful of broccoli to her mouth.

'Ahh,' said Josie's dad, clearing his throat uncomfortably. 'Right. Well, I'm very sorry to . . .'

'What was it?' Mrs Bell wanted to know. 'Heart trouble? Cancer?'

'Mum!' Josie hissed.

'Mel's *mum*, however, is a professor of genetics in Cambridge,' Stu put in quickly.

'A working mother, eh?' Mrs Bell said, nodding as if she vaguely remembered once reading about such a phenomenon.

'Interesting,' Mr Bell said sagely. His knife clicked against a chicken bone as he attempted to lever a last shred of flesh away from it.

Silence fell. 'More potatoes?' Mrs Bell beamed around the table. 'Anyone?'

'My dad's not living with us now,' Toby announced, as if he'd only just remembered.

'He doesn't love Mum any more,' Sam chimed in. 'But we do. And we've decided that we won't like old Meany Beanie, and—'

'All right, love,' Josie said, putting a calming hand on his arm. There was a sharp intake of breath from her parents' end of the table, and now she could feel every pair of eyes burning into her. All except her boys' eyes, of course – they'd gone back to flicking peas. Announcement over, job done. She took a deep breath and looked up at her mum. 'It's true,' she said quietly. 'But perhaps this isn't the time to tell you about it.'

'Well, what's happened?' her mum burst out, her eyes as round as marbles. Any second now they were going to drop out of her head, pop, pop and splash into the gravy. 'So he's not at golf, then?'

'No,' Josie said, through gritted teeth. 'He's not at golf. That was just ... I wanted to pick the right time to tell you, that's all.'

Her mum was still staring. 'Well, where *has* he gone? Has he really left you, for good?'

'Mu-um!' Josie said, trying to rein her in. She cast a meaningful glance at her sons' heads, but her mother was unstoppable, bristling with questions.

'I mean, is he coming back? Is it like a trial separation? Or is it going to end in divorce?' One liver-spotted hand flew up to her throat. 'My daughter, a divorcee! Oh, I never thought this day would come!'

'Mum, for heaven's sake!' Stu put in sharply.

Melanie, Josie noticed, was looking down at her plate as if she were casting a teleport spell and wishing herself at a different, saner dinner table. Me and you both, love, Josie thought fervently.

'Always thought there was something shifty about him,' her dad put in, his eyes dark. 'Should have known we couldn't trust him!'

'Dad!' Josie exploded. 'Not in front of the boys!'

'Shifty, shifty, very very wifty,' Toby sang tunelessly, and the room seemed to freeze in silence.

'The little boys!' Josie's mum said in an anguished sob. 'The little lads!'

'Mel's been working on a research project lately,' Stu said, with a concerned glance at Josie. He took Melanie's hand, and she looked warily around the table. 'Haven't you, Mel? Egyptology. It's for the British Museum, you know.'

'Lovely,' said Mrs Bell absent-mindedly, but she was still staring at Josie, with a look of great sadness in her eyes. 'And I was *so* hoping for another grandchild!' she cried.

Chapter Nine

Loaded up with newly knitted jumpers for the boys, some teeny new potatoes from Mr Bell's garden, cold chicken and a recipe for lemon cheesecake that she'd no doubt never get round to making, Josie pulled away from her parents' driveway in an almost crippling wash of exhaustion. Well, *that* had gone about as catastrophically wrong as it possibly could have done, she thought grimly.

Her mum had embraced her with tears in her eyes, offering to come and stay so that she could help out.

'Thanks,' Josie had said quickly, 'but no thanks.' She'd have to be desperate before she'd agree to that. Or completely la-la.

Her dad had folded her into his arms. 'The man's an idiot,' he'd announced gruffly, patting Josie's back. 'You wait, he'll come crawling back, tail between his legs.'

'Yeah,' Josie had sighed in return. 'That's what I'm hoping, Dad.'

Stu had hugged her too. He was younger than her by

184

a mere eighteen months and they'd been close as children, but these days they had little in common. He was still heavily into the club scene and had a shit-hot career, complete with minimalist bachelor crash-pad in the City. 'Take care,' he said into her ear. 'Want me to beat him up for you?'

He was joking, she knew, but Josie appreciated the sentiment. 'Thanks, Stu, but I'd better pass on that one,' she said, trying to smile.

'Sorry, Melanie,' she'd added, on her way out. 'You must think this family is a bunch of nutters.'

'No, honestly,' Melanie protested. She smiled at Josie, and put a hand on her arm. 'Take care of yourself. Sorry to hear you're having a rough time,' she said. 'Your boys are lovely, by the way.'

'Don't start getting ideas, Melanie,' Stu said warningly.

Josie had driven away feeling as if she was escaping from a bad dream. She wondered how long it would take her mum to get on the phone to her cronies. *You'll never guess what. I can't believe it! My little girl, a divorcee! A single mum! You could have knocked me down with a feather . . .*

Christ. Her mum would milk it until it was dry. It would be poor-me the whole way, forget how Josie was feeling.

Josie sighed. And now she was back home again, and it was all the same. That was the problem. It just went on being the same. Why wasn't she feeling any better? Why did she still feel so utterly crap?

'Help me,' she muttered to her bedroom ceiling. She was lying flat on her back, feeling as if all her spirit and energy had drained away. She was too tired to go and investigate what the boys were up to, even though they were being suspiciously quiet. She couldn't even think what she was going to make for their tea. How was she ever going to fight for her relationship when she felt so weak and punched-out?

'Somebody help me,' she said, pulling a pillow over her head. 'I can't do this any more. I just can't.'

Then the doorbell rang.

Josie sat up. Even that was an effort. Jehovah's Witnesses, probably. Nobody popped round on a Sunday, did they? Unless it was . . .

'Mum!' the boys shouted. 'Door!'

Josie's heart pounded as she got to her feet and headed for the stairs. Unless it was Pete. Could it be Pete?

He'd changed his mind. Seeing the boys had made him realize how much he missed them. And her . . .

Her throat was tight as she ran to the door. She fumbled with the latch and pulled it open. And stared.

'Josie – I hope you don't mind me turning up like this, but—'

'Nell!' It was like a mirage, seeing her there on the doorstep.

'I tried ringing earlier but it was engaged, so . . .' Nell broke off, leaning forwards to stare at Josie. 'Are you all right? You look really pale.'

Was she all right? Oh God. Why did Nell have to ask that?

Josie's shoulders slumped with the weight of the question. That bloody awful question! She shook her head silently and stepped back so that Nell could come in. Was she all right? No, she wasn't. She was a million miles from all right.

'What's happened?' Nell asked, dropping her bags and stepping swiftly over to hug her. 'Babe – what is it?'

'He's . . .' The words stuck in Josie's throat. It had been a whole week now and it was still so hard to say it each time. She leaned her head on Nell's shoulder. 'He's gone. Pete. He's left me.'

Nell stiffened in shock. '*What?*'

Josie sighed. 'Don't make me say it again,' she begged. 'He—'

'Mum, who was at the door? Who's that?'

Sam had come into the hall with a fireman's helmet and light-sabre, and was staring unblinkingly at Nell, resplendent in her scarlet mini-dress and wedge-heeled sandals, as if she was an exotic bird that had just flown in from the rainforest.

'It's me, Nell, your mum's friend,' Nell said with a wide smile. 'Remember? Last time I came here we made a camp outside in the garden. No?' She shrugged. 'I suppose it was a year ago. Are you Sam or Toby, by the way? Let me guess ... Toby!'

Sam shook his head, then disappeared again.

Nell took Josie's hand. 'I've turned up at completely the wrong time, haven't I?' she said apologetically. 'Sorry. Do you want me to go, and leave you in peace?'

Josie shook her head. 'No, I'm glad you're here,' she said. 'Stay, I don't want peace.' She swallowed. 'I want company. I feel like I'm sleepwalking, like this is not really happening. I was just saying before you got here, "Help me, somebody help me."' A tear slid down her face, then another. 'I don't know what to do. I feel like I can't keep going any longer. I still can't take it in, I...' She forced a feeble smile on to her face, even if it was the merest shadow of a smile. 'And I really don't want to do Ten Reasons Why He Was a Wanker Anyway either.'

'No,' Nell said. 'Course you don't. Oh God. I can't believe it, Jose. What happened? Why did he go?'

Josie cast a furtive look towards the living room. The boys seemed to be playing *Star Wars*, which usually kept them engrossed for ages. 'Come in the kitchen,' she said. 'I'll tell you all about it.'

Once in the kitchen, Nell steered Josie to the table and made her sit down while she filled the kettle. 'I'm not ill,' Josie protested. 'I can make you a—'

'No, you can't,' Nell said. 'Least I can do, barging in on you like this. So what's happened with Pete? Do the boys know?'

'A bit,' Josie replied. 'Pete took them out yesterday and told them he wasn't going to live with us any more. That he was in love with someone else.'

'Jesus Ker-rist,' Nell said, looking appalled. 'Fucking Nora. Sorry. I mean – how are they handling it? Did they freak out?'

Josie shook her head. 'Not really. They did ask me if Pete didn't love *them* any more.' A pang of guilt hit her at the thought of Sam's anxious face turning to her in the bath. 'It was *awful*. But ... I don't know. It's hard to gauge. I guess it's going to take a while to sink in.'

'Here you are,' Nell said, stirring milk into Josie's coffee and plonking it down in front of her. 'Biscuits? Toast? Anything else I can get for you?'

'No,' Josie replied. She was still full of roast chicken. She sipped her coffee and took a deep breath. 'Guess what else?' she said. 'It gets worse. Pete told me about Lisa. They *did* have an affair.'

'Oh my God,' Nell breathed. Her eyes glittered and she sat down, an odd expression on her face. 'You know ... I wish I could tell you that surprises me, but it doesn't,' she said. 'I was kind of wondering if that was coming.' She reached over and took Josie's hand. 'The cow. I can't believe she did that. And so ... What? He's left you for *her*?'

Josie shook her head glumly. 'Oh no. That was just for starters. That was all in the past, he said, but I don't know when. No, he's gone off with someone else now.' To her surprise, a hollow laugh fell out of her mouth. 'Talk about Casanova. There was me thinking I'd married Mr Committed, and all the time I was shacked up with Mr Lover-Lover.' Then she looked up, only just register-ing what Nell had said. 'What do you mean, anyway? About not being surprised?'

Nell grimaced. 'Just ... the photo thing, when we were at Lisa's. I did think it was weird,' she confessed. 'I didn't want to say so at the time, because I knew it would send you into a flap, but it did make me wonder if Lisa fancied him.' She put a hand on Josie's. 'You know, it might just have been a shag. Just one stupid shag. We've all done it.'

Josie couldn't help glaring at the photo on the kitchen

noticeboard, a black and white wedding photo of her and Pete, their faces turned towards each other. 'I haven't,' she said fiercely. 'Not since I got married, anyway. Being married is supposed to change all that one-stupid-shag stuff, isn't it?'

Nell nodded. 'It's supposed to,' she agreed. There was a pause. 'So where's Pete now? Who's this other woman?'

'Sabine,' Josie replied tonelessly. 'And he says he's in love with her.'

'Oh fuck,' Nell said. 'Oh God, what a nightmare.' She sipped her coffee, her eyes on Josie. 'But this might just be a blip, right?' she said after a moment. 'I mean, this whole thing just shrieks of mid-life crisis. Totally. Give him a few days and he'll be back, begging you to forgive him.'

Josie glanced up again at the wedding photo, then snatched her gaze away as if it hurt her eyes. 'I keep telling myself that,' she said quietly. 'And everyone else keeps telling me it too. But I don't know if I'm just ... you know, in denial. Because maybe he really has gone. When I spoke to him the other day he was pretty definite about it. So ...' She shrugged. 'So maybe I'm just kidding myself. Maybe this is it, end of. Maybe we'll be getting divorced.'

'Don't go there,' Nell interrupted. 'Don't think about that at the moment. Just bunker down and get through this. We can look after each other.' She gave a wry smile. 'It'll be just like when I split up with Dave and you split up with Nick, remember? All that crying and chocolate in front of *Pretty Woman*, and then jetting off to Cyprus for our girly holiday?'

'Well … kind of,' Josie said. She tried to smile back at her friend, who was so well-meaning, but she knew already that Pete leaving was in a different league.

Toby clattered into the kitchen just then, Darth Vader helmet on, swishing his light-sabre through the air as if he were a demented majorette.

'Careful, love,' Josie said as he whacked one of the chairs with a plasticky thump. She flinched, as if she were the one to receive the whacking.

THWACK! 'I … am … your … father!'

'Use the force!' Nell said.

'But not too much force,' Josie added as he approached, breathing heavily, pointing his light-sabre at her. 'Come here, Darth. Come and give your old mum a cuddle.'

'Darth … Vader … doesn't … cuddle … anyone,' he intoned spookily, and she pulled his helmet off and grabbed him.

'Toby Winter does, though, luckily for me,' she said, wrapping her arms around him until he squealed. She kissed his nose — Pete's nose, it was an exact replica — and felt engulfed by sadness again.

Nell was looking over at her. 'Hey, Tobes, want to show me your footie skills?' she asked quickly. 'Bet you can't score past me. Did you know I used to be goalkeeper for England?'

Toby looked interested. 'Really? Did you?' he asked.

Nell winked at him. 'Not really,' she admitted, 'but I am pretty handy in a penalty shoot-out.' She tilted her head towards the garden. 'I spotted your goal out there. Fancy your chances, do you?'

Toby dropped his light-sabre with a clunk, and it rolled under the table. 'Sam! Sam!' he shouted, wriggling free of Josie and rushing to find his brother. 'Come and play football with that lady, Nell!'

Nell put a hand on Josie's shoulder. 'I'll take them in the garden for a bit,' she said. 'Why don't you go and have a kip? I can always make tea for them later if you want to sleep awhile.'

Josie nodded gratefully, her eyes wet. 'Thanks,' she said. 'I feel like a zombie.'

'Get under your duvet at once then,' Nell ordered. 'And don't come out again until I say you can.'

Josie felt light-headed and woozy as she got to her feet. The whole week seemed like a long, horrible dream that she was trapped in – the sleepless nights, Fulton's Farm, the disastrous dinner at her parents' . . .

She wanted it to stop, this crazy rollercoaster of emotion that had taken over her nice normal world. She wanted to get off now and catch her breath. When was it going to stop?

Cyprus had been Nell's idea. They'd both just been dumped, and were thoroughly gutted about it. After a couple of depressing nights of vodka-fuelled rounds of Ten Reasons ('Number one – he was so stingy with his cash. Remember when he bought me an Iceland own-brand Easter egg at Easter?' 'Tosser!'), Nell had had a brainwave.

'What is the point,' she'd slurred from her position on the sofa, where she'd been for the last forty-eight hours, 'of being pissed off in shitty London when we can be pissed off in the sun?'

'Because we live here,' Josie had reminded her, sploshing more vodka into their glasses. 'And we've got jobs. That's why.'

Nell had waved an arm at the window, where July rain was pattering noisily against the glass. 'But it's crap here,' she'd argued. 'I hate it.' She'd dragged herself up to a sitting position and pointed at Josie with her fag. 'You know what we need, girl? We need a bloody good holiday.'

It had been the perfect, perfect solution. Josie couldn't think of a single reason why not and so, just three days later, with their holiday forms signed by their respective personnel officers and their bags packed, the two of them found themselves at Gatwick Airport, heading for a last-minute package deal to Cyprus.

In Cyprus they'd sunbathed and smoked all day, got trolleyed every night, and snogged whoever they fancied, to take the edge off the pain. It hadn't cured the sadness completely but it had helped. And she'd got the best tan of her life into the bargain.

Josie snuggled a little further into her pillow and closed her eyes. Thank God Nell was here. She had turned up at exactly the right moment.

'You know, I can't help feeling that this is my fault,' Josie said that evening. The boys were in bed and she and Nell were on the sofa with glasses of wine and a box of Milk Tray.

Nell rolled her eyes. 'Please don't say what I think you're going to say,' she warned.

Josie ignored her. 'I mean, maybe if I'd been more fun recently, maybe if I'd been more sexy...'

Nell shoved a hazelnut whirl into Josie's mouth to stop her talking. 'Don't start that, Josie Winter! Don't! It's pants, and I won't listen to it. None of this is your fault!'

Josie bit through the chocolate as if she'd barely registered it was there, and went on. 'If I'd just tried a bit harder, this might not have—'

'Josie! Stop it!' Nell ordered. 'You're sounding like a Stepford! You've done nothing wrong.'

Josie took a slurp of wine. 'You know, when I woke up this morning, I remembered this bet me and Pete had the other week,' she went on. 'I can't even remember what we were arguing about but whatever it was, I bet him a fiver that I was right. And then he laughed and said, "A fiver? Let's make it more interesting. Let's bet a sexual favour that *I'm* right."'

'And were you right?' Nell asked.

Josie hung her head. 'Well, it turned out that I was. And so he was all nudge-nudge-wink-wink, and said, "Babe, your luck's in." And I said . . .'

'You didn't say you'd rather have the fiver?'

'I did.' Josie winced at the memory. Why hadn't she winked saucily at him, and said yes please? Why had she acted like such an old maid? A mercenary old maid at that.

Nell plonked the Milk Tray on to Josie's lap. 'Don't beat yourself up about it. That was one little remark,' she said kindly. 'Husbands don't leave their wives because they turn down a sexual favour. It probably didn't make him feel great, but ...'

'No,' Josie said mournfully. 'What a cow! He looked as if he'd been slapped. No wonder he ran off to Sabine. I bet she never says no.'

The phone rang before Nell could reply.

Ring-ring. Ring-ring.

'Answer it, then,' Nell said. 'It might be him.'

Ring-ring.

'I know,' Josie replied. 'I'm just bracing myself.' She took a deep breath and picked up the receiver. 'Hello?'

'Josie, it's Lisa. *Please* don't hang up on me. I really want to speak to you.'

Josie's skin prickled at the sound of her voice but she kept the phone to her ear. 'I'm listening,' she said begrudgingly.

'First of all, I'm sorry. I'm really, really, *really* sorry. I completely blew my presentation last week because I couldn't stop thinking about you.'

Josie sniffed. 'Oh, boo-hoo, Lisa,' she said, rolling her eyes at Nell and flicking the phone on to speaker. 'I'm sorry if I'm interfering with your work. How very inconsiderate of me.'

'No! I didn't mean—' Lisa sighed. 'I was trying to say, I feel terrible. I shouldn't have done it.'

'No, you shouldn't,' Josie agreed tightly.

'It was wrong of me, it was horrible. And I am really ashamed of myself for doing it.'

'Good,' Josie said. 'I'm ashamed of you too. Call yourself a friend?'

There was a pause. 'I know, I've been a crap friend,' Lisa said in a low voice. 'But I want to explain. Do you think we could meet up and talk about it properly?'

Josie glanced at Nell, who shrugged. 'I don't want to see you,' she said bluntly. 'I don't want to see anyone. Pete's left me.' She shut her eyes as the weight of it rolled over her again. 'I can't do anything right now. I—'

'He's *left* you?' Lisa repeated. 'Oh my God. Why?'

Was it Josie's imagination, or was there a tiny hint of eagerness in Lisa's voice? 'Not because of *you*, if that's what you're hoping,' she snapped. Her fingers clenched into a fist. 'He didn't want me *or* you. So I guess we've got more in common than I thought, Lisa. We're both notches on his bedpost now, aren't we?' She hung up before Lisa could reply.

'You OK?' Nell asked after a moment.

'I'm great,' Josie said wearily. 'I'm just great.' She stayed still for a moment, feeling her heart slow, then looked at Nell. 'How about you? I've hardly asked how you're feeling about Gareth. Sorry – here's me calling

Lisa a crap friend and I've been banging on about myself and not even asking about you.'

Nell gave a small smile. 'I'm cool,' she said. 'It's a bit easier for me to deal with the Gareth thing because I know it's definitely over, and I don't want to see him again. Which is kind of painful, but at least I've drawn a line under it. Whereas you...'

'Want everything to go back to how it was,' Josie sighed. 'But ... don't you want to talk about it? About what happened with Gareth? You haven't really said.'

'There's not much to say,' Nell replied, avoiding Josie's gaze. 'He was ... He turned out to be different from the person I thought I'd fallen in love with. And then...'

'And then...?' Josie prompted as Nell fell silent.

'Oh, nothing. I'll tell you about it some other time.'

Message received loud and clear, thought Josie, finishing her drink. Backing off, at the double! 'Sure,' she said quickly. 'Whenever. Sorry. I wasn't being—'

'Hey, remember Cyprus?' Nell interrupted as if she hadn't heard.

Josie nodded. 'Of course. I was thinking about it earlier,' she replied. 'Why?'

Nell tipped her head back and drank the last of her wine. 'Maybe we should go away somewhere together again. Have some fun.'

Josie laughed. 'Yeah. Nice idea. And back in the real world, would you like another drink?'

Nell sat up straighter. Her eyes were shining. 'I mean it, Jose. Not a shagging holiday in Cyprus, obviously, but just a little … escape. I've got some money saved up. We can take the boys and get away for a few days. Spain. France. America. Anywhere.'

There was a silence while Josie stared at her friend. 'You're serious, aren't you?' she said.

'Too right I am!' Nell said. She rolled the stem of the glass between her fingers. 'What's stopping us? Neither of us has a job. I don't even have a permanent address at the moment. The boys aren't at school. And like I said last time, why be miserable and heartbroken here when we could be miserable and heartbroken on a beach? And—'

'No,' Josie said flatly. 'It's ridiculous. I can't just drop everything like that. Don't you see? I can hardly do *anything* right now. I can't even function, let alone go off gallivanting.' She stood up. 'More wine?'

'Please,' Nell said. She got up and followed Josie into the kitchen. 'Come on, Jose, at least consider it. Are you seriously telling me you'd rather stay here, moping around the house, not sleeping, jumping every time the phone rings?'

'Well, no, but...'

'Let's do it, then!' Nell grabbed Josie by the arm as she opened the fridge. 'Don't you remember how much better we felt on that plane to Cyprus? It was like we were doing something positive about it all. We were having an adventure, being spontaneous. We were on a mission! We were—'

'Totally running away, and you know it,' Josie said. She didn't look at Nell as she filled up their glasses and put the stopper back in the bottle. They were nearly through it already. God. Drinking too much again.

'What's wrong with running away, if you're running somewhere fun?' Nell argued.

Josie passed Nell her glass and looked hard at her. 'Well...' she began. She was trying to think of a good reason to say no, but she couldn't come up with anything. 'You know, when we were in London and you were telling us about your travels, I did really have a pang of jealousy,' she admitted. 'I even came back here and tried to talk Pete into us all going off somewhere exciting.'

'Attagirl,' Nell laughed.

'But that was then,' Josie said. 'That was before all this kicked off. And since Pete left, I've just been so tired. My whole body is tired. I don't have the energy to go anywhere. I couldn't possibly start thinking about packing clothes and ... and ... getting plane tickets while my head is full of Pete.'

'We don't have to go far,' Nell said. 'We don't even have to leave the country. We could go camping in Cornwall for a week. Or up to the Lake District. Or ... wherever. Scotland! The Gower!'

Josie bit her lip, staring at Nell while she mulled it over. She imagined them all piling into the car and setting off into the unknown. She imagined remote sandy beaches, camping under starlit skies, fresh air, new brown freckles sprinkled on the boys' noses ...

Then she imagined Pete's furious face and letters from lawyers about denied access.

'I wouldn't want Pete to think I'm running away with the children,' she said at last.

'You wouldn't be,' Nell argued. 'Tell him we're going for a holiday. That way, you both get some space, and he might realize how empty his life is without you and the boys.'

Josie sighed. 'In my dreams,' she muttered.

'So what's the alternative?' Nell asked. 'Just sit it out here? Hope that all the pain goes away?'

Josie stared at her wine. 'I don't know,' she replied. 'I don't have a game plan. I just can't think straight at the moment.'

Nell nodded. 'OK,' she said. 'But promise me you'll think about it? It might make you feel better.'

Josie nodded. 'Deal,' she said. 'I'll think about it.'

'Has he come back to you yet? Well, what's he doing? You mustn't let him get away with this, you know. You can't!'

'Thanks, Mum. I'll bear that in mind.'

Josie's mum had been phoning – frequently – for updates on her daughter's disintegrating marriage.

Lisa had been phoning too, but Josie hung up on her every time. She didn't want to talk to her. Nor did she want to talk to BT, a double-glazing firm, a cold-calling cat charity, or her bank. Conversely, the one person she did want to speak to hadn't phoned since he'd taken the boys out on Saturday.

Josie's insides were knotting up tighter and tighter at his non-communication, especially as Toby and Sam kept asking when they were going to see him. Sam had wet the bed again, too. Worry lines had appeared on his forehead, like a little old man.

'Soon,' she kept saying to them. 'You'll see him soon. But I'm not exactly sure when.'

'Come on,' Nell said to her, once the boys were asleep the next evening. 'Let's go out for a pint and plan where we're going on our road trip.'

'Hang on a minute,' Josie said, feeling rushed. 'What road trip? I haven't agreed to anything yet. I told you I needed to think about it, remember?'

'Well, let's think about it in the pub,' Nell said. 'There's nothing on telly and we've drunk all your booze. Besides, I fancy getting out. Don't you?'

Josie stared at her. 'What about the boys?' she said. 'We can't just leave them.'

'Phone what's-her-name, Emma, or someone. Can't one of your mates pop round for an hour or so?' Nell replied. She picked up the phone and handed it to Josie. 'Go on. You call someone while I have a quick shower.'

Stunned, Josie gazed after Nell's briskly departing figure, and then down at the phone. She'd forgotten about Nell's calls-to-action. When the mood took her, you got swept along with her, whatever she wanted to do, it had always been the way. She bit her lip, thinking hard, and then dialled Emma's number. Sometimes it was easier to go limp and get pulled along with the current, wasn't it? She didn't have the strength to disagree with Nell in this mood.

Emma said yes, of course, in a pleased-to-help way, and so, just forty minutes later, Josie and Nell were in a taxi heading for the town centre. 'We could have gone to the local,' Josie had tried saying timidly, but Nell was insistent. 'In for a penny, in for a pound,' she'd replied.

'It's a Tuesday night, there'll be nobody in your local. Let's see what's happening in the bright lights of the high street.'

Ten minutes later they were sat in armchairs in The Eagle, a cosy old pub that Josie had been in a few times before with Pete. 'Shame we ate with the boys earlier,' she said as she sipped her beer. 'They do nice food.'

'Well, we could always bring them in for lunch another day,' Nell said, glancing up at the chalked menu above the bar. 'Mmm, and look at the puddings...'

'I know, they're to die for,' Josie said. 'Or to diet for, anyway,' she added with a giggle. 'Me and Pete always shared a sticky toffee pudding when we came in here. It is just the most calorifically sinful thing you could imagine, but—'

Josie stopped talking as Nell suddenly gave a squawk like a strangled chicken.

'What?' she asked, looking around.

Oh God. No. No!

He was there, Pete, standing at the bar with...

Josie swung her face away, not wanting to see.

Then she swung it straight back again, *desperate* to see.

It was her. Sabine. Had to be.

'Oh fuck,' she muttered. 'Oh *shit*.'

'Do you want to go?' Nell asked, putting a hand on Josie's arm.

Josie barely felt it. She couldn't tear her eyes away from Pete and ... and *her*. What should she do? What should she do?

She could tip a pint over Pete's head.

She could throw it in Sabine's face.

She could creep away with Nell before they were spotted.

She could brazen it out, sit there boldly, *waiting* to be spotted.

She could go and introduce herself to Sabine, compare notes. *It doesn't take him much to come, does it? Does that bother you? Have you noticed how spotty his back is yet?*

'Josie!' Nell hissed. 'Let's go. Let's get out of here!'

She was laughing, Sabine. She had shoulder-length dark hair, and dark lipstick. She was taller than Josie. Slimmer. She wore tight jeans and high-heeled sandals and a denim jacket. (Denim and denim. Not a good look. Hadn't anyone ever told her you shouldn't do that?) She was gazing up at Pete, smiling at him. Smiling a wide, lipsticked smile as if he were the funniest man alive.

Josie couldn't help staring at her mouth, Sabine's mouth. The things that mouth had done to Pete. *Her* husband!

Nell stood up. 'Come on. Leave your drink,' she pleaded. 'Josie? Come on. Don't torture yourself.'

They were ordering food, Josie noticed. Ordering food in The Eagle, just like she'd done with Pete over the years. God! Did the man have no originality?

She got to her feet unsteadily. She couldn't stop herself. Her legs were just walking without permission.

'Josie!' Nell squeaked from behind her. She sounded a long way away. 'What are you *doing*?'

Josie walked right up to the bar, and stood between them. 'Don't forget to share the sticky toffee pudding,' she said brightly, then turned to Sabine, who was staring at her in confusion. 'It's very good, you know. Enjoy your meal, both of you!'

And with that she turned on her heel and walked, head high, straight out of the pub.

'Who was *that*?' she dimly heard a woman's voice saying.

She didn't hear Pete's reply. She was out in the cool evening air, feeling as if she was about to throw up and shaking uncontrollably.

'Oh, babe.' Nell had appeared beside her and was cuddling her, and walking her away from the pub. 'Oh, darlin', that must have been horrible.'

'She's pretty, isn't she?' Josie said. 'She looked young, too. Nice skin.'

'Don't,' Nell implored. 'Don't torture yourself, Jose. What a nightmare! I can't believe – of all the pubs we could have gone to . . . Shit. This is my fault. I shouldn't have pushed you into coming out.'

'Did you see the way she was looking at him?' Josie said, still feeling dazed. 'Like she loved him. Like she really fancied him. Like she thought he was just Mr Fantastic. Oh God!'

'I know,' Nell replied, miserably. 'What do you want to do? Shall we go home?'

Josie sniffed, and stopped walking. They were halfway along the high street now, outside Boots. 'I don't know,' she said. 'I can't think about anything.'

Nell wrapped her bare arms around Josie, and Josie found herself staring over Nell's shoulder at the display of Father's Day gifts in the window. Aftershaves, grooming kits, mugs with GREATEST DAD IN THE WORLD! written on them.

'OK,' she found herself saying. 'Let's do it.'

'Let's do what?' Nell asked.

'Let's go,' Josie said. 'The road trip, I mean. Let's get away from here.'

'Brilliant,' Nell replied, squeezing her even harder. 'Let's go home and check out your road atlas. Trust me. I'm an expert in great escapes.'

Chapter Ten

'Mummy! Is it morning yet?'

Josie opened an eye and squinted at Sam, standing with his face just inches away from hers. Slam. Ground-hog Day, all over again. Wake up and smell the divorce papers! 'Hi, baby,' she said wearily, stretching out an arm for him. She could see from the clock that it was just after seven, yet it felt like the middle of the night. She'd barely slept, and whenever she had managed to doze off it had been Sabine's face that had floated up in her dreams, a ghostly pale face swimming up through her subconscious, with that dark-lipsticked mouth wide open in a taunting smile: *He's mine now. You're history!*

'Come in for a cuddle,' she said, pulling Sam into bed with her. He was dry for once, that was some-thing. Her eyelids closed, and then Pete was in her mind again. How had he looked as she'd strode away from him? she wondered. What had been said? Had Sabine been annoyed that he'd brought her to The Eagle, once she knew that Pete and Josie had been there together before?

'Who was that?' Sabine had asked. A surprised, breathy voice. Hadn't she guessed? Wasn't it obvious?

'Toby's downstairs, Mum,' Sam said, kicking restlessly at the duvet. 'Can we have breakfast now?'

Josie sat up and yawned. She didn't even need to look in the mirror to know that her skin was worse than ever. She could feel a rash of pimples around her mouth, along with the red, flaky bits.

Sabine, of course, had lovely skin. Pimple-free. Young and smooth and moisturized.

Oh God. They had looked so happy together, at the bar. Pete and Sabine. Josie, on the other hand, had felt out of place, skulking in the corner like the bad fairy at Sleeping Beauty's christening party, glowering and staring.

Her marriage was so over. Any fool could see that. How could she and Pete ever come back from this?

She pulled on her dressing gown and sighed listlessly. Here we go again. Another day begins. Another day of single-mumhood to struggle through. It was unbearable. It was truly unbearable. She trudged along to the stairs, wondering what would happen if she just threw herself off the top step. Would she break her neck? Would she die?

'Is it playgroup this morning?' Sam asked, hovering behind her.

'Well...' Josie began. She thought back to the night before when Nell had got her fired up about setting off *à la* Thelma and Louise to cheer them both up. 'I'm not sure,' she said vaguely. Now that it was morning, she couldn't help thinking it was all just a stupid idea brought on by too much beer and too little sense. Did she really have the energy to drive three hundred miles today?

'Devon would be nice,' Nell had said thoughtfully, flicking through the road atlas spread out on the kitchen table. 'Or Cornwall, if you want to go further.' She'd leaned over the map and run her finger along the coastline, peering at the village names printed in tiny writing. 'Piddlehinton, the boys would like that,' she'd giggled. 'That's in Dorset ... Ooh.' She'd jabbed at the page with a triumphant look on her face. 'I've found it, Jose. Inner Hope. There's actually a place called Inner Hope! And look, Hope Cove too. Don't you think that sounds like the perfect place for us to go?'

Josie had laughed. 'You're making it up.'

'I'm serious! There, look, in Devon! And God knows we both need a bit of hope back in our lives now. Look – it's right by the sea. I'm sure it's meant to be pretty, that bit of coastline.' She traced the route across the page. 'What do you say? Shall we go for Hope?'

Josie had nodded, finding it hard to believe that this wasn't all an elaborate game. 'I'd love a bit of hope,' she'd said fervently.

That had been last night, though. Today Devon seemed like the end of the earth. And running away from things just seemed ... pointless. The bad stuff would only come with her wherever she was. The bad stuff wouldn't be that easy to push out of her head.

To Josie's surprise, Nell was already at the breakfast table with Toby when they went into the kitchen.

'Hi, guys,' Josie said, raising her eyebrows. Nell wasn't usually the earliest of risers. 'You must have crept down here like little mice. I didn't hear a thing.'

'We did, didn't we, Tobes?' Nell said, grinning at him. *'Squeak, squeak, squeak!'*

'Sam, guess what?' Toby burst out excitedly as he looked up from his jammy toast. 'We're going on an adventure!'

Josie's face froze and she turned to Nell. 'You told him?'

Nell nodded. 'Shouldn't I have?' she asked.

'Sam, Sam, did you know?' Toby shouted, bouncing on his chair. 'We're going to the seaside! Nell said so!'

'I was kind of having second thoughts,' Josie said quietly as she went to boil the kettle. 'But ...'

'Oops,' Nell said.

'Are we, Mum? Are we really?' Sam asked, grabbing Josie's dressing gown and tugging at it.

Josie looked at Nell, and then back at the boys' expectant faces. Then she looked at the washing machine and the cooker and the kitchen sink, and something shifted inside her.

'Yep,' she said. 'Of course we're going.' And as the words came out, she felt a fluttering sensation deep within her, as if she was letting go of a heavy weight and floating free. 'Let's have breakfast, and then we can pack up and go.'

The fluttering sensation lasted within Josie the whole time she was buttering toast and making sludgy Weetabix and pouring apple juice for the boys. By the time she was sitting down with her own breakfast, she was writing lists in her head.

Things to take: bedtime teds, clothes, swimming trunks, favourite cups, books, toys, mobile and charger, plastic sheet for Sam . . .

Things to do: lock up shed, turn off hot water, fill up with petrol and . . . Well. The tough one: tell Pete.

She had to let him know they were going – that was a given. She couldn't just sneak off with no word of explanation; he'd go mental if she did.

But she was dreading having to call him after seeing

him the night before. He'd probably have a go at her for daring to come and speak to him and Sabine like that. He'd be pissed off about the toffee pudding remark, too, she knew already. He might even try and talk her out of going, saying that he wanted to spend time with the boys this week. And what if he said he wanted to introduce them to Sabine?

'Over my dead body,' Josie growled, her hand on the phone.

'Get it over with,' Nell advised, noticing her hovering. 'Just tell him. It's not a crime for you to go away. He's got no say over what you do anyway. Go on. Phone him at work, where he won't be able to have a hissy fit on you.'

Josie pulled a face. 'I know, it's just . . .'

'Do it. I'll go and chivvy the boys along, help them decide how many Power Rangers we need to keep us company.' Nell's voice was authoritative, and Josie found herself nodding obediently.

'Mortimer Insurance, how can I help you?' trilled the receptionist moments later.

'Peter Winter, please,' Josie said, licking her lips nervously.

'Certainly. May I say who's calling?'

'It's . . .' Would he pick up if he knew it was her? 'It's Leia,' she blurted out, remembering her previous alibi.

'Just putting you through.'

Josie sat down on the sofa as she heard the line ringing in Pete's office. Once, twice . . .

'Peter Winter speaking.'

Josie gulped. All of a sudden, she couldn't say anything. That voice. *Peter Winter speaking.* It was so familiar, that voice. It had whispered to her, teased her, even serenaded her on their honeymoon.

'Hello? Is anybody there?'

It had hurt her, too. Told her so many lies.

'Hi,' she said at last. 'Pete, it's me. Josie.'

'Oh.' His voice became gruff. 'What do you want?'

'I'm phoning to let you know that I'm going away for a week or two, to Devon,' she said, getting the words out quickly, 'just to—'

'To *Devon*? What for?'

'To . . . think,' she said, trying to stay calm. 'To have a bit of space.'

'What about the boys?' he asked.

'Well, they're coming with me, of course,' she replied. She felt angry that he even had to ask. Of course they were coming with her! *She* wasn't the one who'd walked out on them, after all.

'How . . .' He hesitated. 'How are they? About the . . . situation, I mean. Have they said anything?'

'No,' she said. She tried not to look at the Cornwall

We Are Family photo but her eyes were drawn to it. Those four smiling faces. Such a nice, happy family. She'd have to take that photo down. It was doing her head in, having to see it every day. 'They just asked if you still loved them. And then they asked if you still loved me.'

'Oh, Josie,' he said. He sounded sympathetic, to her surprise. 'How horrible for you.'

'Yes.' Her eyes stung. 'It just keeps on being horrible, that's the problem.' Her voice shook. 'Sam's wetting the bed, he's gone all anxious. And Toby's whacking everything in sight, like he's mad with the whole world...' She bit her lip. 'Anyway. That's why I'm going. Nell's coming with us. I won't be gone for long. I just need to get away. You know.'

'Yes.' His voice was gentler now. 'Sure. Well ... Have a nice time.'

She swallowed. 'Thank you,' she said. 'I'll call you when I get back. Maybe we could arrange proper times for you to see the boys. They really ... They really miss you.' She sighed unhappily as her gaze wandered back to the Cornwall photo. Oh God. It was awful, just the *thought* of Pete and her arranging visiting times, shuttling their sons back and forth between them like ping-pong balls. It broke her heart.

'Yes,' he said. 'OK, then.' He hesitated again. 'I am sorry, you know. About all of this. I...'

'OK,' she said briskly. She had to get him off the phone before she started blubbing. She didn't want him to hear that. Keep it together just for another minute. Nearly there.

'I'll speak to you soon then,' he said in a formal voice, as if she were one of his clients.

'Bye,' she said, and put the phone down. Then she slumped on the sofa and groaned.

'Oh, love,' Nell said, hearing her and hurrying through, a small red robot in her hand. 'Oh, sweetheart, was he horrible?'

Josie shook her head. 'No,' she sniffed. 'He was actually quite nice. It was just so...' She shrugged. 'It was so bloody formal. Civil. Like we barely knew each other.'

Nell sat next to her on the sofa and put an arm around her shoulders. 'It's really hard speaking to an ex, and you're doing so well,' she said. 'Look at me, I've not even dared phone Gareth, I'm so crap and pathetic. But you... You've spoken to him and you kept it together. So you did really well. Yeah?'

'Yeah,' Josie said wearily. 'And at least we can go now without him accusing me of abducting the children or anything...' She stopped in horror. 'Oh God,' she said, pressing the dial button on the phone again and punching in Pete's number. 'I just had an awful thought.'

'What?' Nell asked, but the receptionist was already trilling in Josie's ear.

'Peter Winter, please,' Josie gabbled. 'It's Leia again.'

Ring-ring, ring-ring.

'What's with all this Leia shit anyway?' Pete asked a second later. He was sounding less civil and formal now, and slightly more grumpy.

'Pete – while we're away, I need you to promise me something,' Josie said. Her voice was trembling. So much for keeping it together.

'What's that?' he asked. There was a wary note to his question, as if his Hysterical Woman radar had just been triggered. *Danger! Danger! Proceed with caution! Hysterical Woman is likely to blow!*

'I'm begging you, I'm seriously begging you, if I ever meant anything to you at all,' she began, 'then...'

'Oh, Josie!' he said, sounding exasperated. 'What is it? Spit it out.'

'Please, Pete, please don't bring her to our house. Please, not in our house, our bed. I can't bear the thought of—'

'All right, all right!' he said. 'I wasn't going to anyway,

but . . .' He lowered his voice. 'Look, I don't want to talk about this at work, OK?'

'It's not *my* fault we're having to have this conversation!' Josie cried, stung. 'It's not like I'm the one who—'

Nell gave her a warning nudge and she bit the words back as she heard the boys tramping down the stairs. 'I'd better go. Bye,' she said, hanging up.

Toby came into the room wearing his Buzz Lightyear costume and brandishing a pirate sword. He gave the sofa a few fierce smacks with it, then held it up in the air. 'I'm ready for our holiday!' he announced, then looked over at Josie with interest. 'Who were you shouting at, Mum?' he asked.

Josie forced a smile on her face, unclenching her hands from their fists. 'Just the . . . postman,' she said lamely, saying the first thing that popped into her head.

Toby's eyes were round and interested. 'Why?'

'It's a secret,' Nell said quickly. 'Right! Will you help me put your things in the car, Tobes? Because then we're going to hit the road, Jack!'

'He's not Jack!' Sam said indignantly.

'It's a song, you silly banana,' Nell said. 'Didn't your mum ever teach you that one? It goes like this . . .'

Josie rubbed her eyes as Nell hustled the boys out, singing loudly, then blew her nose. Suddenly, she really,

really didn't want to hit the road, or go anywhere. She wanted to stay in her own four walls, camp indoors with takeaway food and CBeebies for the boys, willing Pete to have second thoughts about Sabine, and come home.

Devon seemed a bad idea now. A crazy idea, the sort of thing she'd have done back in her twenties when 'responsibility' was a dirty word.

She stood up slowly. There was still time to change her mind. She could take the boys for a day-trip somewhere instead. They didn't have to go far . . .

She watched through the window as Nell supervised them packing their stuff into the boot. They were all laughing about something or other. Then Sam and Toby put their buckets on their heads like helmets and started knocking on each other's heads, chortling as if they were in danger of peeing their pants.

A faint smile twitched at the corners of Josie's mouth. She loved hearing them laugh like that. Things had been so tense at home lately, there hadn't been much laughing. They probably needed a change of scenery, too, just as much as she did.

Oh, what the hell. Devon would be fine. And they could always come home if something went wrong. The main thing was that the boys were happy. That was all she cared about.

Right, where was that list? It was time to get the show on the road...

'And off we go!' Nell said, turning to smile back at Toby and Sam. 'Ready for our holiday, boys?'

'Yeah!' they chorused.

Josie, in the passenger's seat, gave a small smile as Nell turned the ignition key and started up the engine. She was so bone-weary that she'd put Nell on the insurance to share the driving. Making the call had seemed an effort, but her mind had been in a perpetual fog lately, and even driving to Tesco seemed perilous. She didn't feel anywhere near sharp enough to get them all safely down to Devon in one piece.

She gazed out of the window as Nell reversed carefully out of the driveway and into the road.

'Blimey,' Nell commented as she went into second gear, 'this is a bit smoother than Gareth's old jalopy. Ooh, power steering too. Excellent.'

'Make the most of it, I'll probably have to sell it once I'm homeless and destitute,' Josie replied. She was trying to be jokey but the words came out sounding mournful.

Nell glanced back to where the boys were plugged into a double Walkman and singing tunelessly to 'The Grand Old Duke of York'. 'You could always live in it,' she suggested. 'Nice and cosy, put a few curtains up, get a pot plant on the dashboard . . .'

Josie grimaced. 'Don't,' she said. 'I can't even joke about it, I'm so scared.'

'Well, don't think about it then,' Nell said. 'Look, we're leaving Heartbreak Hotel behind, right? Next stop, Hope.'

Nell drove for a couple of hours while Josie dozed, her head wedged uncomfortably between the window and the headrest. The boys were now listening to a *Horrid Henry* tape on the main car stereo system, and Miranda Richardson's bolshy Henry voice floated in and out of Josie's dreams. The boys' guffaws broke her slumber and she wiped her mouth blearily. 'Pete, did you—?'

She blinked as she turned to the driver. It wasn't Pete. Of course it wasn't Pete.

Nell patted her hand. 'All right, Sleeping Beauty? I'm getting peckish. Fancy stopping somewhere for lunch?'

'Lunch!'

'Yeah!'

Sam and Toby had pounced upon the question before Josie could answer. 'Mmm, yeah,' she said, trying to shake the sleep from her brain. She'd really thought she was with Pete again. Just for a second. 'Lunch. Right. What were you thinking? Service station, or . . . ?'

Nell was indicating to come off the motorway. 'Nah.

Let's do some exploring,' she said, turning on to the slip-road. 'Lower Hensall,' she said, reading the sign. 'Never heard of it. But maybe it's got a nice pub.'

'Pub!' squealed Sam. 'Are we going to the pub?'

Nell winked at Josie. 'Just like his father,' she joked.

'Let's hope not,' Josie replied, then wished she hadn't. She was sounding so bitter. 'Let's hope he's even nicer than his father, if that's possible,' she said loudly, for Sam's benefit. Stop moaning, she ordered herself. This is supposed to be a jolly, remember?

'Left or right?' Nell said, coming to a crossroads.

'Right,' Josie said.

'Left,' Sam chimed in.

'Light,' Toby giggled. 'Reft.'

'And I vote left, so the lefts have it,' Nell said, turning into a single-track lane with high beech hedges. She drove another a mile or so, uphill all the way, then the hedges became lower and they could see they were on the peak of a hill, with green meadows sloping down either side of them, dotted with fat white sheep. There was a village, complete with squat stone church, and purple hills and woodland in the far distance. A tractor droned somewhere in the background.

'Nice,' Nell said approvingly. 'Fingers crossed there's a stonking pub down here. It's a perfect day for lunch outside.'

Josie leaned forward as they entered the village. This was actually happening, she thought in surprise. They had actually escaped the house and were here, in the middle of nowhere, with the sun shining. It was a good start.

'Hallelujah and God bless Lower Hensall,' Nell whooped as she slowed the car and parked it outside a sprawling cream-coloured building. 'Thatched roof and everything. Oh, look – and a food sign. This is the life, boys. This is the life!'

Nell's enthusiasm was infectious. Josie let Sam and Toby out of the back and they raced straight to the pub door, bouncing around like a couple of Tiggers under the old wooden porch. She slipped an arm through Nell's as they followed. 'This is a new one for me, you know,' she confessed. 'Doing something like this without Pete. I keep looking around for him, expecting him to be here too.'

Nell gave her a sidelong look. 'And how do you feel when you remember he's not here?' she asked.

Josie thought for a moment. 'All right,' she pronounced. 'Kind of all right. It helps when I think of him in his suit, sitting in his office,' she added, 'when we're off on an adventure.'

'Too right,' Nell said, pushing open the door. It was dim and cool inside, with solid oak beams across the ceiling. Through an open back door, Josie could see a strip of long lawned garden.

'Hello, poppet,' the woman behind the bar said, catching sight of Toby. She looked to be in her fifties, small and neat-looking with shingled coppery hair and a slathering of orange foundation. 'Oh, two poppets!' she added as she saw Sam. 'Double trouble, eh?'

The twin poppets charged outside and Josie followed while Nell ordered drinks. There were ten or so wooden picnic tables spread out on the grass, each with a white parasol stuck through the centre. A pair of elderly women giggled conspiratorially at one another over a glass of wine, and a couple held hands across one of the tables, but otherwise the garden was theirs.

Josie slipped her feet out of her sandals and walked across the grass after the boys, letting the cool blades tickle her toes.

Toby and Sam were right at the far end of the garden, squatting to peer at something in the grass.

'A frog, Mum!' Sam called as she came over. His eyes were shining as if he'd just seen Father Christmas. 'A real frog, Mum!'

'Wow,' Josie breathed, trying to sound suitably impressed. 'Not a real one!' She crouched down with them to watch the small young frog scramble away from Toby's grubby poking finger, loving the way her sons were both so utterly absorbed in this single moment. Toby had grass stains on his shorts already, and Sam had a bramble scratch on one leg – how on earth had he managed that? – but for ten seconds or so, nothing else mattered to them in the world except this one creature.

A couple of birds were calling to one another in the woodland behind the pub garden, and Josie suddenly felt a rush of relief that they were there, barefoot in the grass in a sunny pub garden, gazing at a frog together, instead of on the playgroup run, or anywhere else. If only Pete could have been there too ...

No. Don't let that spoil things.

'So!' Nell's voice broke the spell. Josie looked up to see her striding towards them with a tray of drinks and some menus. 'What does everyone fancy to eat, then?'

Somehow or other, the minutes turned into hours and time slid by in a haze of frog-bothering and chip-scoffing. Nell lay on the grass with her shades on, catching forty winks, while Josie watched the boys trying their hardest to climb up a twisted old apple tree. It was so peaceful sitting in the sunny garden, in no hurry to get back in the car.

'What's the rush?' Nell had said lazily before she fell asleep. 'Devon will still be there tomorrow. We'll move on when the boys have had enough. These things are always better left unplanned, if you ask me.'

A week ago, Josie would have disagreed outright with such a statement. In her opinion, life was better if you had everything mapped out. Husband – check. Children – check. House with all the trimmings – check. If everything was arranged and in its place, there was no room for the bad stuff to sneak in and ambush you.

That was what she'd thought a week ago, anyway. Now that her life had been invaded by turmoil and chaos, Josie couldn't do anything other than get through each day as it came, and be grateful if everyone was OK at the end of it. Forget planning, forget mapping everything out. If her boys were happy right now, this minute, then that was good enough. That was enough to cling on to.

Nell stirred and pushed up her sunglasses to rub her eyes. Then she sat up, shaking grass from her hair. 'Bliss,' she said, stretching her arms above her head. 'Fancy pushing on? We don't have to go far, just look for somewhere to spend tonight.'

Josie nodded and got to her feet. 'I'll get the map,' she said, grabbing the car keys from the table. 'We can see if there's anywhere interesting coming up.'

With a last quick glance over her shoulder at Toby

and Sam — who were both astride one of the lower branches, looking through their curled-up hands like telescopes — Josie slipped on her sandals and walked to the car.

'Off on holiday, are you?' the orange-faced woman behind the bar asked as Josie came back through the pub with the road atlas.

Josie hesitated. 'Kind of,' she said. 'It was a bit ... spontaneous. We only decided to go last night.'

The woman raised her eyebrows. 'Lucky you. I wish I could hop off for a jaunt like that,' she said approvingly.

Not that lucky, Josie thought, but she said nothing, just smiled and made her way out to the garden again. It was funny the way other people made assumptions about your life, she thought. That woman really did think Josie was lucky, but then all she'd seen of Josie's life had been her sons, and the fact that they could afford a nice lunch out together, and that now they were heading off on holiday, on a whim, just for fun!

Josie shook her head at the irony. *Actually, we're going away because my husband has left me for a marriage-wrecker, and I'm trying my hardest to stave off a nervous breakdown and make sure my boys enjoy themselves*, she added in her head. *That do you?*

She spread the road atlas out, and she and Nell pored over the page.

'I've never been to Stonehenge,' Josie ventured, point-ing at it.

Nell wrinkled her nose. 'Salisbury is a bit of a 'mare to drive through,' she said. 'I think we should avoid it.' She leaned over thoughtfully. 'Where are we anyway? I can't spot our village.'

Josie pointed it out for her. 'So if we look around here in a – what? A thirty-mile radius,' she began, 'then...'

'Oh! Look, we're near Lymington,' Nell exclaimed, not paying her any attention. Her eyes sparkled and she reached in her pocket for her phone. 'That's where Rob lives – well, not for much longer actually, according to my mum. Shall I ring him? I'm sure he'd let us stay.'

'What, Rob as in your brother?' Josie asked.

'Rob as in my brother,' Nell confirmed, pressing a button on her phone. She held it to her ear and waited, face alight. 'Hi, stranger,' she said, then laughed. 'I'm OK, how are you? All packed?'

Nell began chatting away, and an image of Rob's face floated up into Josie's mind. Rob! She'd had an embar-rassing crush on him when she and Nell had first been flatmates, gone all coy whenever she'd answered the phone to him and made sure she washed her hair and squirted perfume in her cleavage if she knew he was coming round. Not that he ever seemed to notice, too busy getting ready to go off on another adventure most of the time to give the eye to his kid sister's mate, but all the same . . .

Josie found herself smiling to think of him. Rob was just as well travelled as Nell, and with a permanent tan, it seemed. She vaguely remembered him working in Nepal a few years ago, leading mountain treks or something equally exciting-sounding. Before that he'd been a volunteer in Mozambique, some kind of mechanic, she thought, and before *that* . . .

'Excellent,' Nell said, grinning as she hung up. 'We can stay. I'm dead chuffed I've got a chance to see him; he's off to Zambia at the end of the week. Some new voluntary thing, Mum said.'

Josie rolled her eyes and smiled. 'Of course he's off to Zambia. I'm amazed he's actually in this country at all,' she said. When had she last seen Rob? She'd been kept up to date by Nell of his various comings and goings, but the last time she'd actually clapped eyes on him . . . Oh, yes! Of course. It was just after she'd split up with Nick, before she started seeing Pete. Years ago. Josie frowned. There was something else. Something she hadn't remembered. What had happened that night?

Nell rolled her hand into a tube and shouted through it to the boys. 'Ahoy there, shipmates! This is your captain speaking!'

Toby shouted through his own small hand. 'What?'

'Land ahoy!' Nell called. 'Prepare to lower the gang-plank and become landlubbers!'

'Aye aye, captain!' Sam yelled.

'And then we're going to go and meet my brother,' Nell told them, with a grin. 'You two are just going to love him.'

She'd drunk too much the last time she'd seen Rob, that much Josie could remember. She had a brief flash-back of the beer garden swaying around her. Oh God! She hadn't made a pass at him or something awful, had she? Why wouldn't her brain remember?

'Anchors away!' Toby bellowed suddenly, and hurled himself off the branch.

'Toby!' she cried, just getting there in time to catch the full weight of him as he plummeted headlong. 'Be careful!' She hugged him, and then set him down and held out her arms for his more cautious brother. 'Honestly, Tobes, you're just an adrenalin junkie,' she scolded, too relieved that she'd caught him to be cross.

Nell scooped him up and tickled him. 'Just like my big brother,' she said with a grin. 'Didn't I say that you were going to love him?'

Chapter Eleven

It was almost five by the time they reached Lymington, a pretty town on the edge of the New Forest. 'Nice,' Nell commented as they drove past the old stone quay, where clusters of children were crabbing off the side.

Josie felt prickly with tiredness and almost immune to the charms of the cobbled streets she glimpsed, with their sweet little boutiques and ice-cream shops. 'Look, boys, see all the yachts out there?' she asked, leaning over the back seat to point out of Toby's window. They were getting hungry and grouchy by now, and had started pushing each other in the back seat. They were immune to Lymington's charms too.

'Stop fighting,' she snapped for the tenth time. 'Toby, keep your hands to yourself. Sam, stop winding him up.'

Josie was starting to wish they were back home, jammed safely into the usual conveyor belt of routine. Tea ... bath ... story ... sleep. She was already dreading putting the boys to bed in Rob's house. They'd never been the most brilliant sleepers to start with, but were even worse when they were away from their own bunk bed. And she'd no doubt have to camp in with them – she was sure Rob didn't live in a mansion where they could all have a room to themselves. And they'd be waking each other up the whole night ... How was she going to manage her nightly sobbing session when she had her boys snoring either side of her?

Oh, why had they come? Why had she let herself get talked into this? She wished they were round her kitchen table right now, eating shepherd's pie together like they did every Wednesday night. Rob didn't have kids of his own, he probably hadn't even thought as far ahead as tea yet, he might not even have any food in the house ...

'Mum, he kicked me!' whined Sam.

Josie swung round irritably. Sam's nose was running and he had snot trails on his cheek. His mouth was turned down as if he were on the verge of tears. Toby was kicking a petulant leg in the air as if he might very well lash out again. He grabbed his sword with a glint in his eye and a sidelong look at Josie, deliberately provoking her.

'Both of you just pack it in, or I'll—'

'Here we are,' Nell said at that moment, pulling up outside a small terraced house at the end of a lane.

'And not a moment too soon,' Josie muttered, unclipping

her seatbelt thankfully. 'Right, boys, get your shoes back on.'

Nell got out of the driver's seat and stretched her legs. Josie let the boys out of the back, helped them with their shoes and grabbed their overnight things. 'Where are we?' Sam asked, staring around as they went up Rob's front path. The front garden was scruffy and unkempt, full of rubble sacks and old planks of wood.

'We're at Nell's big brother's house, remember?' Josie said. 'This is where we're all going to sleep tonight. Like campers! Like...'

'Well, I don't like this house,' Toby said loudly, and Josie shushed him as they approached the door.

'It's not very pretty is it?' Nell agreed. 'He's been helping a mate, Mark, do it up,' she explained to Josie, knocking on the door. 'And, by a stroke of luck, Mark's away all this week, hence room for us to stay.'

They stood there waiting for a few seconds, and an image of Rob as she'd last seen him rushed into Josie's head. He'd just come back from a two-month holiday in ... where had it been? Sri Lanka that time? ... and was bronzed and unshaven, his tousled brown hair a shade lighter from the sun as it fell almost to his shoulders. She could picture him at the table in the pub garden now, could remember precisely the way he'd held his pint glass with both hands while he told them stories of his travels. He'd been wearing an unusual green disc pendant round his neck, and a white cotton shirt – really thick, heavy cotton, it had looked. She remembered wanting to stroke it. She remembered the way he'd made them all laugh with his stories.

Had she made a pass at him? She remembered thinking about it, daring herself to . . .

'All right?' Nell asked, cutting into her thoughts. 'You look a bit weird.'

Josie nodded, trying to shut out her memories. 'I'm fine,' she said.

And then the latch was clicking and the door was pulled open and there stood Rob, in a white T-shirt and jeans covered with daubs of paint, his hair shorter now and his chin smooth. 'Hey!' he cried, laughing, and reached forwards for Nell, hugging her to his chest. 'Hello.' His eyes fell upon Josie and he grinned at her, then stood back and crouched down to the boys' level. 'And look at you two!' he laughed. 'Top light-sabre,' he added solemnly, which made Toby wriggle with pride.

Rob stood up and hugged Josie, two strong arms around her back. 'Lovely to see you again, Josie B,' he said into her hair. He smelled of soap and sawdust, clean and honest.

And then Josie had a sudden flashback to that warm, boozy evening: a moment – several moments actually –

when she'd caught him looking at her in a strange, wondering way, holding her gaze with those blue eyes of his . . .

And the way he'd come back from the bar, and deliberately squeezed in next to her . . .

And then the two of them pausing before they said goodbye, something unspoken in the air before they went their separate ways . . . him to catch the night bus, her to walk home with her mates.

She distinctly remembered lying in her bed that night, wishing she'd leaned in for a kiss. Wishing she'd asked him back to her place.

And then, of course, two weeks later she'd met Pete and Rob had been forgotten. Until now.

Don't be silly, Josie, she told herself, as Rob let go of her. You must have imagined it all. Don't be ridiculous!

'Come on in, guys,' Rob said, stepping back so they could walk into the hallway. 'Anyone hungry?'

'Me!'

'Me!' shouted the boys at once.

'Anyone like shepherd's pie? Made with real shepherds?'

There was a pause while the boys thought about it. 'Yes!' 'Me!' they yelled.

'And me makes three,' Nell added, with a laugh. 'How about you, Jose?'

'What? Um ... Yes,' Josie said, snapping herself out of her reverie. She turned to close the front door behind her, thankful that Nell couldn't see the strange expression she knew was on her face.

I've not had enough sleep lately, she told herself sharply. And that half of lager has gone straight to my head. My mind is playing tricks on me!

But there was just something about Rob's low, amused voice, those blue eyes of his that made her feel twitchy.

You're being silly, she told herself again, following Nell as she headed towards the kitchen. This is called Misplaced Attention Syndrome and it's totally because I'm missing Pete. She gave her shoulders a shake in an attempt to throw off her strange feelings. And then she put a big smile on her face and caught up with Nell.

When the shepherd's pie had been well and truly polished off – the coincidence of it hadn't been lost on Josie – Rob showed them where they'd be sleeping. 'The boys can have my room,' he said, 'and you and Josie can sleep in Mark's room, Nell. Is that OK?'

'Where are you going to sleep, then?' Nell asked.

'On the sofa,' Rob replied.

'Are you sure?' Josie asked. 'I can sleep with the boys, and you and Nell go in together if you want.'

'No chance, his feet smell,' Nell said.

'And she snores like a pig,' Rob retorted.

Josie laughed. 'Well, if you're sure . . .'

'We're sure,' they chorused.

To her great relief, the boys were so worn out from the day's travels that they got into their pyjamas without complaint and fell asleep on Rob's double mattress almost immediately. What a result, thought Josie, closing the door quietly behind her as she slipped out of the room.

'And then there were three,' Nell said as Josie came downstairs again.

'And then there was beer,' Rob added, holding out a couple of bottles straight from the fridge.

Josie hesitated before taking one. She was drinking way too much. But . . .

'We *are* on holiday,' Nell reminded her. 'You're allowed to, Jose. Come on, let's drink these outside.'

'How come you're off on this road trip together anyway?' Rob asked conversationally as they headed into the garden. It was a warm evening, and still light. He dragged some deckchairs from a shed, brushed off the cobwebs and started setting them up on the daisy-dotted lawn. 'And what does your husband think about you gallivanting around the country with my wild sister, Josie?'

Josie's smile froze on her face. 'He . . . um . . .' she said.

She didn't want to say it. She didn't want to spoil the nice day she'd just had by reminding herself all over again of what lay behind it.

'He thinks it's a good idea,' Nell said, gallantly stepping in to rescue her.

'He's left me,' Josie said bluntly.

Rob's head turned sharply towards her, and the deck-chair he was setting up swung shut with a loud *clack*. 'Oh God, sorry,' he said, his eyes on her. 'I wouldn't have asked if I'd known ... It's none of my business, I'm sorry.'

'It's OK,' Josie said.

Rob opened up the last deckchair and arranged them in a semicircle. 'Have a seat,' he said. 'Me and my big gob. Sorry, Josie.'

'Really, it's OK,' Josie said, trying to smile. 'That's why we're on the road, anyway. Running away from our broken hearts.'

'You as well?' He turned to Nell. 'Was that "hearts", plural?'

Nell nodded. 'Afraid so,' she said. 'It's all over with the big G.'

'Bloody hell,' Rob said. 'I can't keep up. What happened? Last time I heard, it was all hunky-dory.'

'It was,' Nell said. She leaned back in her chair and swigged from her beer bottle. 'Then it went pear-shaped.'

'Why? What happened?' Rob persisted.

Josie found that she was perching on the edge of her seat, waiting for Nell's response. It had to be something pretty bad, she guessed. Nell had been so cagey about the break-up, and had looked so fragile in London, Josie knew it had to be something serious. Something damaging.

Nell sighed. 'Look, I don't really want to talk about it,' she said, not meeting her brother's eye.

Josie leaned back. Should have known. And it was clear as anything that Nell *should* be talking about it. She couldn't stay in denial for ever, pretending everything was fine. If Gareth had treated her badly, then Nell needed to talk. Had to tell somebody.

'Why not? There has to be some reason. What did he do wrong?' Rob asked.

'Did he hit you?' Josie blurted out.

Nell turned and stared at her, and for a moment there was a terrible silence. Josie held her breath. '*Did* he?' she asked again.

'Did he *hit* me? Gareth? No!' Nell cried, looking aghast.

Josie blushed. 'Oh,' she said. 'Sorry. Stick, wrong end.'

'Gareth would never lay a finger on me!' she went on. 'He loved me!'

'Then ... what went wrong?' Rob asked again. 'Why did you split up?'

'Because he asked me to *marry* him,' Nell burst out, looking down at her knees.

There was an incredulous silence. Rob laughed. Josie's mouth fell open. 'Did you just say . . . ?' she faltered.

'Marry him? What, and so you chucked him?' Rob asked. 'You dumped him because he proposed?'

'Yes!' Nell replied fiercely, rounding on her brother. 'Yes, too right I did! Of all the things . . . I mean, that is *so* what I don't want. It's the absolute *antithesis* of what I want. And for him not to realize that . . . It's like he just never knew me at all.'

'Oh, come on, that's a bit strong,' Rob argued. Josie was still too stunned to speak. 'Couldn't you just say no thanks and carry on as you were? Why did you have to play the drama-queen card and storm off in a tantrum?'

'I didn't!' Nell had tears in her eyes, Josie noticed. She reached over and took Nell's hand.

'Sorry,' Rob said. 'I didn't mean to upset you. I just . . . I just don't get it. Why did Gareth proposing to you have to mean the end of everything?'

'Because for me, marriage is the kiss of death,' Nell said, with a shudder. She turned to Josie, suddenly apologetic. 'No offence – obviously lots of people want all that traditional stuff, but me, I don't. I really, really don't. And I thought Gareth knew that.' She swigged down some beer. 'I just want to be free, that's all.'

'And you haven't spoken to Gareth since this all kicked off?' Josie asked. She still couldn't really get her head around it, to be honest. For Nell to be rejecting exactly what she, Josie, wanted most of all ... It seemed warped.

Nell shook her head. 'We had a massive row, loads of horrible things got said, and then ...' She hesitated. 'And then I kind of ran away,' she mumbled.

Josie and Rob exchanged a look. 'Seems to be your answer to everything,' Rob said. Nell didn't dispute it.

'I think you should go and see him,' Josie ventured. 'I mean ... You've walked out on this good relationship just because he tried to express a bit of commitment.'

'But I don't want—' Nell started saying.

'I know you don't want commitment,' Josie interrupted. 'And I'm sure Gareth's got the message now, loud and clear. But it doesn't have to be The End for you two, does it? Surely there's a midway point you can meet at?'

Nell picked at the label on her bottle and said nothing.

'I can't believe you're being so cowardly,' Rob said, looking amused.

'I'm not!' Nell cried, outraged.

'You are!' Rob shot straight back. 'What are you playing at? You can't keep running for ever.'

'Says you, with your bags packed for Zambia,' Nell retorted, chin up defiantly.

Rob put a hand up. 'Fair point,' he conceded. 'But this is my last trip – really!' he said to Nell's disbelieving snort. 'While I've been helping Mark do up this place, I've found myself thinking for the first time that I can see the appeal of putting down roots for a while. Making a home. Growing vegetables.'

'I'll believe that when I see it,' said Nell with another snort. 'Vegetables, my arse!'

'It's true! It's like ... I've had my adventures. Seen the world. I don't want to be one of those addled old fuckers you always see in India, on their own, still trying to escape from whatever it was they first ran away from.' He finished his beer in one gulp. 'I want a life, too. A life in England.'

'Yeah, yeah,' Nell scoffed. 'I'll remember that when you come back and start getting itchy feet again.'

He shook his head. 'This is a favour, that's all,' he said. 'The Volunteer Africa lot had taken on someone else for this job in Zambia, but the person had to delay starting for six months. Personal reasons, not sure what. So they phoned me, as it's the kind of work I was doing for them in Mozambique, and ...' He shrugged. 'Well, I couldn't say no. That's why I'm going, and it's only for six months. Otherwise I'd stay here.' A grin flashed across his face. 'Anyway, let's stop arguing. We're making Josie feel all awkward and squirmy, I can tell. I'm going to get some more beers, and after that we can stop talking about failed romances and move on to something else.'

He went back indoors, and Josie turned to Nell. 'Are you OK?' she asked. 'That all got a bit heavy.'

Nell rolled her eyes. 'I'm OK,' she said. 'Feeling a bit ... stupid, if you must know.'

'Stupid? Why?'

'Oh, just the Gareth thing. I feel bad for not phoning him. I need to speak to him, say sorry, that kind of thing.' She stared up at the sky. 'I wasn't being cowardly, running away, but it really freaked me out. And I kept thinking I should phone and talk things through, but I couldn't bring myself to. And then the longer I left it, the worse it's become.'

Josie leaned over and squeezed Nell's hand. 'Phone him in the morning, not when you've been drinking,' she said. 'That's my expert opinion in these matters anyway,' she added wryly. 'I mean, not so long ago the guy wanted to marry you. He's not going to have switched those feelings off overnight, is he? He's probably dying to speak to you. And there must be a way you can compromise. It's not like he said *Marry me or it's all over*, is it?'

'No,' Nell said. 'It's just, he was pushing for commitment, that was all. And I can't do that!' She sighed. 'It's not because of him, I'd be the same with anyone. It's because of me, who I am.'

'I'm sure he'll understand,' Josie said. 'He loves you, after all. He loves you enough to want to marry you, for Christ's sake! So I'm sure he'll listen.'

Nell squeezed her hand back. 'Thanks,' she said quietly.

'I should be thanking you,' Josie told her. 'I'm so glad you turned up when you did.'

Nell smiled at her. 'Me too,' she said. 'And I'll stick around for as long as you need me.'

'You sound like Nanny McPhee,' Josie said, thinking how much she loved Nell at that moment.

'Nanny who?'

Josie chuckled. 'It's a kids' film. Nanny McPhee is this witchy kind of old nanny—'

'Oh, thanks a bunch!'

'And she comes to stay with this dysfunctional family. But she's good, really, and she sorts everyone out,' Josie went on. 'And then, as soon as the family stop needing her, she disappears again.' She shot a quick sideways glance at Nell. 'And then she goes back to Wales and tells her boyfriend that she's sorry she was such a melodramatic—'

'All right, all right! Don't go on!' Nell groaned and shut her eyes. 'I said I'd phone in the morning, didn't I?' She sat there in silence and for a moment Josie thought she'd overstepped the mark, but then a little smile crept over Nell's face. 'Nanny McPhee indeed,' she muttered. 'Some friend you are!'

By the end of the evening, Josie felt horribly unsteady on her feet. The garden seemed to be swaying and tipping around her as she staggered through the darkness towards the house. Nell had already gone in to make tea, and Josie kept her eyes firmly on the bright rectangle of light that blazed from the open kitchen door, willing herself to make it all the way there without going arse over tit in front of Rob. The grass felt cold now under her bare feet, and the stars were all out. She could smell night-scented stocks from a flowerbed somewhere, sweet and fragrant.

'Oops,' she giggled, tripping over the back of Nell's deckchair and almost falling over.

Rob grabbed her arm to keep her upright. 'Are you OK?' he asked.

Josie turned to smile at him, but managed to lurch right into his side by mistake. 'Sorry,' she said. 'God, I'm all over the place.'

He caught hold of her again, and she could feel the warmth of his body close to her in the cool night air.

'This is a bit like that evening in The Duke of Edinburgh, isn't it?' she blurted out before she could stop herself. 'I kept thinking about it earlier, you and me, both wondering . . .'

She clamped her mouth shut just in time. Josie, shut up! screamed the tiny remaining part of her that wasn't awash with alcohol. Get a grip, right now!

There was a moment's silence as they both stood still on the grass. Josie's heart pounded. Oh God! Now she'd gone and done it. She had to get inside *immediately* before she said anything else to embarrass herself.

Before she could move, though, Rob spoke. 'I was thinking about that earlier too,' he said slowly. 'You know . . . I probably shouldn't say this, especially with you being . . .'

'Completely trolleyed,' Josie put in, then giggled nervously. Oh, she *had* to get inside. She had to go! This was all getting too personal. She was too drunk. He was too nice. Go, Josie! Get walking!

She swayed on her feet, but they wouldn't move.

He laughed, and for a second she thought he wasn't going to say anything else, but then in a quiet voice he said, 'You know, I was gutted when I heard you were seeing Pete all those years ago. Because that night in The Duke of Edinburgh, I really thought . . .'

Nell stuck her head out of the back door. 'Tea or coffee?' she asked.

'Tea, please,' Josie said faintly. She felt way too sloshed to be standing up any longer. She needed to sit down at the kitchen table and drink tea and go to bed. Yes. That was exactly what she needed.

'Tea for me too,' Rob said. Neither he nor Josie moved.

'Coming up,' Nell said and vanished from sight.

'Right,' Josie said. She shivered suddenly. 'Let's go in then.'

'Josie! Are you still awake?'

Josie rolled over at the sound of the whisper. Nell seemed to have disappeared from the double bed they were sharing ... but there was Rob, perched on the edge. There was just enough light from the half-open door for Josie to be able to see him looking down at her.

She sat up before she could register just how thin the T-shirt was that she'd been sleeping in. 'What's going on?' she asked blearily.

He put a hand on her bare arm, and her skin prickled under his touch. 'We never finished our conversation,' he said. 'You know, about that night in the pub.'

Josie felt wide awake. 'No,' she said, looking him full in the eye. 'We didn't, did we?'

There was a beat of silence while they gazed at each other. Josie's heart quickened. They were on the very edge of something happening, she knew, both poised, waiting to see who made the move.

'Well, what I was trying to say,' Rob began, still looking into her eyes, 'was ...' He paused, and Josie felt her heart thud as his thumb started tracing slow circles on her arm. He smiled at her. 'I was trying to tell you, that night, how much I fancied you.'

'Oh, Rob,' she said, the words bursting out of her. 'I felt like that, too. I so did! But I always thought—'

There was no time for her to tell him what she'd always thought because all of a sudden he was kissing her, his lips stopping the words.

She leaned right into him, his warm, solid body, and then she was kissing him too, sliding a hand around his back, feeling the muscles in his shoulders, and how smooth his skin was under his shirt ...

'Josie,' he murmured, tracing the side of her face with almost unbearable gentleness. Then his hand was moving around the back of her neck and under her hair, and she was kissing him harder, passionately, as if she'd been waiting all those years for this moment. And now his hands were moving down her back, and under her T-shirt, and ...

She opened her eyes, and there was Pete standing watching, his lip curled in a sneer. 'You slag,' he said. 'What about me?'

'Oh!' Josie gasped, and then her voice rose to a scream. 'No! No!'

And then she woke up, panting, a cold sweat down her back.

She swung round at a noise beside her but it was only Nell, fast asleep, the duvet pulled up around her ears, breath sighing out across the pillow.

Only a dream. Of course. Only a dream.

Her heart was hammering, her mouth dry. Just a silly dream. Too much booze. She was going to pay for it in the morning, she could tell already.

She lay down heavily and stared up at the darkness, feeling a huge rush of disappointment. Only a dream. And yet . . .

The disappointment evaporated, and gave way to a burning feeling of embarrassment. God, what was she like? So desperate for a man that she was having horny dreams about Nell's brother, just days after Pete had walked out on her!

Stupid cow. Stupid, desperate, drunken cow. Thank goodness dreams were private. Thank goodness Rob never had to know she'd just fantasized about him like that!

Her cheeks flamed against the pillow and she squeezed her eyes shut. Then she put her arms around herself and tried to get back to sleep, but it eluded her for a long time.

'Mum! Mummy!'

Nell was still motionless next to her, blond head just poking out of the top of the duvet as Josie sat up and rubbed her eyes. A little voice from the next room was calling for her, and she tiptoed out to see which boy it was who'd woken up, and whether she had any chance of persuading him to go for another half-hour's sleep. It was six-thirty and the sun was up, though. Probably not.

She and the boys had breakfast together. The sun shone into the little kitchen and Josie held her mug of tea with both hands, enjoying the feeling of warmth as it spread through her fingers. Soon the weather would be fine enough to have breakfast in the garden. She always loved the first day of the year when they ate it outside. Such a nice way to start the day. It was strange to think that Pete wouldn't be there to share it with them this year.

Her eyes misted over. Such a shame.

'Where are we going today, Mum?' Sam asked, interrupting her thoughts.

She blinked away the tears and smiled at him over her steaming mug. 'To the seaside, sweetheart. To a little place called Hope.'

'Is that in Australia?' he asked eagerly.

She shook her head. 'No, love,' she said. 'Devon.' She sniffed quickly as she heard Rob whistling, and got up to flick the kettle on again for him. She felt faintly embarrassed as a flash of last night came into her head – her leaning against Rob like that in the garden, pissed and wittering about The Duke of Edinburgh. Then the colour surged into her face as she remembered her raunchy dream about him. God! What was she like? Like a dog on heat, that was what. Thank Christ nothing had actually happened. Thank goodness it had all stayed in her head.

It *had* stayed in her head, hadn't it? She hadn't said anything too awful, had she?

'Coffee?' she asked, deliberately busying herself at the kettle as he came into the kitchen, wet-haired from the shower.

He smiled. 'Please. Morning, boys! Sleep all right?'

They nodded at him over their cereal bowls, shy again.

'Seagulls didn't wake you up, did they?' he went on, sawing at a loaf with a bread knife. 'Noisy bunch, they are. Still, this time next week I could be getting woken up by a bunch of hungry lions, so I shouldn't complain.'

'Lions?' Sam echoed, sitting up in his chair.

Toby gave Rob a wary look before turning to his

brother. 'He's tricking us,' he said authoritatively. 'There aren't no lions in this country. Except in zoos.'

Rob jammed his bread down in the toaster. 'Ahh, but that's the thing. I'm not going to *be* in this country. I'm going to be in Zambia. Know where that is?'

Sam shook his head. 'Is it in Devon?' he guessed.

Toby, still narrow-eyed and in sussing-out mode, said nothing.

Rob sat down at the table while he waited for his toast. 'It's in Africa.'

'Like *The Lion King*,' Josie put in helpfully, then felt her cheeks flush even hotter. Good one, Jose — teach your children world geography through Disney, she scolded herself. She changed the subject quickly. 'What are you going to be doing in Zambia, anyway, Rob?'

'District engineer,' he told her. 'For the healthcare service. Repairing all their vehicles and biomedical equipment, basically.' He raised his eyebrows self-deprecatingly. 'I know what you're going to say — too glamorous and thrilling for words, eh?'

'I wasn't going to say that at all,' Josie protested. 'I was going to say how brilliant I think that is. How...' She stopped. *How amazing of you*, she'd been about to say. Ugh. Naff, Jose. Too much. 'Good for you,' she finished instead. 'Really admirable.'

'What about the lions?' Toby persisted. 'Are you really going to see any?'

Rob gave him a wink. 'Tell you what, Tobes,' he said, 'if I *do* see any lions, I'll let you know, OK?' He got to his feet as his toast popped up, and opened the fridge for butter. 'Might even send you a postcard, if you're lucky.'

Toby's eyes shone. He practically swelled with awe.

'Can I have one too?' Sam asked in the next second.

Rob nodded. 'Absolutely,' he replied solemnly. 'I'll make it the first thing I do when I get there – lion-spotting for Toby and Sam.'

Josie watched him spreading butter and Marmite on his toast. Strange, the different paths their lives all took. 'How about me, do I get a postcard?' she said, the words coming out before she'd even processed them properly. She laughed, self-conscious at how forlorn she'd sounded.

'Definitely,' he told her, swinging round to face her. 'As long as you write back to me, that is.' He smiled, and Josie felt her heart give a little flip. He was so *good*. He was so *nice*. Thank Christ there were people like Rob in the world, when so many others had let her down. For a split second she found herself wishing that he wasn't going away at all.

'Take care,' Rob said as he hugged her goodbye later that morning.

She gave him an impulsive kiss on the cheek. How nice it was, standing there, being held by him. 'And you. Have fun in Zambia.'

'I'll do my best. It's only for six months, this one, so I'll be home before I know it.' He let go of her, and she felt a pang of separation. Just hungover, she admonished herself quickly. Being ridiculous. Stop thinking like this!

'Lovely to see you again, Josie, and those boys of yours,' Rob was saying. 'I hope things work out with Pete. He must be mad to have gone off with anyone else.'

Josie gave a wan smile. 'Certifiable, if you ask me,' she said, trying to sound nonchalant. She held his gaze for a moment, then dropped her eyes. It felt strange to be talking about Pete with Rob, after her dream last night. She kept forgetting that Rob didn't know about it. 'I haven't a clue what's going on in his head, but hopefully he'll be hammering on the door when I get home, wanting to make up.' She pulled a face. 'Or something. Thanks anyway. For the hospitality and the chats. It was really nice to see you again.' She glanced out of the front door to where the boys were in the car, along with their bags. 'Right – we'd better make tracks. Where's Nell got to?'

Nell emerged from the hallway just then, clutching her

phone. 'I did it, so you can stop nagging,' she said. 'I phoned Gareth.'

'And?' Josie and Rob chorused.

'And I said sorry,' Nell told them.

'God!' Rob said, pretending to be astonished. 'And?'

'And I told him I'll go up to Wales so that we can talk once I've finished my Nanny McPhee duty,' she said.

'Your what?' asked Rob.

'You don't have to stay because of me!' Josie cried. 'And what did Gareth say, anyway?'

Nell twisted her mouth uncertainly. 'Not a lot. He sounded a bit pissed off with me, to be honest. But he said he'll meet me to talk, so...'

'He's probably married somebody else by now,' Rob said, dodging out of the way as Nell tried to cuff him. 'He'll probably want to introduce you to his new bride. Ow!'

'Oi! You can leave that out for starters!' Nell said, but she was laughing. 'Thanks for the pep talk, anyway, bro. Write me lots of letters and emails, won't you?'

'Course, every day, probably,' Rob said jokily, then pulled her in for a hug. 'Take care. Good luck with Gareth. And don't forget my invite to the wedding!'

'Ro-ob!' Nell moaned, wriggling out of his arms.

'I'll even get myself a new hat,' he went on wickedly.

'Oh shut up,' Nell said, rolling her eyes. 'See you ... sometime. Christmas?'

'Christmas,' Rob agreed. 'Bye, Nell. Bye, Josie.'

They drove for a while in companionable silence, save for the *Horrid Henry* tape and the occasional shouts from the back seat as they drove past roadworks with particularly impressive-looking diggers and bulldozers. Soon they were winding down towards the coast, the roads getting smaller and smaller until they were single-track lanes with jungly green tunnels where the trees arched over the tarmac. Josie had always hated driving down such roads, dreaded having to squeeze against the high hedgerows to avoid oncoming cars, but to her relief the traffic was light. Great sudsy heads of elderflowers foamed in the hedges, shrieking seagulls dive-bombed through the sky ahead of them and tractors burred in the fields. Josie found she was gripping the wheel less tightly as she slowed to appreciate the bosomy green hills all around them. She almost wanted to curl up in their rounded velvety curves, they looked so comforting.

'Mum, it's too hot,' grumbled Toby from the back.

She glanced in the rear-view mirror and saw how flushed his cheeks were. Then, as she moved into third gear and accelerated along the empty road, she pressed the button to open her window. *Zzzzz* went the mechanism, as the window lowered obediently. *Zzzzz ... Clunk.*

'What was that noise, Mum?' Sam asked.

Josie pressed the window-opening button again. Nothing. She jammed her index finger down on it hard, several times. Still nothing. Bollocks. Oh, bollocks!

'I think the window's broken,' she groaned.

'Cool,' Toby said. 'Shall we ask Bob the Builder to fix it?'

Josie didn't reply. Of all the times for something to go wrong with the car, it had to happen when they were stuck in the middle of nowhere. Car stuff had always been Pete's job. She didn't know *anything* about cars!

A gust of wind ruffled her hair and she sighed. Typical! Just when she was starting, ever so slowly, to feel remotely cheerful again, this had to happen. In an instant she felt as if she'd been plunged back into despair.

'Don't worry,' Nell said reassuringly. She was sitting with her bare feet on the dashboard, slim, tanned legs bent at the knee. 'We'll probably be able to wedge it shut again with something.'

'And then what?' Josie wailed.

Nell looked surprised at the question. 'Well, go to a garage, I guess. It depends how desperate you are to get it fixed.' She shrugged. 'It's only a window, Josie. It's not like one of the wheels has fallen off or anything.'

'I know, but . . .' She couldn't explain. It was the loss-of-control thing, that was what was bugging her. It was the wanting Pete to sort it out, and not being able to ask him. Oh, it was just *everything* all of a sudden!

'There's the turning,' Nell said, leaning forward and pointing just then, and Josie jammed on the brake.

INNER HOPE, the signpost read, and Josie steered the car into an even smaller lane than they were already on. 'Inner Hope,' she said, shaking her head. 'I almost thought you were making it up when you saw it on the map.'

'I'm feeling more hopeful already,' Nell said, wiggling her toes with a contented air. 'Right then, who's going to be first to spot the sea?'

It had gone past their usual lunchtime, and on any other day the boys would have been clamouring for food. Today, though, they seemed to have forgotten all about lunch, such was their excitement to be approaching the coast. A tense silence fell upon the car as Josie drove down a leafy lane, past a few houses and into a village.

'There!'

'The sea!'

'I saw it first!'

'No, *I* did!'

It lay in front of them, the cove: a sparkling bolt of blue sea with a sandy beach sloping up from it, and the headland rising a deep forested green beyond. A couple of sail-boats bobbed up and down on the water, and a dog bounded along the sand, its faint barking carried to them on the breeze.

Josie forgot all about the broken window for a moment as she drank in the view. She could smell the salty sea air through the open window and breathed it in hungrily. It smelled of escape. It smelled wonderful.

'We're here,' she said, in a kind of wonder. 'We made it.'

The village at Hope Cove was small, not much more than a pub, a shop and a clutch of hotels and B&Bs. It was quiet, too, after the half-term rush of two weeks before, the owner of one of the B&Bs told Josie. She booked them into two rooms for a week, and told them they'd picked a good time to visit. 'It's meant to be sunny for the next few days,' she added with a smile at the boys. 'I hope you two have got your buckets and spades with you!'

Ten minutes later they were all down on the beach. The boys, in trunks and sun cream, wasted no time in starting a castle and moat. Josie sat on the warm sand with her arms around her knees, staring at the waves as they crashed to shore. There was something hypnotic about the way the rollers came in relentlessly, their white foaming heads rising and falling in a rhythm of sound and movement. 'I feel really happy,' she confessed to Nell. 'Is that awful of me? I can't explain it. I want Pete to be here too, but I've kind of accepted that he isn't, and won't be.' She shifted slightly, feeling the grittiness of the sand underneath her. 'And at this moment, it's actually bearable.'

Nell shuffled closer to Josie and put an arm around her. 'You deserve better than him, you know,' she said lightly. 'He's not good enough for you.' She got to her feet and held out a hand. 'Come on. Those boys are making a right pig's ear of that castle. Not nearly enough shells for my liking. Let's go and help.'

The next few days revolved entirely around beach life. Each morning dawned bright and warm, and the hours sped by in a pleasant haze of paddling, digging, ice lollies, sandy pants and sun cream. They went rockpooling in Thurlestone, the next beach along, catching blennies and red-eyed devil crabs, and even saw a wash of purple-rimmed jellyfish on the sand one day. 'Come on, you two, who dares pick one up and chuck it at Mummy?' Nell had teased, causing Josie to squeal and dart away.

Toby and Sam had barely mentioned Pete now that they were the kings of the cove, with their spades permanent fixtures in their hands. They had peeling noses and freckles, and berry-brown arms and legs. They whooped and yelled from dusk till dawn, and were quiet only when they stopped to eat. There were no more wet beds from Sam, and a whole lot less sword-wielding from Toby. Displacement had definitely been the right solution, Josie thought in relief.

Yes, the days were easy. It was just the nights that were still long and dismal, as she tossed and turned in the sand-scratchy sheets of the bed. It was hard not to be swamped with thoughts of Pete the whole time. Josie still felt haunted by that scene in The Eagle – it seemed like a horrible dream, now, her marching over to the pair of them like that – and had replayed it countless times in her head. She kept thinking she could smell Sabine's perfume, a musky, sexy sort of scent, as if it had caught on her somehow. The scent – phantom or not – made her feel nauseous. And whenever she did manage to fall into sleep, Josie dreamed about her rival every night. It was like being bewitched.

Still. She was glad they were away from home. In fact, she didn't ever want to go back. Why would she? What did she have to go back for? The boys were busy all day on the beach here, and weren't winding around her ankles like they did at home, demanding entertainment. And she didn't have to face all the other mums and their sympathetic faces at playgroup and gym club either.

'Sorry to hear what's happened . . .'

'Let me know if there's anything I can do to help . . .'

'Is it true, that Pete's walked out?'

Yes! Yes! It was true, all right? It was like Chinese whispers, the way her bad news had spread through the neighbourhood, rushing from house to house like the wind, whispering into open windows and gusting through letterboxes. *'Have you heard? Have you heard? He's left her. Yes, for some young girl!'*

If she was brutally honest with herself, she was frightened of going home again. There. She'd admitted it. Frightened of having to mend all the pieces of her shattered life, jigsaw it all back together somehow, when she knew it would never fit properly again. It would be like a broken pot; you'd always be able to see the cracks, however carefully it was superglued. Any pressure and the whole thing would disintegrate again, implode.

It was all very well having Nell here, looking after her for the time being, but Nell wouldn't stick around for ever. She had her own life to sort out. And then, when they drove away from Devon and Nell said goodbye and went up to Wales, it would be down to her, Josie, to soldier on alone. It was terrifying.

She punched her hard pillow into a more comfortable shape and racked her brain for a masterplan. What would feisty Nell have done in her place? Surely she wouldn't have caved in and accepted Pete's decision as pathetically as Josie had done? Surely Nell would be out there, fighting to give the relationship another chance if she believed it was worth it?

'Did you think I'd crumble?' she heard Gloria Gaynor sing in her head. 'Did you think I'd lay down and die? Oh no, not I!'

Josie's eyes opened wide in the darkness as the glimmerings of an idea appeared in her mind at last. Did she dare? Did she have any choice?

'Peter Winter, I'm coming to get you,' she whispered aloud. She went to sleep with a smile on her face, and dreamed of being held.

Chapter Twelve

'Good luck, and thanks. Thanks for everything.' Josie threw her arms around Nell, not quite wanting to let go. Already Devon seemed like a rose-tinted dream. Saying goodbye to Nell felt like putting the lid on it all. Fun-time over.

Nell hugged her for a long time. 'Thanks for having me,' she said at last. 'Thanks for kicking my arse about Gareth. It was just what I needed to hear. Let's hope we both get our men back this week – on *our* terms.'

'Yeah,' Josie agreed fervently. 'Let me know how you get on, won't you? I'll be thinking about you.'

'Same here. You are doing *so* well, you know. Have you got your plan of action all worked out?'

Josie nodded. 'Kind of,' she said. A flurry of butterflies swirled around in her belly at the thought. 'Are you sure you don't want a lift to the station, by the way?'

Nell shook her head. 'I'll walk,' she said. 'It's a gorgeous day.'

'Bye then,' said Josie, hovering on the doorstep.

'See ya,' said Nell, and then she was off.

Josie shut the door. It was Thursday morning now. They'd got back from Devon late last night. No messages from Pete. No Pete camped out on the sofa. Only two terse messages on the answerphone from Barbara wanting to see the boys and demanding that Josie ring her back. Three sympathetic messages from her mum, asking if Josie wanted her to come and stay. And a whole number of beeps, where someone had phoned up and rung off without leaving a message. Lisa, probably. Not that Josie wanted to hear from *her*, of course.

Still. She had her plan now, didn't she? She could wait.

Josie had woken at five-thirty, and had been so wide awake that she'd got up and done the first load of holiday washing before anyone else had even stirred. The boys were at playgroup now, the plants were all watered, the post opened and sorted, and the four cups of tea that she'd already had were sloshing around inside her.

She couldn't put it off any longer. She was going to launch her first strike in the Win Back Pete campaign. The fight to save her marriage started here!

Pete worked in a dull grey office building on a horrible eyesore of an industrial estate, about two miles out of town. No wonder he was having a mid-life crisis, thought

Josie as she parked the car a short while later. It was enough to make anyone feel depressed, coming to work in such an uninspiring place every day. Maybe that was the problem! If she could just persuade him to find a new job, it might be the kick-start he needed. Forget Sabine, forget all this other-woman shit ... Maybe if she sent his CV off to a few recruitment agencies she could find a new job for him!

Josie looked at herself in the rear-view mirror. One step at a time, she reminded herself. She had to get him back before she could start interfering in his career.

She scrabbled in the glove compartment for her lipstick and rolled some on, smacked her lips and blotted them on a tissue. She checked her hair for dandruff – flake-free at the moment, she'd only just washed it that morning. All the same, she'd have to be careful to remember not to scratch her head at any time in his office. Freefall snowstorm was not the effect she was going for. Her chin was still flaky and dry, despite all the Vitamin D it had had from the sun, and her forehead resembled a page of Braille with all the stress pimples on it. Never mind. She had a tan, at least. She always looked better with a tan. Besides, he wouldn't be looking at her chin or forehead, would he? Not with the outfit she was wearing today.

Josie looked down and saw the plunging line of

cleavage she had on display, tanned boobs pushed up together, jostling for space in the low V of her white blouse. Was this top a bit *too* revealing?

She hoicked it up a little, suddenly self-conscious, then pulled it back down two seconds later. Pete had never complained about it before. Quite the contrary. He'd always had a thing about her boobs, so who cared what the rest of Mortimer Insurance thought? Desperate times called for desperate measures and all that, and you had to go into battle prepared, didn't you? She couldn't just stroll in there without making an impression.

She sniffed her armpits surreptitiously. Blew into her hands and smelled her breath. Then she squared her shoulders.

So. Here she was, in the car park, just a few hundred metres away from an unsuspecting Pete. Was she actually going to go through with this? Did she really have the bottle?

She hesitated as she caught a glimpse of her cleavage in the mirror. Maybe this was a bit rash, a bit ... desperate, after all. 'What are you going to do?' Nell had asked curiously, but Josie had avoided details.

'Get him back, that's what I'm going to do,' she'd replied. Lock myself in his office, and seduce him over his own desk to remind him what he's missing, she'd thought. She couldn't risk telling Nell and seeing doubt on her friend's face, though. Even a flicker of uncertainty would be enough to stop her doing this, she knew.

Josie swallowed. The thing was, now that she'd thought about Nell and the doubtful expression she might have — would have — worn at hearing Josie's plan, her nerve was ebbing away. There was still time to abandon the whole thing, still time to change her mind . . .

She *should* change her mind. It was madness to imagine herself strutting brazenly into his office, charlies on display, grabbing him by the tie and pulling him towards her . . .

No. She simply could not do it. Would not.

She was just about to turn the key in the ignition and go home when she happened to see her wedding ring, still there on her finger, shining up at her where a shaft of sunlight had angled through the windscreen on to it.

And then she hesitated all over again.

It was a sign, wasn't it? It was *definitely* a sign.

She took a deep breath. Be brave, Josie! Be bold!

She grabbed her handbag, checked the broken window was still wedged shut — it was, thanks to Nell shoving in a crease of cardboard to hold it up — and got out of the car.

Yes. Oh, yes. She *would* go through with it. She had to put up a bit of a fight, after all, didn't she? She couldn't just give up on her marriage!

'Peter Winter, I'm coming to get you,' she muttered again as she pressed the automatic locking button on her key. 'Ready or not.'

Anne, the middle-aged receptionist, smiled as Josie walked in. 'Hello, dear! Haven't seen you for a while,' she said. 'Lovely weather, isn't it?' she added, waving her through the barrier.

Josie's heart beat fast as she smiled back and strolled as casually as she was able to the lift. So Anne clearly didn't know anything had happened between her and Pete. Josie was relieved, but surprised too. She knew all too well what office rumours were like. One word at the water cooler was enough to set off a whole chain of whispers from desk to desk. Hadn't Pete told *anybody*? Hadn't Sara suspected anything when he suddenly took time off to go on his shagging holiday, wherever that had been? Or had the shagging holiday been booked in all along?

Josie's stomach lurched as the thought struck her. Oh God. Had he really been so calculating? Had he pencilled it neatly in his office diary – 'May 20, *Chuck Josie*. May 21, *Hols*'?

The lift pinged as it reached the ground floor, and she

stepped into it. Come on. Don't think about that now, she told herself.

Going up . . .

She got the shakes as the lift began slowing to a smooth halt at Pete's floor, and doubt swamped her all over again.

What was she doing? What the *hell* was she doing? She was acting like a maniac! This was a mistake. As soon as the lift stopped, she would press the Ground Floor button and slink out of the building and home. The whole thing was the most stupid idea she'd ever had!

Ping! 'Level three,' the automated voice cooed at her. 'Doors opening.'

Josie stabbed at the Close Doors button but the lift paid no attention, and the doors parted in front of her.

'Hello, Josie! I didn't know you were popping in today!'

And there was Sara, standing right in front of her, waiting to use the lift herself. Spotted.

Oh balls. Oh *bollocks*.

'Hi, Sara,' Josie said weakly, making no move to get out. 'Actually, d'you know, I'm not sure I locked the car properly, so . . .'

'Doors closing . . .'

'Oh, stupid bloody lift,' Sara said, jabbing at a button in front of her.

'Level three. Doors opening,' the lift repeated in its smarmy robotic voice.

'I'll go and tell Pete you're here,' Sara said as the silver doors slid back once again. 'He's been working flat-out this week, I know he'll be dead pleased with an interruption.'

Josie stared after Sara as she trotted towards Pete's office. She had to go through with this now, didn't she? If she dodged downstairs and out of the building, Sara would definitely smell a rat. And Pete would get to hear that she'd been sneaking into the office and . . .

'Doors closing . . .'

But she couldn't do it. She just couldn't!

'I've got to go,' she called desperately to Sara as the doors began shuddering together all over again. 'Sorry – I just remembered I—'

'Going down . . .'

Josie leaned against the wall of the lift as it swished downwards. Oh God. Oh God. She'd made such a fool of herself! *I just remembered I . . .*

What? Just remembered what? She'd had absolutely no idea what was going to come out of her mouth next, the excuse had just started spilling out of her in her over-whelming urge to run away.

She put her head in her hands. She was such an idiot! To think that she'd been on the verge of going into

Pete's office to try and seduce him, to win him back! Like that would have worked!

'Doors opening. Ground floor.'

She all but ran back to the car, head down, arms across her chest, not meeting anyone's eye.

Josie went straight to the kettle, direct as a heat-seeking missile. And then, when her hand was on its white plastic handle, halfway to the sink, she hesitated, catching sight of the wine glasses stacked neatly in the washing-up rack, from where she and Nell had tucked away a nice crisp end-of-holiday bottle of white the night before. It seemed ages ago now.

She licked her lips. It was only eleven o'clock. It was too early for alcohol. She had the boys to pick up soon, and the whole afternoon to get through with them . . .

She stood there, quite still, weighing it up. No. She shouldn't. The playgroup staff would smell it on her breath and then the rumours would get even wilder. *She's taking it hard, you know. Oh yes, drinking before breakfast, I heard!*

She tore her eyes reluctantly from the wine glasses winking in the sunlight. Mother's ruin and all that . . .

But if she was already ruined, then what was the point of holding back? After what she'd so nearly done, why not go for all-out annihilation? What else did she have left to lose?

She shuddered at the thought. What had she been *thinking?* Her cheeks flooded with colour at the vision of herself, done up like a dog's dinner, all set to go and humiliate herself in front of the Mortimer Insurance staff.

She put down the kettle abruptly and reached for one of the glasses. Sod it. Sod what the playgroup workers thought. She'd just have one little . . .

Ring-ring!

The noise of the phone made her jump, and she snatched her fingers away, feeling absurdly guilty.

Ring-ring!

Her heart quickened as she went to the living room and picked up the receiver. 'Hello?'

'It's Barbara.'

'Oh. Hello, Barbara.' Josie rolled her eyes, wishing she'd necked the wine there and then while she had the chance. She needed something to get through a phone call with her mother-in-law, that was for sure.

'I have already left several messages,' Barbara said, without preamble, 'so I was wondering why you hadn't phoned me back. I do have rights, you know. I am their grandmother.'

Josie rolled her eyes. *How are you, Josie?*

How's it all been, since my crappy son walked out on you, Josie? Goodness, it must be hard for you. I do sympathize! Oh, and how are my darling little grandsons? You're bringing them up so nicely, you know, have I ever told you that?

Right. Like Barbara even knew how to formulate a sentence without some kind of criticism.

She gritted her teeth. 'The thing is, Barbara, we've been away. All right? Only got back last night. So . . .'

'Away? What do you mean, away? I've read about this in magazines. Suddenly the grandparents get cut out of the picture! And . . .'

'Do you know what? I don't actually have to listen to this,' Josie said, interrupting her in full flow. She suddenly felt very tired and irritable. 'And right now, I don't want to either. Goodbye.' She jabbed at the Talk button decisively, cutting her off. The receiver purred its dial tone as if amused.

Bloody hell. Bloody hell! What was Barbara like? *Her* rights, indeed. Of all the sodding nerve!

Josie crashed the receiver down and stomped towards the kitchen. She *would* have a drink now, and it would be all Barbara bloody Winter's fault if she turned into a raging alkie. So there!

She paused in the doorway as the phone started ringing again. Go away, Barbara. Not interested. Go and tell it to Roy, see if he wants to listen. Or, if you're that bothered, tell the answerphone, get it all off your chest. Then Josie would be able to delete Barbara's rantings with the press of a button, without having to hear a word of them. Sometimes technology was wonderful.

The answerphone was doing its thing. 'You have reached Pete, Josie, Toby and Sam...'

She really had to change that soon. It made her flinch every time she heard Pete's name spoken so cheerfully by her own voice. *You have reached our happy little home...*

Not any more. What should she change it to? *You have reached Josie, Toby and Sam. Leave us a message. If you want Pete, the wife abandoner, you'll have to try him at Liars R Us on...*

She stopped at the sound of the new voice that was speaking – 'Mrs Winter? It's Maddie from the playgroup' – and made a dash for the receiver.

'Hello? Maddie? Yes, I am here. Sorry about that. Is everything all right?'

'Well, no, actually,' Maddie replied. 'Toby seems a bit off-colour, and we think he should be home. Would you mind coming to pick him up?'

'Toby? What's wrong with him?'

'His temperature's up, and he's been very quiet. Not like Toby.'

'No. Poor thing. I'll be two minutes, Maddie. Thank you.'

Josie wriggled out of her seduction top as she hung up, and headed upstairs half naked. There was no way she was going to collect Toby looking like a prostitute, that was for sure. She pulled on some jeans and a T-shirt, then grabbed her door keys and raced out. Poor old Tobes, no doubt the excitement about going on holiday had caught up with him. All the late nights he'd had, too. And even though it had been fun for him and Sam in Devon, he was probably missing his dad.

She'd think about that later, though. Much later.

Josie panted along the road towards playgroup. It was only a few minutes from her house, luckily, and it wasn't long before she was ringing the bell to get in. Maddie answered and took her through to where Toby was slumped on a sofa, not joining in with the singing like all the other children.

Josie went over and stroked his hot head. His eyes had lost their usual cheeky sparkle and there was an ashen look to his face, despite his tan. She cuddled him close to her. 'Let's get you home, pumpkin,' she said, stroking his sweaty hair. 'Sit there a moment and I'll get your sun hat.'

Sam – unusually for him – was less pleased to be taken out of playgroup early. 'Oh-h-h-h,' he moaned, huffing out his bottom lip. 'Do I have to go? I never finished my frog painting.'

'Finish it another time,' Josie told him. 'Come on, Sam. I need to take Toby home, and I can't drag him out again to get you later on.' She ruffled his hair but his eyes were unusually mutinous. 'Come on,' she said more coaxingly. 'I'll put CBeebies on . . .'

That did the trick. 'O-k-a-a-ay,' he sighed.

They walked home together slowly. Toby wanted to be carried, but he was so heavy she couldn't manage it the whole way. 'Come on, tired boy,' she said, lugging him on to her shoulders after he'd dragged his feet a whole ten metres. 'You just need a good sleep, I think. Too much excitement lately, hmmm?'

Back home, she put on CBeebies as promised and busied herself tidying up the living room. The embarrassment of being caught by Sara earlier had ebbed away, but she was still conscious of it prickling uncomfortably under her skin. Had Sara told Pete she'd been in the building? Oh yes, of course she would have done. Sara had always been the one to sidle up to Josie at the company's Christmas parties and fill her in on all the gossip about everyone. Sara didn't know the meaning of the word 'discretion' – she'd have trotted straight round to Pete, pencil-skirted bottom wiggling with importance as she click-clacked through the office . . . 'Josie's just been in! Looked all flustered and ran off, though. Bit odd, I thought! All dressed up she was, too; were you two meant to be having lunch together or something?'

The colour surged back into her cheeks as she tried to shake the scene from her head, but it was no good: she couldn't stop herself imagining the shocked expression on Pete's face as he heard that she'd actually been there, had had the nerve to swish up to the third floor of Mortimer Insurance and—

She broke off from her thoughts at a sudden cry from Toby, and turned to see him frozen on the sofa, a glazed look in his eyes.

'Are you all right?' she asked, going over to him. She felt his forehead. Burning up now. 'Toby?'

He made no response, just seemed to be staring over her shoulder. She put a hand on his back, but he didn't react. 'Toby?' He felt rigid, almost as if he'd stopped breathing. Something was wrong. Something was badly wrong. Suddenly Josie could hardly breathe herself for fear.

'Toby!' she said, louder, more urgent. 'Darling – can you hear me? Toby?'

His cheeks were hot and red, his pupils dilating, his gaze fixed and unresponsive. Oh my God. Josie's heart leaped into her mouth. 'I don't know what to do,' she said in a frightened voice. 'Oh, Toby! Don't mess about! Can you hear me? Can you hear Mummy?'

'Mu-um,' Sam moaned, his eyes glued to the TV screen. 'I can't hear the telly.'

His voice sounded far away, she could hardly focus on what he was saying. 'Toby!' she screamed as his body

started jerking. His arms and legs twitched uncontrollably, his eyes started to close. Josie felt a cold fear flood
through her and lunged for the phone, dialling 999 with
a shaking finger. 'Ambulance, please!' she gabbled. 'It's
my little boy – he's having a fit! He's very hot and he's
just ... jerking, his arms and legs. He can't hear me,
he's not saying anything.' Her voice rose in a wail. 'What
shall I do? Help me!'

'We'll send someone round,' the man on the other end
of the line said, and took her address. 'You need to cool
him down. Get his clothes off, get him on the floor –
don't hold him, it'll only make him hotter – fan him
with a newspaper or something. And don't put anything
in his mouth...'

Josie followed his instructions, her heart thumping.
She had never been so terrified in her life. Toby's eyes
were closed now and she shouted at him to wake up.
Was he dying? Was he actually dying, her boy, right
there on the living-room carpet? No. Please no. Please –
she'd do anything! – please, please, not that!

The ambulance was on its way, she was told, and she
sat there, fanning her hot, naked little boy like a maniac
and calling his name, tears plopping on to his feverish
skin.

Sam was crying now as well, CBeebies forgotten. 'Is he
dead, Mum? Is he *dead*?' he kept shouting, staring at his

brother with fearful eyes. 'Why is he *doing* that? Is he dead?'

'No, love, he's just poorly,' Josie managed to say. 'I'm sure he'll be fine, don't worry.' Her own words mocked her. He certainly didn't look fine, semi-conscious on the carpet in just a pair of Scooby-Doo pants, still making those jerky little movements. Oh God, what was wrong with him? Would the ambulance never arrive?

But yes — there was the siren coming faintly up the street now, getting louder and louder with every second. She could hardly believe this was happening. Toby had been absolutely fine first thing this morning and now — now . . .

Oh Christ. What if this was it? Brain damage, some kind of aneurysm? What if he never spoke, laughed, opened his eyes again? What then?

'They're here!' Sam said, and she hauled up Toby's limp body in her arms to open the front door, his skin still scarily hot against hers.

In came the paramedics, one male, one female. She'd never been so glad to see anybody. Toby's jerky movements were slowing now, then he lay still in her arms, eyes closed, his face a horrible grey.

'Sounds like a febrile convulsion,' the male paramedic said, feeling Toby's forehead. 'Temperature's up. Have you got any Calpol?'

'Yes,' Josie said, setting Toby down gently on the sofa and running to get it. 'Will he ... will he be all right?'

'Has he had a fit like this before?' the female paramedic asked, holding Toby's wrist and taking his pulse.

Josie shook her head, tears rolling down her face. 'No,' she said. 'Nothing like this. He's always been perfectly healthy.' Sam came and pressed himself against her, still crying.

'Is he dead?' Sam asked fearfully from behind Josie's legs. 'Is he dead?'

'No, sunshine,' the male paramedic said. 'He's just having a sleep now. He's worn out, I should think.' He plunged a plastic syringe into the Calpol bottle and squirted a pink dose into the corner of Toby's mouth.

Josie felt bewildered. 'I don't understand. What happened to him? Is he going to be OK?'

The female paramedic was peeling up one of Toby's eyelids and looking at his eyeball. 'Almost certainly,' she said. 'We see this happen to lots of children – pretty much every day.' She put a hand on Josie's shoulder. 'I know it's very frightening for you, but it's more common than you think. Chances are he'll be absolutely fine, and it might never happen again. Still, we'll take him into A&E, get him checked over, just to be on the safe side.'

'Right,' Josie said, feeling dazed. 'I thought he was

dying,' she said in a small voice. 'I really thought he was ...'

The male paramedic patted her arm in a comforting manner. 'Let's get him ready to go, eh? Can you grab a few clothes for him, a blanket, maybe a favourite toy?'

Josie nodded dumbly. Adrenalin was still coursing around her body, and she felt suddenly overwhelmed. She'd really thought that she was losing him, her precious boy, right there on the floor. She would never, *never* take him for granted again. Not ever. She would never let him out of her sight, not for a minute. She ...

'Is there someone who could look after your other son?' the female paramedic put in. 'They're always busy in A&E – there might be a long wait.'

Josie nodded. 'I'll ring a friend,' she said, picking up the phone and dialling Emma's number.

'Course I will – oh God, poor you!' Emma said when Josie explained. 'Is there anyone who'll come to the hospital with you? Do you want me to get Guy to come home and watch the kids so I can keep you company?'

'No, I'll ring Pete,' Josie said. 'Thanks, Em. Will you come as quickly as you can?'

'I'll be there in two minutes,' Emma promised.

Josie swallowed hard. 'I'll just ring my husband,' she said to the paramedics.

'No problem,' the woman said. 'We'll get Toby into the ambulance and wait for you there, OK?'

Josie dialled Pete's office number, feeling numb. Sara took the call. 'I'm sorry, Josie, but he's asked me not to put you through,' she said, sounding very awkward about it. 'I told him you'd been in, and he went all funny about it, and said—'

'Yes, but Toby—' Josie began.

'I'm really sorry,' Sara interrupted, a briskness coming into her voice. 'He was quite definite about it.'

'Could you just—' Josie tried, but the line went dead. She felt like throwing the receiver at the wall. It was as if she was being punished. *His son is going into hospital, you stupid cow!* she wanted to scream, but there was only the dialling tone to hear her.

She put down the phone, Sam clinging to her legs, and it rang immediately. She picked it up, hoping it would be Pete.

'Josie! Don't hang up on me again. I really need to speak to you . . .'

It was Barbara. Of all the times. And yet . . .

'Barbara, I need your help,' Josie said quickly, before her mother-in-law could launch into a tirade. She swallowed. 'Barbara, please – it's really important. Will you help me? Please, Barbara?'

Chapter Thirteen

Cometh the hour, cometh the mother-in-law. That's what they said, wasn't it? That's what they should have said, anyway, because Barbara was fantastic. Unbelievably, wouldn't-have-bet-your-bottom-dollar-on-it fantastic. She was already at the hospital when Josie and Toby arrived, interrogating the receptionist as to their whereabouts as Josie staggered through the door with Toby still limp in her arms.

'Oh!' cried Barbara, hurrying across. 'Josie, there you are! Is he all right?'

'I don't know,' Josie replied, and then, as the paramedics went up to the receptionist and started asking about empty receiving rooms, her bottom lip trembled, and all the fight went out of her. 'I don't know, Barbara,' she said again, as she began to sob.

'Oh, Josie,' Barbara said. 'Come on, don't cry! He'll be all right.'

And then, stranger than strange, Josie found that she

was leaning into her mother-in-law – leaning into barbarous Barbara's cast-iron bosom! – letting herself be comforted and hugged with Toby between them, soothed with reassuring words as the tears came.

'I was so frightened,' Josie sobbed. 'I thought he was—'

'I know. I know,' Barbara said. 'Peter was just the same when he was a boy, didn't I ever tell you? He was always flaking out on me, you know.' She patted Josie on the back. 'Horrible, isn't it? Oh, I know all about it! Really puts the wind up you, especially the first time.' She stepped back and stroked Toby's hair, cupped his head with her lined palm. 'He'll be all right, you'll see. He'll be fine.'

'Do you think so?' Josie croaked, her eyes on Barbara's face as her mother-in-law clucked over Toby. She'd never known the old battleaxe to be so motherly before.

'Mark my words,' Barbara replied firmly. 'He'll be right as rain.'

'Mrs Winter? If you'd like to follow me,' the kindly male paramedic said then, and Josie and Barbara went after him into a receiving room. Josie laid Toby down on the hospital bed, his body still motionless as he slept on.

A nurse bustled in and snapped up the metal sides of

the bed so Toby wouldn't roll off, and started firing questions at Josie, who did her best to answer.

Barbara stayed at Josie's side, her gaze constantly going to the door and back as if she were watching a game of tennis. 'Where is he?' she muttered. 'For heaven's sake, where *is* he?'

'Where's who?' Josie asked as the nurse paused to write something down.

'Peter, of course! Do you think he's been held up in traffic?'

Josie stared at Barbara, uncomprehending for a moment. She'd quite forgotten that Barbara wouldn't know about her disastrous trip to Pete's office that morning. 'He ... He wouldn't take my call,' she said. 'His secretary hung up on me.' She wiped a tendril of hair out of her eyes. 'He doesn't actually know that Toby ... well, what happened. I tried to leave a message but...'

Barbara clicked her tongue. 'She hung up on you? The little madam.' The old ferocity was back, but for once it wasn't directed towards Josie. Barbara rummaged in her large handbag for her purse, a grimness around her mouth. 'I'll go and call him. He should be here with you. Honestly! I don't know what's got into him, I really don't.'

She bustled away, and the nurse flicked Josie a curious

look before going on with her questions. 'So, Mrs Winter, were both arms and both legs jerking? Or was it just one side of the body?'

The questions were terrifying, actually. Josie stood there, the cold metal bars of the bed pressing into her side as she did her best to answer them, all the while smoothing Toby's damp hair away from his head.

Was there a history of epilepsy in the family?

Had he had a difficult birth?

Did he have heart problems?

It was all she could do to keep herself from crying at some of them. It was like being in the very worst kind of nightmare that she just couldn't wake up out of. *Why do you need to know that?* she wanted to ask, between the nurse's questions. *What's the significance of how his body was jerking? What do you think is wrong with him anyway?*

Barbara came back in with a cup of tea for her as the nurse was checking Toby's skin for rashes. Meningitis, that's what she's looking for, Josie thought, a freezing fear slicing through her body. Please don't let him have meningitis. Please don't let him . . .

'Here,' said Barbara. 'I put sugar in it, for your shock.'

Josie sipped it gratefully. 'Thank you,' she murmured, unable to take her eyes off what the nurse was doing.

Then the nurse pulled the blanket back over Toby,

her skin-pressing finished. 'No rashes, that's good,' she said with a brief smile at Josie, and ticked off a section of her notes. 'Doctor will be in to see you as soon as possible,' she added, and left the room.

Meningitis off the list, then. Thank God.

'I got through to Peter,' Barbara said. 'He's on his way.'

'Thanks,' Josie said. What, she wondered, would Pete say to her about her trip to the office that morning?

Then her eyes fell upon Toby, and she no longer cared. Oh, so what if she'd made a fool of herself? It was so irrelevant now. It was nothing.

Barbara sat down on the plastic chair and stirred her coffee. 'Peter was mortified that he hadn't spoken to you about this. And he's very sorry.' She sipped her drink, her eyes meeting Josie's over the rim of it. 'And –' she broke off, looking awkward, then plunged back into her sentence – 'well, I'm sorry too.' The words hung between them for a second, and Josie felt her eyes widening. Had Barbara just said that? Had she really just said . . . ?

'Sorry that all this has happened, I mean. Not just Toby. What *he*'s done, Peter, walking out on you like that.' She spoke briskly, matter-of-factly, then dropped her gaze. 'Marriage was for life in my day. We said those vows and we meant them!'

'Well, yes,' Josie said quietly. 'So did I.'

'My own son!' Barbara tutted, staring into her coffee. 'I didn't think he had it in him.'

Josie blinked, not quite able to take this in. She'd been expecting Barbara to blame *her* for Pete leaving, such was the woman's devotion to her son. Oh, she'd been expecting the recriminations to have started the moment Barbara had heard the news. None of it would have been Golden Boy's fault, of course. Instead, there would be the accusation that Josie had been the wrong woman all along, yes, and that she was a dreadful mother, not worthy to bear Pete's children, and what else? That the house was such a mess, and the children's clothes were never ironed – no wonder darling Peter had left her!

Yet there she was, Barbara, saying she was *sorry*?

'Well, I . . .' Josie mumbled, not sure how to reply. And then, before she could assemble her thoughts into any kind of a sentence, Toby stirred, rustling the crisp sheets.

Josie leaned over him. His eyes opened a fraction. 'Mama?' he said thickly.

'I'm here, baby,' she said, almost choking on the words. 'I'm right here.'

His eyelids flickered. She could see all the tiny purple veins on them, twisted in an intricate design, uniquely him, Toby Winter. He was so beautiful, so perfect, it hurt her to look at him.

'Hot,' he murmured, turning his head. His cheek was creased where it had rested on the pillow, its cotton weave imprinted on to his skin.

She blew on him gently. 'I know, love,' she said. 'You'll cool down soon, don't worry.' She leaned over the metal bars and laid her head next to his on the pillow, feeling his hot, sour breath on her cheek. Her hand rested on his chest, thankful for its steady rise and fall. He was breathing. He was talking. He was still there, her boy. Right now, that was as much as she could ask for.

Josie and Barbara stayed in silence for a while as Toby's eyelids fluttered closed and he slipped back into sleep. Josie held his hand and gazed at him, the adrenalin trickling away. She felt exhausted now, done-in. She hoped Sam was all right. It had been such a rush, Emma coming round and spiriting him away like that, and Josie had been so caught up with worry over Toby that she'd hardly been able to concentrate on anything else.

She turned to get her phone out of her bag. 'I'd better just check Sam's all right,' she muttered. She'd have to go outside to use it, she supposed: there were signs every-where asking people to switch off their phones.

Barbara rose from her chair. 'If you give me the number, I can ring if you like,' she offered. 'Then you can stay here with Toby.'

Josie nodded, touched by Barbara's thoughtfulness. Her mother-in-law was really surprising her today. In fact, she was going to have to check in a minute if that woman beside her in the flowered dress and perm was actually Barbara at all, or some kind of polyester-clad impostor. 'Thank you,' she mumbled, scribbling down Emma's number on a piece of paper. 'Would you tell her that I'll call again as soon as we've seen the doctor and I know what's happening? Thanks.'

Josie turned back to her son, dimly aware of the noises outside the room — a squeaky wheel on a trolley rattling by, the low hum of the receptionists in the next room, the muffled cries of a baby in the waiting area, and . . .

'Where are they? Is he all right?'

. . . Pete's voice down the corridor.

'Just in there. We haven't seen the doctor yet.' Barbara's curt reply, followed by the tapping of her heels as she walked away.

Josie looked around as the door opened and Pete rushed in, his face white, tie askew. 'I came as soon as I could,' he said, his eyes swerving from Josie to Toby. He looked sick and pale, as if he needed medical treatment himself. 'Oh God! What have they said? What happened?'

Josie stroked Toby's hand as she told Pete about the convulsion, and what the paramedics had said. She felt numb now, as if she was watching herself trot it all out. Tired, too. And angry, that Pete hadn't taken her call. Really angry that he hadn't been there when she'd needed him.

He came over and put a hand on her shoulder, and she cringed at his touch, turning her head away so that she could only see her son.

'I'm so sorry,' he said.

'Yeah, well,' she replied. She didn't have the energy for anything else. The words had deserted her, along with her adrenalin. She suspected this was probably her cue to apologize for turning up unannounced at his office, but she just couldn't face it. Somehow it seemed wrong to drag that up now, now they were sitting in the hospital with their feverish, semi-conscious son.

Toby's eyelids twitched, and Josie and Pete both froze as they studied his face. Toby stirred, and opened his eyes. 'Daddy,' he said groggily, focusing on Pete's face. His lips moved in a slight smile.

Pete stepped around to the other side of the bed and ran a forefinger down Toby's cheek. 'Hello, mate,' he said gently. 'How are you feeling?'

Toby blinked as if he wasn't sure how to answer.

'Toby?' Josie asked. 'Can you hear me? Can you hear Mummy?'

He rolled his head around on the pillow and stared at her. 'Yes,' he said after a moment.

'Toby, do you remember what happened?' Josie asked, holding his hand. 'We're in the hospital. Do you remember, you were sitting on the sofa and . . .'

His eyes clouded over, puzzled, and Josie stopped. She'd lost him, she could tell.

'Don't badger him,' Pete said. 'He's only just come round.'

'I'm not badgering him!' she hissed, furious at Pete's nerve. She put a hand on Toby's forehead, which was slightly cooler at last. 'Do you want a drink or anything, poppet?'

Toby nodded feebly. 'Yes please.'

'Good boy. Pete, could you get him some water? There's a sink in the corner, look.'

Pete stiffened, as if he didn't like Josie telling him what to do, but he went over to the sink and filled a cup from the tap.

Barbara appeared in the doorway just then. 'Sam's fine,' she said. 'Having a great time with Emma's daughter in the sandpit, apparently.'

Josie smiled at her gratefully. 'Thanks,' she said.

Barbara gave a little nod. 'I'll leave you to it then, shall I?' she asked. 'Let me know what the doctors say, won't you? And if you need any help at all . . .'

'Thanks,' Josie said, coming across the room to her. 'For everything. You've been brilliant, Barbara.'

Barbara folded her arms in front of her chest. 'Like I say, if there's anything I can do to help . . .'

'Yes,' Josie said. 'And I'm sure the boys would love to see you soon. I'll . . . I'll call you and arrange something, shall I?'

Barbara's face lit up in a rare smile. 'Oh, would you? I'd really like that. I've been worried that . . .' Her gaze flicked across to Toby and she lowered her voice. 'I don't want to lose touch with my grandsons, Josie. I've been so upset at the thought that . . .'

Josie put a hand on her arm. 'We'll sort something out soon,' she said. 'Of course you won't lose touch with them.' She swallowed. 'They adore you.'

Barbara's chin had gone all puckered, and her eyes were moist. 'That's very . . . That's very kind of you,' she said, walking quickly over to Toby, so that Josie could no longer see her face. 'Bye, sweetie,' she said, dropping a kiss on his head. 'You get well for your old nanny, OK?'

'Nanny,' Toby said wonderingly, gazing up at her.

'And Peter...' Barbara turned to him, the warmth disappearing from her voice. 'I'll speak to you soon,' she said formally.

'Thanks, Mum,' he said, stepping towards her, his arms outstretched.

Her mouth tightened as he hugged her. She didn't hug him back.

Weirder and weirder, thought Josie, trying to stop her eyes boggling at the sight. Barbara taking sides with her, Josie. It was shocking to see such a display of sisterhood, from Barbara of all people. She hardly would have believed it if she hadn't witnessed it for herself. And all this time Barbara had been worrying about not seeing Toby and Sam!

Josie pushed her hair out of her eyes as she went to sit down by Toby again. She'd never even thought of Barbara's take on it. How awful, as a grandparent, to think that your precious grandchildren might be taken from your life like that! No wonder she'd been phoning so much. She must have felt vulnerable too.

The door swung shut, and it seemed as if the walls closed in a fraction around them all with Barbara's departure.

'Where's Sam?' Toby mumbled, staring up at Josie.

'He's playing with Clara,' she replied, trying to sound

casual about it. 'And we're going to stay with you until the doctor comes and has a look at you, OK? And then hopefully we can go home.'

She was aware of Pete shifting around on the other side of the bed, and felt the anger rise up in her all over again. That's if Daddy here doesn't have to rush off on a hot date with his mistress, of course, she added venomously in her head. That's if good old Daddy can spare us a few minutes of his time!

Pete ruffled Toby's hair. 'I'll go and see what's happening,' he said, and made for the door. 'Want another tea or anything?' he asked Josie in his politest, best-behaviour voice.

'No thanks,' she said dully. She squeezed Toby's hand as Pete slipped out of the room. 'Want me to tell you a story while we're waiting?'

He nodded. The colour was starting to come back into his cheeks, although he still felt clammy. Josie kissed him. 'Once upon a time,' she began, and he closed his eyes in satisfaction and snuggled into the pillow, 'there was a boy called Toby, who had a brother called Sam. And one day, Toby and Sam went down to the beach. And what do you think they saw coming out of the sea?'

She paused, waiting for him to reply, but his deep, even breathing was the only sound. She kissed him again.

'A magical sea monster who made Toby all better,' she murmured, stroking his hair. 'Oh, Tobes,' she whispered, 'you *are* going to get better, aren't you?'

'There's nobody around,' Pete said after a few minutes, coming back in with a coffee. His face was strained, anxious. 'Is he asleep? Oh.' He sat down on the other side of the bed. 'We need to talk, don't we?' he said. It was a statement rather than a question.

Josie nodded. 'I suppose you'll want to get your things soon,' she said. 'And there's legal stuff, maintenance payments, what we're going to do with the house . . .' She said it all quickly, so that he didn't have the chance to get in first with the list. Coming from him, the words would have felt like an attack. Coming from her, they gave her a feeling of control.

Pete passed a hand over his brow. 'We need to set up some kind of regular arrangement for me to see the boys,' he said. 'That's the most important thing.'

Josie felt nettled, as if he were criticizing her for not having said it herself. 'Well, of course, that goes without saying,' she replied irritably.

'And obviously you can stay in the house for the time being,' he went on.

'Very big of you,' she muttered, feeling ungracious. 'For the time being' was very vague. What did he mean by it, exactly? That they could stay in the house until he decided he wanted to sell his share of it?

Pete ignored her remark. 'Perhaps I could take the boys somewhere this weekend?' he suggested. 'Give you a break. And maybe pick up my things too.'

Josie squeezed Toby's fingers. 'Well ... Let's see how Toby is, shall we?' she said after a moment. There was no way she wanted him out of her sight as early as that. No way, after what had just happened.

'Of course,' Pete said. 'I—'

'Mr and Mrs Winter?' came a voice just then, and a female doctor came in, tall and rangy, with a clipboard in her hand.

Pete and Josie looked at one another. 'Yes,' they replied.

'For the time being,' Josie added under her breath.

The doctor examined Toby and announced that he had a nasty-looking ear infection. 'The spike of high temperature is what probably caused the convulsion,' she explained. 'It's fairly common among young children. The brain can't cope with the temperature, and basically short-circuits and cuts out.'

'Oh God,' Josie said, clutching a hand to her mouth.

'Most children grow out of it by the age of five,' the

doctor went on. 'Toby's four, did you say? It's very late, actually, to have a first convulsion. Most children we see for this are toddlers. It's quite likely that he'll never have another one, anyway. Or, on the other hand, he may have several more. I'm afraid there's no way of telling.'

She prescribed a course of antibiotics and gave Josie a leaflet about febrile convulsions. And that was that.

Toby was awake now, and pinker in the cheeks. 'Can we go home?' he asked, sitting up. 'Can I have something to eat? I'm THIS hungry.'

Josie hugged him, suddenly unable to talk. She felt choked with emotion. He was hungry – good. She could feed him, and make him feel better – good. 'Of course, baby,' she said, wiping her eyes on her sleeve. 'Let's go.'

Pete drove them back home and sat with Toby in front of a dinosaur video while Josie raced round to Emma's to collect Sam.

She got back to find Toby lying on the sofa alone while the sound of the radio floated down from upstairs.

'Sit here with your brother,' she instructed Sam through gritted teeth, trying to keep her voice neutral. 'Shout for me if anything happens to him again.'

Then she ran upstairs to where Pete was in their bedroom, clearing out his wardrobe into sports bags while Radio 5 burbled about the cricket. She'd forgotten his annoying habit of needing the radio on in every room he was in – bathroom, kitchen, bedroom, car – as if he couldn't bear a single news story to pass him by, even when his own son had just come back from being rushed into hospital. Talk about priorities. Talk about *clueless!*

She marched over and snapped off the radio. 'Why did you leave him? Couldn't you sit with him for two minutes?' she berated him shrilly. 'What if it had happened again? You'd have had no idea, would you, being up here, radio blasting out?'

'Whoa!' he said, putting up his hands in protest. He'd packed some books, she noticed, seeing gaps on the shelves, and the drawers were sticking out at angles from the chest where he'd emptied out all his socks and boxers. Both wardrobes were open and Josie stiffened as she saw a flash of Rose's pink baby things spilling out, where he must have knocked them. Clumsy oaf! 'We don't have to watch over him day and night! He's got an ear infection, that's all!'

She stared at him, hands on her hips. 'You have no idea, have you?' she said accusingly. 'No idea at all! You didn't see him when it happened,' she went on, glaring. 'It was *horrible*. And I never want to see him like that again.'

'What, and you think I do?' he countered, ramming a pile of T-shirts into a holdall. 'Don't be so ridiculous!'

Josie shook her head, not trusting herself to speak.

And then her face crumpled. 'I … am … not … ridiculous,' she spluttered defensively, putting her arms around herself.

'Oh *Jose*, come here,' he said, abandoning his packing and coming over. 'I'm sorry, I …'

She backed away from him. 'No, don't "Oh Jose" me,' she said bitterly. She glared at him, hating him. 'Don't you dare! I've just had the worst, scariest time, and you tell me I'm ridiculous?' She shook her head, daring him to come any closer. 'You carry on,' she told him. '*I'll* go and sit with Toby.'

Downstairs, Sam was staring at Toby with interest when Josie came back in to the living room. 'I thought you was dead,' he was saying, looking at his brother as if he were a particularly fascinating museum exhibit. 'Really and truly dead. Cos you were going like *this*.' He lay on the floor and started jerking his arms and legs around on the carpet. 'And me and Mum were saying—'

'Sam! Stop it!' Josie snapped. 'That's not funny!'

'I was only showing—'

'Well, don't,' Josie said. She sighed, feeling as if she might fall apart any minute. Deep breath, come on. Don't freak them out any more by shouting at them. 'I'm just going to put the oven on for tea. I'll be back in one second, all right?'

'I nearly *was* dead,' she heard Toby boasting as she left

the room. 'Very very nearly. And then you would have had to bury me in the garden!'

Josie didn't know whether to laugh or cry as she turned on the oven, then filled the kettle. She leaned against the kitchen worktop as she waited for it to boil, gazing dispiritedly at the sink. The washing-up bowl was dirty. The draining board was smeared and there were pools of cloudy water at the back. The windows needed cleaning . . .

Out of habit, she looked up as she heard the chittering of the magpie outside. And there, to her disbelief, was a second magpie on the lawn, pecking at something in the grass. Two for joy. Yeah, right.

Yeah, *right.*

Pete came downstairs ten minutes later with a couple of over-stuffed sports bags. Socks snaked out of the zip of one of them. A paperback book poked out of the top of the other. Josie was watching a Tyrannosaurus Rex tear a smaller dinosaur into bloody shreds on the telly as she sat on the sofa, one arm around each boy.

'I'll be off then,' Pete announced, dropping his bags on the floor and letting his arms dangle by his sides as if he wasn't quite sure what to do with them. Was he waiting for the boys to rush into his arms for a farewell hug?

Neither boy moved a muscle in response.

'Say bye to your dad, then,' Josie ordered them.

'Bye,' they droned, eyes still glued to the screen.

'Cool,' Sam breathed, as the smaller dinosaur fell limply to the ground and the T-Rex chewed into its side.

'That is so *gross*,' Toby said, his eyes delighted at the bone-crunching noises that ensued.

'So, boys, do you fancy coming out with me at the weekend?' Pete said, with a rather forced air of joviality.

No reply.

'Do I have to switch it off?' Pete asked. 'Boys?'

'Don't turn it off, this is the best bit!' Sam protested.

Pete turned to Josie. 'Shall I pick them up on Sunday morning, say, ten o'clock?' he asked. 'It *is* Father's Day, after all,' he added lamely.

'Sure,' Josie said sarcastically. 'Can't miss *Father's* Day, can we?'

Pete hesitated. 'OK. Take care, then. Ring me if you need me to do anything, yeah?'

Josie nodded, turning back to the screen. The small dinosaur gave one final whimper as the T-Rex crunched through its leg, and then lay still. Josie leaned back wearily as she heard the front door close. Goodbye and good riddance, she thought. He'd been no help at all to her in the hospital. She didn't need him.

She blinked at the revelation. She didn't actually *need* him.

On screen, the T-Rex licked its lips and thundered away, alone.

Chapter Fourteen

A feeling of anxiety settled upon Josie that she couldn't shake off. It weighed her down, worries constantly goosing her. Was Toby getting another temperature? Was he too hot, too cold, too anything? Was he looking flushed, pale, blotchy? Would it happen all over again?

The responsibility – the sole responsibility – for his health and happiness lay around her neck like a millstone. If he had another convulsion, it was up to Josie to spot it, nobody else. There was no way she could trust any other single person to monitor him with the same fierceness that she could. Pete didn't even come into it. Not after the Radio 5 clothes-packing episode. It still made Josie clench her fists whenever she thought about that. It was as if Toby and Sam had slipped off his radar now that he'd walked out. And that hurt Josie more than anything, knowing that one day the boys would realize that for themselves, see that they'd plummeted straight down Daddy's list of priorities like a stone down a well.

God. How did a child deal with something like that anyway? It was crappy enough for an adult to discover they weren't loved as much by another person as they'd thought. But for a kid . . .

It was all too much. Josie felt as if she couldn't face the rest of the world any more. It was enough for her to worry about, Toby and Sam being under her own roof just breathing and existing without anything bad happening, let alone venturing out there, in the wider world, with germs just waiting to attack them, cars waiting to knock them over, psychos waiting to steal them away and molest them . . .

No. None of that. She simply would not let that happen.

Instead, Josie ordered in her supermarket shopping online from the safety of the desk in the spare room, and set up the camp-bed in the boys' bedroom so that she could bunk in with them at night. She told them playgroup was closed for the rest of the week even though that was a complete lie, and joined in every game they thought up so that she could watch over them.

It was as if she'd been bungeed straight back to the newborn days, Josie thought, where she was continually checking her babies were still breathing, still alive. She slept badly on the camp-bed every night, lying there listening to them breathing, unable to fall asleep for fear that she'd miss the last breath. How would she know if Toby had another convulsion in his bed? How would she *know*?

Each time one of them whimpered or muttered she was bolt upright, wide awake with anxiety, anticipating a dash downstairs to call an ambulance. Then, as they quietened again, she'd lie back, staring up at the ceiling through the velvety darkness, her heartbeat as loud as a clock.

By day, she was washed out and stressed. The shock was slamming through her now. She'd thought he was *dying*. She'd thought it was all over. Her son, lying there in her arms, dying. It had been so terrifying, so awful. She'd felt so out of control. She could hardly bear to think about what would have happened if—

No. Stop. It *hadn't* happened, she had to keep reminding herself. Toby hadn't died. And luckily, within just a few hits of the penicillin, he was running about, as cheeky and funny as ever, temperature down and staying down. He was fine. Sam was fine. It was only her, Josie, who was finding it hard to pick up the pieces and carry on.

The one and only thing that made her feel better was cleaning the house. God, it had never looked so spotless, not ever. She'd Dustbustered the corners of all the rooms, and wiped down each and every grubby skirting board. She'd scrubbed out the microwave. She'd disinfected the entire bathroom and kitchen. She'd even alphabetized all the books and CDs, *and* cleaned their shelves.

The whole house looked and smelled like a Flash advert. Her fingers were wrinkled and sore from the chemicals. But she didn't care. She didn't stop. It soothed her to scrub and scour and wipe away all the dirt and dust.

No more germs. No more bugs. No more ear infections. No more terrifying siren-shrieking ambulance rides to the hospital. No more misery. She hoped.

Pete came at the weekend to take the boys out, and Josie seized up with tension as he led them away to the car. 'Can't I come with you?' she begged. 'I just … I just don't want to let them out of my sight. Not yet.'

'But they'll be with me!' Pete countered, palms up. 'I'll be looking after them!'

That's what I'm worried about, Josie thought desperately, watching him drive away. That's the problem, pal.

No doubt he already had the radio yapping in the car, he'd be concentrating on the cricket scores rather than his own sons – his own flesh and blood! – in the back seat. It was terrifying. It felt like letting them go off with a stranger. She'd lost all faith in Pete; in fact, she could hardly believe she'd ever trusted him in the first place – to be a faithful husband, to be a diligent father, to tell the truth.

She spent the first hour they were away cleaning the hob and oven. She used a baby wipe to bring the surface of the hob up to a silvery sheen. And then she remembered someone in a magazine who'd advised using cotton buds to clean around the outside of the stove, so she did that, too. It was amazing, the grease and dirt you could get off that way. Then she put her arms into the oven and squatted there, on her haunches, scraping the charred bits of food off its black bottom and scrubbing the wire shelves free of their burned-on fat drips, and then the grill pan, and then even the oven door.

And then she phoned Pete for the fourth time to check everyone was OK.

'We're still fine,' he said with an aggrieved note in his voice. 'No, no one's injured themselves since you last phoned, half an hour ago. We. Are. All. Fine. OK?'

She moved out into the garden next, feeling white and pasty as she stepped, blinking, into the sunshine for the first time in days. She'd hardly been out there lately, save to hang out the washing, or supervise the boys on the climbing frame.

Pete had never been interested in the garden, other than as another place to sit and read the paper. It was Josie's territory, always had been, right from its early incarnation as a rectangle of turf.

The first summer she'd been too bound up in baby-world to do much else, and the garden had stayed a rectangle of turf. But by the following autumn, she had found the occasional burst of energy to dig in flower-beds and put in a few bulbs. A rowan tree had gone in next, and an apple tree, then four or five low-maintenance shrubs. The summer after that, she'd really got stuck in. Every weekend she'd found time to weed and plant and water, adding in perennials and annuals, putting up trellises for the climbing plants . . .

She gazed around critically, wondering where to start today. She'd neglected it over the last few weeks, and the ground was parched and cracked. The delphiniums were just stumps where the slugs had got at them. The rock rose, which was usually covered in flowers by now, looked yellowy-leaved and droopy.

She'd let it all die. Her lovely garden, which she'd nurtured like a third child, had withered away neglected. Even the grass was patchy and brown.

She went to fill up the watering can, the sun hot on her face. She felt like a murderer.

The boys returned rosy-cheeked and in high spirits, having gorged themselves on fast food and sweets at a wildlife park all day. Sam had a new elephant mask that he refused to take off, even while he ate his tea. Toby had a Hyena Blasta, a horrible gun-shaped toy that made an awful cackling hyena laugh whenever you squeezed the trigger.

Ha-ha-ha-ha-ha-HA!

Ha-ha-ha-ha-ha-HA!

It set Josie's teeth on edge within five minutes of them being home. And Pete knew damn well she wasn't keen on the boys having toy guns. So what was he doing, buying Toby a Hyena Blasta? Was he bent on finishing off her nervous breakdown? *I've started so I'll finish . . .*

'They've been fine,' he said casually at the door. 'We've all had a great time, haven't we, boys?'

'YEAH!' they cheered, kicking off their shoes and racing past her, Sam trumpeting, Toby cackling along with his hyena toy.

Ha-ha-ha-ha-ha-HA!

'Well, thanks,' Josie said uncertainly, lingering at the door. 'And Toby was OK? No temperatures? Did he have plenty of water to drink? Did you remember to give him his antibiotics?'

'Oops – I knew there was something. What did I do with it?' Pete held his hands up. 'Must still be in the car, hang on.'

'What, you forgot his antibiotics?' Josie shouted after his retreating body. He didn't answer – pretending not to have heard, no doubt – and she felt a fury whirling up inside her like a tornado. Unbelievable, that he could be so cavalier about his own son's health after what had happened. Unbefuckinglievable!

Ha~ha~ha~ha~ha~HA!

Pete came back, the bottle of penicillin in his hand. 'Slipped my mind,' he said, shrugging. 'Not to worry.'

She glared at him. Not to worry? Not to bloody worry?

'Great,' she said tightly, snatching the bottle from his fingers. 'That's probably wrecked the whole course now, and it won't work. Thanks a lot, Pete!'

'Hey – no need to—' he started, but she'd already slammed the door in his face.

'Toby!' she called along the hallway, striding down it in search of the boys. 'Tobes – you need to have your yellow medicine now. Daddy said he *forgot*,' she added in a bellow, just in case Pete happened to be listening through the letterbox. 'The incompetent moron,' she added under her breath.

And as she poured a yellow spoonful – the yellow spoonful he should have had before his *lunch* – and watched Toby swallow it obediently down, she could feel the horrible anxious feeling closing in on her, even tighter and heavier now. She'd let the boys go, after all her worries – she'd let them go out with Pete for the day, and the stupid cretin had just confirmed what she'd suspected all along: that he wasn't fit to look after them.

Ha-ha-ha-ha-ha-HA!

She put the bottle back in the fridge, rinsed the plastic medicine spoon, dried it and put it away. That was when she noticed the forgotten Father's Day mugs sitting on the work counter where she'd left them, meaning to get the boys to give them to him.

It was only the fact that Toby and Sam had painted the mugs themselves that stopped her from smashing them into little bits.

'So please ring me, won't you, if you think there's anything unusual about them . . .' Josie bit her lip as she watched her sons scamper into the home corner at playgroup a few days later. She'd agonized over whether or not to bring them – it was relinquishing the control, that was the hardest thing – but eventually she'd been so worn down by their clamouring to go that she'd held up her hands in defeat, and agreed.

Now that they were here, in the noisy, hectic playgroup environment, she couldn't help wondering if she'd just made a terrible mistake.

'Of course we'll ring,' Maddie said reassuringly. 'Don't worry. I'll keep my beadies on them, Josie.'

Josie tried to smile, but her insides were churning. Maddie and the other three staff had twenty children to look after. They couldn't possibly pay the same attention to her sons as she, Josie, would have been able to give. And really, when you thought about it, there was so much that could go wrong here. Another child could pass on a virus or infection – something really nasty that could hospitalize them. They could trip over, fall, bump their heads. They wouldn't wash their hands properly, nails and all, before they had a snack . . .

'Um . . .' said Josie hesitantly. She wished she hadn't just thought about all of that. Because now she really, really wanted them back home with her. Safe.

Maddie was watching her. 'You don't have to leave straight away, you know,' she said. 'Stay for a while if you want, if that'll make it easier for you.' Maddie knew the full story of Toby's convulsion, of course. The hospital had sent the playgroup details of what had happened, and for a few frightened days Josie had been afraid she'd get a call: 'Regret to inform you . . . play-group policy . . . no children liable to fits allowed on site . . .'

No such line had been issued, of course. In fact, Maddie and Sheryl had both assured her they'd seen it all before, had known lots of children come to playgroup who'd suffered from febrile convulsions, and it hadn't been an issue. Sheryl's daughter had had them as a tot too, so she fully sympathized, and knew what to look out for.

'Could I really stay?' Josie asked. 'Do you mind?'

'Maddie, did you know, my daddy doesn't live with us now,' Toby said just then, bounding up to them. 'Mum said he was an incorent moron,' he added, in an airy manner. 'Can I do some painting?'

'Incompelent, not incorent,' Sam told him.

'Incompetent,' Josie corrected weakly. She forced a smile, knowing the colour was rising in her cheeks. 'Why don't you do some paintings to put on your bedroom wall?' she managed to get out through gritted teeth.

Maddie waited until the boys had rushed off to the easels. 'I'm sorry to hear ... if things have been difficult,' she said. 'And do stay, as long as you like today. Sheryl's going to make clay pots with some of the children in a while, and I'll be making jungle collages once everybody's here.' She put a hand on Josie's arm, and suddenly Josie wished she was four and had Maddie to look after her all morning. 'Just join in, do whatever you want.'

'Thanks,' Josie replied. 'I appreciate this.'

'Not half as much as we do,' Maddie said with a laugh. 'Always glad of an extra pair of hands, we are! Now – coffee? Tea? What can I get you?'

Josie ended up staying the whole morning. She helped a group make animal masks, read countless stories aloud, and went into the garden with everyone at outside time. How simply children saw things! No mind games, or second-guessing, it was all black and white. When they liked something, they laughed or smiled. When they were hurt, they cried and wanted cuddling. And of course, when they were cross, they hurled things around, or lay on the floor shouting and kicking things. If only it was so simple for adults.

She found herself thinking about the bare flowerbeds in the playgroup garden as she helped tidy all the toys away at the end of the morning session. It was a small space, granted, but it was a shame to leave them empty like that. It wouldn't take much effort to put in a few rows of beans, maybe buy a couple of strawberry plants, get some sunflowers going...

'You look very cheerful,' Emma said just then, interrupting Josie's plans.

Josie started at the sight of her friend in the doorway, sunglasses perched on her dark hair, a string of aquamarine beads around her throat. Of course, it was pick-up time for all the morning children. This was where she herself usually came in, waving to the boys, weaving her way across to the art table to collect their work, trying to listen to both their accounts of the morning at once...

She smiled at Emma. 'I am, actually,' she said, feeling

surprised. She laughed. 'God. I'm actually cheerful! It's been a while since I've said that.'

Normal order was restored that night. The boys in their room, Josie back in hers. The double bed felt luxuriously enormous after all those nights on the camp-bed. They all slept soundly until morning.

Josie took the boys to playgroup and found herself staying again – and again. In fact, she stayed every morning that week. Not just to be with Toby and Sam, although that was still part of it. By the end of the week, she was more confident that they weren't going to get hurt or fall ill suddenly, but now she was staying to help out purely because she was enjoying being there. Besides, the house was already clean enough, and she didn't have anything else planned. So why not?

The other children were getting to know her now. She'd dug over the flowerbeds in the garden and they'd watched with interest as she'd pulled out the weeds and turned the soil, mixing in compost. A few of them had wanted to help as she'd made the trenches for the beans – and they'd all been keen to plant the seeds where she showed them. She'd had to draw up a watering rota to prevent the ground being flooded where they'd all wanted to wield the watering can, too.

It was fun. It was nice, having those expectant, wide-eyed little faces all crowding around her, hanging on her every word, as if she were performing magic for them. She had to tear herself away when it was time to go home that Friday.

'Bye, Harry, bye, Lola, bye, Mia,' she said as other people's children ran up and hugged her. It was touching, really. It was ever so sweet.

'Ever thought about doing this as a job?' Maddie asked as Josie collected up Sam and Toby's artwork and tracked down their sunhats. 'I'm serious! You're a natural!'

'Well...' Josie laughed. It was a far cry from her last job, the London design department she'd worked in where everyone was a chain-smoking fashionista with a degree in clubbing and takeaways. 'Well, I hadn't before, no,' she said slowly, 'but ... I do kind of like it here.'

'That's her, Mum! That's Josie!'

A voice piped up before any more could be said on the subject, and there was Oliver, Sam's friend, dragging his mum over to her.

'Hello,' Josie said, smiling at the woman. 'I'm Josie. Nice to meet you.'

'Annette,' the woman replied. 'Are you new here? My son is certainly very taken with you.'

'Oh, is he? That's sweet.' She winked at Oliver. 'I'm taken with him too, but I'm not ... Well, I'm not actually working here. I've just been helping out because ...' She flapped her hands awkwardly, suddenly self-conscious. *Because I'm completely neurotic and can't bear to be away from my children for a single morning.* She shrugged. 'Well, just because,' she finished lamely. 'I'm Sam and Toby's mum.'

'Oh! I've heard about Sam. Oliver talks about him a lot,' Annette said. She had the same periwinkle-blue eyes as her son, and long brown hair that looked as if it had been through the straighteners. She was wearing a cream suit with a pale pink scarf knotted at her neck, and looked cool and summery.

'They seem to be really good friends actually,' Josie replied. 'We could swap numbers if you like, so that Oliver can come round and play one day?' She grabbed a bit of scrap paper from the drawing table and wrote down her number. 'Here. We're on Edmond Road, just around the corner.'

Annette wrote down her number. 'We're just off Edmond – on Howard Terrace? Just moved in a few weeks ago after ...' She glanced at Oliver, who had drifted over to the fish tank where he was gazing in at the goldfish. 'Well, my divorce actually. We're just getting to know this area – so yes, I'm sure Oliver would love that. Thanks.'

'Great. And actually ...' Now it was Josie's turn to glance around for her boys' whereabouts, checking they were out of earshot. They were. 'Actually, I'm kind of going through the same thing myself. So I sympathize.'

Annette gave a nod. 'It's awful, isn't it? Horrible.' That same quick check over at Oliver, who was still tapping on the fish tank with his thumbnail. 'I'd better go, anyway. This is my one and only afternoon of the week with Ol now that I'm working, so I'd better make the most of it. Nice to meet you, Josie, anyway . . .'

'You too,' Josie said. 'And give me a ring. Have a good weekend.' She gave Annette a last smile and went to round up her boys. 'Come on, guys, time to go home.'

Josie and the boys stopped by the bakery on the way home for fresh bread, plus sausage rolls and gingerbread men for lunch. It was a glorious June day, and she was smiling again. She'd had another good morning. She'd met someone new, who seemed nice. Almost another week had gone by without anyone falling ill or hurting themselves.

Best of all, she felt as if she was finally starting to mend. Not completely, of course – God, no, that was going to take ages. But she'd stopped crying all the time. She'd stopped waiting for Pete to call, expecting him to come back. She'd stopped being haunted by dreams of Sabine.

I'm doing all right, she realized, once they were back

home. Life is beginning to settle down again, ever so slowly. I'm getting by without Pete. I'm managing. The bills are paid, the fridge is full, the boys are happy. On the surface of things, we're OK.

She was feeling so all right, she phoned Barbara to see if she'd like to come over sometime.

'Ooh yes,' Barbara said at once. 'Oh, I'd love to. I could do Monday. Or Tuesday, actually. Or – well, to be honest, the rest of the week is only WI stuff and I can change that, for the boys. And any time you need a babysitter, Josie, do say, won't you?'

'Oh, cheers,' Josie said. 'I will.' She put the phone down once they'd made arrangements, smiling. She'd actually had a friendly chat with Scary Barbara. And Scary Barbara had even offered to help her out! Who would have thought it?

Josie's good mood lasted all afternoon, and she treated herself and the boys to fish and chips in the garden for tea. It was almost midsummer now, a point in the year that she always loved, with its promise of warm days, her birthday, bucket-and-spade holidays just around the corner. Things were looking up. They were definitely looking up!

But then, later that night, when the boys were asleep and she'd just poured herself a large G and T, there came a knock at the door.

Josie glanced towards the hallway in dismay. *Coronation Street* was just starting and she had some cake from the bakery she'd been saving all day. She wasn't expecting anyone to call round. Her friends would all be tucking into gin and cake on their own sofas by now, surely?

The knocking came again as the *Coronation Street* music warbled to a close, and Josie sighed in annoyance as she went into the hall. This had better be something important, she thought crossly.

She opened the door – and then stared.

'Josie? Is it Josie?'

It was her, Sabine, standing on the doorstep.

Chapter Fifteen

For a second, Josie couldn't move. She felt winded, as if someone had landed a punch in her stomach. Then she was overwhelmed by a surge of fury. 'I don't want to speak to you,' she said, pushing the door shut.

Sabine stepped in front of it, stopping her. 'Please! I know you must hate me but—'

'Too right I do,' Josie shouted, shoving the door against her. 'Get the fuck out of the way. I mean it!'

'I didn't know! Josie, I didn't know he was married!'

Crash! The door slammed and Josie stood there for a moment, reeling from the shock. On the other side of the glass, just centimetres away, was Sabine, the slut, the tramp, the whore. Sabine the backstabbing bitch who'd stolen her husband, wrecked her marriage, destroyed her children's lives.

Had she really just said what Josie thought she'd said?

The letterbox rattled open. 'Did you hear me? I didn't know he was married. I swear!'

Her vowels were northern-sounding. Her tone was beseeching, but Josie was too tightly wound to be able to produce sympathy.

'Go away,' she said, heart hammering.

There was a pause, then another rush of words. 'I've only just found out. He lied to me, too. And ... I'm really sorry. I'm really, *really* sorry. I feel awful. I ...'

Josie wrenched the door open again, almost sending Sabine flying from her position at the letterbox.

Sabine got to her feet, dark eyes apprehensive. Josie's eyes raked over her, taking in her blow-dried hair, her cropped jeans and high heels, her sexy, strappy black top. Was that the sort of thing Sabine wore to pop out of an evening? Or had she dressed up for the occasion?

Josie wished she'd changed out of the top she'd been wearing all day. It had got painty round the cuffs from playgroup, and she hadn't really cared enough to take it off. Now she cared. Now she felt a scruff next to scrubbed-up Sabine. Off out with Pete after this, was she? Duty call followed by booty call?

'If I'd known about you, I never would have got involved,' Sabine said quietly now. Her eyes hung on Josie's. She fiddled with her hands. 'I'm not a home wrecker, no way. My dad left my mum for another woman; I know the kind of damage it causes, and ...'

Josie shook her head. She didn't want to be in this

conversation. She didn't want to start feeling sorry for Sabine. She twisted the knife instead. 'Did he tell you he has kids, then, as well as a wife? Did he tell you that bit yet?'

'Yes, he—'

'Very big of him! Very honest of him!' She was sneering, she couldn't help herself. 'So, what do you want now? Why did you come here? For a cosy little chat about Pete, eh? Compare notes? Or are you just trying to salve your own conscience? Make yourself feel better about destroying my marriage?'

'Don't take it out on me!' Sabine shouted. Her eyes flashed with emotion. 'I came to apologize, but—'

'Well, save it. I'm not interested. I don't want to speak to you. I don't want to know anything about you,' Josie said, spitting the words out. Sabine's face hardened, but she ploughed on. 'As far as I'm concerned, you're welcome to him. So why don't you both fuck off together?'

She slammed the door shut, panting, before Sabine could reply, and gripped the radiator for support. She felt as if she'd been in a fight, a physical fight. She hadn't actually done anything except stand there shouting, but her whole body throbbed from the exertion. Blood pounded through her veins, and her fists were clenched so hard her nails dug into her palms.

There was a moment's silence. Come on, then! Let's

have it! What have you got to say for yourself now, Sabine?

'Fine!' Sabine yelled through the letterbox. 'If that's what you want, we will!'

Josie held her breath as she heard Sabine's heels tip-tapping their way down the drive and out on to the pavement.

Then there was silence, and Josie let out a great rag-gedy sigh of relief. Her hands were trembling. She felt *sick*.

Oh God! Sabine had actually come here, to her house, for peace talks! And she'd ignored the white flag of surrender and gunned her down instead.

But what else could she have done? *Oh, you didn't know he was married? Well, that's all right then! No probs — cheers for clearing that up!*

As if. As if!

She slid down the wall to a crouching position. She rested her head on her knees, adrenalin draining away. It had been all too easy to paint Sabine as the villain of the piece, the self-centred husband-stealer who'd ruined every-thing for Josie and Pete. It had been convenient to blame her, rather than Pete.

It was disturbing to find out that Sabine was actually a victim of Pete's lies as well. And it was disturbing to come face to face with her, close enough to see her smooth skin, sexy hair and Friday-night clothes. Disturbing that she was gutsy enough to rock up at Josie's on a bridge-building mission.

Sabine might be lying too, of course. Playing the innocence card, making herself out to be a victim as well as Josie.

But why bother? Evil villainesses didn't do that. She'd got her man, after all. Why should she care about what remained in his wake? Why stop to look back at the abandoned wife and children, bobbing about like debris?

Josie sighed. It had all been so much simpler when Sabine had been anonymous and loathsome. And now she kept seeing those troubled dark eyes, that nervous buckle of the other woman's mouth.

I am not going to start feeling sorry for Sabine in all of this! she told herself forcefully, getting to her feet with a burst of resolution. I will NOT!

The morning brought a nice surprise. Not one, not two, but three postcards from Zambia. The boys fell upon them as if they were pirate gold on the doormat. 'Look! An elephant!' gasped Sam, staring at the glossy print on his.

'And I've got a lion!' Toby cheered, waving the lurid picture in Josie's face. 'See? "Toby", it says there. Read it, Mum. Read it! Did Rob see a lion?'

Josie smiled at their faces and, as they clambered on to her lap at the table, one boy on each knee, she felt a beat of excitement herself.

'Let's start with Sam's,' she said, turning it over. '"Hello Sam, I'm in a country called Malawi, in Africa (a long way from Devon). This morning when I was having breakfast, a herd of elephants came down to drink from the dambo, a little river, just near me. Love from Rob."'

'Wow,' Sam breathed, eyes wide. He gazed around the kitchen, as if half hoping to spot some elephants drinking at the sink, rubbery trunks draped over the work surface. 'Elephants!'

'Read mine, read mine,' Toby urged, jiggling on Josie's thigh.

'OK, OK, take it easy,' she laughed. 'Let's see: "Dear Toby, I'm staying in a big park called Kasungu in a country called Malawi. Last night when I was in bed, I heard lions roaring outside. It was very exciting! Love from Rob."'

The boys were silent, drinking it in. 'Can we go to Africa?' Toby asked, his face alight. 'I want to hear lions too!'

'And me!' Sam chimed in.

Josie hugged them both. 'Maybe, one day,' she said vaguely. 'When you're a bit older.'

They jumped down, clutching their postcards. 'Let's go and play Africa!' Toby suggested, running into the garden.

'I'll be an elephant!' Sam shouted, barrelling after his brother.

Josie picked up the third postcard, a vivid sunset over rolling grassland, the wide sky streaked with orange and purple. It was funny to think of Rob being somewhere so different, so *foreign*, when it was only a few weeks since she'd seen him. She read her own message eagerly.

Dear Josie

I don't start my job for a week, so I couldn't resist getting in a safari first (cheaper here in Malawi). Flew into Kamuzu a few days ago, and took a bus up to Kasungu. Dry season here, so fires have burned off all the tall grass — perfect for game-viewing. Have seen zebras, elephants, buffaloes, antelopes, leopards and hippos. The boys would love it! There's also an extensive collection of roaches in my rondavel (had to turf out a snake last night too). Off over the border to Zambia tomorrow, and work! Take care. Hope things are looking brighter. Keep in touch, tsalani bwino, love Rob x

Josie looked at the picture again, feeling warm, as if the heat of the African sun had stretched all the way to her own little kitchen.

'The boys would love it . . .' Oh, they would. Wouldn't

they just? But how was she ever going to be able to afford to take them somewhere like that?

Still, it was sweet of him to write, and to the boys as well. She could already hear the roars and brayings through the back door.

She checked the postmark. He'd posted it ten days ago. Maybe he'd started his new job by now. 'Hope it's going well, Rob,' she murmured aloud to the empty room, then, on impulse, pressed the postcard to her cheek.

'Oh, at last! I was starting to think you were avoiding my calls!'

Josie rolled her eyes and swung her legs underneath her on the sofa. 'Of course not, Mum. I've just been busy, that's all.'

'With Pete? Has he come back to you?'

Josie sighed. 'No. He hasn't come back to me. You don't have to keep asking me that, Mum, you know. If he comes back, you'll hear it first, OK? But I don't think that's going to happen.'

'Nonsense! You mustn't give up that easily! What happened to Stand By Your Man?'

Josie gritted her teeth. 'I've tried that already, Mum. I can't chain him to my ankle, though, can I? It doesn't work unless he wants to Stand By Me.' This was turning into one of those games she and Stu had played as music-mad teenagers, where you had to talk in song titles.

Don't Leave Me This Way.

Please Don't Go.

Come Back and Stay.

Stay With Me.

Back For Good...

'How are the boys taking it? Must have hit them hard. I bet they miss their daddy, don't they?'

Josie glanced out of the window to where the boys were digging in the sandpit. 'They're fine, Mum,' she said tonelessly. It was like getting flayed alive speaking to her mum these days. *Hit me! Go on, again! Harder! Got any salt? Pour it into the wound, rub it in with a scouring pad, why don't you?*

'It's so common, these days, isn't it, for men to walk out on their families? I keep reading about it in magazines. Honestly – your generation don't seem to know how to stick with anything!'

'Mum!' Josie yelled. 'You're not helping!'

'I said to Louise next door, I said, marriage should be for life, if you ask me. Why don't people seem to respect their vows any more?'

'Mum, I need to go now. I've got something in the oven.' It was a lie, of course. There was nothing in the oven – not even any burned black bits these days – but it was the sort of lie that worked for her mum, because Mrs Bell was the kind of person who always *did* have something in the oven, even on a hot summer's day.

'Oh well, I won't keep you, then,' she said. 'Give the boys a kiss for me. Oh – any more fits, by the way?'

'No,' Josie replied. She'd already had the epilepsy conversation with her mum, who had advised her to take Toby for an MRI scan at the double. 'Bye, then. See you next weekend. Yeah – love to Dad. Bye.'

Any more fits, by the way? Asked in passing, as if she'd just remembered. God! Maybe that was why Pete had dumped her, because the thought of Josie becoming more like her mother was too much to stand. It would scare away any sane man, she thought gloomily, replacing the phone.

It rang again straight away and Josie glared at it. What now? More marriage-guidance tips? Another article her mum had seen on epilepsy and was thoughtfully going to post her? Or something as banal as a recipe for her lemon drizzle cake?

'Oh, Josie, hello, it's Annette, Oliver's mum.'

'Annette, hi! How are you?'

'Fine, thanks. I'm sorry to ring on a Sunday – I'm not interrupting anything, am I?'

'No.' Josie let out a short, self-conscious laugh. 'No. Weekends have become a bit of a different concept now that ... Well, you know.'

'I do know. That's why I'm ringing. I don't suppose you and the boys fancy coming over for the afternoon, do you? We've got a paddling pool set up and a bubble machine, and with a bit of luck they can all get stuck in, and me and you can have a chat.'

Josie smiled. 'I'd like that. Cheers.'

'Oh, great. I was hoping you'd say that. We're at number 17 so just ... come over.'

'Will do. See you soon!' Josie put the phone down and ran to the window, feeling a renewed sense of purpose. Something to do, somewhere to go. And on a Sunday too! 'Boys!' she shouted, waving and smiling at them. 'Come in and find your trunks. We're going out!'

'Tea or coffee? Or something stronger?'

Forty minutes or so later, she and Annette were in Annette's kitchen, watching through the window while the boys splashed noisily outside in the paddling pool. It was a tiny room, basic and bare, with bright white walls broken only by Oliver's paintings from playgroup tacked up.

'Tea, please,' Josie said decisively. She'd had way too much booze lately. And besides, it wasn't as if she knew

Annette well enough to launch into an afternoon on the lash with her. She certainly didn't want to do anything embarrassing like go off on one about Pete – which she was highly likely to do, given even a sniff of alcohol.

'You'll have to excuse this place,' Annette said apologetically. 'We only moved in a month ago and I still haven't got everything sorted. Gary was always the one who did the Handy Andy stuff, so . . .'

Her sentence hung unfinished in the air. Josie nodded sympathetically, stepping in before Annette had to complete it. 'I know what you mean,' she said. 'I'm like that about the car. I'm terrified of something going wrong, I'm clueless about all that.'

Annette flicked the kettle on at the wall, and there was silence for a moment.

'So . . . Where were you living before? Did you grow up round here?' Josie asked, trying to steer the conversation away from ex-husbands. She didn't want to have to answer any questions about Pete yet. She was tired of talking about Pete.

'We had a house on the other side of town, me and Gary,' Annette replied, getting out a couple of mugs from the cupboard. 'It's been a bit of a whirlwind, really, this year. New job, new home, new life to get used to . . .'

Toby rushed in just then, dripping wet and wild-eyed. 'Mum, come and see what we're doing, Oliver's got this water-gun, and it shoots water at you and ... Oh, just come and see. Come *on!*'

His wet hand tugged at her trouser leg and Josie laughed at his excitement. 'All right, all right,' she said. 'I'll be out in a minute. You go back out there, go on, you're getting water all over the floor.' She turned back to Annette. 'Sorry – you were telling me all about your life changes.'

Annette opened the fridge for milk, and Josie saw piles of ready meals on the shelves and a green line of beer bottles in the salad drawer. She pulled her eyes away hurriedly, not wanting Annette to think she was being nosy.

Annette had already clocked her though. 'I know, I know, I'm not exactly a domestic goddess, am I?' she said, shrugging as she took out the milk bottle.

'I never said—'

Annette laughed. 'I know you didn't, but...' She shook her head. 'Cooking just isn't one of my priorities, that's all.' She sloshed milk into the mugs, spilling some on the work counter. 'Come to think of it, cleaning isn't really, either.'

'Well, so what?' Josie blurted out. 'That's all I seemed to do when I was married, domestic stuff, and it didn't do me any favours.' She shut her mouth quickly, aware that her voice was loud. Too loud.

'MU-U-U-UM!' the boys were shouting from outside.

'You don't have to justify your fridge to me,' Josie said. 'Or your cleaning skills. It's all overrated anyway, if you ask me.'

'Yeah,' Annette said. She finished making the tea and passed Josie a mug. 'Let's go outside,' she said. 'The garden's a bit titchy but I've got a couple of deckchairs, and they're just about out of splashing range from the paddling pool.'

They sat down in the shade of a fig tree, and suddenly Josie felt awkward. It was all a bit unnatural, being here with Annette, who she hardly knew, with the elephant of their broken marriages trumpeting loudly in the background. She sipped her tea and wished they were sitting in the sun, so that she could at least pull down her sunglasses and close her eyes.

'So, if you don't mind me asking . . .' Annette began.

Here we go, Josie thought.

'Was it another woman?'

Knew it. Josie nodded. 'Yeah,' she said. She sipped her tea again. This was her invitation to launch into the story, she knew, but she dodged the cue. 'How about you?'

'Yeah,' Annette replied. There was silence for a moment, and they both studied the boys wrestling energetically in the pool. 'Shit, isn't it?' Annette said.

Josie nodded. 'Yeah,' she said again. 'And ... Is it still shit for you? Does it ever stop being shit?'

Annette paused to consider her answer. 'The angry phase was quite fun,' she said thoughtfully. 'I went totally out for revenge – slashing his car tyres, ripping up his best suit, just trashing loads of his stuff basically.' She giggled at Josie's face. 'Ooh, I've shocked you, haven't I?' she said. 'Bet you're wishing you hadn't come round now you know what a psycho I am.'

'No,' Josie said, only half truthfully.

'Don't worry, I've got through that,' Annette said. 'Did angry. Did sad. Oh yeah, I missed out denial. Did that, too. Did hating. What else? Oh, a bit of slagging around. And now ...' She shrugged. 'I'm on to acceptance now, which is a bit boring, but actually, after that lot, I don't mind boring at all.' She grinned. 'Weary resignation, that's where I am.'

Josie laughed at her frankness. 'Weary resignation sounds bloody great from where I'm sitting,' she said. 'I'd take that over angry and sad any day.'

'Is that where you're up to?' Annette asked, peering over her sunglasses.

Josie thought. 'Well, I certainly haven't done any slagging around,' she replied.

'God, that's the best bit,' Annette told her, leaning

over like a conspirator. 'You definitely can't miss that bit out.'

Josie laughed again. 'That's a million miles away from what I want now. Ugh. Sex with anybody else. No way.'

Annette grinned. 'Yeah, I remember saying that too, in the beginning,' she assured Josie. 'But ... well, whatever gets you through the night, that's my motto.'

Josie sipped her drink, surprised at the way the conversation was going. She'd been expecting some man-bashing, a dollop of *They're all bastards* from Annette, but all this honesty ... It was fantastic.

'So life goes on, then,' Josie said. 'That's good to know.'

'Yeah, life goes on,' Annette repeated. 'How are the boys doing with it all?'

Josie gazed over at them. 'Up and down,' she replied. 'Toby's been angry. Hitting everything, you know. Sam's gone the other way. Anxious, and insecure.' She sighed. 'I hate it. That's the worst bit, what it's done to them.'

'They'll come through it,' Annette said. 'It *is* grim, I know, but I promise it gets better. Oliver was angry too, blamed me for it all, like I'd driven Gary away, but he's fine now. We've both got our heads round it.' She smiled. 'We've moved here – fresh start and all that – and I've got a new job, plans again. It feels good. Not how I thought my life was going to turn out, but it's all right.'

Josie was silent for a moment. 'Thanks,' she said. 'It's good to speak to someone who's been through it. Someone who truly knows how I'm feeling.'

'Takes one to know one, right?' Annette said. 'You'll get there. And don't forget the getting-laid bit. It's a crucial part of the recovery process, feeling fanciable again. You just wait.'

'It might have helped her, but for me? It is so not going to happen,' Josie said to Nell on the phone that evening. She'd been thinking about Annette's predictions, and the idea still filled her with despair. 'I mean, it's terrifying, for starters. I haven't slept with anyone other than Pete for years – eight years! And, more to the point, I don't want to. The thought of letting someone else see me naked – all the stretchmarks and dimply cellulite, and handfuls of fat...'

'Oh, listen to yourself! You can stop that right there,' Nell said firmly. 'You're lovely. And no woman gets to be our age without a few disfigurements along the way.'

'Yes, but yours are interesting ones – like your dog-bite scar from Thailand, and your motorbike-crash scar from the Philippines...' Josie sighed. 'There are glamorous disfigurements, and there are ugh-yuck-what's-that?

disfigurements. And I know which I've got.' She stretched her legs along the sofa. 'Anyway, that's enough about my non-existent sex life. How about you? What's happening with Gareth?'

Now it was Nell's turn to sigh down the phone. 'Well … We got back together…'

'Great!'

'…And then he dumped me.'

'Oh no!'

'Yeah, not so great. He was angry with me at first, for walking out on him, so I've had to do a lot of grovelling, and arse-kissing. And I do mean that literally.'

Josie giggled. 'You can spare me the details, thanks,' she said. 'So what then, you got back together…'

'Got back together, yes. For a week. Then he started up with all these questions about the future. "But where is this all going? Where do we go from here?"'

'Ahh. And what did you say?'

'Well, I said, don't ask *me*, I haven't the faintest! Because I'd rather not have it all mapped out like that. I don't want us to be saying, *We'll buy a house in a year, have a child a year after that, have a second child two years on from that*…' She sounded exasperated. 'I know some people like all that planning. But I don't. So I couldn't really answer his questions, because I don't know!'

Josie clucked sympathetically. 'It's a difficult one.'

'It is. And that's why he dumped me. Because he *wanted* me to know.' She groaned. 'We kind of hit a deadlock over it.'

Josie felt her eyes drifting to the postcard from Rob, still up on the mantelpiece, as she and Nell discussed a few other things, then said goodbye. It was always so complicated, wasn't it, trying to make a relationship work? Maybe Rob had the right idea, taking off and doing his own thing. On impulse, she reached for a pad of paper and pen.

Dear Rob, she wrote. *How are you? Thanks for the postcard. I was only a tiny bit jealous to hear about what you've been doing . . .*

She licked her lips, wondering what else to write. He was sure to think her life was very humdrum compared to his. She couldn't compete with roaring lions, and elephants at breakfast time. And surely he wouldn't want to hear about her marriage breakdown in all its gory detail.

She put the pen down and switched the telly on instead. She'd write to him when she actually had something interesting to say. She just hoped she wouldn't have too long to wait.

Chapter Sixteen

Before Josie knew it July had come, and her birthday. She'd been dreading it. She couldn't help remembering last year, when Pete had brought her breakfast in bed, and taken her out for dinner in the evening. He'd sneaked the boys out shopping to choose presents for her, and they'd done scribbly pictures in birthday cards, too. She'd felt truly loved, special, like it mattered that she was in the world.

But this year . . .

This year, who would remember? The boys, bless them, had no idea. They were too young to know about dates. It was just another morning to them – breakfast, being nagged into getting dressed, suffering a wet flannel over their Weetabixy mouths . . .

'It's Mummy's birthday today,' Josie said that Thursday morning when it became apparent they didn't know. She tried to sound casual about it, like it didn't matter, but she couldn't help a sigh escaping with the words.

'We did you a card,' Sam said through his toothpaste.

'When are we having the cake?' Toby wanted to know.

Josie stopped brushing Sam's teeth in surprise. 'Did you really do me a card?' she asked him. 'With Daddy?'

'No, with—'

'Ssshhh! It's a secret!' Toby said, scowling at his brother.

There was a knock at the door just then, and Josie quickly rinsed their toothbrushes before going down to answer it. Emma was standing there, with Clara hanging back behind her mum's legs, and Millie in her school uniform. 'Happy birthday!' Emma said, handing over a present and card.

'Have you got the surprise?' Toby asked, hopping from one foot to the other behind Josie.

Emma smiled. 'Yes, love. Here you go.' She handed them a couple of brightly painted cards. 'The boys made these when I was looking after them the other day,' she explained. 'God, do you mean they actually kept it secret?' she laughed, seeing the surprised look on Josie's face.

Josie nodded, not trusting herself to speak suddenly. Catch a grip! she told herself. They're only cards! But it was the feeling-special thing, that was what had got to her. The thought of Emma and the boys spreading newspaper on the table, getting out the paints and brushes, daubing on the colours in great messy splodges, and then Emma clearing the lot up afterwards – all for her. For *her*.

Toby pushed his card into Josie's face. 'Open it, open it!' he shouted, jigging up and down. Josie opened it up to read, in Emma's handwriting, *To a brilliant mum on her birthday, love from Toby.'*

'And look, I did the T for Toby – there, look, see?'

Josie bit her lip, feeling tears well in her eyes. 'Oh, sweetheart, well done,' she said. 'It's lovely. Sam, is that for me too?'

She took the other card from Sam's outstretched hand. 'It's a picture of me and Toby on the beach at Devon,' he explained. 'And that's a lion.'

'Oh, of course it is,' Josie said, grateful for the information. She'd been just about to ask if it was a frog. *To Mum, Happy birthday, love from Sam.*

'And I did the smiley face there, too,' he said, pointing proudly at a lopsided oval under his name.

'They're brilliant,' Josie said, kissing both boys. She smiled at Emma. 'Thanks, Em. That was really sweet of you.'

'And I've booked a table in Browns for a load of us tonight,' Emma went on. 'Babysitter's all sorted too,' she said firmly. 'I thought you needed a treat.'

'Em … thanks,' Josie said, feeling dazzled. 'You're a superstar!' She opened the present Emma had given her, to find a necklace with pretty blue stones on it and a matching bracelet. 'These are gorgeous – and the cards . . . Oh, I'm going to cry in a minute!'

'Don't do that!' Emma said, hugging her. 'Not on your birthday! It's meant to be bad luck, isn't it?' She knelt down to address the boys. 'Right, you two – shall I walk you up to playgroup this morning? Give your mum a break?' She straightened up and winked at Josie. 'You'd better start thinking about what you're going to wear tonight.'

Josie nodded, lost for words. Emma was so kind, so thoughtful. She'd totally gone the extra mile for her today. She kissed the boys again and waved them off. For all her worries, she was actually feeling more special than she had done on her last birthday. Sure, breakfast in bed and dinner out with Pete had been lovely. But they were your classic birthday rituals, weren't they? No-brainer choices.

Letting the boys mess up your kitchen then organizing a babysitter, girly mates and a restaurant . . . it was a good friend who would do all that. A very good friend.

Josie made herself a pot of coffee and took it out into the garden. The sun was shining and she sat on the wooden bench at the back of the patio to catch the early morning rays. The garden was reviving now: she could smell the fresh, perfumed scent from her lilies, the sweet peas were clambering up everything they could reach and the cornflowers were starting to unfold their jewel-bright heads. The cat from next door came and sat with her companionably, a throaty purr rumbling as Josie stroked its warm fur.

She sipped her coffee. Another birthday. If she could have foreseen this day a whole year ago, she would have been horrified at the way her life had fallen apart. But slowly, slowly, she was rebuilding it.

It was six weeks now since he'd walked out on her. Six whole weeks. She had stopped crying every night. She had stopped cleaning everything in sight. She still felt frightened by what lay ahead in the future – the thought of spending the rest of her life on her own was too terrifying to contemplate – but she was taking it gently. One day at a time. And so far, today was going well.

The postman knocked at the front door just then, and she jerked out of her thoughts and went to get her mail – a parcel, and a pile of cards. She sat at the kitchen table with it all, back door still wide open, and tackled the parcel first. It was from her mum, and contained ... Oh, thanks, Mum. A book called *The Single Parent's Handbook*, and a recipe box.

Josie wasn't sure if she felt more like laughing or crying. You couldn't make it up. Not with her mother.

Pete had sent a card, and Josie held her breath as she

opened it. She wasn't even sure what she wanted him to have written inside. A tender message, offering her baby-sitting and apologies? Or would he have been so cruel as to have signed it from Sabine too?

Neither. *To Josie, Happy birthday from Pete.*

Very bland. Very safe. Not even risking a *Love from.*

She sighed. Oh, whatever. At least he'd remembered. She was surprised he'd managed that much. Things had been strained between them after Toby's hospital rush and Pete's resulting crapness. Since then, he had been civil to Josie, and she was managing to be the same back. But all the hopes she'd cherished of him realizing his mistake and returning to her were dying, little by little, every day. It was over, it was over, it was over. She couldn't let herself even dream otherwise.

She opened the envelope with Nell's handwriting on next, for some light relief. Nell had sent a funny card with a few condoms inside and a scribbled message – *Make sure you get through these by Christmas, Slapper's Orders.*

Yeah, right, Josie thought, rolling her eyes. What was Nell like? Christmas in five years' time, maybe.

The next envelope was addressed in Lisa's sloping handwriting. Lisa had always been good with birthdays, never missed one. Organized, that was what she was, noting everything in her beautiful leather-bound diaries, always in control. But what on earth had given her the idea that Josie might want a card from *her*?

Josie picked it up, then hesitated. She was quite tempted to stuff the thick, cream envelope straight into the dustbin. She felt detached from Lisa now, removed, as if Lisa was someone from a former life. She'd done the angry time, hating Lisa and calling her every name under the sun, but things had moved on now, and the sting had been taken out of the wound. Weary resignation, as Annette might have said.

She got up to pour herself another coffee, but her eyes kept flicking back to the card, lying there on the table. Should she open it? Or would it be more sensible to ignore Lisa full-stop, cut her right out of the picture? What could Lisa possibly have to say that would make things all right again?

Josie leaned against the worktop, stirring her coffee so hard it slopped over the side of the mug. She busied herself wiping the surface clean, wiping the bottom of the mug and washing up the teaspoon.

Then she sat down and took a deep breath. And opened the card.

It was a classy one, of course. No naff cartoons in lurid colours for Lisa. No jokes about getting old and wrinkly, or drinking too much. It was an abstract Liberty print, all blues and greens, woven in an elegant design. Josie rolled her eyes. Very Lisa. Pete would have taken one look at it and said, 'What's with the wallpaper?' It was amazing to think that he and Lisa had ever got it together when...

Anyway. She wasn't going to think about that. Not today.

She opened the card. It felt thick and expensive between her fingers.

Dear Josie, she read. *Thinking about you on your birthday. I hope it's a happy one. I know you must still be angry with me—*

Damn right she was!

but I'd love to be able to explain, if you'd give me the chance. If our friendship has ever meant anything to you—

Cheap shot, Lise. Cheap.

then please call me, so we can talk.

Your friend, Lisa

'Your friend'? Your *friend*? Yeah, right! What planet was Lisa on?

Josie's fingers tightened on the card, seized by the urge to crumple it up. She put it face-down on the table instead. She's trying her best, a voice reasoned in her head.

'Should have tried harder not to shag my husband then, shouldn't she?' Josie said out loud.

She picked up the last envelope, recognizing her brother's handwriting. The card inside had a picture of a pissed-looking woman with a fag hanging out of her mouth, brandishing a full glass of wine. Subtle, Stu was not.

Happy birthday Josie! he'd written inside. *Love Stu and Mel. PS Party at the flat this Saturday — can you come? Spare bed if you fancy a weekend away.* x

Josie could feel the excuses brimming inside her, was already composing them in her head — *Sorry, would love to, but too short notice, impossible to get a babysitter, can't leave the boys . . .*

Then she stared around the kitchen, empty as it was of the boys' chatter and laughing. Her whole life, her whole world, had been lived out in the confines of these walls lately, it seemed. Maybe . . . maybe she should say yes to Stu's invitation. Just this once. Maybe she should get out there, dress up for a party, have an evening of fun away from the boring safety of her own house.

Should she?

Well, why not? Why shouldn't she have a night off for once? The boys were well. Stu's flat was only an hour or so away. And it had been a long, long time since she'd been to a party.

She munched through a biscuit. Sod it. She deserved a

treat. She'd think of herself for a change, just like Pete had done for so long. And it *was* her birthday today. Surely Pete couldn't say no to her on her birthday?

She went and dialled his work number before she could change her mind. Already, she felt giddy at her daring. What would she wear to a party? What would she *talk* about? Could she really do this?

'Pete, hi, it's me. Josie,' she added when he answered.

'Oh, hi,' he said, sounding apprehensive. She hadn't called him at work for some time. It was safer to leave messages on his mobile, she'd found. That way she didn't have to actually speak to him. 'Um ... Happy birthday.'

'Thanks,' she said. She took a deep breath. Go for it. 'Are you doing anything this Saturday? I was wondering if you could babysit. Have the boys overnight.'

'Well, I . . .'

'It's just that I haven't been out for quite a while. And Stu's asked me over for the weekend.' Probably best not to mention the party, she decided. 'So – what do you say?' She bit her lip as she waited for his reply, so hard she drew blood. It tasted hot and salty in her mouth, and she licked it away, heart thumping. 'Pete?'

'Um . . .' He sounded like she'd caught him off guard. She could almost hear his mind whirring down the phone line.

'I'll ask Barbara, if you're busy,' she said while he thought. Ha – stroke of genius, Josie.

'No need for that,' Pete said quickly. 'Yeah. Yeah, I'll have them Saturday night. Why not?'

Josie grinned, feeling exultant. It had been so easy, after all.

'Great,' she said. 'So, shall we say you pick them up at about two? And I'll be back by ... Well, midday on Sunday, I guess.' She was light-headed at the thought. Practically a whole day away. Wow. Should she really be doing this? Should she really trust him with them for all that time?

'OK,' he said. 'Two o'clock, Saturday. I'll be there.'

They would be fine. He was their dad, they needed to spend time with him. And she wouldn't be far away, after all. She could hurry back really fast if anything went wrong.

'Thanks,' she said, clicking the phone off. 'I think,' she added.

There were five of them going out that night – herself, Emma, Laura, Harriet and Sophie. The usual gang, in other words. On impulse, Josie phoned Annette and asked if she'd like to join them.

'I know it's a last-minute thing, but it was only sprung

on me this morning and I just wondered ... You would? Really? Brilliant. See you later!'

Later that evening, she got the boys in bed early and poured herself a glass of wine to slurp as she had a quick bath. She hovered in front of her wardrobe before picking out a scoop-necked turquoise top and some white, wide-legged trousers. The top was a good match for the jewellery from Emma, and she could pin up her hair to show off the necklace around her throat. She pulled on the trousers, her favourite summer going-out ones, which she hadn't worn since last year. She did up the button, and gasped. God, they were so baggy on her now! The fabric swung loosely around her thighs like a couple of flour sacks, and she could nip in the waistline by a good inch.

Christ. So there was a silver lining to your marriage falling apart, after all! She looked so thin!

Josie let go of the waistband, and the trousers dropped straight down to her hips. Right. Maybe she wouldn't wear those after all. She'd only get drunk and flash bum cleavage at the whole restaurant, stumbling drunkenly to the loo or something. She pulled on a floaty skirt instead that was gathered by elastic at the top, and couldn't help turning on her side to look at herself in the mirror. Wow. She really *had* lost weight. She ran a hand over her tummy. Where had it all gone?

She turned and leaned closer to the mirror, gazing at her face. Definitely some cheekbones there. She had cheekbones again! Her spots were all but gone now, too. Dandruff – yep, that had been blitzed. Bags under her eyes … well, one thing at a time, eh. She still wasn't sleeping brilliantly, but she did have a good concealer in her armoury.

She sorted through her make-up box, looking for the foundation. It had been ages since she'd got dolled up for a night out. In fact, it had been weeks since she'd had a night out full-stop. The last time had been when Nell was staying and they'd had that disastrous venture to the pub. The less said about that the better.

Tonight, as birthday girl, she would make an effort. And she had a bit of time before the babysitter was due to arrive, so hey, trowel it on. Why not?

'And then he snored all night, like a pissed-up warthog! All night long, I'm not exaggerating! I'm telling you, sometimes I wonder if I married a bloke or some kind of throwback. It's like living with an animal half the time!'

Everyone was laughing at Harriet and her eye-rolling account of her husband's misdemeanours. Then they all seemed to have a contribution.

'Matthew's just as bad, he farts like a wildebeest in his sleep,' Laura complained. 'The whole bed shakes, it's disgusting.' She fanned a hand in front of her face. 'There's no mystery left in our relationship, I'm telling you. And I *so* wish there was – especially on the farting front.'

'What gets me with Jake is the way he's completely monosyllabic when the football's on,' Sophie moaned. 'Grunts at me like a . . . rhinoceros, as if he's lost all powers of speech.' She tipped back her glass of wine and giggled. 'We should set up some kind of zoo. Between us, we've got a right assortment of beasts.'

Josie met Annette's eyes briefly, then looked down at her food. Suddenly she'd lost her appetite. Up until then she'd been having a brilliant time. The babysitter arriving, the cab speeding her and her friends into town, clinking glasses as the first bottle of wine arrived at the table, singing 'Happy Birthday' over the second bottle . . . Now they were on to their fourth or fifth bottle and the confessions were flowing. But why did everyone keep talking about their *husbands*? Had they forgotten that she and Annette were sitting at the table, husbandless?

Annette seemed unbowed by it, and put down her fork. 'The worst thing about Gary was the fact that he left *stuff* everywhere,' she said conversationally. 'Smelly socks. Pants. Shirt from work. He'd just take it off and drop it, wherever he happened to be standing. Didn't seem to understand the concept of a laundry bin.

Didn't seem to have grasped that you could actually put dirty clothes in the washing machine!' She swigged her wine, eyes glittering. 'Whenever I've gone back to a bloke's place since then, I've totally checked out the mess factor. And if there's any stuff lying around, any mess, then I'm out of there, "Nice to meet you, bye!"' She grinned. 'Well, after the shag, of course.'

Josie spluttered with laughter at Annette's honesty, but her friends didn't. Laura gave a polite titter and Emma smiled, but the other two sipped their drinks and looked down at the tablecloth.

'When did you say you split up with him?' Sophie asked, spearing the last cherry tomato from the mixed salad.

'About a year ago,' Annette replied. She eyed Sophie steadily as she bit into it.

'Sorry to hear that,' Sophie said, dabbing tomato juice off her chin. 'Must be hard.'

'Oh, don't be sorry,' Annette told her. 'And it's fine. In fact, it's good now, just me and my son. I wish I'd ditched Gary earlier, when I first had an inkling that he was being unfaithful to me.'

'Really? You guessed?' Harriet leaned forward, her long dark hair dangling over her tortelloni.

'I had a feeling, you know,' Annette said. Her lips twitched as if she was about to say something else, but she picked up her glass instead and drank her last mouthful. 'Shall we order another bottle?'

'Of course! Is that one dead already?' Laura exclaimed.

Emma nudged Josie as the others started waving to the waiter. 'You all right? You've gone very quiet.'

Josie gave an apologetic smile. 'I'm fine. Bit tired, that's all.' She didn't really want to join in the conversation, that was the problem. She didn't want one of the girls to turn to her next and say brightly, *So, how about you? Did you guess Pete was shagging around too?*

She swirled the last few drops of wine around in her glass. She was glad she'd come out: it had been kind of Emma to organize it all. But she couldn't help feeling that she didn't fit into the old gang the way she once had. She'd been squeezed out of the Happily Marrieds and relegated to the Dumped and Dealing With Its. And while the six of them could have talked about their children all night – that much they still had in common – she didn't want to. She talked about them enough in the daytime.

The waiter came over with another bottle of wine and uncorked it with a flourish. Laura poured it out between them and raised her glass, smiling across the table at Josie. 'Cheers, darlin', happy birthday,' she said, shiny-faced, hair spilling loose from her French plait.

'Cheers,' everyone chorused.

'Thanks,' Josie mumbled. All of a sudden, she was longing to go home. She'd had enough of feeling special, thanks all the same. She just wanted to be like everyone else again now. Was that so much to ask?

It was a relief to crawl into bed and pull the covers over her head. And then she cried and cried and cried.

She cried because it was her birthday and she had nobody to cuddle up to, arms and legs comfortably tangled together.

She cried because she was alienated from her friends; however nice they'd been about the separation, she was still set apart, different. Not one of them any more.

She cried because her boys were going to grow up without a father figure in the house, making them laugh, teaching them to ride their bikes and catch tennis balls, taking them to the football ... all the things that *her* dad had done for her and Stu.

She cried because she couldn't imagine feeling truly happy ever again. Not properly. She would always feel broken, for the rest of her life.

She cried because Pete didn't love her any more, and she was washed-up at thirty-six, and no one would ever fancy her again, or want to have sex with her.

She cried because she didn't want to have sex with anyone else anyway.

She cried because she was completely trashed and she was going to feel like shit in the morning.

And then she fell asleep.

The memory of her despair came back to her on Saturday as she waited on the platform for the train. Now that she was here though, weekend bag at her feet, return ticket to London stuffed in her pocket, her goodbyes with the boys still ringing in her ears, she felt much better again, thank goodness.

Pete had been surprisingly pleasant when he'd picked the boys up earlier. He'd reached forward impulsively and given her a hug as she'd said goodbye. Josie had stood stiffly in his arms, not knowing what to say, her brain fogged by the scent of him. It felt natural, to have his arms around her, yet wrong too. And the way Sam was looking at them, with that light of hope in his eyes . . .

She had pulled free then, conscious of her son's gaze. No mixed messages, right? Keep it simple.

Pete had stepped back, looking awkward. 'Sorry,' he'd said. 'It's just . . . You look really nice. And I miss you. Sorry, though. Overstepped the line, and . . .'

'No, no, it's OK,' she'd replied, startled. Had he really just said that? 'I . . . I miss you too,' she found herself saying in a low voice.

'Dad, Dad, where are we going? Where are you taking

us?' Toby had shouted out, tugging at Pete's arm, and the moment had gone. But still ... He had said it. They had both said it. 'I miss you.'

What had got into him? What did he *mean*?

She leaned back in her seat once she'd boarded the train. Here she went again, off to London, same journey, different person. Christ, she was altered beyond recognition, Josie thought – inside and out.

She could almost see a mirror image of herself sitting on the next seat, how she'd been back then – gazing excitedly out of the window, pink coat on, looking forward to seeing Nell and Lisa, missing the boys but really pleased to be away on her own too...

She'd had no idea what had been about to hit her. Not the faintest. And imagine if she, her self now, had been able to tap the not-knowing Josie on the shoulder and say, *Hey, guess what? Make the most of this weekend, because it's all going to change, you know. It's all about to go totally pear-shaped, darlin'!*

She wouldn't have believed it, would she? The not-knowing Josie. She'd have wrinkled up her nose and said, *As if!*

And yet today, with Pete ... 'I miss you', he'd said. It kept playing in her head, on a loop. She hadn't expected him to miss her. Surely he wasn't ... Surely he wasn't regretting what he'd done?

Was he?

She realized she was sitting forward in her seat, fists clenched, a tense expression on her face. What would she say if he *did* change his mind now, six weeks on? Could she forgive him and welcome him home?

She stared, unseeing, out of the window as the train rattled through a station. The platform blurred in front of her gaze as she tried to make sense of her feelings. At the bottom of everything there was still a deep, unshake-able sadness that he'd gone. And if he wanted to come back . . .

She shut her eyes. Don't torture yourself. Don't even think about it. So he said he missed her. Big deal. It didn't mean anything. He was probably only being slick. Once a charmer, always a charmer. She shouldn't trust a single thing he said to her again, not now she knew what a liar and cheat he had been.

'A leopard doesn't change his spots,' her mum always pronounced, in that annoyingly sage way of hers. And while it was slightly galling to admit to agreeing with her mum about anything, Josie did on this occasion. Pete had cheated once – well, twice, actually, with Lisa as well – so he was sure to do it again. No. She was well rid of him. She would forget him and move on.

Her mind drifted back to the birthday card from Lisa.

Imagine, again, that same self of hers going up to London those few weeks ago, being told, *Oh yeah, and by the way, Lisa's been stabbing you in the back too.*

She twisted her fingers in her lap as she thought about it. She could hardly believe Lisa had betrayed her like that, even now. And she still didn't really know why, or how it had happened in the first place.

What was it Lisa had written in her card?

I'd love to be able to explain, if you'd give me the chance. If our friendship has ever meant anything to you then please call me, so we can talk. Your friend, Lisa

Josie gazed out of the window. They were rattling through the outskirts of London now, tower blocks looming on the skyline. It was unfair of Lisa to word it like that – 'if our friendship has ever meant anything to you', indeed. Of course it had meant something! For years, the friendship Josie had had with Lisa and Nell had been everything, her whole world. And she'd believed the entire time that Lisa felt the same way too. So for Lisa to then turn around and do what she'd done was just so devastating of her. So unforgivable. How could Lisa even *think* of signing off that way?

I'd love to be able to explain, if you'd give me the chance.

Should she? Could she even bear to see her?

She glanced down at her watch. Two-thirty. She was

earlier than she'd told Stu. And the party wasn't due to start until the evening anyway.

Impulsively she fished her mobile out of her bag and punched in Stu's number.

'Hiya,' she said when he answered. 'Listen, I'm going to be a bit later than I said, is that all right?'

Chapter Seventeen

Josie walked along the road, heart knocking inside her ribcage. Her hand was sweaty as she heaved her bag along, her mouth dry. What was she going to say? And what would *Lisa* say in reply?

Her car was there. The baby-blue Honda, parked neatly outside the tall, elegant house. Of course, that didn't mean anything in London, though. Lisa might well have gone out on the bus somewhere today, caught the tube into town ... She probably wouldn't be in at all. And if she wasn't, then so be it. Fate, and all that.

I'm giving you your chance, Lisa, Josie thought with a shiver, as she walked up to the front door. For one day only. Here I come, ready or not.

Her fingers closed around the black iron loop of the door knocker and she hesitated. Still time to walk away. Still time to change her mind and go off to Stu's. She didn't have to do this ...

She gripped the knocker and banged it against the

door. Then she stood frozen on the step, waiting. Silence. She gave it a few seconds ... tick, tick, tick ... but there was no noise from inside the house, no movement through the frosted glass. She breathed out in relief. Nobody in.

She was glad, actually. She'd tried, hadn't she? Nobody could say she hadn't tried. And now she could walk away, conscience clear ...

There was a shift of light through the glass panels in the door. A pale, ghostly figure loomed up through the hallway, closer, closer. And now Josie could hear the latch turning on the other side of the door.

Oh God. Lisa was in. She was actually in. She was ...

'Josie!'

... She was surprised. In fact, Josie registered dimly, Lisa was clutching at the door jamb, she was so surprised.

Josie cleared her throat. 'Hello,' she said. Her heart was really hammering now. Lisa was standing there like a startled animal, eyes wide, colour draining from her face. She had bare feet and no make-up, and wore a sweet little cotton sundress, and a pair of sunglasses pushed up on her head.

'I was just passing,' Josie said, 'and I thought ...' Her voice petered out. She felt too nervous to speak now. All the brave words of confrontation she'd planned on the train, all the poise and calm she'd hoped for – they had vanished. She pressed her lips together and took a deep breath. Come on. You're here now. Might as well do this. 'Can I come in?'

Lisa nodded dumbly, then seemed to recover herself. 'Of course,' she said, stepping back and pulling the door open. 'I was in the garden, I ... Were you knocking for long? Only I just came in to—'

'No,' Josie said, cutting into her rambling. 'I only knocked once. I just got here.'

Lisa glanced down at Josie's weekend bag but said nothing, merely stood there while Josie walked past her into the hallway. It felt cool and quiet inside. Josie's hands were shaking, and she had to clench them both around the leather handles of the bag to still them. Don't let her see that you're nervous. Don't give her the edge.

'Come in,' Lisa said, leading her along the hallway. 'How come you're in London, anyway? And where are the boys?' She gave Josie a sickly smile over her shoulder as they walked through into the kitchen. 'You look amazing, by the way. So slim! Have you lost weight?'

'Mmm,' Josie replied non-committally. She put her bag down and folded her arms across her chest. She was finding it quite hard to believe that she was actually here, in Lisa's kitchen. The last time she'd been here, she'd been standing on the cold stone tiles in her pyjamas waving a photo of Pete — *that* photo! — and asking why it had been under Lisa's bed. And Lisa had said...

Yeah, yeah, all right. Forget that now. Back to the present.

'Stu's having a party,' Josie said. She was trying her hardest to modulate her voice so that her words came out even and normal-sounding. 'The boys are with Pete.'

There. She'd said it. She'd dropped his name into the conversation.

Lisa lowered her gaze. Good. Quite right, too. Josie could feel her pulse rushing as she stared hard at Lisa's bent head. She could almost hear a ponderous David Attenborough narrative as a voiceover to the scene.

And the attacking female eyes the second female. The second female displays clear signs of submission, so the attacking female...

'We need to talk,' Josie said bluntly. 'That's why I'm here.'

... moves in for the kill.

Lisa's head jerked up, as if it were on a string. She met Josie's eye and nodded, her mouth curled in a sort of grimace of — what? Pain? Fear?

'Do you want something to drink?' she asked. Her voice was artificially bright. 'Fizzy water, or...'

'Yeah, whatever,' Josie said. She didn't want to get

steered off course, going through Lisa's beverage collection.

Lisa opened the fridge door and pulled out a bottle of water. Of course, being Lisa, she also popped out a couple of ice cubes and cut half-slices of lemon too before pouring. *Standards, darling! Even when under attack!*

Josie took the glass. The bubbles were racing to the top of the water, knocking the ice cubes against each other. She took a sip, wondering what was going to happen next.

'Let's go and sit in the garden,' Lisa said. She had taken control of the situation, Josie realized with a jolt. How come *Lisa* was calling the shots all of a sudden?

The second female leads the attacking female away from her territory where she ...

Where she what? Attacks her right back?

Lisa hadn't waited for a reply, she was already padding across the floor to the back door, glass in hand. Josie followed, her resolve shrinking away. *Come on. She's in the wrong, remember? Moral high ground? She's miles from it. Whereas I ... I'm right at the highest point of the moral high ground. And we both know it.*

Lisa's garden was long and rectangular, edged with mature trees. The sun streamed through them, casting a dappled light on the small patio area at the back of the house. A round mosaic table and chairs were set up, sheltered by a low stone wall. Lisa sat down at the table and looked at Josie expectantly. 'Have a seat,' she said.

Josie sat. This was all so very civil of them, she couldn't help thinking. All so controlled, so English. Afternoon tea – all right, afternoon *sparkling water* – on the patio, no slapping, no shouting. Well – not yet, anyway.

She cleared her throat, feeling as if she ought to lead the conversation, reclaim a bit of control. 'You said in the birthday card you sent that you wanted to explain,' she began. There. Gauntlet thrown. Over to you, Lise.

Lisa nodded. She took a long slug of water, dark eyes upon Josie. If she felt under pressure at all, she wasn't letting it show. How extremely irritating, Josie thought, crossing her legs under the table and shifting uncomfortably on the slatted metal seat.

'I do want to explain,' she replied after a moment. She pushed her hair back behind her ears, making a ponytail of it with her hand and twisting it around. 'Where do you want me to begin?'

Josie sighed impatiently. 'Just ... I don't care,' she replied, batting a hand through the air. 'Wherever you want. It was you who said you wanted to talk. "If you ever valued our friendship", you said. And I did. So that's why I came. So just tell me.'

Lisa nodded, releasing her hair again. It fell in a thick, shining mass around her shoulders, and Josie felt her fingers tighten on her glass. It was a mistake to come here, she thought. A mistake. If Lisa thought she could wriggle out of this one, then . . .

'It started not long after the boys were born,' Lisa said, looking down at the table.

Josie's stomach lurched and suddenly she wasn't sure she wanted to know after all. 'What a cliché,' she said coldly to cover up her feelings. 'I should have guessed.'

Lisa merely nodded, as if agreeing. She traced a finger around the line of tiles on the table, and Josie felt herself staring at the polished red nail as if it were a hypnotist's chain. 'You were knackered, of course, and wrapped up in the boys,' Lisa went on, 'and . . .'

'How inconsiderate of me,' Josie said. She could feel the rage creeping through her, the pressure building now that they were finally discussing this. It had been restrained inside her the whole time since Lisa had opened the front door, wide-eyed, but now she could feel the anger building like a rising tide. 'What, so you offered Pete a shoulder to cry on, and . . . ?'

'Josie, please,' Lisa said. 'I'm trying to tell you.' Josie fell silent, and there was a small pause before she pressed on. 'I bumped into Pete when he was in London for a meeting with one of the guys one day. It was purely chance. Nothing premeditated. He was looking a bit tired, and . . .'

Josie clenched her fists under the table. *Oh, my heart bleeds*, she wanted to say sarcastically. *Poor, tired Pete — let Lisa make it all better for you!*

'He was looking tired, so I asked if he was OK, and how it was all going at home,' Lisa went on, with a wary look at Josie. 'And he asked if I fancied going for a drink, because he was worried about you and wanted to talk to me about you.'

Josie snorted. 'So worried about me that he jumped into bed with *you*,' she said scornfully. 'What a nice little story.'

Lisa sipped her water. 'It wasn't like that,' she said. 'Nothing happened that evening. Nothing at all. We just talked, and he went back to you, and I came home. Then, a week or so later, he sent me an email saying he was going to be up in London again, and did I want to have lunch sometime. So we went for lunch. And then one thing led to another . . .'

Josie glared at her. 'One thing led to another? For fuck's sake! How does going for lunch with your friend's husband lead to having an affair with him? How does that happen?'

'I—' Lisa started to say, but Josie was already on her

feet. Her chair squawked as she pushed it back, hands shaking.

'I thought I wanted to know,' she said, stalking away. 'But I was wrong. I don't. It just makes it even worse.' Then something clicked in her mind and she stopped, swivelling around again to face Lisa. 'Hold on,' she said slowly. 'I thought that was when you started seeing *Guy*, when the boys were babies. I thought that was when you fell in love, had your big, this-is-it romance?'

Lisa's face was pale, and her eyes glistened with tears. She nodded, as if she were afraid to speak. 'Yes,' she said after a moment. 'Yes, that's right.' She bit her lip. 'Guy was Pete. It was a kind of code, so that I could say, "I'm in love with this guy," and nobody would know . . .' Her voice trailed away to a whisper. 'It was kind of a joke.'

Josie felt as if she'd been slapped. 'A joke? A *joke?*' she said, her voice hollow. 'Well, excuse me if I don't wet myself laughing.' She clenched her fists. 'Excuse me if I don't find that very funny!'

'Josie, please – let me explain,' Lisa said. 'Please!' She started talking quickly, before Josie could get away. 'Yes, I lost the plot a bit. I was infatuated, crazy about him. And no, I didn't stop to think about you. And I'm sorry. That was selfish of me, and—'

'I'll say,' Josie spat. She stood there, glaring at Lisa, despising her.

'And stupid of me, too. I've been a crap friend, I betrayed your trust, I crossed the line,' Lisa said. 'And I'm so sorry for that. I know you'll never forgive me, and I don't blame you.' She shook her head. 'I don't expect you to forgive me.'

Silence hung between them. A faint breeze rustled the leaves in the trees, and Josie rubbed her bare arms.

'So ... how did it end?' she asked. 'Who dumped who?' She licked her lips while she waited for Lisa to reply, feeling vulnerable. She really wanted Lisa to tell her that Pete had ditched her. Pete had seen sense, had realized he loved Josie more. It mattered.

'It was complicated,' Lisa said. She hid her face in her hands for a moment, before looking up again at Josie. 'Sit down, won't you?' she asked. 'I'd really like to tell you. I've never actually told another person what happened, and it's kind of...'

Josie hovered, her angry feelings wrestling with her curiosity. Sod it, she was here now, she might as well listen. If she walked away without knowing how the story ended, she'd forever be wondering. She sat down rather ungraciously, and picked up her glass of water, draining it in a single gulp. She clattered it back down on the table and faced Lisa, a hard look on her face.

Lisa took a deep breath. 'I was always more into the relationship than Pete,' she started baldly. 'I know that now – well, I suppose I knew it then, too. He always held back – because of you, I'm sure. Whereas I...' She shut her eyes briefly, as if it pained her, then looked Josie full in the face. 'Well, I was mad about him. Sorry. I know it must sound awful. Such a bitch, I know, for me to fall in love with your husband like that, but...'

Josie said nothing.

'...I did. It was like I was blind to the fact that you were one of my best friends; I just couldn't see past my infatuation to get a grip on the situation.' She sighed. 'Sounds pathetic, I know, but there you go. And no, before you ask, it was nothing to do with what happened with Nick.' Her voice rose half an octave. 'Nothing at all. It wasn't revenge or anything like that. It was separate. Anyway. Sorry. I didn't mean to drag this out. I...' She raked a hand through her hair, and sighed again. 'The long and the short of it was, I got pregnant.'

Josie gasped in surprise. 'Oh God,' she said. Her mouth fell open. 'So ... So what happened?'

Lisa gave a rueful smile. 'He didn't want to know, is what happened. He was furious, actually. Said he already had two kids, didn't want a third—'

'Oh, no!' Josie felt winded. Had Pete really been so harsh?

'Oh yes.' Lisa stared into the middle distance. 'And that was it – I never saw him again. Well, apart from Bev's wedding last year, when you were there too. Didn't you wonder why I kept avoiding you the whole time?'

Josie's hand flew up to her mouth. 'Well, I...' She paused, not able to move on from Lisa's pregnancy. 'So did Pete ditch you, just like that?'

'Just like that.'

There was a moment of silence. A cabbage-white butterfly zigzagged across the garden, ghostly wings fluttering.

'Fuck,' Josie said, looking hard at Lisa. 'What a bastard.'

Lisa traced a pattern on the table. She didn't raise her eyes. 'Absolutely,' she agreed.

'So, what happened? With the baby?' It was hard to take everything in. To think that all this had happened without her knowing about it! There she'd been, staggering through the zombie months of early motherhood, haggard and irritable, and meanwhile, in another part of the world, there had been this relationship, the sex, conception ... the baby?

Lisa bit her lip. 'She died,' she said flatly. She looked up, and Josie could read the pain in her eyes.

'Oh, no,' Josie said. She reached over the table and took Lisa's hand. 'Oh, Lisa.'

'Despite everything, Pete being such a shit, me brokenhearted, you in the dark, despite all of that, I decided to keep the baby,' she said. There was a heaviness in her voice. 'I know it probably sounds mad to you: me, the career woman, considering dropping it all to become a single mum, but that's the decision I made.'

'God,' Josie said. 'I'm so—'

Lisa shook her head. 'Don't. This is really hard to say. Just let me say it.'

Josie nodded. 'Sorry. OK.'

'It was like, I wasn't sure if I would ever fall in love again,' she went on. 'I wasn't sure if I would ever have the chance to be pregnant again, without getting a donor or ... well, you know. Turkey-baster job and all that. And I wanted a child. I really did.' She sighed. 'Still do, but ... Anyway. I didn't tell anyone about the pregnancy. It was easy enough to keep secret at first. By the time I started showing, it was winter and I could cover up the bump with layers and ... Well, you know. And even though I was scared about doing it all on my own – Pete had made it absolutely clear he wanted nothing to do with the baby – I'd made my mind up. I'm a tough person, I can do stuff without a man around.' She took a deep breath. 'And then, when I was twenty-five weeks pregnant, she died. Stillbirth. Just one of those things, they said to me.' A tear rolled down her cheek. 'Sometimes it happens, they said. Something wrong with the placenta. We don't know why.'

'Oh, Lisa,' Josie said again, gripping her hand. 'Oh, God, I'm so—'

'I had to go through the birth and everything,' Lisa said tonelessly. 'They induced me to bring on the labour, and I was all on my own. Told work I'd been rushed in to have my appendix out, when all the time I was delivering my dead baby, all on my own. Delivering Rose.'

'*Rose?*' Josie echoed. A shiver went down her back, even though it was hot and airless in the garden.

'That's what I called her,' Lisa said. 'It was my nan's name.' Her gaze rested on the rose bush nearby, which was covered in fragrant white velvety blooms. 'I always wanted a daughter,' she said. Another tear rolled down her cheek, and splashed on the table. She turned back to look at Josie, her mouth trembling. 'So you see, I was punished for it. I was punished for what I did with your husband. And while you may hate me for the rest of our lives, I've paid the price. I lost my baby. I lost my little girl.'

Josie pushed herself off her chair and threw her arms around Lisa. 'Sweetheart,' she murmured into Lisa's shiny hair. 'How horrible. How awful.'

'And I'm so ... so sorry,' Lisa sobbed brokenly. 'I'm so sorry, Josie.'

'It's all right,' Josie soothed her. 'It's all right.'

*

Lisa cried and cried. And as Josie sat there, arms around her friend's shaking back, she could feel the hard lump of anger and bitterness dissolving, draining away. Lisa was right: she'd been punished enough.

After a few minutes Josie rummaged in her bag for a tissue. Four years of looking after the boys meant she was never without one. 'Here,' she said, passing it over.

'Thanks,' Lisa said, wiping her eyes. 'Thanks for letting me say that. I've kept it in for such a long time.'

Josie shrugged awkwardly. 'It's all right. I'm just sorry you've had such a horrible time,' she said. 'And that you had to go through it alone. That must have been really tough. I can't imagine how tough it must have been.'

Lisa blew her nose. 'It was awful,' she said quietly.

'What a shitty thing for Pete to do,' Josie said. She sat back down. 'You know, when I came here, I hated your guts. I was thinking to myself on the train, What can she possibly say that will change the way I feel about her? But you just said it.' She turned her glass around on the table, making a churring noise on the tiles. 'Now I don't know what to feel. Sorry for you, I suppose. And sad for Rose. She would have been a half-sister to the boys. Although . . .' She raised her eyes. 'Although I guess you'd never have told me that, right?'

Lisa gave a small smile. 'No.' She glanced again at the

roses by her side. 'I planted those when she ... After she ...'

Instinctively Josie got to her feet and went over to the flowers. She crouched on her haunches and carefully pulled one of the rose heads towards her, burying her nose in its soft petals. And then her eyes swam with tears, as its perfume caught in her nose, and she thought about her own phantom Rose, the daughter that she too had wished for.

'Are you all right? This must be a bit of a head-fuck,' Lisa said from behind her. 'I'm sorry to spring all of this on you, but ...'

Josie shook her head. She didn't want to start telling Lisa about her Rose. It was too private, too painful. 'I'm all right,' she said. She got to her feet, wiping the tears away with the back of her hand. 'I'd better go to Stu's – although I don't exactly feel in a party mood now.'

'I'll call you a taxi, shall I?' Lisa asked. 'Or do you want to stay a bit longer? You're welcome to.'

The smell of the roses was catching in the back of Josie's throat; it was making her gag now. She stepped away from them, towards Lisa's back door. Suddenly the garden felt too bright; the sunlight hurt her eyes. 'Could I have a coffee, do you think?' she asked.

'Course,' Lisa said, standing up and going inside.

Josie followed, turning one last time to look at the roses. 'Bye, Rose,' she whispered under her breath.

Josie hugged Lisa when the cab arrived. It was almost six o'clock now, and she'd phoned Stu to let him know she was on the way at last. 'I had a bit of catching-up to do,' she'd told him.

'No worries,' he'd said. Punctuality was never an issue for Stu. 'See you when we see you.'

Now she was on Lisa's doorstep saying goodbye, with a taxi purring at the kerbside. 'I'm really glad I came,' she said truthfully, heaving her bag on to her shoulder. 'And I'm glad you told me all of that.'

'Me too,' Lisa said. She looked wan and pale in the sunlight, Josie thought, giving her hand a last squeeze.

'And I kind of understand,' Josie said after a moment. She hesitated. 'Sure you don't fancy coming with me to Stu's?'

Lisa shook her head. 'Not tonight,' she said. 'But maybe if you're in London again, some other time . . . ?'

Josie nodded. 'That would be good,' she said. 'Bye, Lisa.'

'Bye,' Lisa said. 'Take care. And . . . thanks.'

Josie slid on to the back seat of the taxi as the driver put it into first and drove away. Lisa waved from her doorway and then they were gone, winding through the Islington streets towards the river. Josie shut her eyes, feeling red-faced from too much sun. What an afternoon. What a revelation. It had all been so much bigger than she'd anticipated. So much sadder, more intense. She could hardly bring herself to think about how awful it must have been for Lisa to go through alone.

Poor Rose, as well. At twenty-five weeks, she'd still have been so small. How tragic, how unbearable that Rose, *Pete's* Rose, had been so briefly alive, kicking and somersaulting in her watery red world. Until one day . . . what? What had gone wrong? Her heart would have stopped, its tiny drumbeat falling still. Her brain would have closed down. Her miniature arms and legs would have stopped flailing, like a clockwork toy winding down. But why had this been allowed to happen? Why? It was so unjust!

Josie shivered and rubbed her arms, feeling goose-pimply. The death of a child, even an unborn one, surely had to be the worst possible thing, too painful even to think about. She had dreaded it herself when she'd been pregnant with the boys, become frantic if she hadn't felt them tumble and squirm every day in her belly. And then to have brought them into the world, both alive and healthy . . . it had felt monumental. Her greatest achievement, without doubt.

She stared out of the window. Love, life, death, sex. It went on and on, everywhere, all around the world. Right now, while she was sitting in the back of this taxi, babies were yelling their first yells in every corner of the globe, while others whimpered their last breaths.

She found herself thinking about Rob, in Africa. Rob, fixing ambulances or mending a piece of medical kit that might just save a baby's life in Zambia. It put things in perspective, Josie thought, as the taxi crawled over London Bridge, but it didn't make her feel any better.

Stu's flat was a total bachelor pad, with its floor-to-ceiling windows, white walls, fancy gadgets and sprawling sofa. Melanie hadn't actually moved in, but had definitely made her presence felt, Josie decided with a smile, as Stu showed her in. There were a couple of new framed black and white photographs on the living-room wall that were far too tasteful to have been chosen by Stu, a pile of paperbacks on one of the shelves (including some fat, well-thumbed Marian Keyes novels), and a colourful kilim on the floor.

The flat also had a tiny balcony – just room for a small patio table and a few chairs – but it overlooked the river, so gave an illusion of space. Sitting there on the rickety wooden chair, feet propped up on the edge of the balcony, mug in her hands, Josie gazed down at the Thames as it rolled along in front of her, sunlight twinkling off the water, while Stu went to answer the phone. She'd known this stretch of the river quite well once upon a time. The boys had been born in a hospital less than a mile away. She and Pete had rented a scuzzy flat in Elephant and Castle down the road. And she'd worked for a while as a junior designer for one of the free London magazines a short walk along the riverbank.

She'd liked working there. She'd just started seeing Pete, and he'd had a job not far away, in Oval, so she'd often hop on a number 8 bus to meet him for lunch. And oh, the lust that had shot through them both in those days! The knee-tremblers they'd had, panting and giggling, in all sorts of places – down alleyways, in that deserted churchyard, once even in the park, behind the derelict toilet block. They'd been mad for each other. She could still remember going back to the office without her knickers on when Pete had flung them off into the undergrowth somewhere and she hadn't been able to find them again. Could still remember the way she'd sat so primly on the bus back to work, knees tight together, hoping there wasn't a wet patch on her skirt . . .

Still. That was a long time ago. She wondered if Pete ever thought back to those heady days. Surely not. He had a whole new set of sexual exploits to enjoy right now, after all. Why would he bother harking back to ancient history?

She shifted uncomfortably on her chair as she remembered what Lisa had said about him. The way he'd treated her, dropping her like a stone when she'd told him about the baby ... It was breathtaking.

She'd always thought Pete was fundamentally a kind person, a good guy, yet he'd behaved so callously. And after ditching Lisa he'd gone on to start things up with Sabine. Not so very kind after all, then.

'Everything OK?' Stu came back to the balcony at that moment, his expression quizzical.

Josie realized she was frowning, and tried to snap her features into a smile. 'Fine,' she said. She took another slurp of tea, and tried to push both Pete and Lisa out of her head. 'I'm fine.'

It was a relief to strip her clothes off and get into the shower cubicle a little while later. She tipped her head back, letting the water sluice over her face, slicking back her hair to rinse out all the London grime. Then she put her hands over her face and leaned against the wet tiled wall, the hot hiss of spray on her body. It was a refuge, this small steamy space, but she knew before long she'd have to slap on her party face. God. She was so not in the mood. She was *so* not up for this.

The minutes passed. She shampooed her hair, scrubbed her pits and bits. She shut her eyes and stood there, motionless under the downpour as it needled her skin. And then, with a sigh, she switched off the water and stepped through the steam to wrap herself in towels. Her body was warm and clean. Her hair smelled good. Retreat over. Time to look happy.

She went through the motions as best as she could, blow-drying her hair and styling it, putting on her face, squirting perfume on her neck. She borrowed a clingy, flattering wrap-dress of Melanie's ('God, you cow, it looks much better on you than me,' Melanie said, wrinkling her nose and pretending to be miffed), and then with a heavy heart proceeded to eat Stu's food, and drink Stu's drink, and schmooze with Stu's mates.

She caught up with Bridget and Eve, two women she'd known since sixth form.

She managed a laugh with Melanie about Stu's crap taste in music. (Melanie was lovely! Definitely the nicest girlfriend Stu had ever had.)

She fended off slimy Jake's wandering hands, and batted away creepy Trev's compliments.

She even flirted mildly with someone called Andy, knowing full well it would come to nothing.

But the whole time she was aching inside for poor dead Rose.

Chapter Eighteen

'It's all back on!'

Nell's voice was breathless down the phone. 'What is?' Josie asked, rubbing her right temple gingerly. It was the morning after the night before – OK, technically it was the early afternoon after the night before – and she was back home, feeling dog-rough with a hangover.

'Me and Gareth. We're sorted. One hundred per cent. Everything's hunky-dory. In fact...' She paused a little self-consciously. 'In fact, I've got an announcement to make.'

Josie sat up at once, from where she'd been slumped immobile on the sofa. '*What?*' she cried, wincing as the blood rushed to her head. An announcement? Surely Nell wasn't going to say what Josie thought she was going to say? 'You're getting...?'

Nell laughed. 'I *knew* you'd think that. No, we're not getting married or engaged or up the duff. It's *me*, remember. But we *are* going travelling together. Central

America, in January.' Josie could hear her smiling. 'Now tell me *that's* not commitment.'

'That's commitment,' Josie said, smiling too, despite the ringing headache she'd had all morning. 'Oh, Nell – that's brilliant news. That's perfect.'

'I know,' Nell went on. 'Him dumping me made me really think about our relationship. How much I was going to miss him. It was like a total reality check.' She paused. 'And I'm dead grateful to you and Rob for kicking my arse in the first place, you know. I wouldn't have gone back for our summit talks if it hadn't been for you two. So cheers. You were a total friend in need – in fact, you were a proper Granny McFadden yourself.'

'You don't have to thank me,' Josie told her. 'I'm just glad things have worked out all right.' She tried to stifle a yawn as she lay back down on the sofa. God, she was knackered. She hadn't even seen Stu's spare bed until well after three this morning. 'And it's Nanny McPhee, by the way.'

'Whatever, guardian angel, fairy godmother. Same difference. How about you, anyway? What's happening in your life?'

'Well, I've just got back from London, actually,' Josie replied. 'Went to a party at my brother's.'

'Ooh!' She could almost hear Nell raising her eyebrows. 'Nice one.' Her voice was rich with approval. *The old maid, out on the lash again! Who would have thought?* 'And? Any disgraceful behaviour to report?'

'No. And no, I haven't used one of those condoms yet either, before you ask.' She shut her eyes suddenly, remembering the conversation she'd had with flirty Andy the night before. She'd been in the kitchen, leaning against the fridge, twiddling a tendril of hair round and round her finger. God, she must have looked so coy and girly. Shame she'd blown him out as soon as he tried to sneak a hand around her arse. 'But ... D'you know what, I'm really glad I went. I actually felt *attractive* again. I've lost loads of weight since Pete dumped me, and I've obviously turned into a bit of a babe.' She giggled. 'Three blokes tried to chat me up. Three!'

'Course they did. I'm surprised it wasn't thirty,' Nell said. 'I bet they were all after you in there, darlin'. So ... Any lookers, then?'

'We-e-ell ...' Josie laughed. 'There was this one guy, Andy, who was really nice. But no, nothing happened. I was in a bit of a funny mood, to be honest. And even though I enjoyed all the chatting-up and attention, I wasn't up for anything else. It was just ...' She paused, trying to get the right words. 'It was just nice to have a break from normal life. Time off from Misery Central, I mean.' She yawned again and stretched out her legs. 'And now I'm back, and ...'

'Back at Misery Central?'

Josie was silent for a moment, reflecting. 'No, I wouldn't say that. I don't feel miserable today. Just a bit rough.' She paused, wondering whether or not to tell Nell about Lisa. Not, she decided. It was Lisa's story, not hers.

'Well, that's all right. At least with a hangover you know you'll be OK by tomorrow,' Nell said comfortingly. 'Trust me. I'm an expert on these matters. But anyway, I won't keep you if you're suffering. I was just ringing to tell you our news, and ask you to our leaving do. We're going to have a bash in London before we go away. A big party, with all our mates and family...'

'Sounds a bit like a wedding to me,' Josie teased. 'Sure you're not tempted to ask a registrar along too?'

Nell chuckled good-naturedly. 'Leave it out, you're as bad as Gareth,' she said. 'Actually, that's a point. Talking of weddings and sparring guests and all that – you just reminded me. How would you feel about Lisa coming? Because obviously, you two are both my mates, but I don't want any aggro or anyone feeling awkward. So if it's going to be too difficult, I can always catch up with her separately – not invite her, I mean.'

Josie gazed out of the window. From her position on the sofa she could see into the back garden, where her own roses were bobbing their heads in a breeze. For an instant she felt a tearing sadness inside again, and turned her head away quickly, not wanting to look at them. 'Actually, it's funny you should mention Lisa,' she said, trying to sound casual about it. 'Because I saw her yesterday, and we've sorted things out. So don't worry about any sparring or aggro. We're all right, me and Lisa, now.'

'God. Really? Wow. What did she say?'

Josie hesitated. 'It's kind of private,' she said at last. 'But things are OK, anyway. Let's just leave it at that.'

'OK,' Nell replied. 'Sorry – I didn't mean to sound nosy—'

'Course not,' Josie said, smiling. 'You?'

'All right, so I *was* being nosy, but ... Well, I'm glad you've sorted things out. So mature and grown-up, dahling!'

'That's me,' Josie agreed. Her gaze drifted to the African postcards on the mantelpiece and she seized on them as a good means to change the subject. 'Have you heard from Rob lately?'

'Yeah, we've been emailing. He asked about you, said he hadn't heard from you and were you all right?'

Josie nodded, even though Nell couldn't see her. 'Tell him I'm fine,' she replied. 'In fact, I'll tell him myself. I've been meaning to write back to him – top of the To Do list.'

'Oh good.' Nell paused. 'Because I think he'd really like to hear from you. He's always had a bit of a thing for you, and . . .'

'Nell!'

'And he'd kill me for saying as much to you, but—'

'Nell!'

'I think he—'

'Nell, shut up!' Josie said quickly. 'Just . . . don't. Let me get things straight with Pete first. I can't think about anything else right now, OK?'

'O-k-a-a-a-y,' Nell replied. She sounded like one of the boys did when they'd been told off. 'Better go anyway. Speak to you soon, yeah?'

'Speak to you soon, Nell. Bye.'

Josie was asleep when Pete arrived with the boys. The knocking at the door filtered into her dream, and she struggled to surface. She'd been in Africa, riding an elephant with slimy Jake from the party and . . . No. No, she wasn't. She was in her own living room, with dribble down the side of her face, and bed-head hair. She tidied herself up quickly and went to answer the door. The boys were shouting to her through the letterbox and she was suddenly desperate to see them again. Then she was struck by a pang of guilt at hardly having thought about them at all while she'd been away. Slack mother! Dreadful mother!

'Mummy!'

'Mum!'

'Hello, you two, had a good time?' She hugged them to her, her twin bouncing puppies of boys, kissing them, and almost falling over in the enthusiasm of their embraces.

She heaved them up, one in each arm – God, they were getting so big! – and straightened to look at Pete. 'Have they been all right? Behaved themselves?'

Pete nodded, smiling at her. 'We've had a great time,' he said. 'Haven't we, boys? Football in the park . . .'

'And ice creams!' Toby put in.

'And we took the bikes out, too, didn't we?'

'And guess what? I had a go without my stabulizers,' Sam said proudly.

'We *both* did,' Toby corrected him. 'We both did it without our stabrilizers.'

'Well done! Without your *stabilizers*! Wow,' Josie said, smiling at each of them in turn. They both seemed really happy, full of it. 'Thanks, Pete,' she added, in a more formal tone.

'Any time,' he said. 'How about you, was it a good night?'

Josie was slightly taken aback. She'd been expecting to whip straight into the usual polite goodbye, close-the-door, sigh-of-relief routine. They hadn't exactly been *doing* conversation, she and Pete, apart from the brief handover chat each time they exchanged the boys. 'Um ... yeah,' she replied. 'Yes, it *was* good, actually, thanks.'

'So, er, what did you get up to?' he asked.

She frowned. 'What did I get up to?' she echoed. Why was he asking? 'Well...'

Toby, yanking at Pete's T-shirt, interrupted. 'Dad, Dad, come and see our room. You know I told you about the drawing I did of the T-Rexes fighting, and all the blood? Mum put it on the wall for me. Come and see!'

Pete looked questioningly at Josie, and she shrugged. 'Fine by me,' she said.

She stood there as Pete kicked off his shoes in the hall – the way he'd done every evening, once upon a time – and followed Toby up the stairs. And there was Sam, running after them to catch up, slipping a hand into his dad's. It was almost as if nothing had ever gone wrong.

She glanced down at her own hand, bare of its wedding ring. *Almost.*

She paused in the hallway, unsure of what to do. What was the protocol? She hadn't a clue. She shut the front door, thinking hard. 'Want a coffee?' she called up the stairs after a moment. Why not? It would be nice for the boys to have their dad here, on their own turf, again. Hopefully it would give them some extra security, demonstrate that hey, Mum and Dad could still be pleasant to each other, even if they hated each other really.

She paused, her hand on the banister, then corrected herself. Well, not 'hated'. She didn't *hate* him. She wasn't really sure what she felt about him any more.

His voice floated down. 'Please!'

'Can we have biscuits?' Toby bellowed.

She found herself smiling as she went into the kitchen, put on the kettle and took out two mugs – Pete's favourite Arsenal one still lived in the cupboard – and poured some juice into cups for the boys. Two mugs, two cups and a packet of biscuits. It was all so familiar, yet so very peculiar at the same time.

She took her time with the coffees as they tramped into the kitchen moments later, Toby, Sam and Pete. She deliberately kept her back to the table, trying to pretend it wasn't a big deal. Really, though, her cheeks were burning. And when Pete sat down in his old place, head of the table, she pressed her lips together very hard so as not to smile too obviously.

Oh, it was nice to have him sitting there again, back in his place. She could hardly look at him, she felt so stupidly pleased. It was ridiculous, she knew. Daft. He was only staying for a *coffee*. But the boys were loving it, having him here at home again. They went around the kitchen, pointing out all the pictures they'd done at playgroup, their bean shoots that were growing crazily on the windowsill, the photos that she'd taken of them in Devon. Josie watched. It was enough to take her hangover right away, like magic.

Then she thought about Rose, and what Lisa had told her, and stiffened. Hardened herself to him all over again.

She put his coffee on the table without looking at him. Then she stood back against the work surface with her own drink, unable to join them at the table. I can't just pretend nothing's happened, she thought. I can't just switch into Happy Families, play along with this.

She could feel his eyes upon her and made a point of looking up at the wall clock. 'Is that the time?' she said coldly.

To: Rob
From: Josie
Date: 18 July
Subject: Hello

Dear Rob,
How are you? Sorry it's taken me so long to reply.

Josie stared at the computer screen, wondering what to put next. She was feeling guilty for not having written earlier, after Nell's prompt that afternoon. But what should she say?

We're all fine – just about. I'm getting by without Pete and it's gradually becoming easier, but I still have my down days where I feel really sad about it.

She stopped typing and popped a cherry into her mouth from the bag next to her, chewing it thoughtfully as she read back her words. That was a bit heavy, wasn't it? Rob wasn't going to want to read that sort of thing while he was away. Her finger searched for the Delete button, then she hesitated. Maybe it was better to bash out how she felt now, then she could edit it afterwards, before sending it. It might be quite cathartic.

She nodded to herself – decision made – and began typing again.

I actually had 24 hours on my own this weekend for the first time since me and Pete split. Beforehand, I kept swinging between panicky (Toby has been ill recently, in hospital, and Pete was a bit useless when it happened, to be honest) and this sort of exhilaration, I

suppose, at doing something on my own again. Stu, my brother, was having a party, that's why I went, but on the spur of the moment I decided to drop in and see Lisa. Remember her?

She paused, wondering how Lisa had been since they'd said goodbye on Saturday, then more words spilled on to the screen.

Well, anyway, she told me some awful stuff. She had an affair with Pete, you see, which I discovered just before he walked out. I'm trying not to think about how many others there might have been that I didn't know about. But Lisa actually fell for him, seriously involved, huge love etc. On her side, anyway, she was quick to stress. I've no idea how Pete felt. Probably played along with it, to get his end away.

She bit into another cherry, pained at the idea. It hurt, analysing their affair like this, in hindsight, when at the time she'd been blissfully ignorant.

It all went into meltdown when Lisa found out she was pregnant – at which point Pete promptly did a bunk. I hate thinking of him doing that to her. So cowardly and crap. Even worse, Lisa decided to keep the baby, but had a stillbirth. She had to go through the whole thing all on her own.

So now my feelings are all mixed up. I don't hate her any more – well, a bit, I suppose, for being weak enough to go off with my husband, but more than that, I feel so desperately sorry for her. And I feel sorry for myself, too – you see, when Pete walked out on me, we'd been trying for another baby. I got a bit obsessed about it actually, had it all planned out, that I was going to have this little daughter, Rose. We'd tried and tried, but it just wasn't happening.

The slap in the face is that that's what Lisa called *her* daughter, the one who died. So Pete got to have a Rose after all, even though he doesn't know about her. And I

Josie sniffed and wiped her eyes. This was a mistake. She shouldn't have started this now, not when she was so hungover.

She moved the mouse to the Save Draft button, blowing her nose, and clicked, thinking absent-mindedly about taking a bath and getting an early night.

Then she froze in horror at the page that popped up on screen:

Your message has been sent. Add this name to your contacts?

She stared at the words, as if her brain was tricking her. Your message has been *sent*? How had that just . . . ?

She slapped a hand to her forehead and groaned. Oh shit. She must have clicked on the Send button, instead of Save Draft. And now that message, all that personal stuff about Lisa, was in Rob's inbox in cyberspace, just waiting for him to click it open and read it. Oh God. Oh *God*! Disaster!

She'd have to try and retract it, beg him not to open it. She really *really* didn't want him to read all that heartfelt rambling. It was too emotional, too much information. He'd be embarrassed – she already was – oh, it was just a complete non-starter.

With shaking fingers she typed a new heading: **READ THIS ONE FIRST!**, and tabbed down to the message area.

Rob – being a complete fuckwit, I have just sent you a message you weren't supposed to see. Please, please, PLEASE don't read it.
    Josie xxx

She clicked the Send button – staring fiercely at the screen all the while – and sat back in her chair.

Your message has been sent. Add this name to your contacts?

God. He was going to think she was a complete nutter now. An utter loop-the-loop. She laughed, despite the awfulness of what she'd just done. Oh, well. She *was* a complete nutter, let's face it.

She ate a couple more cherries, tart and juicy. The pile of stones next to the computer was growing bigger by the minute. Then she started a new message, hoping to redress the balance.

Hi again, Rob
You're going to be so surprised when you check your emails and see three from me, aren't you? Especially when only one of them – this one, I hope – is a proper letter. I'm feeling embarrassed about what a moron you must think I am, but am comforting myself with the thought that, in cyberspace, no one can see you blush.

Anyway! How are you? How are those lions? And how is it all going out there?

We are all right here. Almost into the summer holidays now which means the end of playgroup for the boys . . . sniff! . . . as they'll start school in September. I know already there will be tears, and I don't mean from them. And, with the two of them out of the house all day, I'll have to reluctantly return to the real world and get a job. I quite fancy a career in

She stopped typing and paused to think. She and Pete hadn't had the big money-chat yet but she knew it was coming. Maybe that's why he'd been acting so friendly earlier, because he was building up to telling her she'd have to move out of the house. Perhaps he wanted to sell it, and claw back some of the capital to use as a deposit for a new flat. She had to be prepared. She had to have some kind of defence lined up. But what?

She backspaced over her last half-finished sentence. She didn't know *what* she fancied doing, that was the problem. I've always worked in design, she typed.

But that was when we lived in London, before the boys were born, and I don't want to have to commute there now we're out in the 'burbs. I suppose the sensible thing to do would be to try and take on projects at home, set myself up as a freelance, but I don't really have the contacts any more. Besides, a lot of what gets farmed out these days seems to be web design work, and I don't have much experience of that.

A thought struck her, and she stopped typing. Nothing was stopping her from *learning* some web-design skills now, though. If the boys were out all day from September onwards, she could go on a course, get savvy with the latest software. She felt a rush of excitement at the thought. Why not? It would be a good direction to go in, something she could do from home, work around the boys . . .

Smiling, she put her fingers back on the keyboard. I'm going to look into taking a course, she typed. Why hadn't she thought of this earlier? It would suit her down to the ground. I think it'll be quite fun to be a student once again, even if I won't have the same social life this time around . . .

She finished the email quickly — there, she sounded perfectly normal this time, not bonkers at all — and winged it off. Then she went to a search engine to find herself a suitable part-time course.

This is where it all starts, she told herself happily as the list of results came up. And yes! There was her local college in the listings. *This is how I'm going to get back on my feet.* The boys starting school was the end of a chapter in so many ways, the end of that precious time she'd had with them at home, but it was also a beginning. The beginning of the rest of her life. Maybe even the beginning of her recovery.

To: Josie
From: Rob
Date: 20 July
Subject: Hi

Dear Josie

came the email a few days later.

First up, an apology. Our email access is a bit intermittent here (there is a shared computer at the healthcare centre that I can use but there isn't always an internet connection) and for some reason your emails came through in the wrong order. So I didn't get the 'Read This One First' email until late yesterday, having already read the other two. I'm *so* sorry – on two levels. One, that I (mistakenly) read all those private things you didn't want me to know about. And two, that you had such a horrible time of it with Lisa. It must be a really tough one to get your head around, finding out about the affair, and about Rose too. I wish I could do something to help. When I'm back, we can talk properly, if you want. In the meantime, I'm thinking about you.

It's been pretty full-on here. Zambia is in a desperate state – one in five people is HIV-positive, and TB is rife. Sanitation is really basic where we are, and there's limited electricity. And the roads are just appalling, so it's difficult for the health workers to deliver drugs and other services to the local communities without wrecking their vehicles on a daily basis – which is where I come in. I'm in the workshop most of the time, trying to juggle the meagre equipment there is on woefully limited resources. I've got to say, for the first week, I felt pretty depressed, like, what can I possibly do for these people, when the situation seems beyond repair? But I'm getting on with it. It almost feels like cheating, though, coming here for just six months. Feel a bit guilty, that it's not enough to make a difference.

The people are amazing, falling over themselves to be welcoming and friendly. I'm sharing a house with another volunteer, Michael, who's working as a community nurse. We've both been invited to our manager Grace's house for dinner this weekend – she keeps winding us up that she's going to serve some truly Zambian delicacies for us: caterpillars and locusts. I'm not kidding either.

Have you found yourself a course, then? I think it

sounds a good idea. I've always been partial to student life, probably because I've been putting off that 'proper job' experience for all this time. But I might actually have got something lined up for the New Year – I know, I know, bit unlike me, being sorted and having plans. Anyway, nothing definite yet, am waiting to hear, but January could see a few life changes for me too.

Better go – always worried that the PC here is going to die on me in the middle of a long email. I'll write a proper letter next time, but wanted to email you straight back after reading yours.

Take care of yourself, Josie. Sorry things have been so tough.

Love Rob x

PS Am sending the boys a banknote each – 5,000 kwacha, not worth much – but they've got lion pictures on. Hope they are suitably impressed!

To: Rob
From: Josie
Date: 2 August
Subject: Re: Hi

Dear Rob
Thanks for your email. Hope the caterpillars were nice.

I told the boys about that, and they were all for running out into the garden and trying some! I had to tell them quickly that English caterpillars are different to African ones, and make your willy drop off. I don't think they believed me, but they weren't taking any chances all the same.

Sorry it's taken me a while to reply. We're in a heat haze here at the moment, and it's all I can do to lie on the sofa eating broad beans from the pod once the boys are in bed. The raspberries are in the shops, too – proper seasonal English ones, I mean, not ones freighted in from New Zealand or wherever. Sorry. Shouldn't go on about yummy English summer food, should I, when you're having to make do with caterpillars and locusts?

I've actually got loads to tell you! I've got a job! Don't laugh, it's nothing glamorous, and I won't be power-dressing or carrying a BlackBerry any time soon. But I've been helping out at the boys' playgroup recently, and a job came up there so I thought, Why not, might as well. It's a lovely place, and it fits in perfectly with the boys' school hours. I know it's not much. Pete actually asked why the hell I wanted to work *there*, and wasn't it a bit beneath me, but I'm not doing it for the money, or to look good on my CV. I'm doing it because I like being there. Plus, I've got to get some money in from somewhere. I can't ask Pete to subsidize us for ever. (More to the point, I don't want him to.)

Second life change – I found a web-design course and have got a place. It's been so long since I've applied for anything like that, I was half expecting a knock-back – *What, you? On our course? We don't accept house-wives, thanks very much, darlin'!* – but the fools have given me a place. I'm a bit excited, actually.

Third life change – for the boys, really, not me. They've left playgroup and are in a weird pre-school limbo. They're excited, but I think it's a bit overwhelming, too. We went in to meet the teacher and look around the classroom before the summer term broke up, and I couldn't help getting all emotional at the thought of my babies in school uniform . . .

Anyway. Sorry. Didn't mean to get all mumsy on you. Not what you wanted to read about, I'm sure!

It sounds amazing, what you're doing – so admirable. And I don't think you should feel guilty, or as if you're cheating, just staying for six months. No way. I think you're

Josie broke off from typing. She was gushing, wasn't she? **I think you're brilliant**, she'd been about to write, but it was a bit much, probably. She backspaced over the last three words.

Take care. Write soon. Love Josie xx

PS The banknotes arrived – thank you. My sons both think you are a hero!

Chapter Nineteen

'So remember to do everything your teacher tells you to, OK? And look after each other, won't you?' Josie sniffed. She couldn't believe that the two boys standing in front of her in brand-new school uniform were actually her sons. The grey trousers, white shirts and navy-blue jumpers seemed to have added three years on to them overnight. 'And be nice to the other children, and—'

'Look, there's Oliver!' Sam said, interrupting. He waved excitedly as Annette and Oliver came through the school gates and towards the boys' new classroom.

Josie was outside with a huddle of parents, all dropping their children off for their first morning at school. She was having to try really hard – *really* hard – to keep herself from going all mushy. It was the beginning of September, and the pre-school days were officially over. From here on in, her boys were in the system. Institutionalized. Just two blond heads in a room full of twenty-eight other children. God. It was heartbreaking!

The summer had flown by. She'd taken the boys to the Gower for a week, meeting up for a few days with Nell and Gareth, who seemed blissfully happy. Another time she, Toby and Sam had taken the train to London, doing the London Eye, the Natural History Museum and the Science Museum all in one exhausting day. They'd also spent a few days staying with her parents, which had been more than enough for all concerned.

Thanks to Pete, she'd squeezed in a second child-free weekend, too. This time she'd gone it alone, using the last of her savings to treat herself to a day out in London – visiting the latest Tate Modern exhibition, ambling around Covent Garden, watching the buskers with an extortionately priced sandwich and coffee, and then trying on lots of gorgeous clothes in the boutiques before sighing and returning them all to their hangers. The only treats she'd allowed herself had been a smart folder and some new pens and paper for college. She dithered enjoyably over what she wanted, feeling as if it were she who was going to school for the first time, not the boys.

And now suddenly it was September, and the whole look of her week was changing. Tomorrow, Tuesday, she'd have her first morning's work at the playgroup, and again on Thursday. And from now on Wednesdays and Fridays would be her college days, as she got stuck into her web-design course. It was all so different. So exciting. But she was so going to miss her sons!

Annette came over, immaculately dressed for work in her trouser suit and high-heeled boots, with a pair of dark glasses covering her eyes. 'I've started already,' she whispered to Josie, raising them above her nose so that Josie could see how bloodshot they were from crying. 'I just feel so upset, I can't believe it!'

Josie nodded. 'I know what you mean,' she said, blowing her nose.

Emma appeared then, with Clara and Millie. She looked agitated and out of breath. 'Jose – I've just seen Pete,' she gabbled. 'At the office. He was asking where the reception classroom was.'

'Pete?' Josie echoed. 'What, my Pete?' *My Pete indeed,* she chastised herself, as soon as the words were out of her mouth. He certainly wasn't her Pete any more.

'Yes,' Emma said, just as Josie saw him for herself. There he was, walking straight towards her, a hand up in a wave.

'Daddy! Dad!' the boys shouted, racing over to him. 'Look! This is our school! We're starting school!'

He crouched down and held them to him. Josie could almost see the lump in his throat. 'Just look at you two,' she heard him saying. 'Just look at my schoolboys, all grown up!'

Emma glanced sideways at her. 'Nice of him to turn up,' she said, but it was a question rather than a statement.

'Very nice,' Annette agreed. 'Gary would never dream of being late for his precious job so that he could be here.' She put a hand on Josie's arm. 'You OK?'

'Yes,' Josie replied, swallowing down the enormous lump lodged in her own throat. She put on a smile as Pete walked over, flanked by the boys. 'Hi,' she said. 'I wasn't expecting to see you here.'

'Couldn't miss seeing these two off on their first day,' he said, gazing down at them and ruffling their hair. He looked misty-eyed as he turned back to Josie. 'I can't believe it, can you?'

'No, I—' she started, but then there was a great bustle of excitement from all the children and parents as the classroom door opened and Mrs Archer, the reception teacher, stood there. 'Good morning everyone,' she said. 'Come on in!'

'Well. So that's it.' Josie stood outside the school gate, not quite sure what to do with herself. Annette had gone to work. Emma was off to the supermarket. All the other parents seemed to have dispersed, some dabbing at their eyes, some looking positively jubilant.

Pete nodded. 'I know. I hope they're all right,' he said,

glancing back over his shoulder in the direction of the classroom. 'She seemed nice, though, didn't she, Mrs Archer?'

Josie nodded. 'Yeah,' she said. 'It's weird, isn't it? It's like ... that's it now. Job done. Into the system they go.' She wiped her eyes with a bit of tissue.

Pete rested an arm on the school gate. He didn't seem in a hurry to get to work. 'I found myself thinking about the day they were born last night,' he confessed. 'I'll never forget holding Tobes for the first time, when he was so wrinkly and red ... Remember that funny little sucking thing he used to do with his mouth when he was asleep?'

Josie nodded, feeling choked. She'd been thinking about the births herself last night, as she'd ironed their new school shirts and set their book bags out ready. Because, whatever else had happened since, she and Pete had shared that amazing day when the boys came into the world. They'd been there in the delivery room together, holding hands through it all, meeting their sons for the first magical time. Nobody could take that away. She wiped her eyes again, thinking about it. 'Don't!' she said to Pete. 'You're going to set me off in a minute.'

'Sorry,' he said. There was a pause. 'Fancy a coffee?'

'Haven't you got to get to work?' Josie asked in surprise.

He shook his head. 'I took the morning off,' he told

her. 'What? Why are you looking like that?' he asked, seeing her eyebrows shooting up. 'There was no way I was going to miss seeing them off today, not for anything!'

Josie managed a smile. 'That's ... that's nice,' she said lamely. 'I'm glad you did that.'

'And I've been meaning to say, any time you want me to pick them up from school, just ask. I can be flexible about it if need be.'

She looked hard at him. Part of her was scoffing and saying, *Well, that's all great, but I've sorted it out, thanks. How come you're only just offering this now, when I had to think about it weeks ago, and make arrangements then?*

The other part of her was glad that he cared enough to make the effort. Cared about the boys, of course. And she knew without thinking twice that they'd love him to be waiting for them after school every now and then, to take them to the park, or out to tea.

'That's ... great,' she got out after a moment. 'Thanks. They'd really like that.'

'So ...' He was smiling at her. Properly smiling, in that soft-eyed friendly way she hadn't seen for months. 'How about that coffee then?'

It was only a five-minute walk home from school, but Josie suddenly felt lost for words as she strolled along, Pete by her side. She couldn't think of the last time they'd walked down the street, just the two of them, without the boys there too.

'Seems quiet, just you and me,' she said, for want of anything better to say.

He smiled at her. 'I know, it's weird, isn't it? I keep wondering how they are.'

'Me too,' Josie said, with a pang of missing them.

She jumped as Pete slipped a companionable arm through hers and felt goosepimply, despite the warm, muggy morning. 'I can't quite believe they've gone,' he said.

Josie glanced at him out of the corner of her eye. Peter David Winter, ex-husband. He was wearing a shirt she hadn't seen before, she realized, and wondered if Sabine had bought it for him. It seemed a bit louder than his usual style. A bit younger, somehow. And then she had another pang, but this time because it was Sabine who got to walk along with Pete like this now, not her. Hand in hand, arm in arm . . .

She felt as if she were borrowing Pete, going back for coffee with him. In fact, it almost seemed for a moment as if she were the one Pete was having a fling with, when of course that was miles away from the truth . . .

She sniffed. 'Sorry,' she said quickly. 'I'm all over the place.'

His fingers groped for hers and gave them a squeeze.

'Course you are,' he said affectionately. 'Like you were ever going to be any other way today!'

She laughed. Like she was ever going to be any other way today. Exactly. He knew her inside-out still.

The thought made her feel trembly, and she was glad to be approaching the house; it gave her an excuse to slip her hand out of his and rummage in her handbag for her keys. For some reason, her heart was thumping harder than usual. Or was it all the starting-school emotion that made everything seem magnified?

'So, here's to our boys,' he said, raising his coffee cup in Josie's direction. 'And their first day at school.'

'Cheers,' Josie said, lifting her mug of tea. She and Pete were sitting at right-angles to each other at the kitchen table, the room quiet save for the kitchen clock marking time. As on the walk home, it was odd to be here with Pete, and without the children. She kept expecting one of them to burst in – *Can I have a biscuit? Mum, he hit me!* – but the house was still.

Josie put her cup down, untouched. 'I wonder how they're getting on?' she said again. 'I wonder how long it'll take Mrs Archer to tell them apart.'

Pete smiled. 'It took us long enough, didn't it, when they were born? Remember how we used to get them muddled up all the time as babies?'

Josie was shocked. 'You did, but not me. I always knew them apart.'

He lowered an eyebrow at her in a yeah-right way. 'I don't think so,' he said. 'I distinctly remember you calling them Tam and Soby one evening because——'

'Because I was frazzled, that's all,' Josie laughed. She sipped her tea. 'I always knew who was who.'

'Just me, then,' Pete joked. 'Crap dad, forgetting his own children's names.'

'You're not a crap dad,' Josie said. She found her eyes were drawn to his lips as he drank his coffee. Both of the boys had inherited that mouth, with their wide, easy smiles and . . .

She shook herself suddenly, pulled her gaze away. It wasn't her mouth to look at like that any more, was it? Sabine held the rights over that mouth.

'So, what have you been up to?' she asked, to fill the silence.

Pete didn't seem to have heard. He was leaning on his elbow, chin resting on his palm. 'Do you remember coming home from hospital with them? Both of them crying in their car seats, and both of us almost crying too, by the time we finally made it home?' His eyes were soft. 'It seems so long ago that they were so tiny and helpless and freaked out by the world, yet I can remember it like it was yesterday.'

Josie nodded. 'Me too,' she said. 'Sometimes I'm sitting in the bath and just for a second I think I feel a twitch inside me, like I'm still pregnant and—'

She broke off. Pregnancy had become such a touchy subject with Pete before he walked out. She didn't want to put him on the defensive again.

He was smiling though. 'It was so weird, wasn't it, the way you could see an elbow or foot sticking out of your bump?' he said. 'I can't imagine what it must have felt like.'

'Nice,' Josie said, without thinking. 'So nice.' Her thoughts slid to Rose. Both of the Roses, the real and the imagined.

There was a silence. A mournful feeling stole over Josie. One of these days, Pete might tell Toby and Sam they were going to have a brother or sister, only she, Josie, wouldn't be involved. Wouldn't that be a killer? Wouldn't that be simply—?

'I suppose I'd better make a move,' he said, interrupting her thoughts.

She got to her feet. 'OK,' she replied.

'Nice to see you, Jose,' he said. 'Like this, I mean, us two sitting here again. Maybe—'

She grabbed his cup and took it to the sink, not sure if she was ready to hear a 'maybe' from Pete. 'Yes,' she said. 'Thanks for dropping in.'

*

By mid-week the boys looked done-in, Josie thought sympathetically as she reversed into a parking space in the college car park on Wednesday morning. Sam had grizzled all the way to school earlier on, saying that he didn't want to go, and that he'd learned enough already. Toby was complaining that he wanted to go back to playgroup, and missed Maddie. And then — it had been so awful! — Sam had actually wept at the classroom door, clinging to her, both arms wrapped around her legs. She'd had to unpeel him from her, dry his tears and take him into the classroom. When she'd looked back for a last wave through the window, he had turned away from her as if betrayed, eyes still pink.

She sighed as she pulled on the handbrake. They were still so young to be at school, she couldn't help feeling. Sam struggled to do his shoes up on his own. Neither of them could do up the zip on his coat. They still sometimes needed reminding to go to the loo . . .

Josie switched off the car engine and gathered up her new folder and pens, forgetting about the boys temporarily as her hand touched the lovely smooth writing pad she'd bought. And now here she was, about to re-enter the education system herself. She'd barely thought about it, being so caught up with the boys starting school. Now that she was here, actually in the college car park, ready to go in for her first lesson at 9.30, she found herself having the same jittery feelings as she'd had about the boys. She hoped she liked her teacher. She hoped the rest of the class were nice. What if nobody liked her?

She rolled her eyes at herself in the driver's mirror. Honestly! She was a grown woman, not a four-year-old! Pull yourself together, Josie! she told her reflection.

All the same, she rolled on a red slash of lipstick and tossed her hair so that it fell around her shoulders. She was wearing a confidence-boosting new top and a jangly bracelet with her cropped jeans and flip-flops. She looked good, actually. Still had the vestiges of her Gower tan, and she'd blow-dried her hair rather than scrape it into its usual ponytail. Other students in the classroom wouldn't know that she'd been a housewife for the last four years, would they? The thought gave her a *frisson* of excitement.

She giggled, thinking about *Educating Rita*, one of her favourite films. And there might even be a fanciable teacher into the bargain. What was she waiting for?

'So, how did it go?'

It was early evening, and Nell had phoned for a catching-up session. Josie had been out in the garden when she'd called, in the middle of raking up the grass clippings where she'd mown the lawn. The scent of cut grass followed her through the house as she ran in to grab the receiver.

'It was great,' Josie sighed, settling back on the sofa. 'Really interesting. The teacher's lovely, too – dead funny and artistic. I feel like my brain is buzzing with ideas already.' She smiled, thinking back to the morning. They'd been looking collectively at an assortment of websites, discussing the merits and flaws of each design. Then, in the afternoon, the teacher had put them in small groups and they'd spent some time researching different subject areas, and comparing website styles within each subject. Josie's group had been looking at music sites, and she'd been amazed at the variety there was out there, ranging from the most amateurish to the slick, big-budget sites, packed with different features.

'Cool,' Nell said. 'And what are your classmates like? Any friend material in there?'

Josie laughed. 'You sound like me, haranguing the boys after school,' she said. 'Well, the people in my group were really nice – Jack, he's an interior designer, mid-twenties, I reckon—'

'Ooh, the younger man, lovely—'

'And *gay*,' Josie added firmly, cutting Nell off mid-flow before she got any ideas. 'Then there was Steph, who was about our age, jobbing actress. Said she'd been in *Casualty* a few times, but I didn't recognize her. But she was dead friendly and funny. Yeah, the whole day was great.' She beamed, thinking about the way they'd all gone for lunch in the refectory together and chatted about politics, soap operas, where they'd been on holiday that summer ... 'It's fab. And hardly anyone there is a parent, so I actually had to talk about things other than children. So refreshing!'

'Good for you,' Nell said warmly.

'I know,' Josie giggled. 'I think it will be.' She paused, wondering whether or not to tell Nell about her new reconciliation with Pete. Oh, what the hell. She couldn't keep it to herself any longer. 'The other thing is that Pete and I have been getting on really well.'

Nell's tone turned suspicious. 'Oh yeah?'

'Yeah – he came to see the boys off with me on Monday, and ...'

'And?'

'Well, he came back here for coffee, and ...'

'You didn't.'

'Didn't want?'

'You didn't ... do anything stupid, did you?' Nell sounded horrified rather than pleased at the idea of anything happening.

Josie felt nettled by her friend's response. 'Well ... What do you mean?' she asked.

'I mean, you didn't ...' Nell hesitated. 'Sorry. Being judgemental. Presumptuous. Just tell me.'

'Well, it was really nice, that's all,' Josie said. 'Nothing *happened*, not in the way you're thinking, we just ... talked. In a friendly kind of way. About the boys and stuff.'

'Right.' There was a pause. 'So ... you're not about to tell me you're getting back with him or anything?'

'No, but ...' Josie felt confused. She hadn't been expecting Nell to react like this. She'd been *pleased* that Pete had been so nice the other day. Hopeful, too, even if she hardly dared admit it to herself. So why was Nell being so negative all of a sudden?

Nell changed the subject and launched into a story about some drama concerning getting her visa for Panama, but Josie felt rattled for a while after she'd put down the phone.

She poured herself a glass of wine and sat down at the table with her notes from that day's seminar.

Design flaws in HTML itself (no separation between content, structure and presentation of data) and the Netscape/Microsoft strategy ('extending' HTML to include features which only worked with their browser) combined to create ...

But all she could think about was having sat here just a few days ago with Pete. How good it had felt. How nice it had been to reminisce about the babies with him.

'Get a grip, Josie,' she told herself, staring at her own scribbled words until the letters jumbled before her eyes. 'Get a grip!'

Chapter Twenty

A few weeks of consolidation passed while everyone got used to their different routines. The boys made a new friend each at school and stopped looking quite so tired. Josie was loving her course, and had already had a raucous night out with a bunch of the other students. And she and Pete...

Well. Things had moved from civil to positively matey, actually. He'd come round one evening, ostensibly so that they could sort out their joint finances, but somehow or other they'd managed to drink a whole bottle of wine between them, and had ended up laughing fit to bust on the sofa about old times.

For a moment – a single moment – she caught him looking at her and wondered, with a twisting thrill inside, whether he was on the verge of saying something serious. Something important.

She'd made an excuse to go to the kitchen – 'Fancy some olives?' she'd blurted out – and jumped to her feet

so quickly that she'd kicked over her wine glass. So that
had been that. Moment over.

She was terrified of him making a move again. Terrified, but at the same time longing for it.

'I just *miss* him,' she confessed to Annette over the
phone. 'Even after everything he's done, I still fancy him
and I still miss him. And if he tried it on, I just don't
know what I'd do.'

'Oh, Jose,' Annette replied. 'He won't change, you
know. If you got back with him, chances are he'd only
cop off with someone else six months down the line.'

Josie sighed. 'I know that. That's why I'm keeping him
at arm's length,' she said. 'But he's still my husband, and
the boys' father, so . . .'

'And he's still a cheat,' Annette reminded her. 'Sorry,
Josie, but I've got to say it! And what about the guy in
Zambia, anyway? I thought you were hoping—'

'Oh, I haven't heard from him for ages,' Josie replied,
interrupting quickly. She didn't want Annette to say any
more about what she may or may not have been hoping.
She'd told Annette about Rob during a one-glass-too-
many night down the pub a few weeks ago, and now
regretted opening her big mouth. 'That was probably all
pie in the sky, anyway. Me imagining stuff that wasn't
there. I think I went a bit mad over the summer. He
probably just felt sorry for me, did his Good Samaritan

thing, etc. Anyway, he's so lovely, some gorgeous Zambian woman has probably snapped him up by now.'

'Hmmm,' Annette said. 'When's he back, this guy? What's his name again? Rob, was it?'

'Yeah, Rob,' Josie said. She sighed again. Her and her stupid crushes. Her and her silly pipe-dreams. 'I think he's back at Christmas time.'

'Well, I'd forget Pete and hang out for riding off into the sunset with Rob, if I were you,' Annette said. 'He sounded great.'

'Yeah, but he's probably not interested,' Josie argued. 'Whereas Pete . . .'

'Whereas Pete let you down big-time,' Annette finished. 'Remember?'

Of course she remembered. How would she ever be able to forget? Yes, he'd let her down. Yes, he'd lied and cheated and stabbed her in the back, but . . .

She groaned. Stop it, Josie. *Stop it!*

Of course nothing was going to happen with Pete. It was definitely all over. They'd had the money-chat now, sorted everything out fairly, so if he *did* have any intentions towards her he'd hardly have gone through all the paperwork for nothing, would he? And he was talking about buying a flat, for God's sake! People didn't start spending thousands of pounds on surveys and property when they were hoping to move back into the family home, did they?

She was feeling good about heading towards financial independence for the first time in years, anyway. Pete had agreed to pay for the mortgage and a share of the bills until Easter, after which time she was hoping to manage the bulk of the payments herself. Her course ended at Christmas, and she'd already got some design work lined up for the New Year thanks to Lisa throwing a few contacts her way.

So really, everything was flowing smoothly. She actually felt as if she was starting to come through the whole mess of separation with her sanity intact, just like Annette had predicted.

Then it happened. She was lying on her bed one evening, reading a book, when she first heard it. A scratching sort of a noise. She sat up, putting the book face-down, and strained her ears to listen. It was windy outside, and for a moment she wondered if it was just a branch from the tree at the front of the house scraping against the window.

There it went again. No. It wasn't the window. Wrong sort of sound.

Feeling edgy, she got off the bed and went to look outside. It was dark now, punctuated only by the yellow pools of light from the streetlamps. The trees were groaning in the wind. The cars seemed to be hunkering down on the road, their aerials lashed by the gale. A bad sort of a night to be out, she thought with a shiver.

And there it came a third time, the scratching noise. It sounded as if it was right outside the house. She froze as she heard it – and then her eyes widened as she realized that it was the sound of a key in the door. *Her* door.

Her heart bumped in alarm. Someone was trying to get in! Someone was on the other side of her front door, trying to pick her lock, just a few centimetres of wood and glass away from being in her house. Oh fuck. Shit! This was what she'd been dreading.

She padded out of the bedroom, along the landing to the top of the stairs. The boys, got to protect the boys. A burglar could take everything else – whatever they wanted – as long as the boys were all right. But you heard such awful stories, didn't you, about deranged crackheads completely out of control, hurting people for kicks, even little kids like her two . . .

Oh God. This was the worst thing about being a single parent. The fearful locking up every evening, each time knowing that this could be the night when someone tried their luck, gave the door a kicking or smashed a window, forced their way in past the locks and bolts, sneaked through her house . . . It could happen, she knew damn well it could. It was a nice enough area, their estate, there weren't dead-eyed feral kids roaming the streets, stuffing petrol bombs through letterboxes or stomping over car bonnets, but that didn't mean her safety was guaranteed. Laura's car had been pinched by joyriders a few weeks ago. Emma's shed had been broken into over the summer. Why wouldn't someone want to have a go at Josie's house? Especially if they'd been watching it; they'd know she was on her own in there, just her and the children.

Oh *shit. SHIT.*

Her mind raced for a weapon she could use, something she could defend herself with, if need be. A hammer? Rolling-pin? Meat cleaver? Sod it, she'd do it, if anyone tried anything with the boys. She wouldn't hesitate, she'd have a go at anyone to protect her sons. But if she could just get to the phone first, call the police, maybe she could avoid any of that . . .

She started down the stairs. The letterbox was rattling, and she pressed herself against the wall, into the inky shadows, trying not to gasp as she saw a pair of eyes peering through. And then a voice.

'Jose! Josie! Let us in, will you? It's me.'

She almost fell down the rest of the stairs. 'Pete!' she cried, feeling awash with relief at his voice. She strode across to the door and pulled it open, unable to stop herself berating him. 'What the hell are you doing? I thought you were trying to break in. I was all set to call the police! I—'

He held up a hand to head her off, and she could hear how shrill her voice was, how scared and accusatory.

'I was just passing,' he said. 'And I wondered . . . can I come in?'

There was something about the way he was enunciating his words so carefully and deliberately that roused Josie's suspicions. She narrowed her eyes, leaned forward so as to get a better look at him. 'Are you drunk?' she asked, not moving an inch.

'No!' he exclaimed, sounding wounded. His breath stank. 'Just been celebrating a bit, that's all. Celebrating my freedom.'

'Your what? Freedom? What do you mean?' She leaned against the doorframe, her arms folded.

He spread his palms upward, a fluid, definitely drunken movement. 'It's over,' he said dramatically. 'Sabine, I mean. It's all over. And I've seen the light.'

'What, you've found God?' Josie asked sarcastically. Her heart was quickening all over again, though, at the thought that Pete and Sabine had split. Why? she couldn't help wondering. What was wrong in Paradise all of a sudden?

He laughed. 'No, not God,' he said. His expression

was earnest under the glow of the hall light. He put a hand on his chest — was she really meant to take that seriously? — and took a deep breath. 'I got it wrong, Jose. I made a mistake. And...'

She stared at him. 'And you've come round here, pissed, to tell me that? Well, thanks. Thanks a lot, Pete. But you're going to have to do a bit better than that, I'm afraid.' Of all the cheek! 'Trying to let yourself in, too! God! You frightened the life out of me.'

He shrugged. 'Sorry,' he said. He flashed her an aw-shucks smile. 'It felt nice though, the thought of letting myself in here. Just like I used to before ... Well, you know.' The smile looked strained suddenly, and his arms fell limp by his sides. 'Go on, let us in, Jose,' he said. 'It's freezing out here.'

The wind battered the side of the house, as if proving a point. Josie thought quickly, trying to decide what was best to do. A quick chat and maybe a drink wouldn't hurt, would it? And she was curious to hear what had happened with Sabine anyway — just so that she could gloat in private once he'd gone. She hesitated. The thing was, she was tired, and he was half-cut, and it would surely be better to have this conversation in the civilization of daylight rather than in the darkness of evening. Wouldn't inviting him in now muddle all the boundaries that had been set?

Pete was still smiling at her. 'Go on, Jose,' he said. 'For old times' sake, eh?'

And, infuriatingly, she felt herself smile back, and roll her eyes at him. 'What are you like?' she said. 'Come on, then. Come in.'

'Cheers,' he said, stepping into the hall. He stood there while she shut the door, waiting for her to lead him in. 'Where are we going, then? Kitchen? Living room?'

'Come in the kitchen while I get us a drink,' she suggested, walking briskly past him. She felt tingly, strange, having him in the house again after dark. She was conscious of her body moving, with him walking behind her there, and went a bit faster, trying to shake the thought from her mind. It was disturbing. She didn't want to dwell on it. She pushed open the kitchen door and snapped on the lights.

'So, what do you want?' she asked, turning to face him.

He was blinking and sallow-faced under the unmerciful spotlights. 'Well, as I said, I feel like I've made a mistake, and—'

Now it was her turn to cut him off with a hand. 'No, to *drink*,' she said.

He had the grace to laugh at his mistake. 'Oh, right, I thought you meant—'

'Coffee? Tea?' Josie wasn't sure why she was reining him in so much, interrupting every time he started getting personal, but she felt on edge. It was too close to what she'd dreamed about, perhaps, too near the knuckle. He was saying things that she'd longed to hear him say, but she almost couldn't bear to hear them, because she knew he was just drunk and probably didn't mean a word of it.

Annette's words rang in her ears. *He let you down big-time, remember?*

Yeah. She did remember.

'Glass of wine?' Pete said hopefully. He took his jacket off and slung it around his old chair at the head of the table, then parked himself in it, eyes twinkling at her.

She felt herself soften, just a fraction. She still missed him, after everything; that was the problem. She still cared.

'Glass of wine it is then,' she said, turning away so that he couldn't see the flush of feeling creep through her cheeks. Keep your cool, she instructed herself. Play it cool. Don't let him take control again, whatever you do.

She pulled a bottle of white out of the fridge, one she'd started the night before, and was easing the cork out of the bottle's neck when he got to his feet and came to stand next to her. 'Josie,' he said quietly.

He was right in her space, too close. She could smell him – beer, aftershave, soap – and could hear her blood roaring in her ears. She stepped sideways, away from him, but he caught hold of her. 'Josie,' he said again, taking her hands. 'Look at me a moment, will you?'

She let go of the bottle and slowly swivelled her head to meet his gaze, feeling tense. She didn't feel prepared for this, like an actress without a script. She didn't know where it was going, what he was doing. But he was looking straight at her, those soulful brown eyes, as serious as the day she'd looked up at him in the church on their wedding day.

Do you, Josie Catherine Bell, take this man, Peter David Winter, to be your lawful wedded husband?

'Josie, I want to come back,' he said bluntly. One of his hands stole around her waist. 'I must have been mad to have walked out the way I did. Mid-life crisis, I guess – but that's over. I know now that it's you I want. You and the boys. And if you'll have me back, then . . .'

She wrenched herself out of his hands, stepped away, her heart thumping. The walls seemed to be closing in around her, the strip lighting too bright overhead. 'Don't,' she said, not able to look at him. 'You're only saying this because you're pissed and feeling sorry for yourself.' She bit her lip. 'You can't just come here and say all that, and think we can carry on like it never happened. Because—'

'I know I let you down,' he said, interrupting her smoothly. His eyes were on her face, his gaze steady.

'And I'm sorry. I am so, so sorry. I totally lost the plot for a while, but...' He held his hands out to her, palms up. *Look, no weapons.* 'I've come through that now. I've come out the other side. And I miss you, Josie.' His eyes were liquid under the bright kitchen lights. 'And maybe it's taken me some Dutch courage to come round here and say it, but that's the truth, the bottom line. I miss you – and I want things to go back to the way they were.'

Josie felt unsteady on her feet and leaned against the work surface for support. She could hear Nell's doubtful voice in her head now. *You're not about to tell me you're getting back with him or anything?*

Nell thought she shouldn't. Annette thought she shouldn't.

Then she thought of the boys. Sam had come home just that afternoon and said, 'Everyone else in my school has got a daddy.'

'*You've* got a daddy too!' Josie had protested. 'Even though he doesn't live with us.'

'We were drawing house pictures,' Toby had put in. 'And we had to draw who lived in our houses. And there's only me and Sam and you in our house. Not Dad.'

'I drew Dad looking through the window,' Sam said. 'But you weren't letting him come in.'

'Oh, Sam!' Josie cried. 'I always let Daddy in!' She felt hurt at their words. 'And you're not the only ones, anyway. What about Oliver?'

'*His* dad bought him a PlayStation,' Toby replied. 'Can we have one?'

Josie shook the conversation out of her head now, feeling Pete's gaze still resting upon her. 'I don't know what to say,' she confessed. She really didn't.

You're not about to tell me you're getting back with him or anything?

He let you down big-time, remember?

Everyone else in my school has got a daddy . . .

The voices churned in her head, and she could hardly think. The pressure to speak was immense. This is it! Make your decision!

'I . . .' she faltered. He was right in front of her, an imploring expression on his face . . . Oh God. She could feel her resolve crumbling. Despite everything that had happened between them, all the tears and betrayals and hurt, she still fancied him. That hadn't changed. She still had a physical reaction to him.

Her fingers remembered how the back of his neck felt underneath his hair, her mouth remembered the imprint of his lips, her body remembered the way it felt to be held by him . . .

He seized upon her hesitation, stepped forward and cupped the side of her face with a hand, gently lifting her chin so that she had to look at him. 'You want it too, don't you?' he said quietly. 'Mr and Mrs, Happy Families, both of us there for the boys.' He paused, and inched his way forward a little more, so that he was closer still. His body was almost touching hers now, and he slid his other hand around her waist again, fingers resting lightly on the small of her back. 'You want me, don't you? I can tell,' he said into her ear, and then he was kissing her, gentle butterfly kisses in her hair, and down her neck.

Josie stood frozen in shock, clutching the worktop and trying her hardest not to respond.

'Oh, Jose,' he groaned, as his hand slid down on to her bottom.

She could feel his heart beating through his shirt as he pressed her against him. She could hear the slow tick of his watch. It was nice, so nice, to be held again, and she shut her eyes for a moment to savour the sensation.

You're not about to tell me you're getting back with him or anything?

He let you down big-time, remember?

'Stop,' she said. 'No. I can't do this.'

He hadn't stopped. He was still nuzzling the side of

her neck, still caressing her. 'Yeah, you can,' he said into her hair. His hand slid under her top and she stepped away from him, breaking contact.

'No,' she said sharply. 'No, I can't.' She folded her arms across her chest. 'I've just spent the last few months picking myself up after you trampled all over me,' she told him. 'You can't just ... *do* ... that. You can't. It's not fair.'

'But Josie, I—' he said, but his mobile chose that moment to ring, interrupting him. He fished it out of his jeans pocket. 'Just a minute,' he said, holding up a finger. Then his face blanched as he saw the screen and he clicked it off without answering.

'Who was it?' Josie asked, feeling a new tension in the air. She knew, though. She already knew. Damn him. Damn him!

'Oh, no one. Someone from work,' he replied without looking at her.

She glared at him. 'Like you were ever going to change,' she said coldly. 'Someone from work, my arse. At this time of night?'

He opened his mouth to argue, but something in her face seemed to stop him. He said nothing.

Do you, Josie Catherine Bell take this man, Peter David Winter, to be your lawful wedded husband?

No, she thought. No, I don't. Not any more.

'Look at you,' she said. 'You're the man I fell in love with. Married. Planned a future with. The man who let me down, told me all those lies, made me cry so much.'

'All right, all right,' he muttered, but she ignored him.

'How can you *possibly* think it would work with us again, after that?' she went on. 'Every time your mobile rang, every time you were late back from work, I'd be wondering, Is that another one? Is he at it again?' She sighed. 'Don't you see? I don't want that. I need more. If you came back here, I'd need to know that you were one hundred per cent madly in love with me, proper love, this-is-for-ever love.' She looked him full in the face. 'You can't give me that, we both know it. So I'm not going to settle for second-best.'

He looked back at her. 'You've met someone else, haven't you? That's why you're saying all this. Because—'

'No,' she cut in. 'This isn't about anybody else. It's about me and you.'

'*Have* you met someone else?' he asked.

Josie felt irritated by the question. It was as if he couldn't believe she was turning down his offer without some other guy waiting in the wings. That was the way *he* thought, clearly – couldn't leave Sabine without lining up Josie as bedmate again. But Josie was different.

'Have you?' Pete prompted.

Josie sighed. She wanted him to go now. 'Pete, that's just none of your business any more,' she said. 'It's late, anyway. Shouldn't you be . . .?'

He got to his feet, looking dejected. 'Well, I think it *is* my business,' he blustered. 'I don't want the boys having to meet all sorts of blokes that you're—'

'Get out,' she said. 'You're drunk, and you're about to say something really offensive. So just get out.'

Josie was trembling as she deadlocked the front door and turned out the hall light. She could hardly believe she'd just sent him packing like that. But it was the right thing to do. It was definitely the right thing to do. Give him a few days and he'd be back with Sabine anyway, she reckoned. Or someone else he'd given the eye to at work. It wasn't her problem any more.

She went into the living room and picked up the phone. 'Nell, it's me, Josie,' she said. 'Sorry it's a bit late to phone, but I had to speak to you. You'll never guess what's just happened . . .'

Nell cheered at the end of the retelling. 'Thank fuck for that!' she said. 'For a minute I thought you were going to tell me you'd just had a rebound shag on the kitchen table.'

Josie laughed. She was feeling light-headed with what she'd done now, buoyed up by her own self-belief. 'Nah,' she said. 'Just for a second, I thought I might snog him – you know, I was tempted, when he tried. It's that closeness, I do miss it. But I kept hearing you and my friend Annette saying, "Don't do it! No!" in my head. So I stopped him before he got his hand in my bra.'

'Good work,' Nell said. 'Ooh, I can't wait to tell Rob this. He'll be dead pleased.'

Josie frowned. 'What do you mean? I haven't heard from him in ages. I thought he must have . . .' She shrugged. 'I dunno. Met someone else, or—'

'No, he hasn't,' Nell said. 'He was giving you a bit of space, I think. I'd told him a while back that Pete had been cosying up to you again, and he thought he'd back off in case you two wanted to make a go of it. But now you've told Pete where to stick his cosying-up . . .'

Josie felt her pulse quicken. 'And all this time I thought he'd just gone a bit cold on me,' she said.

'He hasn't gone cold on you,' Nell assured her. 'I promise.'

Six weeks later, Josie tramped up the steps of the underground and out into the crisp December air. She opened her *A–Z* and a cold wind snatched at its pages, howling around her legs before sending a tin can clattering into the gutter nearby.

Let's see ... Blackfriars, there it was on the map. There was the Thames, a snake of blue on the paper. And there was the pub where Nell and Gareth were having their send-off. Which meant she needed to turn right, go up to the Strand, then cross over and turn right again ... She snapped the book shut, suddenly feeling like a tourist. She'd find it. A two-minute walk away, Nell had said. No worries.

Josie pulled her coat a little more tightly around herself as she set off, walking into the wind. It tugged at the overnight bag on her shoulder, pulled at her hair. God, it felt truly wintry today. It had been frosty at home that morning, the garden covered with sparkling ice crystals, and the car had played awkward buggers and refused to start at first so that they'd all sat there, dragon breath steaming out from their mouths, as she tried the engine again and again. Barbara was having the kids for her this weekend; Pete and Sabine had gone away somewhere hot and tropical. You could do that when you didn't have the school terms to book your holiday around, couldn't you?

Josie grimaced as she walked a little faster, her kitten heels echoing on the pavement. He was so predictable, Pete. Straight back to Sabine, after she'd turned him down that night in October. Flat purchased and moved into. Talk of introducing Sabine to the boys after Christmas ... she was *dying* to meet them, apparently ...

Josie paused as she came out on the Strand, feeling taken aback suddenly by the rushing red buses, the beeping taxis, the people bustling along loaded down with carrier bags. The Christmas lights twinkled above the road, it would be dark soon, even though it was only three o'clock. She turned left, frowning a little as she tried to get her bearings. She still wasn't sure how she felt about the boys meeting Sabine. Rationally, she knew that they'd always love their mummy best, no matter how many sweets and treats another woman might bribe them with, but all the same ... They were only four. They were well up for a bit of cupboard love and bribery, ripe for the picking.

She plunged her hands deeper into her pockets as she passed a coffee stand, sniffed appreciatively at the smell of roast coffee beans that mingled with the exhaust fumes and fag smoke all around. She was looking forward to Christmas, and then the year being over. New Year was a good time to make plans for the future.

Oh, there it was, the pub, right on the corner across the road. She smiled to herself as she waited for the traffic lights to change, shifted her bag into a more comfortable position on her shoulder. She was going to stay at Stu's tonight, was looking forward to catching up with him and Melanie again. She was definitely up for a bit of silly dancing with Nell after a few beers, and maybe even with Lisa too. She'd always been a bit of a mover on the dance floor, had Lise.

The green man was flashing, and Josie crossed over with a crowd of other people. Her, Nell and Lisa, all back in London together again. It was a kind of symmetry. But how everything had changed!

She reached the other side of the road and headed for the pub. She was hoping that Rob would be there too. According to Nell, his plane should have arrived at Heathrow yesterday but of course delays happened, flights were cancelled, jetlag kicked in. He might not show.

He'd been in touch regularly over the last few weeks, with news of a job here in London at the Volunteer Africa office, plans to share a flat with a mate in Crawley until he got his own place . . .

Josie tucked her hair behind her ears, suddenly nervous as she approached the pub doors. It wasn't as if she'd been pinning all her hopes on this big reunion with Rob. She'd proved to herself and everyone else that she could manage without a man. And yet . . .

Crawley was just a fifteen-minute drive from where she

lived. If Rob was interested, it would be easy enough for them to meet up.

It was a big 'if', of course. She might have misread the signals back in the summer, have flattered herself that he liked her as anything other than a friend. But the main thing was, Josie felt ready for something to happen again. She was over Pete. She was mended, cured of him. She was ready.

She pushed open the door, heart thudding, looking around for a familiar face as she walked in. There was Nell, holding court, of course, regaling everyone from where she sat at a long table over on the left. Gareth was next to her, rolling his eyes at what Nell was saying, a protective arm slung around her shoulders. A couple. A happy couple. Oh, and Lisa was on her other side, tipping back her head laughing so that her dark hair fell in long, glossy waves over her shoulder. And there was Melanie, spotting her and nudging Stu, who looked around and waved.

Josie waved back, smiling at them all as she went over to the table. Her eye flicked through the crowd of Nell's other friends, her mouth suddenly dry.

There was no sign of Rob. Maybe he wasn't going to show after all. Never mind. It was still great to see the others.

'Hiya,' she said, as she reached the table. 'I'll just get a drink. Anyone need anything?'

No one did. Nell flashed her a wink and then, as Josie turned and made for the bar, she saw him. Rob, leaning on an elbow as he stood there, waiting to be served.

Her heart skipped a beat. She forgot all about Nell and Gareth and Lisa and Stu. She forgot about catching up, and beers, and silly dancing. She walked up to the bar, set her bag down on the floor and stood next to him. Rob.

He turned his head and grinned at her. He was tanned and fit-looking, his hair short, his eyes a brighter blue than she remembered.

'I was hoping you'd be here,' he said, reaching out on impulse and hugging her. 'Hello, Josie. It's good to see you.'

She smiled and put her arms around him. I am ready for this, she thought, filling up inside with joy. I am ready.

She hugged him tightly, close enough to feel his heartbeat. 'It's good to see you too,' she replied. 'Welcome back.'

Epilogue

Eighteen months later

'Look! Over there! An elephant!'

Josie thought Toby's eyes were about to fall from his head at the sight. He could hardly get the words out in his excitement.

'*Two* elephants!' Sam cried, clutching the side of the Jeep. 'Look, there's another one!'

Rob turned the video camera towards them. 'Here we are in Kenya, first day of the holiday, on safari in Tsavo National Park. Tobes, Sam, are you having a good time?'

'YEAH!' Toby bellowed, throwing his hands in the air.

'This is so COOL!' Sam beamed, waving into the camera then turning back to the elephants. 'Oh, look, that one's picked something up in his trunk!'

'Why are they all red?' Toby wanted to know.

'It's the dust,' Rob explained. 'Look — see how red the earth is? Maybe those elephants have just had a dustbath.'

The driver of the Jeep slowed so they could have a closer look. 'There are giraffes in the distance, see?' he said, pointing them out.

Josie looked over to where a procession of slow, stately giraffes were making their way across the sweeping plain, necks bobbing slightly as they walked.

'Giraffes!' Sam marvelled, bouncing up and down on the seat. 'Giraffes, Toby!'

'Wow,' Toby breathed, pressing against the window. 'Real, live giraffes!'

Josie smiled at their faces, alight with happiness. 'This was such a brilliant idea, Rob,' she said. 'I'm so glad we're here.'

Rob turned the camera on her. 'Go on, say it again for the record, Jose. The bit about my brilliant idea.'

She winked at the lens. 'You're just brilliant full-stop, darlin',' she told him. 'Did you know that?'

He put the camera down and leaned over to kiss her. 'You're not so bad yourself, you know,' he replied.

'Ugh, yucky,' Sam moaned. 'Mummy and Rob, sitting in a tree . . .'

'K-I-S-S-I-N-G!' Toby joined in. 'Yuck, do you have to?'

Josie laughed, and ruffled his hair. 'Sorry, guys, but yeah, we absolutely have to,' she replied.

Rob looked over at the elephants thoughtfully. One

was tromping heavily across the ground towards a pool. 'Actually, do you know what, boys?' he said. 'That elephant there, that really enormous one, reminds me of someone. Can't quite think who...'

Josie narrowed her eyes. 'I hope you're not trying to say...'

The boys hooted with laughter. 'Mummy!' spluttered Toby, prodding her belly.

'Big fat Mummy!' Sam chortled.

'Oi!' Josie said, clutching her belly protectively. 'Leave it out, this isn't fat! This is your new baby brother or sister in here!'

'She's right, boys, she's right,' Rob said, in a more serious voice. 'In fact, Jose, I was wondering... Maybe if it's a girl, we could call her... Ella?'

'What, after the elephant? You cheeky...!' But Josie's words were lost in the volley of guffaws from her boys. The baby somersaulted in her belly just then, and she stroked her bump tenderly. 'Just ignore them, baby,' she said. 'No elephant names for you, my love.'

Rob reached out to grab her hand. 'Only joking, Jose,' he said. 'You're nothing like an elephant. In fact, I can't believe Toby and Sam could even suggest such a thing.'

'Hey!' they cried. 'We never said that!'

'That's a relief,' she said. 'Because there's still three

months to go, and I'm only going to get more elephantine.'

'Jose, even if you're a whale, you'll still be a gorgeous whale,' Rob said, his eyes crinkling at the edges. 'The most beautiful whale ever to wobble through the ocean.'

Josie laughed. 'Darling, you say the nicest things,' she said, rolling her eyes.

Rob put his arm around Josie and hugged her. 'I do my best,' he said.

Sam let out a theatrical groan as he saw them. 'Oh no, not more kissing,' he said, turning away to look at the giraffes again.

'Yeeeeuck,' Toby said, pretending to vomit over the seat.

Josie laughed again and leaned against Rob. 'Come on, let's ride off into the sunset together,' she murmured to him.

He stroked her hand. 'But we've only just got here,' he replied.

'I know,' she said happily. 'Aren't we the lucky ones?'

If you enjoyed

Over You

you'll love these other books
by Lucy Diamond . . .

The Secrets of Happiness

The best things in life can be just around the corner

Rachel and Becca aren't real sisters, or so they say. They are step-sisters, living far apart, with little in common. Rachel is the successful one: happily married with three children and a big house, plus an impressive career. Artistic Becca, meanwhile, lurches from one dead-end job to another, shares a titchy flat and has given up on love.

The two of them have lost touch but when Rachel doesn't come home one night, Becca is called in to help. Once there, she quickly realizes that her step-sister's life is not so perfect after all: Rachel's handsome husband has moved out, her children are rebelling, and her glamorous career has taken a nosedive. Worst of all, nobody seems to have a clue where she might be.

As Becca begins to untangle Rachel's secrets, she is forced to confront some uncomfortable truths about her own life, and the future seems uncertain.

But sometimes happiness can be found in the most unexpected places . . .

The House of New Beginnings

One life-changing summer . . .

In an elegant Regency house near the Brighton seafront, three tenants have more in common than they know . . .

A shocking revelation has led Rosa to start over as a sous chef. The work is gruelling but it's a distraction . . . until she comes up against the stroppy teenager next door who challenges her lifestyle choices. What if Rosa's passion for food could lead her to more interesting places?

Having followed her childhood sweetheart down south, Georgie is busily carving out a new career in journalism. Throwing herself into the city's delights is fun, but before she knows it she's sliding headlong into all kinds of trouble . . .

Nursing a devastating loss, Charlotte just wants to keep her head down. But Margot, the glamorous older lady on the top floor, has other ideas. Like it or not, Charlotte must confront the outside world, and the possibilities it still holds.

As the women find each other, hope surfaces, friendships blossom and a whole new chapter unfolds for them all.

On a Beautiful Day

Treasure every moment. Life can change in a heartbeat.

It's a beautiful day in Manchester and four friends are meeting for a birthday lunch. But then they witness a shocking accident just metres away that acts as a catalyst for each of them.

For Laura, it's a wake-up call to heed the ticking of her biological clock. Sensible Jo finds herself throwing caution to the wind in a new relationship. Eve, who has been trying to ignore the worrying lump in her breast, feels helpless and out of control. And happy-go-lucky India is drawn to one of the victims of the accident, causing long-buried secrets to rise to the surface.

This is a novel about the startling and unexpected turns life can take. It's about luck – good and bad – and about finding bravery and resilience when your world is in turmoil. Above all, it's about friendship, togetherness and hope.

Praise for Lucy Diamond

'A hugely satisfying read' *Heat*

'An absolute treat' Katie Fforde,
bestselling author of *A Summer at Sea*

'Warm, witty and wise' *Daily Mail*